Rose turned to Jean Pierre as she shed her grimy outer garments. "Do you suppose I could get some water for a bath?"

"Nobody is going to see you tonight," Jean Pierre replied in exasperation, forgetting that no matter how tiring the day, he now had a bride to consider. . .and woo.

"I know that," she hissed, her eyes shooting blue fire. "You may enjoy looking and smelling like an animal, but I don't." She picked up her discarded, dirty vest and threw it at him where he sat upon the foot of the bed, taking him by surprise.

The rough fabric hit Jean Pierre in the face, a button scratching his cheek and adding fuel to his smoldering temper. Not stopping to think, he lunged and hauled her, struggling and protesting, onto the bed, backing her up against the headrails until they sat with only inches between their bodies.

"Now, you wildcat," he asked, a one-sided smile on his face, "what next?"

Her response both surprised and pleasured him. . .

Cajun Rose

Cajun Rose

Myra Rowe

WARNER BOOKS

A Warner Communications Company

WARNER BOOKS EDITION

Cover art by Sharon Spiak

Warner Books, Inc.
666 Fifth Avenue
New York, N.Y. 10103

 A Warner Communications Company

Printed in the United States of America

First Printing: February, 1987

10 9 8 7 6 5 4 3 2 1

For rough spots smoothed over, for dreams made possible through their belief, and for steady love returned through the years, we dedicate this book to Joe and W.C.

Acknowledgment

Cajun Rose is the single collaborative work of two longtime, close friends. Co-authoring the fictional *Cajun Rose* under the name of Myra Rowe, they give special thanks to their agent, Adele Leone, and to their editor, Judith Stern, for their encouragement and judicious editing.

Please look for future books by these two authors. Margie Jordan will be writing as Margie Jordan. Myra Rowe will be writing as Myra Rowe.

PART
ONE

Chapter One

An ordinary step from a pirogue onto black gumbo soil bordering the Bayou Teche—or so it seemed to Rose Guilbeau that June afternoon in 1775. The grayed boat carved from a log was as familiar to the beautiful young woman as the muddy waters of the broad Louisiana bayou. How could she have guessed that she was moving toward events that would shake her, whirl her about, and turn her life upside down?

Jean Pierre, the eldest Guilbeau child at twenty-three, turned to Rose once they reached the path leading to the two-story mansion ahead and said, "Straighten your ribbons and don't you stare when we get inside." With his free hand he reached to remove a piece of bark from her unbound hair. He carried a roll of clothing in the other.

"Don't touch me," snapped Rose, darting to avoid his hand and sending her pale fingers to smooth down the laces of her black waist girdle. They had loosened during the two-hour trip down from their simple, unpainted home near Attakapas, the center of the Acadian settlement along the Bayou Teche. "You've no right to order me around just because Papa named you to look out for me," she said defiantly, tossing long blond curls and rolling fiery blue eyes up at him.

Though others among the Acadians seemed to admire

the handsome Jean Pierre Guilbeau for his commanding voice and personality, Rose shrank each time he called her to task in matters she thought none of his business. All she had ever wanted was to please him, to recapture the old camaraderie she recalled from early childhood. Now that he was home so seldom, Rose sometimes caught her breath at the sudden sight of the tall, broad-shouldered young man with the piercing dark eyes and deep-timbred voice and wondered when they had become strangers. As eagerly and as often as she confided her innermost thoughts to her fraternal twin, Jarrette, she had never been able to talk with him about her feelings for Jean Pierre. Somehow words couldn't express them. But she had no wish to think upon anything so serious on this special afternoon and cast such thoughts aside.

As Jarrette caught up with them after he tied up the pirogue, Rose linked her arm with his, ignoring the older cousin whom their parents had reared as a son. Not so tall as Jean Pierre, Jarrette, with similar dark eyes, hair, and even features, also had claim to the title of handsome. He was her dearest friend and constant companion.

"Jarrette, you could look after me just as well as Jean Pierre, couldn't you?" she teased with open affection, her blue eyes capturing the brown ones of her twin.

"Sure, if you ever needed looking after," Jarrette responded with a grin as the three young people moved up the long path leading to the imposing white house called Grenfall.

Rose checked to make sure the sometimes-careless Jarrette carried the portmanteau holding her gown. She beamed at the thought of the splendid night that lay ahead: Acadians attending a Creole party at the elegant mansion up ahead. What good fortune! She hoped it was an omen of good times to come. All kinds of fantasies had danced inside Rose's pretty head ever since the invitation came.

From the shadows of the second-floor veranda, Louis Brearde stood watching the three Guilbeaus walk toward his home. He sipped brandy and thought back to the day three weeks before when Jean Pierre and he had returned from trapping in the Northwest. A practiced hand loosened his white cravat, then unbuttoned his blue brocaded vest as he leaned back against the tall-backed rocker there on the upper veranda, concealed by towering oaks. His brooding, handsome features softened as he recalled the last time he had seen Rose. Of course he had no way of knowing that she had relived it at least a thousand times already—most recently, a few moments earlier.

Louis, wanting to stop by for a visit with the elder Guilbeau before going downstream to Grenfall, had paddled up the small finger of bayou beside their house to tie up at the private dock used by the family. His cargo, he knew, was too tempting not to conceal from the view of casual passersby. But what Louis had found on the little platform reaching over the water had astounded him, pleasured him—even tempted him. The younger cousin of his trapping companion had apparently just bathed and washed her hair there in the privacy of the secluded spot and was stretched out in the noon sunshine with her thick, gleaming blond tresses spread out behind her.

When Rose heard the intruder, she flushed and quickly sat up. Not until she tried to cover her still-wet chemise with a towel did she realize that she no longer had one.

"What, sir, are you doing here?" she asked in surprise, staring at the sodden towel his paddle thrust toward her.

Puzzled blue eyes met laughing brown ones. Astonishment became vexation as suddenly as a turtle sunning on a stump nearby plunked into the brown water, setting off ripples. Farther up the narrowing stream, a redheaded woodpecker ceased its hammering attack upon a bald-headed cypress and flew off, its raucous protest echoing in the forest beyond. A velvety-skinned chameleon paused in the shade at the edge of the pier, its tiny green head tilting in query while the red balloon swelled beneath its neck in obvious anticipation of attracting a whining, circling mosquito. The pirogue nudged the pilings then, the hollowed-out log clacking against the solid, upended ones, the sound bouncing off encircling, low-limbed cypress trees and changing the preening green lizard into a little brown blur of frenzied escape. Rose could have reached to touch the handsome trespasser.

Louis Brearde, her cousin's friend and trapping companion, she noted while feeling that she was seeing him for the first time. About his full lips was a new, wondering expression. Had his eyes always had such unfathomable depths, like bayou water on a cloudy day? All hint of treachery was gone from them, and she realized that those dark eyes were feasting on the sight of her barely covered body. Glancing down, Rose saw her nipples visible through the thin, clinging material and crossed her arms across her breasts. Growing up around teasing males had taught her that speaking one's mind gave one a distinct advantage. She was never one to sidestep an issue and simper like an ordinary, helpless female.

Rose demanded in a sharp tone, "Louis Brearde, did you steal my towel?"

"And if I did, what would you do, little Rose?" he responded, amused at her maidenly blushes and unsuccessful efforts to hide her chemise-molded body from his blatant looks. While Jean Pierre and he had been away, she had developed into a stunning young woman. Dark eyebrows shot up in appreciation, and his white teeth flashed when he let dance across his face the smile that few young women had ever resisted.

"When did you and Jean Pierre get back?" She glanced down the small stream, expecting her cousin to be close behind Louis. She dreaded the scolding he would give her for having been caught in such a predicament. Each time he returned from trapping, he seemed to pick on her more and more; thus, she was always relieved to see him off. Although Rose and her twin, Jarrette, as well as their younger sister and brother, had always doted on the tall handsome Jean Pierre before he began trapping, now that Rose had grown into womanhood there were times when she felt she couldn't have stood it had he lived at home year-round.

"Just now. Jean Pierre is out front unloading his furs, but I thought I'd bring my pirogue down here out of sight. I wanted to visit awhile with your father before going home." Lean and agile, Louis stepped upon the pier, squatting to tie his boat before turning to look at her again.

Something told him that Rose, hiding now behind suddenly lowered lashes, had been studying him with an intensity akin to his own. "Had I known you were waiting for me, I would've paddled a little faster," he added teasingly.

Everything about her was exquisite, Louis noted, his lips parted a bit in admiration. Big eyes, widely spaced, framed above by delicate brown hairs in arched appeal, fringed with pale silky lashes tipped with that same rich brown—long, thick, curling outward as if to draw one's gaze into those blue depths flecked with dark, intriguing pinpoints. Creamy skin . . . a satiny gloss over sweet features—cheeks rounded high, blushed with rosy tones; nose straight and dainty, with little flare at the nostrils; chin both feminine and strong at the same time; neck regal, slender, its pulse a hummingbird hollow begging to be calmed. Generous, inviting mouth nipped upward at the corners even when unsmiling, as now . . . the lips, a luscious pink bordering on red, swollen as though just bee-kissed, the fuller top lip resting a bit over the bottom in an attempt to hide the charming little protrusion of small front teeth. But her hair was what really set Rose apart, Louis thought; it would make her unique in any collection of beauties.

Blond hair was rare among the colonists in Louisiana in 1775, where French, Spanish, and Indian blood dominated. Never was it found in Acadian settlements on the Bayou Teche, those peopled by the French who had fled twenty years earlier from British rule in Nova Scotia to seek land in the colony of their home country. That Rose's waist-length hair was not only blond but had a pinkish tint was unheard of . . . and caused much talk. A luscious image of strawberries and cream such as he had been served in an elegant restaurant in New Orleans flashed into Louis's mind as he gazed at her.

Even in the unrelenting sunlight Louis could detect no flaw in the young woman with saucy waves and curls springing to life in the golden warmth right before him on the weathered pier. Rose resembled an exotic jewel fixed into an everyday setting—much like the winking ruby dangling from a simple gold chain around her neck, nestling between the top curves of her breasts as proudly as though she were preparing to dress for a ball. Jolted at the sight of the gem, he tried to recall if he had seen it before; but then, he reminded himself when he failed, he had not seen her as anything but a pretty, precocious child until that very May afternoon. Yes, Rose Guilbeau had indeed become a strikingly beautiful, desirable young woman; and during his twenty-five years, Louis Brearde had made it his business to become something of an expert in that fascinating field.

"I wasn't waiting for you . . . or for anyone else," Rose declared, all breathless from his close-up examination and not, at first, understanding why. He had never paid her any special attention before. What was different this time?

"Don't tell me you aren't already having callers." Louis cocked his handsome head in disbelief, letting his dark eyes wander again over her tempting body. The winter had been long, with few Indian maidens willing to incur the wrath of their fathers to sneak into his blankets.

"Papa says I must wait for my seventeenth birthday next month." She was suddenly aware that Louis was no longer eyeing her as the "little sister" or "cousin" of his friend; he was seeing her as a young woman. She had noticed how over the past few months the three or four young bachelors in the settlement, and even some men Papa's age, had begun sending new, appraising glances her way when they thought she wasn't looking. Stirrings deep within had whispered to her that she was indeed becoming a woman, and she looked forward to having callers and being courted—or wooed, as Grandmère called it.

Never had Rose expected to attract the attention of any other men than the young Acadians, those with whom she went to church and school, and none of whom showed promise as the kind of husband she longed for. All year at school and at community gatherings they had fawned over her at every opportunity, stammered when they tried to talk to her, and sparked not one whit of the fire she suspected lay banked inside her. She dreamed of being sought after by someone new and exciting, someone who would overpower her with love and teach her all she burned to know of life . . . and passion. What did the dashing, older Creole have in mind . . . courtship? The daring thought brought a new racing to her pulse, a graceful arch to her neck, an instinctive, coquettish smile to her lips.

Louis stepped back deeper into the shadows of the upper veranda, now that the Guilbeaus were halfway up the walk. He recalled that Pierre Guilbeau, ever the wise father, had listened later that afternoon to Louis's invitation for Rose to attend his sister's birthday party but had declined. Only when the grandmother and mother had begged him to reconsider had Pierre agreed that, if accompanied by Jean Pierre and Jarrette, Rose might attend the party.

And now, Louis sighed from his hidden spot on the upper veranda, she was here for Celeste's celebration. He noticed for the first time that masculine voices floated from below. Obviously the earlier arrivals were talking on the downstairs veranda and, judging from their conversation, were also watching Rose and her escorts walk toward the two-story mansion.

Casting aside the half-formed thought that for the reputedly vicious nephew of the governor to have arrived unexpectedly the day of the party would likely lead to trouble, Louis directed his mind toward a more obvious problem. If only things had worked out as he had hoped that day three weeks earlier when he invited Rose. . . . He killed off the remaining brandy and went inside for more, unaccustomed remorse nibbling at him with each step Rose took toward Grenfall. How could Fate have been so cruel?

"Who is she?" asked one of the three young men lounging on the lower veranda of Grenfall, none aware that the son of their host stood directly above them, watching the same scene and getting caught up in reverie. Their eyes had centered on Rose from the moment the three Guilbeaus reached the dock. Two of the idlers had only recently arrived from a downriver plantation and were polishing off lemonade and cakes a slave had set before them. They had paddled since early morning to reach the Brearde mansion before dark.

"I hope the two with her are merely kinfolk," remarked

Phillip de Cordoza, the only Spaniard. The others were self-proclaimed Creoles, those sometimes arrogant children born in Louisiana to families that came from France to settle in the colony. "She is the first true blonde I've seen since I came to this godforsaken place just before Christmas." Long of face and noticeably thin-lipped, Phillip turned with a world-weary air of disbelief to his companions. "Even I have never seen hair quite that color." His black eyes moved back to Rose in calculated appraisal. "A man with her on his arm would be the envy of the entire court back in Spain. Look at the way she walks, like some duenna had drilled her for hours on how to move without bobbing her head. I'd like to add her to my collection of things rare and beautiful. Would you think such a lovely creature could come from bayou country?"

"Phillip, your snobbery is showing," intoned Henri D'Argent with obvious disapproval. "I doubt she would appreciate being sized up as though she were nothing more than an object for someone's collection." He, too, kept his eyes fixed on the young woman, letting an appreciative smile drift across his face.

If Phillip realized he was tolerated by the clannish Creoles living along Bayou Teche only because Luis de Unzaga, his uncle, was governor of Louisiana now that France had ceded the colony to Spain back in 1762, he made no show of it. The young Spaniard shrugged with a bored air and said, "As my uncle's new keeper of land records, I traveled all the way from New Orleans to inspect the Acadian settlements and consider new requests, gentlemen. To arrive and find my host throwing a party to honor his daughter Celeste on her sixteenth birthday did brighten such a dull assignment. Celeste promises to be a tasty morsel, but now that I see this blond vision getting closer and looking more and more delectable—" He paused to let his tongue wet his upper lip before going on, "Surely you can't begrudge my finding a dish to whet my appetite." He narrowed his eyes to study the young woman moving up the long, tree-shaded walkway between her escorts, deciding to keep further thoughts to himself. None of the colonists seemed to appreciate him; instead they seemed to work at thwarting his every move, he reflected. That some were already finding he was not one to cross delighted him.

"Phillip, who's to say yours is the only appetite being tempted?" asked William, Henri D'Argent's brother. The beauty of the approaching young woman obviously prompted him to join in the lazy conversation. He ran his fingers through hair almost too curly to comb. "Wonder who she is?"

"Judging from her clothing, I'd guess she's from an Acadian village up-bayou," his brother Henri replied, cocking his dark head as though he were an expert eyeing the petite blonde's white blouse, dark skirt, and black, laced waist girdle. "And judging from the proud way she carries herself, I'd guess she descends from royalty," he added, causing his companions to jeer under their breaths at the dramatic exaggeration. Everyone knew that Acadians— shortened to Cajuns, despite objections from the ones bearing the label—were about as far removed from royalty as one could get.

Out on the walkway, Rose was unaware of the stir her arrival had created on both verandas. Though one part of her wanted to exclaim over the beauty of the vine-covered pergola off to one side of the path and to ask about the small elegant building far on the other side, she couldn't. She was too busy giving her cousin a piece of her mind.

"Ever since you returned from the winter's trapping up north, you've been cross as a bear," Rose grumbled, irritated at Jean Pierre's harping on how she should act, what she should say and wear. "I hear about how you see all the sights and visit all the fancy women in New Orleans when you go down to sell your furs each spring. But even you've never been invited to a Creole party before, have you?" When his reply was a mere dagger of a look from beneath heavy brows, she went on, "You know well that both Maman and Grandmère have painted me a good picture of how I should act. I do have a little sense, despite what you choose to believe about me."

A dainty thumb and forefinger worried at the ruby hanging from the ever-present gold chain around Rose's slender neck, a sure sign of inner agitation. It was too much to expect Jean Pierre to see her as anything other than a flighty girl, she reflected. The way he pursed his finely etched lips and cocked his head to send smiling dark eyes to size her up during her little tirade let her know he didn't pay much attention to her objections. She sighed, letting her mind dart to more pleasant prospects. Would Louis be as attentive as his actions that afternoon beside the bayou had promised? She felt hemmed in by more than the masculine bulk of her escorts and let out a loud breath of longing for something unknown.

"She's right, Jean Pierre," Jarrette interposed, looking up to catch his cousin's eye. "Give her a chance."

"Just like always," Jean Pierre shot back, his deep, musical voice laced heavily with a bass vibrato which set it apart from any other. "Since you two are twins, you think you have a special set of rules." He paused to grip Rose's arm and make her look up at him. "Rose, people in our settlement are different from those out in other areas. Whether or not you like it, Papa looks on me as the eldest son and charged me with your care. I have only your interests at heart. You're too young to be aware of what men are really like."

With a sinking heart, Jean Pierre realized for at least the tenth time that day that Rose had no idea how beautiful and desirable she was—or how naïve. How was it that at home and everywhere he went, people seemed to seek his opinion, believe in him—and that she never showed any respect for his thoughts? Why couldn't she see that all he wanted for her were the rewards she deserved? Somewhere there was a man good enough to win her, and he felt compelled to see that she learn all he could teach her in preparation for a life of happiness.

Something Grandmère had confided to Jean Pierre a few years back flitted into his mind, but he pushed it aside, keeping it secret as the loving old woman had insisted he do until Papa was ready to make the announcement to Rose and the world. That Pierre Guilbeau had chosen from the beginning to claim that Jean Pierre, at two, was the orphaned son of his first cousin—and Marie's and his son only by choice and church announcement—seemed more in keeping with Pierre's frank manner, but . . . The main thing was that the family formed a close-knit, loving unit. Did it truly matter that Rose had not been born a Guilbeau, as everyone believed?

"How can you say I'm too young to know what men are really like? Fiddle-faddle," Rose retorted, easing from Jean Pierre's grasp in case anyone from the mansion ahead might be watching. "I know *you*, don't I?" But did she? an inner voice chided insistently. Her arm tingled where he had held it, and her blue eyes shot a fiery look his way. "You haven't liked anything I've done since I was a little girl, so how could I expect today or tonight to be any different?" Jean Pierre had already made his annual trip to New Orleans to sell his pelts, and she thought she had heard Papa and him talking about his not staying home much longer. Maybe he would go back up north right away and leave her alone, lend his unwelcome, forceful personality to someone else's cause. All winter she had looked forward to being courted in the spring and summer, and she could think of nothing she needed less than to have him around during that special time. He wasn't at all understanding like the soft-voiced Jarrette. Surely, she told herself, it could have nothing to do with the fact that Jean Pierre was a cousin, not truly a brother, despite the fact that everyone called him her father's son.

"Hush," Jarrette cautioned when he glimpsed the three young men on the lower veranda watching their approach. "We're getting too close for your bickering to look like anything except what it is." His fine features took on the pleading look of a practiced peacemaker, and a stain lay beneath the olive skin of his face.

"Are you afraid you might not please Miss Celeste if we don't keep up appearances?" Jean Pierre teased with a little laugh of indulgence for the inexperienced Jarrette. His seven years of seniority sat comfortably on his broad shoulders, lent him a compassion easily called forth. Standing a head taller than the younger man, he was lean, hard, and virile, while Jarrette bore a delicate look. Both had black hair and intelligent, dark eyes, but the resemblance stopped there.

"Louis assured us that his sister would want us to come just as much as he did," Rose reminded him testily. That feeling that she didn't know Jean Pierre anymore, that the easy-gaited young man walking beside her might be someone she had just met, washed over her . . . a feeling that had plagued her more than once since his recent return. "All three of us were invited, and I, for one, intend to have a grand time." She tossed her long hair in annoyance, unaware that fingers of sunlight probed through the trees to dance on it and turn it into a cloud of pinkish gold. "Jean Pierre, you're trying to rile Jarrette and me because we haven't seen anything but our world." In the old days, before he left home to trap, she would have stuck out her tongue at him.

"You'll both see that Celeste is no more than a spoiled child, but a likable one," Jean Pierre remarked, his congenial tone and handsome features showing his enjoyment of Rose's dramatics. If his eyes lingered on her shimmering hair and pouting lips, no one noticed, least of all him. Having stayed overnight several times with Louis when the two young men were on their way to or from New Orleans, where they sold furs and sampled the capital's spicy night life, he spoke, as he usually did, with what he believed was total honesty. Despite what they might think, he wished as much as Jarrette and Rose that they would enjoy the party.

"She's sixteen, just as I'll be until next week," Rose reminded him as they neared the end of the long walkway from the bayou. "Mayhap this Celeste and I are both more woman than you think." She gloried in his shocked look, his narrowed eyes. Not often did anyone best Jean Pierre. She added an extra swish to the movement of her long black skirt and upped her chin before asking, "If I'm so young and childish, why all the lectures?" They were underneath the last trees shading the walkway, and she watched the play of light and shadow on his face as his dark eyes studied her with a disturbing new intensity. Aware that they were being watched from the shadowed veranda ahead, Rose lowered her voice. "From the way you've been carrying on, I'm half-expecting every man here to grab me and take me off into the dark and—"

"That's enough," Jean Pierre interrupted, his tone warning her that he was no longer amused at her antics. "Maybe you are more grown-up than I'd realized. Far be it from me to play chaperon to one who knows all the answers." He forced a smile to his face, one that did not reach his eyes. "Let's leave it that you'll send for me if you need any help." They were at the steps.

The three admiring, curious young men on the veranda stood politely while their host, Antoine Brearde, came from inside to welcome his children's guests. Mr. Brearde's warm greetings to all and brief conversation with the newcomers told the captive eavesdroppers what they wanted to hear. They exchanged secretive smiles, shuffling their feet . . . and waiting.

"Gentlemen," Mr. Brearde said to them, a smile upon his aristocratic face, "allow me to introduce Miss Rose Guilbeau, her twin brother, Jarrette, and her cousin, Jean Pierre, my son Louis's friend and trapping partner in the Northwest for the past three years."

As if she had been coached in how to appear both innocent and worldly, Rose acknowledged the introductions with the right degree of pleasure and boredom. This didn't go unnoticed by her admirers. Her heart fluttered with excitement at the appreciative glances from all of the young men.

So this was how it felt to be admired by handsome young men not of the Acadian settlement! She had felt such exhilaration only once, when Papa had allowed her an extra glass of cherry wine at the Mardi Gras celebration on the Commons. Her eyes, however, moved past the handsome, smiling young men in the hope of seeing the brooding face of Louis Brearde.

"I shall look forward even more to my visit next week to Attakapas," Phillip de Cordoza said once he managed to maneuver Rose off to one side. "In New Orleans there are many stories about you Acadians." When Rose kept her look of polite interest but made no reply, he went on,

"One, that their young women are beautiful, which I've already found to be true."

"Thank you," Rose murmured, as she pondered why it was that up close, this young Spaniard was not nearly as handsome as she had at first believed. Something about his features seemed out of kilter. She wished the others had not become involved in a heavy conversation with Jean Pierre about the alligators in the bayous now that the reptiles had become so numerous. Even when he didn't seem to try, she marveled, Jean Pierre ended up dominating whatever group he happened to be in. She found that talking one-on-one with Phillip was not nearly as exciting as talking with all three young bachelors. He was unlike anyone she had ever met, but she couldn't put her finger on what made him so different. Surely Louis would join them soon.

"Another story which I find intriguing is that Acadians have fortune-tellers who can rival those among the gypsies in Spain." Phillip watched her face and eyes take on a closed, guarded look, and he hastened to add, "No doubt such talent is one to be proud of. In caves outside Granada there are those who collect many gold coins for their ability to see into the future. Not that I've traveled there for such a purpose, but I've known several who have." With a barely perceptible movement, his tongue wet his upper lip before he smiled down at the wide-eyed beauty.

That was what distorted his good looks, Rose thought with distaste: his smile didn't alter the cold, almost reptilian glaze of his black eyes.

But Phillip's words made Rose think back to some shadow-shrouded evenings of her childhood when, at nightfall, neighbors and kinfolk in the settlement would gather for a *veillée,* the custom of getting together at the end of the day for companionship. The activities, sounds, and smells of those gatherings were as much a part of a Cajun's childhood memories as the taste of his first glass of wine.

The men would sit around the kitchen table, often repairing their tools as they chatted and smoked their curved pipes. Keeping watchful eyes on the ever-present pot of steaming coffee, as well as on the men's cups, the women usually mended clothing or carded wool or cotton near the fire, their voices soft and low so as not to disturb the men. The young children would gather around the hearth, whispering and listening to the talk, while the older ones sat among the adults, also listening, but learning to perform the handiwork and crafts.

No matter what the weather was, the large kitchen holding the *veillée* appeared illuminated by more than the sputtering candles and, if it was winter, the dancing flames of giant logs. The very spirit of the Cajuns, joined by mutual need and love, added an almost mystical glow to whatever humble home sheltered them. At times a mood of merriment led the young people to ask for songs of the homeland to be sung by all, requests the adults granted with loving indulgence and appreciation for those who would follow in their footsteps. The old people sometimes held everyone's undivided attention with their tales of witchcraft, goblins, and miracles.

Rose recalled one night in particular, several years back, when an old woman visiting from a settlement farther upstream claimed to be able to predict the future and insisted on telling what she could see ahead for Rose. A mysterious silence seemed to pervade the room and even the forest and the swamp outside, as if the animals, along with those at the *veillée*, might be listening to the white-haired old woman pulling her chair to perch in front of the chosen one. From where she sat quietly beside her mother, Rose felt the beady eyes of the professed seer stare into her blue ones as though looking beyond her, even through her, to some point in eternity.

Bony finger pointing at Rose, the old woman shut her eyes then and lifted her sharp-featured face to the ceiling. A keening sound floated from her trembling mouth into the eerie silence, followed by a reedy, singsong voice:

"Oh, child of dawn, the spirits send their message. Never forget it. 'Tis a beacon for your darkest hours:

White on Black.
Someone close.
Search for the Fang.
White blossoms beneath Flame.
World of Water.
Lifetime of Love.''

When the old woman let her hand fall and stopped chanting the mysterious words, which had made no sense, those in the dimly lighted kitchen snapped out of their trancelike state. By the time the old woman opened her eyes and peered around as if awakening from a deep sleep, even the night animals had once more begun to call. Cheeks pink, Rose had joined the other women in nervous giggling.

Now, Rose reflected uneasily, Phillip de Cordoza had brought up the unsettling memory with his talk of fortune-tellers. She wished she could think of some glib answer. She didn't like the way he looked at her so boldly, so hungrily, as though she were a newly hatched chick.

Antoine Brearde may have overheard Phillip's question and sensed that it had upset Rose, for before she had to answer, he said to her, ''Portia has come to take you upstairs so that you may rest before dressing to meet us downstairs for dinner.'' With a courteous nod to the young men on the veranda, he added, ''My family and I are delighted that you could join us for the party.''

Escorting Rose inside, he presented her to the black woman waiting there before he disappeared down the hallway.

''I'll take you up to find a resting place,'' the smiling older woman said, having taken Rose's portmanteau from her master. ''Miss Celeste and her houseguest from New Orleans have already gone to sleep.'' She watched Rose take in the handsome foyer and the ballroom across the way. ''Since I've belonged to the Breardes a long time, even before Mrs. Brearde died ten years ago, I know this is your first visit. We're happy to have your brothers and you join our other guests in spending the night with us tonight. You'll be sleeping upstairs, but the young men will stay in the *garçonnière* built near the bayou for just such overnight stays. I hope you'll have a good time at Grenfall.''

"Thank you. It's the most beautiful place I've ever seen,'' Rose managed to say, her awe of the luxurious home stealing part of her voice, Jean Pierre's warning not to stare ignored. So the little house she had seen out front served as a sort of guesthouse for young men. Wealthy Creoles seemed to think of everything to add to their guests' comfort, she reflected, noticing tempting smells floating from the long hallway that obviously led to the back of the house.

A huge crystal chandelier in the ballroom seemed to draw Rose's eyes in some mysterious way, and she wondered if it had anything to do with the way great gilt-framed mirrors bordering the walls of the high-ceilinged room reflected it and sent her numerous images of its splendor in the shadowy afternoon sunlight. Myriad unlighted candles with wicks already upended awaited the touch of a taper, their readiness for the night's festivities seeming to represent her own anticipation.

With a slight shiver, Rose tore her gaze from the chandelier and left the lovely surroundings to follow Portia, trying to get a good look at her without seeming to stare, for she was the only slave Rose had ever seen. She moved up the curving staircase, delighting in the feel of her slim fingers against the dark polished wood above a white, hand-carved balustrade. A hint of prickles feathered up her spine. Were masculine eyes watching her? Hoping that she might catch a glimpse of a late-arriving Louis, she turned with an expectant smile.

Almost concealed in the shadowed corner beside the front door, a tall figure stood looking in her direction, his face a blur, his eyes burning up at her with an expression both haunting and vulnerable. Not until he moved with easy, tall-framed grace into a patch of slanting sunshine did Rose's heartbeat slow a bit. That was not Louis Brearde sending her ardent looks, nor was it a handsome stranger appraising her. A hand flew to her parted mouth and smothered the startled whisper of recognition: "Jean Pierre!''

Had his sudden movement from the sunlit veranda into the shadowed corner blinded Jean Pierre for a moment, led him to mistake her for some other guest? Or was her cousin at last seeing her as the grown-up young woman she had become while he was away? The latter thought pleased her for some reason she couldn't fathom. Flipping long blond tresses over her shoulder with a new, heady assurance, Rose sent him a haughty wave and continued up the stairs.

Chapter Two

"This is such fun," Celeste exclaimed, smothering a giggle. The pretty, dark-haired Creole sat upon the canopied bed where Rose had tried to rest after Portia removed her gown from the portmanteau to press it. "I was so glad when Louis told me he had invited you and your brothers to my party."

Within minutes the two young women were talking in half-whispers about the party as though they had known each other for years.

"Why are we whispering?" Rose asked after a while, her eyes full of wonder at all that was happening and promised to happen.

Celeste laughed before answering in a more normal voice, "Because Portia would scold us if she found we weren't napping. She swears we'll get bags underneath our eyes if we don't rest before a party."

"Is she a kind of mother to you?" Rose had heard Jean Pierre tell Papa and Maman that Mrs. Brearde had died when Celeste was very young. Now that Rose thought about it, she realized that Portia had not seemed unhappy about being a slave; in fact, she acted as if Grenfall were as much hers as the Breardes's. Even so, Rose was glad that the Acadians didn't embrace slavery.

"She probably thinks so," Celeste replied. "Sometimes she gets on my nerves being so bossy, though." Her generous lips pouted more fully than they normally did as she told of yesterday's session with the older woman about the gown she would wear tonight. "Portia has no knowledge of the styles being worn in New Orleans, and I almost cried at her remarks about the low neckline of my gown made in the capital. I just finished my schooling at the Ursuline convent, and I'm hardly a child anymore."

"Portia was kind to take my gown to press." Feeling more than a year older than her baby-faced hostess, Rose smiled at Celeste's exaggerated pose. Both were young and blessed with natural beauty of face and limb, but their differences went beyond contrasting color of skin, eyes, and hair. The dark-haired Creole handled her body with a practiced assurance gained from instruction in ladylike movements at the convent, while the blond Cajun moved with God-given grace refined to an art through a lifetime of walking and playing in the forests, riding horses, carrying baskets of laundry and goods about her home, and performing household tasks.

"Oh," Celeste agreed airily, "Portia's nice enough when she's in charge." She stepped from the tall bed to the floor-to-ceiling shutters, opening them with a clatter onto the upstairs veranda and letting in the last golden rays of the sunset. With the little wafting rush of wind came a blend of the late afternoon smells and sounds of Louisiana bayou country in early summer: fresh water laced with a pleasant hint of fish; oak trees stirring from the damp, freshening breeze; scolding house wrens flitting to guard their nests perched above the lintels of the white columns; the sweet scent of late-blooming yellow jasmine climbing the far end of the veranda.

"I didn't see Louis when we arrived," Rose prodded, desperately hoping to learn the whereabouts of the young man who had made her feel so grown-up that afternoon beside her house.

Celeste became interested in a flaw in her fingernail and

replied carelessly, "Oh, he's probably busy." With a rush
of skirts against the plush Persian rug, she moved to the
door. "I really must go now and wake Madeline, my
roommate from school. I'll come back in a little while to
introduce you to her and see if you need any help." Her
dark eyes didn't quite meet Rose's that time.

"Please do hurry back," Rose invited. "I'm eager to
meet your friend from New Orleans."

Soon after Celeste left the room, a young slave tapped
on the door and brought in Rose's gown, the one Maman
and Grandmère had made for her to wear tonight. With all
the wrinkles gone, the sprigged muslin looked just right,
the blue background a match for her eyes. Not knowing
how to turn down the persistent girl's assistance, Rose
reluctantly accepted her help in bathing.

Behind a latticed door was a small room containing a
gleaming brass tub, one end tapered and lengthy enough
for Rose to lie back against. The tub pulled into the
Guilbeaus' kitchen for bathing was a wooden one used
during the week for laundry, one prohibiting any such
luxury as half-reclining; and never had Rose heard of
perfumed oil being added to one's bath water. She knew
she would have enjoyed the heavenly warm bath far more
had the kind-voiced girl not insisted on staying with her
and sponging her back. No one but her younger sister,
Yvette, had seen Rose naked since she had curved into
womanhood. Accepting help in slipping into her full petticoats and gown was far less embarrassing.

Rose was sitting uneasily on a bench before the dressing
table allowing the attentive girl to brush her cascade of
hair when a light tap came at the door. Celeste and her
friend entered.

"Oh, you're as beautiful as Celeste described," breathed
Madeline Harchard after introductions were made. Lovely
in her own right, the young woman showed no jealousy.
"How do you keep your hair so blond?" From the tone of
her voice, she seemed as surprised at the color of Rose's
hair as the young men on the veranda had been. "What do
you use to lighten it?"

"Nothing," Rose answered, a bit flustered at the scrutiny from the two pretty, young Creoles. Madeline's hair was a lighter brown than Celeste's but was far from blond. "It's always been this color."

"How are you going to wear it tonight?" Celeste asked, after whispering to the young slave that she could go now. Obviously keyed up about her birthday celebration, she preened before the mirror behind Rose, tugging at the dark curls falling across a hefty exposure of bosom above her deep pink gown. The vibrant color accentuated her brunette beauty.

"I haven't decided," Rose countered, still seated before the dressing table. She knew little about hairstyles. The Acadian women usually pinned theirs up beneath white caps for everyday wear at home and under starched bonnets for outside gatherings, while the girls and young women wore theirs as she did, long and unfettered.

"Let me help you put it up high and interlace the curls on top with ribbon or flowers, with the back curls falling to the front over one shoulder," Madeline offered, her voice bubbling with enjoyment. "That's the latest fashion from Paris, and it'll be perfect for you." A similar style framed her olive face with beguiling perfection.

Later, when Rose stood there in Grenfall's guest bedroom before the first full-length mirror she had ever seen, she gasped in surprise. Could that slender, curved body really be hers? The gown was even lovelier than she remembered. After Celeste had excused herself to see about the preparations downstairs, Madeline took charge of the young Acadian woman, insisting that she pull the round neckline flounce down over her arms to expose her shoulders, assuring the reluctant Rose that such was the grand style.

And most of my bosom is exposed as well, Rose thought as she stared at her image in the mirror. Right where her breasts began to swell, the ruby pendant lay in its accustomed spot. The oval stone was beautiful, but the intricate setting of varied shades of gold was so unique that when people first noticed the necklace, they often commented on the leaves and scrolls in the setting before mentioning the gem itself. Rose leaned forward to see how much cleavage showed and grinned at the thought of her own daring behavior.

What would Louis think about the way she looked tonight? The mere thought brought a little skip to her heart. She marveled that Madeline had worked such wonders with her hair.

Over Rose's left shoulder, the long hair left out of the top cluster hugged her slender neck and fell forward in golden curls across the tops of her swelling breasts. The pink of two miniature roses at the crown called attention to the sprigs of pink and green in the blue muslin, as well as to the flawless pink and white of Rose's skin. She wondered if she was experiencing what a flower must feel when it first blooms and first meets the world for which it was created.

The excited Madeline rushed to her room and returned with a small bottle of perfume, touching little dabs on the insides of Rose's wrists and urging the shocked young woman to place a drop at the base of her throat. Rose had only read about such heavenly fragrances and felt she could have sniffed at the bottle all night. As Grandmère probably would have said, she mused, anything that smells so good must be sinful. Then the girls stood side by side before the oval mirror in the mahogany frame, one beauty in golden satin, the other in simple muslin, and smiled at the picture they made.

"Do you know Louis?" Rose couldn't keep from asking, aware that Madeline was breathtaking and overflowing with charm. What if she, too, had come to the party hoping to see more of Celeste's dashing brother?

An instant dimming of the lights in her tawny eyes and a slight fading of her smile made Madeline look more grown-up. "Yes, I first met him years ago when he was staying with Celeste and her father at their townhouse in New Orleans during school holidays." Watching Rose in the mirror, she asked, "When did you meet him?"

"He's my cousin Jean Pierre's friend and trapping partner," Rose replied, puzzled at Madeline's obvious withdrawal. What did she know that she wasn't telling? "When they returned three weeks ago from up north, he stopped at our home and invited us to Grenfall for Celeste's party.''

"Let's go down and give the bachelors a treat," Madeline said in a tone suggesting that she had had practice in such matters. She pinched her cheeks once more, then gave her bodice one more adjustment to do her unusually full breasts justice, no doubt dismissing the topic of Louis Brearde as unworthy of further talk.

As they descended the curving staircase with breathless smiles and dancing heartbeats, their full skirts lifted to their ankles, Rose and Madeline halted the talk among the four young men standing in the spacious foyer. Several feet outside the circle of light from the overhead chandelier, Jean Pierre and Louis stood talking together. Champagne glasses held in midair, they turned to see what had brought about the hush; they found themselves joining the silent tribute to the pair of young beauties descending like fluttering butterflies into their midst.

"How could I have forgotten what a lovely sister you have, Jean Pierre?" Louis whispered, draining his crystal glass with one gulp. The brief, triumphant smile Rose sent her twin brother, Jarrette, touched Louis in some uncommon way. Perhaps inviting her hadn't been a mistake; she seemed to radiate happiness. Passion rose unbidden as he took in each of her features, his gaze wavering between her temptingly full lips and the creamy curves of her partially exposed bosom. Only the ruby pendant seemed familiar to him, so different did she look from what he remembered. Her guileless perfection seemed to have taken on a new dimension, now that she was dressed and coiffed so fashionably. His heart pounded in punishing beats. "Just the sight of her leaves me dizzy."

"If you're a gentleman, you'll forget the dizziness and tell her what must be told right away," Jean Pierre replied in demanding, unsympathetic tones; the spell cast by the young women was broken by Phillip de Cordoza's bowing over Rose's hand and starting a conversation with her. William D'Argent soon joined in, despite the Spaniard's obvious disapproval. Henri, the elder D'Argent brother, captured Madeline's attention, though he politely allowed an enthusiastic Jarrette to take part in their talk.

Jean Pierre had difficulty in accepting the poised beauty in blue muslin as Rose. From his standpoint in the partial shadows, she seemed like someone he might never have seen before. Only the unique color of her hair seemed the same, although its modish style topped with rosebuds was a surprise. Where had she learned to arrange it so attractively?

Her eyes were wider, bluer, more star-filled than he had ever seen them, Jean Pierre noted. While Louis left to refill their glasses, his trapping partner mused. Like the lined-up dominoes he had seen tapped into rippling, falling motion in a New Orleans gaming house, memories of Rose's eyes looking at him with varying expressions during her early years flipped through Jean Pierre's mind in one dizzying swoop: the proud shine in the blue depths when she looked for the thirteen-year-old Jean Pierre's approval of her reading from her first hornbook; the devilish laughter in those eyes when a horse threw her and the tall, gangling teenager he was, mouth dry and fearful of serious injury, rushed to turn over the fallen girl's body to find her playing a trick on him; the worshipful, bright-eyed approval drinking him in when he donned his first tailored breeches and coat and strutted for the family to admire the eldest son—for never was Jean Pierre referred to as the child of a cousin. He remembered everyone's praise, but Rose's wide-eyed, wondering look he remembered in vivid detail.

There was more: the shy, pleading expression flicking blue and silvery from beneath silky lashes above flushed cheeks when she served the sad, lopsided cake she had baked for his eighteenth birthday. And then—here his heart no longer sang—the questioning, pained flickers deep in the black-flecked blue when he reached full manhood and let an uncharacteristic, flaring temper govern his reaction to Rose's normal, spirited ways of teasing and following him about the farm, accompanied as always by the equally frolicsome Jarrette. But never had Jarrette's playful actions and dogging of his tracks affected Jean Pierre as Rose's had.

With difficulty, Jean Pierre focused his thoughts on the Rose of the moment. Giving in to an urge to look her over openly and frankly, an urge he had denied himself since returning home this last time, Jean Pierre saw that her waist was smaller than he remembered from last year—a mere span of a man's two hands. At once his fingers tingled at the disturbing thought. Her breasts were fuller, more womanly—enticingly so, he realized with a start when he eyed the daring décolletage. At the sight of those provocative swells, he sensed a tightness deep in his belly, a fullness of throat . . . an inner chastisement. Feeling protective, or guilty, or just plain at odds with the way things were, Jean Pierre changed his stance and swallowed hard. Back now into the role Papa had assigned him—Rose's guardian—he wondered how Maman and Grandmère had come to sew such a revealing gown.

For some strange reason he couldn't fathom, Jean Pierre felt as if he had just belly-flopped into the bayou and lost his breath. Louis arrived with the champagne at just the proper time.

Too caught up in the lively chatter to be aware of Jean Pierre's secretive scrutiny, Rose was miffed that Louis didn't come from the shadows to speak with her privately, even after Celeste made her grand solo entrance and claimed the attentions of William and Jarrette. Was Louis sorry that he had invited her?

Rose saw Louis send her a brief nod and smile before Antoine came to invite everyone into the dining room, but they seemed no more special than those coming from Jean Pierre, and she did her best to ignore the trapping partners standing off to themselves. When Antoine asked the hovering Phillip to escort her in to dinner, Rose could barely hide her disappointment. Despite his handsome coat of gold satin and ornate brocaded vest, she was finding Phillip no more palatable at the second meeting than she had at the first, earlier that afternoon. Moving along with the chattering group and trying to pretend all was well, she lay her arm upon the Spaniard's proffered one in the way she saw Celeste do to William's and tried to smile.

The huge room with its grand furnishings didn't impress

Rose nearly as much as did the realization that she was seated between Louis and Phillip. Phillip sat at one end of the mammoth table next to Antoine and across from Jean Pierre, and despite Phillip's obvious wish to spend more time talking with Rose, the three men soon became embroiled in talk of land holdings and grants.

"Are you having a good time?" Louis asked her after white-coated slaves served soup in gold-bordered bowls.

"Yes," Rose replied, so aware of him sitting next to her that she feared she might not be able to lift the shining soup spoon. Accustomed to the plain, dull pewter utensils at home, she guessed the delicately shaped ones on the table must be of silver. She had felt Louis's intense gaze upon her, but had held off meeting it until he made some move to acknowledge her presence in a private way. Earlier she had sneaked looks at his stylish clothing, thinking that the black broadcloth coat molded his wide shoulders in the nicest way. Below black knee breeches, white stockings gleamed above square-toed slippers, revealing manly calves. She knew he stood shorter than Jean Pierre, but Louis was still a tall man by any standard, especially to one measuring little more than five feet, as she did. Above a heavily ruffled cravat of white linen, his face with its even features seemed far more handsome now that she was close to him.

Louis's thick, dark hair always seemed in place, Rose thought, as though it grew in the proper direction. What she longed to see in those brown eyes were the same devilish glints as she had noticed that day on the pier. General talk at the table had given her time enough to put her thoughts in order, but her breathing kept making up new patterns.

Rose decided to initiate more talk herself, and said, "I must confess, Louis, that I've wondered where you've been since my arrival." Blue eyes met full-on those brown ones she had dreamed of. She sighed. No glints.

"This is Celeste's night," he answered in a voice far more casual than the searching look he gave her. God! She was even more beautiful up close. Not that she needed the trappings she wore to enhance her beauty, but he conceded that she did indeed appear more grown-up, less vulnerable than that afternoon on the pier. "Besides, I think the younger bachelors are due their share of the attentions of you three young ladies this evening."

Rose digested his unwelcome remarks while dawdling over her soup. Idly she noticed the massive arrangement of roses and daisies in the center of the table. And not so idly she saw that Jean Pierre took time out from the discussion with Antoine and Phillip to send both Louis and her dark looks. Why? she wondered. Angling her chin, she glanced around at the other guests.

At the other end of the table, a glowing Celeste and a flush-faced Jarrette were laughing and talking. Good, Rose thought with an adoring smile. When Jarrette left the next day to travel up the bayou past Attakapas to meet Arlee Simpson, master trapper among the Cajuns, and become his helper, he would have happy memories to take with him. A sadness at the proposed drastic change in their lives flitted to mind and erased her smile. What would she do without the ever-present Jarrette, his teasing, and his sympathetic ear? She would miss her twin, but she counted on his learning much and becoming a fine trapper like Jean Pierre. Trapping, she knew, was one of the few ways in which young Cajuns could earn gold.

"But if the French set aside the entire area along the northern banks of the Bayou Teche for us Cajuns, why would the Spanish not honor it now that they're in control?" Jean Pierre asked in his compelling voice, snatching Rose's attention—and that of the other guests.

"Before I attempt to answer, Jean Pierre," Phillip drawled with something akin to a sneer, "perhaps you'll answer a question of mine. I've heard that the Acadians do not smile upon being called what you just called yourselves, Cajuns—but that they quite freely employ the term among themselves. Why is that?" He lifted his head in a way to suggest that he knew he had placed the man across from him in an awkward position and that he didn't care in the least.

"When our people left Acadia some twenty years ago to escape the British and settle on land owned by our mother country, they suffered many hardships. Among them was the bearing of a derogatory term, Cajuns. In keeping with our determination to prosper, we began referring to ourselves in like manner, mainly, I think, to show that no terminology could keep us from our goals. Whether as Acadians or Cajuns, we intend to survive . . . even prevail.'' Jean Pierre's deep voice had never sounded stronger or more forceful than during this pronouncement, and Rose found herself in awe of his loyalty to their people and his articulation. ''The Cajuns' contributions to this colony are enormous, even though Louisiana no longer belongs to France, and ours is not the official language.''

''Hear, hear,'' Antoine intoned, lifting his wineglass in salute to the young man sitting on his right. He shot an amused glance at Phillip. ''And now, sir, if the ladies will forgive us for one moment more, I believe Jean Pierre has earned the right to hear the answer to his question.''

''I gather that when Jean Pierre was in New Orleans last year, he petitioned for the section of land down-bayou from his father's. This year when he returned to secure the title, no decision had been made, and he must have put up quite a fuss to my uncle, the governor. Actually, I'm here as a guest in your home, Antoine, because as official keeper of land titles, I'll be investigating the recent requests from Jean Pierre as well as other Cajuns for additional land,'' Phillip said, sending a challenging look at Jean Pierre as he used the slurring term for his people. ''My approval or disapproval will determine the assignations. We Spaniards aren't bound to agreements made with any group by the French. Whether the Creoles or Cajuns like it or not, Louisiana is now a Spanish colony. I believe the attempted revolt in 1768 proved that beyond doubt.'' Only the slight sputter from candles in the overhead chandelier kept a dead silence from reigning at what had started out as a festive affair.

Phillip's narrow eyes glittered, and his tongue moved against his top lip before he seemed to remember who sat beside him and turned to say, ''My apologies, Rose, for such serious talk.''

Rose ignored the Spaniard's apology and asked in a soft

yet haughty tone, "Does the talk in New Orleans about us Cajuns, the talk that you referred to this afternoon on the veranda, include stories about our settlements being almost totally self-supporting, free of crime and poverty, and in need of little governing by anyone?" Rose was glad that snatches of a recent, fiery outburst from Father Sebastian had stayed in her mind. Ever since Jean Pierre's impassioned statement, the phrases had begged to be mouthed. From the corner of her eye she saw Jarrette grinning and nodding from the end of the table. She stole a glance at Jean Pierre to see if he, too, approved of her boldness. A steady beam from the dark eyes warmed her, as did the half-smile kicking up the corners of his well-shaped lips.

Red-faced, Phillip cleared his throat, hitched his shoulders to a new level, and replied in a frosty tone, "It seems I've carried this matter too far." With an imperious wave of his hand, he looked down the long table at a stunned Celeste to add in unctuous tones, "And to you, Celeste, I apologize and pledge to conduct myself in a more seemly manner from this moment on." He made no apology to Jean Pierre, didn't even glance his way again.

"Hear, hear," exclaimed both Henri and William, their intelligent faces showing their disapproval of the arrogant Spaniard's behavior and their determination not to pick up the gauntlet flung so defiantly before every man there. The dark looks they exchanged seemed to suggest that even if the Spaniard had no manners, they, as Creoles, did and would adhere to them.

"How goes the fur-trading company you and Louis formed last year, Jean Pierre?" Antoine asked in the awkward silence. "He tells me you've found a good market in New Orleans."

"Right, sir," came Jean Pierre's enthusiastic response. "One or two more trips to the Northwest should provide us with enough suppliers to prevent our having to be gone each winter."

Rose glanced down the table at Jarrette, their eyes locking in mutual understanding of the earlier awkward conversation with Phillip. Their looks seemed to be asking, *What are we doing here?* Then Rose sneaked a glance at

Jean Pierre as he talked congenially with Louis and their
host, surprised that a new surge of pride in his having
spoken so well for their people broke through her disapproval of him and his high-handed ways upon their arrival.
But the feeling persisted that he was more a stranger than
the Jean Pierre she had once known so well.

Like Louis, Jean Pierre wore a black broadcloth coat
with satin lapels. Earlier Rose had noted how the rippled
cravat spilled white down his embroidered satin vest of
pale yellow and softened the manly features of his weather-
browned face. Above the table his broad shoulders seemed
far wider than those of any other man there. Black hair
tumbled in waves across his well-shaped forehead as it
always did in humid, warm weather, and she knew that it
would be only a matter of minutes before a large hand
would slap at the offending waves and try to force them
back into place. She almost giggled to think that in spite of
Jean Pierre's usual successes in dominating almost everything and everyone around him, he could never control his
wayward hair.

In a more serious vein, Rose thought of how she had not
known of Jean Pierre's request for land of his own. Why
hadn't he talked about it with her? But then, it had been a
long while since he had confided in her about anything.
Toying with her food, she confessed to herself that she
admired Jean Pierre for pushing Phillip for an answer,
despite the fact that it might be a breach of good manners.
No one could bandy around the cocksure young Cajun
without his complaining about it in forceful tones, she
reflected with approval. Not even Spanish officials.

Papa would be proud, Rose told herself, that neither of
them had passed up an opportunity to speak out for the
often-misunderstood Cajuns. He was always encouraging
the young Guilbeaus—Yvette, Rose, Jean Pierre, Jarrette,
even little Robert—to stand up for their rights. But it
seemed to her that Jean Pierre's petition resting upon the
goodwill of the wily Phillip de Cordoza boded nothing but
failure. Aware that the hot eyes of the Spaniard had raked
over her face and breasts all evening, she pondered how

she might help the causes of other Cajuns and Jean Pierre. Mayhap she should be nicer to him.

"I had no idea that my cousin had petitioned for land of his own," Rose said to Phillip when he kept trying to lure her into private conversation.

"I thought Mr. Brearde introduced Jean Pierre as your brother," the Spaniard said, puzzlement bringing a line to his forehead.

Rose laughed and explained, "He isn't my brother, actually. But in our community and our home, he's always thought of as a son. He's been with my parents since he was two. For some reason, I never think of him as a brother. Maybe it's because my twin has first call on that title." When Phillip seemed to understand, she asked, "Did you say you'll be coming to our settlement right away?"

"Yes," Phillip replied. "Perhaps I'll see you."

Rose concentrated on the garlands of flowers edging her plate so as to avoid the Spaniard's unwelcome gaze and murmured, "Perhaps you will."

Celeste played her role well, ably turning the general conversation among the guests to lighter matters and pretending nothing had ruffled her. Throughout the ensuing courses, everyone followed her lead, and the meal finally ended.

"We'll take a stroll over the grounds," Celeste announced to the others after Jean Pierre and Louis left with Mr. Brearde. "I asked Lije to set up torches beneath the trees in front and also in the rose garden out back." She tossed her hair and smiled at both Jarrette and William, the two young men she had favored at dinner by placing them on either side of her at the table.

"How romantic," said Madeline, sending a flirtatious look at Henri, who had not left her side all evening.

"Let's begin in the rose garden behind the house," Celeste said, hooking her arms in those of her willing escorts and walking down the hall toward the back.

"I much prefer that we begin out front, Rose," murmured Phillip. "I've been wanting to see the pergola up close ever since my arrival yesterday. It looks so intriguing from my bedroom window in the *garçonnière*. Perhaps you noticed it when you arrived?''

Rose nodded, irritated that Louis had made no effort to be with her after the dismal meal. They had exchanged only three or four personal remarks, and she felt she would burst if she did not have more time alone with him. She had seen him wander toward the veranda.

''Phillip,'' she said, wearing the nicest smile she had given him all evening, ''please go with the others, and I'll be along after I get my shawl.'' When he balked, a sullen look upon his long face, she added, ''I promise I'll come find you.''

Rose waited until she heard Phillip's steps die away before going out onto the veranda. A tiny red glow at the far end guided her.

Chapter Three

''Louis, I think you've ignored me far too long,'' Rose said when she approached the figure leaning against the wrought-iron railing in the shadows. She felt as if some thread drew her to the man smoking the cigar. Her heart seemed to be pumping blood at an alarming rate; her face was hot, and her head felt light. ''I thought you invited me to come because you wanted to . . . to see more of . . .'' Her breath ran out, and she stood looking at him now that her eyes had become accustomed to the darkness. There was nothing she wanted more than to hear him say that her coming to Grenfall hadn't been a mistake.

Louis flipped the cigar into the night, watching the little arc reflected for an instant in the questioning blue eyes lifted to him. ''I guess I do owe you an apology.'' One hand moved over his face in a washing movement, as though to remove an accumulation of guilt visible there. When he took his hand away, he saw a new look of bewilderment on her beautiful face and let out a half-groan. "God! You're more temptation than a man can bear, Rose." In one liquid movement he stood and reached for her, hating himself more than a little, but giving in to a great rush of passion.

Letting out a sigh of delight, Rose moved the half-step it took to meet him, her upturned face and gently rising breasts a blur of pink and white. Her heart raced; her pulse sang. Louis did want her, did care for her. His head lowered. Warm lips met hers, setting her insides to quivering, tumbling all her girlish dreams into one giant blazing star. When his arms tightened and crushed her to him, Rose felt she would melt. Or maybe even explode! Never had she dreamed that a kiss could create such bewildering, delicious sensations—

"I see you're telling Rose your news," came a familiar voice from the doorway. Jean Pierre could see the figures at the end of the veranda, but his eyes hadn't adjusted from the lighted foyer.

Louis dropped his arms and allowed a breathless, flushed Rose to back away. She stared at him before turning to ask over her shoulder, "Jean Pierre, why are you spying on me . . . and what are you talking about?"

"Don't tell me Louis hasn't given you the big news." He had reached the couple now and peered at Rose. "And what makes you think I would spy on you?" Her eyes were big and fixed on Louis. What had he interrupted?

"What news, Louis?" Rose asked, aggravated at the intrusion, her senses still reeling from the feel of Louis's mouth and body against hers.

"Tell her, or I will." Jean Pierre's deep voice was firm and brooked no argument. In confusion Rose looked from one to the other, aware that some kind of tension stretched between the two young men.

Louis gazed at the beautiful blonde as if hypnotized, saying in a voice devoid of its usual color and warmth, "I married Arlene Duhon three days ago."

With disbelief Rose looked at Jean Pierre and then back

at Louis. "Tell me this is some kind of ridiculous joke you two have hatched up," she said to the man who had made her lips tingle only moments before.

"I wish I could."

"But how? Why? Who is this Arlene Duhon? Why isn't she here beside you?" Tears of pain and humiliation formed, but she refused to let them surface. She fought to find enough breath to ask more, but failed. Why had he asked her here . . . and why had he kissed her? Something within her felt soiled.

"Let's just say that Arlene's father caught Louis in a rather compromising position and marched the couple to the priest," Jean Pierre explained, a bit shocked that his usually glib friend was offering little information. After all, Louis did owe Rose some explanation, since he had been the one all fired up to have her come to Grenfall. Something about Louis's insistence on her attending the party hadn't set right with Jean Pierre from the beginning, but he had pushed down the niggling thoughts. The pained look on Rose's face spurred him on. "Arlene and her father live on a riverboat an hour away down the bayou. Louis has been seeing her off and on since he came home and—"

"Hush up," Rose interrupted. "I don't know why you made this your business, but I don't need to hear more." On the inside she was screaming that for someone to force a couple not in love into marrying was obscene, indecent. No matter that Louis might have been caught kissing Arlene—and she would not dare think it could have been more than that—he shouldn't have had to ruin his entire life, or this Arlene's, simply because of the area's ridiculous customs about the sanctity of womanhood. And what had it done to her life? Not that Louis had indicated he was interested in courting her, but— Her pride battled to erase all other feelings. She didn't want pity from either of the men watching her with wide, soulful eyes. "Forget it," she snapped, pride having won and put her back in control. It was not her way to be found vulnerable a second time, once she recognized the root of the temporary weakness. "Go find your wife, Louis, and act like a husband." With a swish of angry petticoats and sprigged muslin skirt, she tossed her head and started back inside just as Phillip appeared in the doorway.

"Rose, I've been looking for you," the Spaniard said, trying to see who was at the end of the veranda. In his hand he held two stemmed glasses. "Would you like a glass of champagne to sip while we explore the grounds?"

"But of course I would, Phillip," she replied in an agreeable voice loud enough for the two in the shadows to hear. Never would she admit she'd not tasted any before. "This old veranda has become quite boring." With a half-look over her shoulder toward Louis and Jean Pierre, she lied, in an exaggerated tone, "And I just love champagne." Taking the glass in one hand and slipping the other through the crook of his offered elbow, she allowed Phillip to lead her down the stairs and toward the torchlighted path ahead.

"This is delightful to have you all to myself," Phillip said. They had walked all the way to the pier, where they finished the champagne, and were now crossing beneath the trees toward the pergola. Obviously encouraged by her warm greeting when he found her on the veranda, he had held his arm across her back as they walked. When she tried to draw away, he said, "Since the torchlights don't light this area, I feel I must keep you from slipping upon the wet grass." She made no reply but continued to move away from his touch.

"I know how to walk on grass without falling," Rose said, a hint of steel behind her soft voice. Something about the way he looked at her had bothered her ever since she met him, and now she was finding that to have him put his hand on her was almost repulsive. Her anger at what she viewed as Louis's betrayal had eased a bit, and she regretted having accepted Phillip's invitation. And her head felt funny.

Phillip lightly touched her elbow when they reached the open side of the pergola. "Beautiful," he said, making no pretense of meaning anything but that she was the object he praised.

Hating the way his eyes raked her breasts, Rose wished

she could restore the altered flounce to her shoulders. She
no longer cared for a stylish look. It hadn't been for those
hot eyes to see more of her that she had consented to
display so much of her bosom. Foolish. She had been
foolish ever to have come to Grenfall, where she didn't
belong. Doggedly, she determined to get through this
evening and replied, "Yes, the bougainvillea vines are
lovely, but I'm ready to go back inside now."

"Not yet, my little flower." He leaned closer then, and
she could detect more than fresh champagne on his breath.
A strong, sweetish smell brought a pang of nausea. He had
been drinking whiskey.

Suddenly Rose despised his long face and skimpy lips
and everything about him. She snapped, "I'm not your
little flower." His hand went to her waist and she slapped
at it. A brush of goosebumps slithered up her spine when
the hand tightened its hold. "Don't put your hands on
me!" Never had any boy or man made a move around her
body that she hadn't controlled. Willing her head to act
right, she tensed in awful indignation.

"And why not? You've been flirting with me all evening." His arms imprisoned her then, pinning her, arms
and all, against his lanky frame. "You've no idea what
you do to me—or what I can do for you, Rose. Your
beauty is wasted here." The thin lips split into something
resembling a smile.

Shuddering in the half-light, Rose watched his tongue
wet his upper lip and spat, "Let me go, you Spanish
dog!" The smell of him, the touch of him sickened her.
Surely he would free her before he allowed her to scream
for help.

Phillip stiffened but did not ease his hold. "Is that a way
to talk to one who can give you the world? Wouldn't you
like to go to New Orleans with me and then to Spain?
What a pair we'd make!" When she continued to struggle,
he lost control and hissed beside her ear, "How dare you
turn me down and call me names, you dumb little Cajun?
Who do you think you are to hold yourself holier than me,
the governor's nephew? You need me to grant land to your
precious Cajuns."

He jerked her closer to him then and kissed her, his mouth voracious and punishing. As she fought to free herself, he kept his cruel, wet mouth on hers and reached to the front of her gown. Her arms still pinned against him, Rose kicked out, but she was too close to inflict any noticeable pain. When his hand reached to grab a breast and free it from the low neck of her gown, she struggled harder, almost gagging from his tongue's hateful intrusion, wanting to cry out from the pain of his rough handling of her tender breast.

Rose squirmed as though she were in the center of a consuming fire, not believing the liberties Phillip's free hand was taking. She heard the flounce at the neckline of her gown rip just before he forced her protesting body to the ground beneath him. Once she thought she might get out a scream when he lifted his ravenous mouth for a moment while fumbling with his pants and her skirts, but all sound lay trapped behind the searing knots of nausea in her throat. Then he caught her lips in his again, his teeth biting greedily, his tongue savaging . . . and that dreaded part of him hard and frightening, stabbing at her down low. If only she could get her arms free—

"You dirty Spaniard!" came a low, powerful voice from right above where they lay panting and struggling on the ground. Muttering other foul terms, Jean Pierre swooped to grab Rose's attacker and jerk him up. "I ought to kill you!"

"You're nothing but a lousy Cajun, and you'd best think who you're threatening," Phillip snarled, too angered and aroused to do more than make a feeble attempt to escape Jean Pierre's powerful grasp. "If it's the last thing I do, I'll make you pay—"

With one loud crack, Jean Pierre smashed his fist into Phillip's distorted, surprised face. Rose crawled to the edge of the pergola, gasping and wondering how her heart could beat so fast, allowing the nausea to have its way. One more sickening blow followed by a guttural groan and Phillip lay sprawled on the ground, still and making no further sound.

"What the hell—!" Louis rushed into the pergola. He

had disobeyed Jean Pierre and followed him, thinking at the time that his friend was being overly zealous in his attempts to look after Rose. "You were right, Jean Pierre," Louis said when he took in the scene. "The louse was up to no good."

Jean Pierre had reached Rose by then and was cradling her in his arms. "Are you all right?" he asked, ignoring his bruised hand and using it to smooth back her hair, to fondle her grieving face. "Tell me, Rose. Are you all right?" He saw for the first time that the torn gown exposed her breasts, and he turned and called, "Louis, throw me your coat."

Within minutes Rose had mustered enough control to look at the two young men. "Thank God you came when you did," she said to Jean Pierre between hiccuping sobs, humbled at the thought of what would have taken place in the shadowed pergola had he not come when he did. "I'm glad you spied upon me this time." When his face showed none of the anger at her that she expected, she went on, "Thank you for rescuing me. I don't have to be told that I was foolish to be out with Phillip like this." Was that sympathy on his face? Surely not. It was too dark to read expressions well.

"What are we to do with this...sad piece of a Spaniard?" Louis asked, feeling guilty for having delayed telling Rose of his marriage and then letting her wander off with Phillip when she was plainly upset. "Fortunately, Celeste and the others stopped off at the house to listen to her play the harpsichord before coming to the front grounds, but from what I overheard, they'll probably be here soon. They asked where Phillip and Rose were. We need to get this baggage over to the *garçonnière,* don't you think? He's one mean flea and will be out for blood when he comes to."

Louis tried not to stare at the miserable young woman clinging to Jean Pierre. He hated to admit it, but he realized that both would have to withhold further retribution against the nephew of the governor. It would take all the effort he could muster to persuade his hardheaded friend to leave Phillip alone. He knew that he himself longed to pummel Phillip senseless when he awoke and figured that Jean Pierre had even more vile punishment in mind. But what should be done about Rose's predicament? No breath of scandal should sully her name, and certainly not one connected with Grenfall.

"How do you feel about marrying this man, Rose?" Jean Pierre asked, his voice husky, almost sorrowful.

She pushed away from his cradling arms there on the ground to hiss, "Have you lost your mind? I'd like to kill him, not marry him. I never want to see him again!"

"You know that such an attack cannot be ignored." His voice sounded heavier, deeper, but threaded with a new softness. He leaned to pull Louis's coat up closer around her neck, his hands gentle. "I must answer to Papa about this, but I first want to learn your feelings." His eyes questioned hers in the near darkness.

Her small, pale face still revealing shock, Rose retorted, "Do you mean you'd tell Papa about this . . . monster's attacking me and that he'd want me to marry him? That's outrageous!" Jean Pierre's snuggling the coat closer about her face and shoulders had brought a fuller sense of redemption. Where his fingers had brushed her face and chin, a warmth had lingered, seeming to reassure her that all was well. Now she wasn't sure. With more bravado than she felt, she said, "Papa would never ask me to marry someone I didn't choose myself." What she had learned earlier about Louis's forced marriage nagged at her. Holy Mother! Was such a fate to be hers as well? Little waves of nausea returned.

"You know the customs among our people as well as I," Jean Pierre replied, studying the troubled face before him.

"And among all the colonists," Louis said miserably, coming over to kneel near where they sat upon the ground. "Rose is right, though. No matter if Phillip had succeeded with his vile attentions, she shouldn't be forced to marry someone so cruel and despicable. What a loathsome custom— it adds insult to injury." Even in the pale light, he didn't miss the indignant look she shot him. "Perhaps you could tell your father that you can't identify the man who tried to force himself upon you.''

"Why do I have to tell him at all?" Rose asked, her body trembling, her mind racing from one improbable thought to another. "If you two will keep quiet, we can pretend this didn't happen and go on as before."

"You know that news of what took place tonight will spread, no matter how hard we three try to squelch it. I don't like lying to Papa," Jean Pierre confessed while rising and walking to where Phillip lay still. "But what about him?" He prodded the Spaniard's prone form with his boot. "He'll want revenge and cause endless trouble over this. He may be the governor's nephew, but he's filth."

"Well, I would rather lie to Papa than end up with his forcing me to marry. . . ." Scalding tears formed, and Rose almost gave in to them at the horrible thought of becoming the Spaniard's wife.

"Let's lug him to the guesthouse before the others get out here," Jean Pierre said to Louis after he briefly outlined his plans for the morrow. "The fewer who learn of this, the better."

"You take him on over and dump him while I go with Rose around to the back and sneak her upstairs without anyone seeing her," Louis replied. He offered his hands and helped her to stand. "Are you really all right?"

Rose heard the sorrow in his voice, and felt her heart echo it. Did he, too, regret the way Fate seemed to have altered what might have developed between them? The evening hadn't brought any of the joy she had dreamed of.

As Louis led her in a large circle beneath low-limbed trees toward the back of the house, they heard Celeste and her guests leaving the veranda and wandering down the path toward the bayou. Jarrette called her name, and then Phillip's. A sob tore at Rose's throat at the thought of all that had gone wrong that night.

"Jean Pierre and I will tell everyone you became overly tired and went to bed early," Louis told her when they reached the safety of the guest bedroom. He led her inside and closed the door. "Then in the morning, Jean Pierre and you can be well on your way home before anyone here is awake." The agony on her small face tore at him, but he knew that he had contributed to it, and he swore he'd keep his hands to himself. He should never have invited her here . . . certainly should never have kissed her.

Suddenly overcome by fatigue, Rose nodded her head. "Please leave now, Louis." She heard the door close and began shedding her torn, rumpled gown. Tomorrow seemed unimportant. All she could think of was blocking out the events of the evening and escaping into the comforting arms of sleep. Jean Pierre would work out something.

In the Guilbeau kitchen the next afternoon, Papa's words, like a stump looming ahead suddenly in a fog-shrouded bayou, startled Rose. The mists clouding her brain since Phillip's attack receded a bit, uncovering the keen edges.

"You're not my parents?" Rose asked, realizing she echoed Pierre Guilbeau's very words, but unable to come up with others. Had he lost his mind? "What do you mean I'm not your daughter?" The back of her hand against trembling lips stifled a rising cry as she looked from Papa to Maman and then to Jean Pierre, trying to comprehend. Was this another part of the nightmare she seemed to have been living for the past twenty-four hours?

Clearing his throat, Pierre seemed hesitant to speak. "It's true, Rose." Finally he lifted troubled eyes to look from his wife, Marie, to Rose. "Our decision not to tell you those many years ago seems now to have been a mistake. Jean Pierre was two when Cousin Jean Henri gave him to us to take on the ship from Acadia, so of course he remembered his parents at that time. But you were a newborn infant. . . . All along we had planned to tell you on your seventeenth birthday . . . next week."

Rose recovered her voice, but not yet her composure. "Do you mean that Yvette isn't truly my sister—that Jarrette and little Robert aren't my brothers?" Wide blue eyes filled with bewilderment, pleaded for retraction. "If I'm not your daughter, who am I?"

Jean Pierre glanced at his wife with fondness and a

noticeable touch of sadness. "Marie, it's time we heard from you."

The afternoon sunlight streaming through the windows caught the strands of gray in Marie's black hair and seemed to multiply their number. Her face pale and unsmiling and her normally twinkling eyes full, she said, "You've been our daughter almost seventeen years, Rose, though other people were your God-given parents. We've loved you as our own and find it hard to believe that I didn't give birth to you along with Jarrette, as we led everyone here but close family to believe."

"Who are my parents, and how did you get me?" Rose asked with a catch in her voice.

"Your parents were Charles and Margaret Winstead, our dearest friends when we stopped in Maryland after the British removed us from our farms in Acadia," Pierre said. He was already wondering if his decision to tell Rose the truth had been the right one. Causing pain to one he loved so much tore at his heart. How much better it would have been if Rose had been told about her parents at an early age and grown up with that knowledge as Jean Pierre had. He sighed; Grandmère had been right. Marie and he had overridden her wise old mother's warning, and they must live with that mistake now.

As if needing busy hands, Marie went to the fireplace for the coffeepot and refilled the cups while Pierre continued.

"Your mother and father were from England. Your grandfather, Elgin Winstead, the Earl of Wanington, disowned your father when he married your mother, a commoner. With your pinkish golden hair and blue eyes, you're the spitting image of your mother as we knew her in Maryland. Your father was so much in love with her that he told me often how giving up an inheritance was a small sacrifice."

No one spoke until Marie added, "Meg, as we called your mother, died right after you were born. Since I was nursing Jarrette, who was actually born on the same day as you, your father brought you to me."

"Did Jarrette come by on his way to meet Arlee Simpson before we got here? I want to see him," Rose demanded, her need for his moral support crying out. She was relieved that Yvette and Robert had gone fishing, but she longed for Jarrette's comforting presence. He had always been the only one who understood her, she agonized. Last night when she had wished for him, he had been dancing attendance on Celeste, and now—

"No," Marie replied. "But he'll probably be along shortly. Does he know . . . ?"

"No," Jean Pierre answered, his first contribution to the conversation. "Louis wasn't to tell anyone but his father."

Rose hid her face in her hands. Would it truly help to talk with her twin . . . or the one she had believed to be her twin, she reminded herself with a pang. "Go on, Maman," she said, regaining her self-possession and uncovering her face.

"We asked your father to come and stay with us," Marie continued, her voice steadier now that Rose seemed to be holding up. "He seemed to have lost all desire to live after his beloved Meg was gone. You had a brother Courtney, Jean Pierre's age, who needed looking after, too. Charles was not hard to convince that all of us would be better off living together. We were a happy group for a short time—two big boys and two beautiful babies! Charles recovered from some of his heartbreak over Meg when he began holding you and playing with Courtney again."

"Where is . . . that man now?" Rose asked, still too stunned to understand all she had heard. She balked at calling anyone her father but the big man sitting at the table. Seeing the scarred, gnarled hands nursing his coffee cup reminded her of the countless times they had paused in making furniture or hoeing in the fields to stroke her hair and soothe away hurts, both real and imagined.

Pierre broke the silence this time. "One day when you were two months old, your father took Courtney fishing with him. A storm came up and capsized the boat. Both drowned. We laid them to rest by your mother's side."

"Your ruby necklace was your father's wedding gift to your mother," Marie said. "When Meg died, Charles gave it to me to pass on to you." Marie wiped at a tear, then brushed at an imaginary crumb on the gleaming oak surface of the table.

Rose fingered the pendant on its long chain, nestling it in her palm. Such jewelry was rare among Cajuns, as was the coloring of her skin and hair, yet no one, to her knowledge, had ever made an issue of either oddity. She didn't remember when it was given to her, but she knew that she had never taken it off. Had she always known it held some special meaning? Strange, she mused, that she had never before wondered why the younger sister, Yvette, wore no such impressive jewelry. To what other things had she been blind?

"When did we come to the Bayou Teche?" Rose asked, the events in her past begging for answers before she was willing to face the problems of today. It wasn't like Jean Pierre to sit back and say nothing. Once or twice she had glanced his way, but he seemed hesitant to meet her puzzled looks. What had he told Papa about Phillip de Cordoza and—? No. She would not think of that right now. There was no link between that and this strange tale about her real parents.

"We came to Louisiana the following year. By then we had earned enough money working for farmers to pay our passage here and join those from our village of Grand Pre in Acadia," Pierre replied.

"Why are you telling me this now?" Rose asked. She shot an accusing look at Jean Pierre. He knew something she didn't—why else the withdrawal, the refusal to meet her eyes? His brooding silences were one of the major changes that made her feel she no longer knew him. Before he had left home to trap, Jean Pierre had been as full of fun and laughter as Papa and Jarrette. She resented his shutting her out of his life and sometimes recognized that she taunted and teased in an attempt to regain his earlier attention. More often, though, she chose to put the blame on him for their alienation. All the way home that morning, he had talked very little while paddling the pirogue . . . and she had not spoken at all.

"Because you and Jean Pierre must be married right away," Pierre replied, killing her thoughts. His voice was so low and strained that Rose wasn't sure she had heard correctly.

"Marry Jean Pierre! Why would I marry Jean Pierre?" Rose protested, stiffening. Nibbling at her bottom lip, she continued, "He's not the one who...attacked me." A part of her noted that Pierre looked tired and older than she recalled. How long had the gray hairs outnumbered the black on that familiar head? She regretted any part she might have had in causing him grief, and was willing to do almost anything to put a smile back on his face—short of marrying Jean Pierre. An inane question popped into her mind: What was she supposed to call Pierre now? He had always been "Papa" since she could remember, not this Charles Winstead. Surely she wasn't expected to feel anything for a man she never knew? "I can't seem to think straight, but I know I can't marry Jean Pierre. Can't we forget everything that happened?"

"No, my little Rose." Pierre shook his head, a finger tracing inadvertent circles around the rim of his cup. He shot a look at his namesake before going on, "You've been wronged, and Jean Pierre will take the responsibility. We trusted you to his care at the party, and now your name is likely to be bandied about in degrading terms."

"Papa," Rose urged, placing her hand on his work-muscled arm, "you know Jean Pierre and I haven't gotten along well in a long time. I'm trying to stand up for my rights, as you've taught me. I prefer to live with the reputation I might have acquired than to spend the rest of my life with someone I don't love...and one who doesn't love me." Her pale fingers clutched at his arm; her blue eyes held his gaze with desperation in the ensuing silence.

Even though Rose sat in her accustomed position on the side bench near Pierre, she felt strangely out-of-place, and her hand loosened its hold on the unrelenting arm. The spacious room, serving as both kitchen and sitting room, did not offer its usual comfort. It struck her that the major portion of her time at home had been spent in this room, that it was somehow the nucleus of the entire family. Here they prayed together, ate together, talked freely, teased and laughed with one another, read and studied, entertained visitors—myriad happy memories connected with the Guilbeau kitchen flooded her mind and heart. Now it was the stage for the bizarre scenes that were shaking her world.

Still musing in the silence, Rose looked to the other end of the big table to see Maman studying her work-worn hands folded on the polished surface, her normally smiling face grave. A quick glance at Jean Pierre across from her showed a countenance as frozen and pale as hers probably was. She was grateful that his dark eyes were staring into the black depths of the coffee mug he held with white-knuckled firmness and that she could avoid seeing what lay in them. Surely he must be as opposed to Papa's plan as she. Why wasn't he throwing his weight and deep voice around as he usually did to gain whatever he wanted? Only the tick of the clock on the mantel broke the silence.

Had Jean Pierre suggested to Papa that he marry her? Rose wondered. Exactly how much had he told? Surely he knew, as she did, that he had rescued her before Phillip de Cordoza had done more than kiss and maul her and tear her gown; but as terrible as those actions were, she hadn't actually been raped. If she told the sordid details of the attack in the pergola now, she well knew that Papa would seek out the despicable Spaniard and force him to marry her. The unsavory thought held her tongue . . . but marry Jean Pierre? Believing that she had only those two choices, she sat confounded, unable to force her thoughts into any sort of rational channels.

Chapter Four

Directly across from Rose in the Guilbeau kitchen, Jean Pierre had sat with his own jumbled thoughts throughout the incongruous conversation, sometimes staring at the familiar, giant fireplace with its adjoining brick oven for baking. Even if he were to hold his hands out to that smoldering fire as he had done as a child, he knew he wouldn't gain the comfort he needed. He tried to concentrate first on the black kettle sitting in its accustomed place on the hearth, next on the trivet at the edge of the red-topped coals holding the coffeepot, then on the iron rod angled against the side brick, its end curved to serve as a poker. But, as the others talked, not even the sight of everyday objects eased his mind, could make him feel that the world would ever again be right.

What was it about Rose that had seemed to fascinate him ever since his return from that first trip north two years ago? Since then, he had never stayed home more than a few weeks in the spring and summer, but while there, Jean Pierre had felt a mysterious uneasiness in watching how the pretty, vivacious Rose was turning more each year into a beautiful, desirable young woman. He had come to realize that he sometimes felt like a moth being drawn to a flame, and more than once had blamed his frequent lashing out at her on his reluctance to be attracted to such forbidden fruit.

Apparently sensing Jean Pierre's inner restlessness about Rose, Grandmère had secretly told him two years ago that the pretty blonde wasn't his cousin, but he had never allowed himself to dwell upon her words, preferring instead to keep down nagging thoughts—at least until Rose herself learned the truth from Papa. Wondering at first if he had spoken too hastily in offering marriage during his earlier talk with Papa, he knew that he couldn't allow her to be married to the cruel and hateful Phillip de Cordoza.

Rose deserved better—that was what Jean Pierre had often told himself whenever he would insist that her actions and looks be beyond reproach. Something whispered that he might be a bit in love with the beautiful blonde. Now came the hard part: Was he the reward she deserved? Even if he found he did love Rose, was he the one who could give her happiness?

"Rose," Jean Pierre began, knowing the time had come

for him to speak. Three pairs of eyes swung his way. He
inhaled deeply and let out the air before he went on.
"What do you want? You do have a choice in this matter."
Suddenly he had the urge to smash his fist again into
Phillip's arrogant face.

"Choices? What are they?" Rose asked, pushing back
her hair from her face, unaware that the same shaft of
afternoon sunlight that pointed out Marie's gray strands
transformed her own curls into a golden mass tinged with
pink.

Knowing that Pierre was no different from any of the
men in the area about seeking marriage for the young
women in their families at the first hint of scandal, Rose
stared across at Jean Pierre. Choices? She could either
confess that she knew who had attacked her—by now she
was fairly certain that Pierre did not know all the facts—
and allow Papa to force the repulsive Spaniard to marry
her, or else she could consent to marry Jean Pierre. *Some
choices,* she thought with disgust.

But wait! Her chin lifted, and her mouth pursed. There
was a third to consider. She could become a nun, as her
twelve-year-old sister planned to do. Never, she realized,
could she think of Yvette or any of the Guilbeaus as
anything but what they had always seemed: they were her
family, would always be.

When Yvette was very small and talked of being a nun,
Maman and Papa had expressed joy that she seemed
dedicated and eager to go into the Church. Yvette's decision had removed a burden from Rose. For generations a
female member of the Guilbeau family had worn the cloth,
but Rose had felt no such inclination. Even now, that
choice seemed to run a poor second in her estimation.
Mayhap joining the Ursulines would be wiser than marrying a man she didn't love—and one who didn't love her,
she thought.

But, she agonized while the other three wordlessly
watched her with varying degrees of love and bewilderment, all of her plans for her future dealt with love and
children and family closeness. Could she bear to toss them
away and strive to serve God alone?

Thoughts flashing like jagged bits of lightning in a summer storm, Rose recognized that a dark stream of passion flowed within her veins and that to attempt to ignore it would be impossible. To embrace life to the fullest was her goal, not to be cloistered away from it. She sensed that she could never be fulfilled if she turned away from what seemed her only chance to pursue the major portions of her dreams. At least marriage to Jean Pierre would offer all except one . . . love. Mayhap the talk she had heard about how some husbands and wives marry without love and yet find contentment in their devotion to children and work was true. Resolutely she watched all but one choice fade.

"Come on, Rose. Tell us what you're thinking," Jean Pierre coaxed, reaching across and covering her hand where it lay palm-up on the oak table. She had never looked more beautiful . . . or more vulnerable. What punishing thoughts tore at her?

Rose snatched away her hand as though his touch were a burning coal. "We've never been forced to tell our thoughts, Jean Pierre Guilbeau," she snapped, "and I'm not about to start now." A thumb and forefinger found the pendant, sliding it back and forth against the chain. She tried to recall the warm feelings she had felt for him on the previous night when he rescued her, but to no avail. His deep voice and great size no longer comforted her. All she could think of was that they had become strangers, that she had never pleased him since he left home . . . and she doubted she ever would. Not that she cared to, she reminded herself. Her stare evolved into a glare.

His dark eyes pained, Jean Pierre softened his deep voice. "I wasn't giving an order, just letting you know I care what you're thinking."

Pierre stood up, slid back the heavy chair, and motioned to Marie. He sensed their presence was no longer needed. Throughout Rose's life, she had seemed to possess a will unlike any he had ever come up against in Cajun females. Both Marie and he had tried to teach her to channel it toward wholesome goals, but ever since she had reached her teens, Rose often had run rampant over the peace-

loving members of the family when things had not gone to
her liking. She was never disrespectful, just obstinately
convinced that her way of thinking was the only right one.
Jarrette could sometimes reason with her, but only Jean
Pierre had ever been able to fence with her effectively
when she became riled.

"Come, dear," Pierre said to Marie. "Let's leave the
young folks to talk privately."

Rose had no desire to be alone with Jean Pierre, but she
felt too numb to protest. Watching the couple leave the
room, Papa's callused hand resting lightly on Maman's
plump back, she envied their apparent love and closeness.
Such a marriage was what she longed for.

Another uncomfortable silence claimed the room still
fragrant with the smells from the earlier noonday meal. A
half-eaten peach cobbler sat on the sideboard, its tart,
fruity smell escaping from beneath the clean, ironed flour
sack covering the large stoneware dish. Beside it sat a
cookie jar of like ware, its top nicked from countless
careless hands fingering forth the ever-present, spicy mo-
lasses treats—sometimes by invitation, sometimes by stealth.

As skittering thoughts crammed her mind, Rose looked
at the young man who had offered to marry her. No longer
"brother" from custom, no longer "cousin" in actuality,
who was he? For the first time, Rose scrutinized him as
she might any man she would consider as a prospective
husband. She knew from having seen him occasionally
without a shirt down at the bayou that his body was lean
and muscular, proof of an infrangible strength. Often she
had heard Pierre brag that Jean Pierre stood so tall and
straight because his father, Pierre's beloved cousin, had
been a leader among men and that Jean Pierre could be no
less himself.

And, Rose confessed silently, she could honestly say
that others respected this man she had believed to be her
cousin. He was, indeed, a handsome, fascinating young
man to those of the opposite sex, if the mere numbers seen
trying to attract his attention were any measure—not that
she was swayed by popular opinion. She puzzled over why
such a man, who, she felt sure, could claim any other

woman along the bayou as his wife, would offer to marry her . . . until she remembered: the Guilbeau name was in jeopardy, one long since concordant with pride and honor, judging from all the family tales told over the years in that very room. Jean Pierre was upholding the unblemished family name. The habitual contemplative look she had come to associate with him over the past few years masked his face, lending the usual air of mystery as to what was going on behind those sharp eyes. Did she see compassion?

Not compassion but indecision better identified the ponderings rambling through Jean Pierre's mind there in the kitchen. Many times during family discussions through the years he had heard Rose say that her goals in life were to be married to a Cajun who loved everything about her, to live on the Bayou Teche, and to raise babies just as Maman had. Now that she knew the truth about her English parents, would she be content with such a simple lifestyle? Or would she seek different goals now that she had learned of her aristocratic father?

Looking at the delicate beauty in the face before him, Jean Pierre suddenly realized what had gnawed at him ever since he had escorted her to Grenfall, especially since he had rescued her in the pergola. He was more than a little in love with Rose. His heart did a flipflop. He truly loved her . . . and probably always had. The truth jolted him, brought a dryness to his mouth, a new rhythm to his pulse. To lose her now that he understood what drew him to her would be a fate he couldn't bear. Yet, because of this startling admission to himself, he felt compelled to speak.

"What's your decision, Rose?" Jean Pierre asked, his deep voice hiding a sudden storm of heartbeats. He moved from the bench across from her to take Papa's vacated chair at the head of the table. How he would love to know what was going on in that brain he had already learned was equal to any he had encountered. Papa's revelation had swept away all need to pretend that Rose was a kinswoman, and Jean Pierre felt a profound gratitude for his new sense of freedom. All at once he felt there was nothing he couldn't master.

Panicking on the inside, like an animal suddenly caged,

Rose commanded, "Don't try to push me around, Jean Pierre! I'm in no mood to take orders from you."

"In the mood or not, I'm afraid that this time you'll have to listen. And don't be such a touchy wildcat. I'm not trying to push you around. Can't you see I'm only trying to help?" The defiance in her voice ruffled his earlier thoughts that there was nothing he couldn't master.

"Help me?" Rose hissed. Then, "Help me?" The last words came out in a half-strangled sob. She crossed her arms below her breasts, fixing him with an accusing look. The white blouse made her face appear even paler than it was. "Why did you have to meddle and tell Papa you'd marry me?"

"Would you rather I told the entire truth so you could marry Phillip?" He saw her lift her chin, as if preparing for a real battle; he heard her catch her breath and retain it. "Or are you holding out for Louis?" She reeled a bit from his last question, then shot a haughty look his way. Jealousy—labeled accurately for the first time—nibbled at him, and he couldn't keep from taunting, "He's married, you know."

Caught unawares by the turn in the conversation, Rose stared open-mouthed at the black-haired young man beside her. Never would she let him know he had rattled her.

Leaning toward him, her jaw set, she retorted, "How dare you rub that in! You know that Louis invited me to the party before that horrible business of having to marry that Duhon girl. How do you know that things would not have turned out beautifully if—" She couldn't complete the thought. Blue eyes flashed in fury at all the injustices of the past twenty-four hours. "You're despicable."

"My God! Didn't you hear what I said? You have a decision to make. There's no point in rehashing what might have been or dragging up our past quarrels. We are two adults now, aren't we?" Jean Pierre rose from his chair, stepped around the end of the table, and gently but forcefully pulled Rose to her feet. His hands on her shoulders, his fingers digging through her blouse, he willed her to look at him. "Granted, your choices may be all bad—and maybe marrying me is the worst of the lot—but you must choose."

Releasing her tensed, protesting body to return to its place, he straddled the bench to sit facing her, running spread fingers through his unruly black curls. "Is it because you can't think of me as a husband that you can't agree to marry me?" The deep voice had tempered now, as though his energy had been spent moments before. A part of him longed to pull her into hungry arms and tell her he loved her, had always loved her, that he would do his best to win her love, make her happy.

Rose swallowed hard. What was different about the bass vibrato in his voice? Maybe it was because he sat so near that she could feel his erratic breath on her face. She sensed an unleashed power in him, and almost leaned away to escape its subtle intrusion into the small space between them.

"No," she answered in a slow, puzzled way. She had never before thought of such a thing. "Jarrette and I've always been as close as any twins can be—but I've never felt as though you were kin . . . not even a distant cousin."

The startling truth of her words fell on Rose's ears, ran rushing through her, and found a nestling place in her mind. That Jean Pierre had seemed a stranger for some time now was certainly not a new thought. An unaccustomed shyness made a claim on her, brought a warm flush to her face. What did she really know about this young man who had been gone for the major part of the past three years? Had the muscle always twitched in his jaw like that when he seemed deep in thought? She returned his measuring gaze but made no comment. Startling her, a half-burned log shifted and then fell in the fireplace, the thud and crackles loud in the room.

"I've known for a number of years we weren't kin," Jean Pierre told her, his confession both cleansing and exhilarating to his mind and heart. He watched the blue eyes darken with a new comprehension. "For some time now, you've been someone dear to my heart in a way that has nothing to do with our growing up in the same house." There. He had said as much as he dared for the moment.

"You don't expect me to believe that, do you?" Rose

flipped her long hair with disdain and centered her interest on the fireplace.

Jean Pierre, who usually had a strong opinion about everything and seldom hesitated to express it, hushed then. True to his heritage, he had accepted the wishes and ways of the couple he had always considered his parents until some foreign urging had led him three years ago to seek for himself a code of behavior more suited to his temperament. Maybe he really did embody the spirit of his dead father, a man reputed to be as skilled at trapping as at farming.

All Jean Pierre knew was that he had enjoyed life in the North Wilderness. He had liked making his own decisions and had learned again and again that one must sometimes suffer for making bad ones, that mistakes shouldn't prevent one from trying again. No coward at home or in the wilderness, he never ducked a challenge. But neither did he make many unplanned moves. He sensed that this was not the time to be completely honest with her.

In an uncommonly gentle voice, one not quite steady, he said, "I want to marry you, Rose. What happened was my responsibility. I was too busy drinking and visiting to watch out for you as I should have. I'll do my best to make you happy, if you'll have me. Any man would be proud to call you his wife, just as I'll be."

"Why would you say that?" Rose quipped, surprised at his quiet statements, yet feeling defensive. Her eyes flew to those suddenly soft, assessing brown ones. Why was he staring at her mouth? Certainly, she realized with a jolt, she was sizing him up in a new light.

"Because you're so beautiful." Jean Pierre saw from up close that her skin was even creamier, her full lips even pinker than he had believed. The way her top lip eased over the slightly protruding upper front teeth charmed him anew. For the first time he allowed himself to imagine how it might feel to kiss that pouting mouth. Hope sang through his veins.

"Grandmère says beauty fades, that it shouldn't count for a lot." Rose went on with her study of the young man so close to her. Below the unruly black hair, which delighted her in its daring to fight back, his skin was dark olive and glowing with good health. She had to confess that heavy black brows above intelligent brown eyes, a straight but manly nose, and a chiseled, determined jaw belied any weakness of character or courage, features she would have chosen in a husband—if she had had a real choice, she reminded herself with a pang. His finely shaped mouth drew her gaze. He smiled just enough then to remind her of the little laugh wrinkle in his right cheek . . . one too long to call a dimple, but just as intriguing, she reflected.

"All right," Jean Pierre said agreeably, "let's say it's because you're a good cook."

"How would you know? You've not been home much over the past three years," she retorted.

Lips pursed as if in deep thought, Jean Pierre tried again, determined to soften the frozen look deep in Rose's blue eyes. "Because you're great at riding horses . . . especially spotted ones." His teeth gleamed white, the first true smile of the day dancing across his handsome face.

Rose dropped her belligerent gaze then and let silky, brown-tipped lashes hide her eyes. Her lips quirked a bit before she replied, "The ride on Calico didn't speak any better for you than for me." She fixed him with a level look then, half-mockery, half-admission.

"Who would've thought that pony had such hatred for females?" The smile turned into a boyish grin that set lights sparkling in his dark eyes. His pulse took off on a new race. She was no longer shutting him out completely.

"And," Rose shot back with a trace of her old good humor, "who would've thought you'd bring me an Indian pony from your first trip north and not learn more about it before telling me to climb on? It's a wonder I didn't fall and break my neck before you finally stopped that crazy runaway."

"So let's face it," Jean Pierre quipped, shrugging broad shoulders. "I'm not perfect." When she lifted her chin and seemed about to squelch him, he said, serious once more, "I meant it when I said you'll make a fine wife."

He backed off the bench and walked to the door, not

sure how much longer he could stay so near and not touch her, not confess all. Taking his cap from the peg, he plopped it on his head before turning back to her. He well knew how the entire family had spoiled her, had given in to her moods, and that she had always exercised a will far stronger than any young woman he had ever met. But he also knew that she revered Marie and Pierre and their wishes as much as he did. She would give her decision and make the best of it. He knew that about her, too. "Let me know when you've made up your mind."

Watching as Jean Pierre moved through the doorway in that cocky, squared-shouldered way of his, Rose felt a kind of panic grip her, as though when the door closed his offer would no longer be one of her options. Images of a leering Phillip and the confining walls of a convent strode through her mind. "Wait!" she called.

Jean Pierre retraced his steps to face her. "Yes?" he asked, an unreadable look clouding his handsome face. Inside, his heart beat wildly.

"Uh, I've decided," Rose stammered. Unable to meet his eyes, she stared at Grandmère's spinning wheel where it stood in the corner. "I choose to . . . marry you, Jean Pierre." The words rankled, left an aftertaste in her mouth.

Jean Pierre heard Rose's consent, but his heart recorded the hesitation in her voice and the pain in her blue eyes. Despite the overwhelming realization that he was going to win the young woman he loved, he felt no real happiness. If only once she had smiled . . .

As though eavesdropping—and she probably was—Marie came into the kitchen just then, clapping her hands in excitement. Pierre wasn't far behind, a huge smile wreathing his lined face. "We're happy that you two are going to marry!" She kissed and hugged Rose first, then reached high to embrace Jean Pierre. A serious expression washed over her features as she stepped back to the pale-faced Rose. "Pierre and I sometimes discussed telling you about your natural parents. We see now what a mistake we made not to tell you sooner, and we're sorry. Rose, we always loved you and Jean Pierre in the same way we loved our other children. I believe you know that."

Unshed tears brightening her eyes, Rose met the concerned gazes of the two she would forever think of as her parents and nodded. "I know," she whispered.

"Jean Pierre has always watched over you and Jarrette," Pierre said. "But always it was you he went to first. Jarrette was your playmate, but Jean Pierre was the one you wanted to please." As if he feared he might be on dangerous ground, Pierre went to add a log to the fire.

"The truth is, Rose," Marie explained with a catch in her voice, "that we noticed as you started turning into a young woman how the two of you began sizing each other up. We dared hope that someday . . ." Rose's unbelieving stare compelled Marie to go on. "Grandmère saw it, too, and confided to Jean Pierre that first time he came home from trapping that you two weren't kin. She told us she sensed Jean Pierre and you were destined to marry. We should have listened to her and told all then. I guess we thought we could keep you our little girl awhile longer." Her plump hand brushed nervously at her hair. "Maybe this marriage was meant to be."

"How will we explain it to our neighbors?" Rose asked, her voice trembly and sounding like someone else's. "It'll be a shock for them to hear of our marrying."

"No," Pierre said reassuringly from where he stood backed up to the fireplace. "Our relatives have always known that you weren't born to us, but they went along with our desire not to tell you until you were grown."

Marie added, "We felt sure that others suspected, but you know how we Cajuns believe in 'live and let live.'"

Relieved a bit by these explanations, Rose sat without answering, daring to hope that marrying Jean Pierre might be the best solution. Inside she trembled, felt weak all over. The past twenty-four hours had deluged her with far more than she could absorb readily.

"Maman is right, Rose," Jean Pierre assured her. "Some have hinted to me that they found it hard to believe that a woman with your coloring could be from a Cajun family, but no one seemed interested in kicking up a fuss. Of course, it has always been common knowledge that I wasn't born their son.'' His bass tones were soothing and rang with conviction.

Then Pierre spoke. ''Jean Pierre and I were talking earlier about how it might be best for the two of you to go ahead and leave for Fort Arkansas after the wedding. It won't be long before trapping season, and when you come back in the spring, folks will be used to the idea of your being married. Do you still feel that way, son?'' The term fell from his lips as readily as it did when he addressed Jarrette or Robert.

Jean Pierre looked thoughtful for a moment, glanced at Rose's uncommunicative face, and said, ''I do. I was planning to leave in a week or two anyway.''

When no other comments followed, Marie exclaimed, with love and excitement dancing in her black eyes, ''We must get busy with plans for the wedding.'' She turned to call, ''Come on in, Maman,'' to Grandmère, who was waiting just outside.

Grandmère, an older, withered version of her pretty daughter Marie, appeared in the doorway then, reaching out her arms for Rose and whispering endearments against her hair. ''Jarrette came a little while ago,'' she confided after stepping back and sizing up the pretty, woebegone face. ''We brought him up-to-date on things. He wants to see you before he goes up to Attakapas. He's waiting out on the porch swing.''

Rose caught her breath in gratitude and hurried outside.

''Rose,'' Jarrette said after she settled beside him on the swing. ''I hated learning from Papa what went on at Grenfall. I guess I was too involved with flirting with Celeste to think it strange that Jean Pierre and you had left me to borrow a pirogue to come home in.''

''There was no need for you to know any sooner than now,'' Rose answered consolingly, touched at the concern on his beloved face.

''Maybe, but I did wonder why Phillip acted so mean when I questioned him in the *garçonnière* about his awful black eye and bruised cheek. He was getting ready to leave before noon, and he glared at me and barked that it was none of my business, that it was between Jean Pierre and him alone."

She shuddered and looked away. "What did he actually say?"

Jarrette paused, took a deep breath, then blurted, "That he'd be getting even with him, even if he had to track him down, and that Jean Pierre hadn't heard the last of Phillip de Cordoza." He looked at her then, puzzled and more than concerned over the evil threat. "He seems the kind who'd be full of hot air, don't you think?"

In no uncertain terms, Rose gave her impression of Phillip, her voice low yet vehement.

"You see," Jarrette told Rose after she had vented her anger and disappointment over all that had happened since they'd left home the afternoon before, "folks aren't always in charge of their lives. I guess we'll have to face that more and more, now that we'll be seventeen this week. It doesn't matter that we're not actually twins . . . or kin at all. One way to look at it is to think how lucky we are that something . . . luck or fate or whatever . . . did allow us to grow up together and become close. No matter what happens or what names belong to us, Rose, we'll always be brother and sister. Don't you agree?"

"Oh yes!" she exclaimed, her hand resting against his as they talked in their accustomed way there in the porch swing, the supporting chains squeaking at each lazy, backward movement, just like always. "But I wanted to be wooed and made to feel special. How can I bear marrying Jean Pierre? You know how he's been so against me ever since—"

"Ever since you grew up?" Jarrette finished her sentence for her in the way that, from early childhood, they had come to read each other's thoughts. "While Papa and Maman, and now you, were going over all that happened, I kept thinking about that very thing. Do you suppose Jean Pierre might have begun seeing you as more than a cousin, maybe liking you as a man might like a pretty woman? Papa did say that Jean Pierre has known—"

"Yes," she broke in, sensing the rest of his thought. "Grandmère told him a while back, but I can't believe what you're suggesting is true." She shook her head, blond curls brushing against the back of the swing with a whisper. "He doesn't seem to like anything about me anymore." Rose's free hand captured the ruby pendant and slid it back and forth along the gold chain. Her eyes focused on a white crane settling onto a limb reaching out over the far side of the bayou, but her mind wasn't registering that at all.

"Then pay no never mind and think about your future," Jarrette responded cheerfully now. "I've noticed you hold your own with him pretty well, and you know Jean Pierre will take good care of you... and I know it too, or I couldn't keep myself from going to Papa and begging him to find some other way out of this mess."

Rose removed her hand from one of his lying between them on the swing and joined it with the one in her lap. Jarrette's world and hers were truly separating. "Then you think I'm not going to regret not becoming a nun?" The lump of remorse she had tried to swallow all day still pained her throat; she gave it one more try, but failed to dislodge it. Jarrette was leaving to learn to become a trapper. She, to become a... wife.

Jarrette hooted in a teasing way. "You want to know what I think?" When she nodded, a glimmer of the old spark deep in her eyes, he went on, "I think God would walk straight down from Heaven and block the doorway if you ever made such a move, Rose Guilbeau!" Noticing washes of color in her pretty cheeks and the tiny lift to her mouth he was hoping to see, the fine-featured young man went on in a caring voice, "If ever there was a girl meant to be a wife and mother, it's you. Think about it. What have you ever done but 'play house' and talk about being like Maman and Grandmère? Maybe everything does happen for the best." At her round-eyed expression of disbelief, he added, "What if Maman and Papa hadn't been neighbors to your natural parents back in Maryland? You can't wish away a part of chance without wishing away all of it."

Rose calmed at Jarrette's familiar, reassuring voice. He always made so much sense, she reflected. By the time he hugged her and left to tell the family goodbye, she was feeling a bit more like herself.

Obviously, Rose thought, alone in the gently moving swing with its hypnotic, rhythmic squeak, Marie's penchant for order and detail blinded her to the ludicrousness of the situation. One foot trailing just above the porch floor to push at intervals and keep up the soothing motion, she sat as if in a trance, knowing that inside, Marie, Pierre, and Grandmère were planning every detail of the wedding. It didn't matter that a Cajun wedding was one of the most festive of their celebrations; Rose wanted no part of the preparation. Until today, she had dreamed of her wedding as something special. Now it seemed a mockery. Maybe Maman and Papa believed they were doing what was best for her, but she needed time to think.

If she refused to marry Jean Pierre, where could she go? the dazed young woman agonized. Certainly not to England, where her natural parents had been ostracized. Discounting the people she had met at Grenfall, she knew no one except those who lived along their section of the Bayou Teche, sometimes called Curve Bayou. And she couldn't imagine life without Maman, Grandmère, Papa, and the others.

One hand busy again at worrying the pendant against its chain, Rose wished she could summon an alternative to thinking about the trio planning her wedding to Jean Pierre, which they seemed to view as a joyous occasion. She couldn't forget the way he had sat across from her with a peculiar, faraway look in his eyes, as though accepting his fate. *His* fate? she questioned testily. What about *hers?*

A part of her saw the crane across the bayou swoop from its perch in a white flash, its long yellow beak disappearing into the bayou water for a moment, then lifting with a wriggling brown fish clamped through its middle. As quickly as the long-legged bird had seized its prey, it soared out of sight into the deep forest beyond, its broad white wings flapping in rising rhythm. The suffering part of Rose dwelt upon the realization that she would need to dig deep to summon enough patience to live in peace with the forceful Jean Pierre. *But,* some inner voice shot back, *he won't find living with you any easier.*

"Maman," Rose called, going to the front door long after she had waved to Jarrette as he paddled off toward Attakapas, "where did you say Yvette and Robert are fishing? I think I'll take a walk and see what they've caught."

On her way to the side pier, Rose noticed that the late afternoon sun already hid beyond the surrounding forest of spread-topped oaks draped with hanging moss, the sparsely limbed cypresses, and the wide-leafed cottonwoods. Beneath a sagging oak limb swathed heavily with curling gray moss, she turned back and saw a peaceful light bathing the familiar house and outbuildings, lending a softness to the grayed cypress planks. Never again would she view home with the wide-eyed innocence of her yesterdays, she realized. When she eyed the swing, still swaying, then the steps beyond it leading to the sons' bedrooms beneath the rafters—a peculiar touch of architecture she had noticed on almost every Cajun home—she sighed.

Jarrette was gone, and, according to the plan for the newlyweds to depart for Fort Arkansas immediately after the upcoming ceremony, she would be leaving soon, too. A mosquito circled her head, and for the first time she heard its song as a high-pitched whine of sympathy.

The lump in Rose's throat swelled at the remembrance of all she had longed for and lost—especially the dreamed-of courtship by some unknown, romantic young man. She clapped her hands and drove away the pesky mosquito. Self-pity held no prominence in the proud young woman's constitution, and she squelched it, turning away and moving resolutely down the path to find her younger sister and brother. Thinking of them as siblings was easy, and she knew she would always think of them that way.

From the deepening shade up ahead, Rose could hear the familiar peals of Yvette's laughter and then Robert's; and she hurried, the first genuine smile of the day lighting her face. At that very moment, even she was unaware that somewhere deep inside, the seed of a plan struggled to take root.

Chapter Five

Rose yawned and stretched lazily before her eyes flicked open to see her bedroom brightening in the fast-approaching day. Birds sang to one another outside her window in a hauntingly beautiful cadence that ranged from flutelike notes to rich organ tones. The household was quiet, unlike the last few days, when all the family had been caught up in the excitement of the marriage that would take place the day after tomorrow, on Saturday.

The Guilbeaus, like most Acadians, were fun-loving and never missed an opportunity for a party, or *fais–do–do*. A wedding was an even better reason to celebrate. From what she had observed during the past week, Rose realized that both Maman and Papa must have truly longed for Jean Pierre and her to marry someday. Both acted as if a dream had come true, and Rose found she could not bear to mar their happiness with last-minute pleas to call off the ceremony—not that anything she might do or say could change things. And *she* had made the final choice, Rose reminded herself.

Determined to fill her mind with more pleasant thoughts, Rose left her bed to admire the majestic scene before her. A big orange sun was rising over the bayou, sending feelers of filtering sunlight through the low-hanging, moss-draped branches of the soaring trees and causing twinkling diamonds to dance on the dark water. The bayou moved in a serpentine path around the wide-rooted cypress trees dotting it, often with movement so slow as to be impercep-tible, but it was always moving. Like her thoughts, she reflected. Restless beneath an exterior of calmness. Headed for a destination unperceived.

A gentle breeze sneaked in through the open window, billowing the starched white curtains around the young woman and molding her cotton night dress to her dainty curves. Shivering a bit, more from the dreaded thoughts of all she would soon be facing than from the coolness of the wind, Rose turned away from the window and dressed hurriedly.

Rose, alone in the kitchen, filled her cup from two pots resting over banked coals in the fireplace, the stream of hot, creamy milk blending instantly with that of thick, black coffee—generously laced with chicory, South Louisiana style. A couple of appreciative sips later, she placed the nearby spider over the live coals to heat for cooking pancakes from the leftover batter someone had mixed earlier. Hearing a breathy whistle, Rose turned to see seven-year-old Robert rush into the kitchen on long legs almost as wobbly as a newborn colt's. The youngest Guilbeau was growing fast.

Rose's arms opened wide, and the boy ran into them, catching and holding her around the waist.

"Guess what, Rose?" Robert asked as he moved to sit on the bench at the table.

"What?" Rose answered, smiling at his childish way of telling something.

"I found a bird's nest yesterday in the woods," he said, his eyes wider than usual. "And guess what? There were three blue eggs in it with brown spots all over them. Will you go with me so I can show you?"

"I sure will. Just as soon as I can. First I'll cook us some pancakes for breakfast."

"You spoil that child unmercifully," Maman said teasingly as she entered the room. "He ate breakfast with Pierre and me not over an hour ago." Maman was plump and pretty and cleanly fragrant, with silver-streaked black hair and warm, dark eyes that smiled even on the rare occasions when her mouth didn't. She looked from Rose to Robert and stooped to kiss the cheek of her youngest child before clapping her hands and saying, "Well, I must go outside

and get Yvette to help me catch some chickens to cook for
the wedding reception on Saturday. That girl is such a
dreamer, she's probably wandered down to the bayou.
What a crowd there'll be with all the family and neighbors
there!''

Marie hurried out the back door, calling for Yvette.
When she was preparing for a party, Maman was at her
best, Rose thought with indulgence.

Once Rose and he had settled on the bench and sampled the pancakes covered with slabs of butter and golden
honey, Robert asked, ''Will Jean Pierre bring you back
with him when he comes home next year?''

''Of course he will.'' She tried not to think of next year.

''Will he still be my brother, and you my sister, even
after you're married?''

''Marriage doesn't change everything,'' Rose assured
the puzzled boy. ''You know that Jean Pierre has never
truly been your brother, only a cousin, don't you?''

The dark head nodded. ''But everybody wants him to be
a brother, and Papa calls him 'son.' ''

''Then think of him any way you want,'' Rose replied,
her tone sharp. As for her, she'd had too much thinking
about the man she would soon marry—was it really the
day after tomorrow at sunset? A knot in her stomach told
her to push aside her plate. Her appetite had fled.

''Maman says no matter what, I can still call you my
sister, and I'm glad.''

''So am I.'' Though she loved the boy and usually
enjoyed being with him, Rose felt hemmed in, felt the
need for lighter talk. ''Did you tell Maman about the
bird's nest you found?''

''No, I forgot.'' Eyes sparkling, Robert dropped his fork
onto his plate with a clatter and left the table. ''I'm going
to tell Maman,'' he called as he scooted out the door,
letting it slam in his haste.

The dishcloth moved in frantic circles on the polished
surface of the oak table as Rose spent her frustration. This
was what she needed . . . total peace. She could feel it
flowing through her, relaxing her body and soothing her
mind.

"Rosalind," Grandmère called as she entered the big room and went to sit at her spinning wheel. She always called Rose by her given name, not liking nicknames. "I'd like to speak with you." In one fluid motion, she arranged her black skirt and smoothed the long white apron over her lap.

Rose moved to the stool beside the spinning wheel, automatically picking up the cotton to hand to the white-haired woman so that it could be spun into thread. "Yes, Grandmère?"

Her feet moving the worn treadle to turn the wheel, her fragile fingers twisting cotton into strands, Grandmère spoke. "I've watched you droop around all week, and I think I know how you feel about marrying a man who hasn't won your heart by wooing you with gentle words and loving ways—but, Rose, I believe Jean Pierre truly loves you."

A welcome satisfaction warmed Rose as she performed the movements to assist the spinner. She allowed Grandmère's words to drift about in her mind. The familiar kitchen fragrances of coffee, spices, and soap-and-water cleanliness wafted beyond her nose and went straight to her heart.

Raising glistening eyes to meet her grandmother's wise ones, she replied, "You say Jean Pierre loves me, but he doesn't show it. Even if you're right, he can't love me as I want to be loved. There can never be anything romantic in a marriage between two people who have grown up together." Rose leaned forward and placed a ball of thread in the basket on the floor. "How can you know how I feel?" She added with a shuddering sigh, "I feel so trapped."

"I know. I know," Grandmère crooned. "I was young and full of dreams once." Her small feet stopped moving then, and they both watched as the big wheel gradually slowed down and stopped with a tiny squeak. She tucked a stray wisp of silvery hair neatly under her white, starched cap. "You see, Rosalind, you already know your intended, but I had never even seen my Paul until a few days before our wedding."

Astonishment marked the young woman's face, and her

mouth opened slightly. "You'd never even seen him! How could you marry someone you'd never seen? That would be even worse—"

"There are lots of things worse than what you're doing," Grandmère interrupted with a knowing look. "You're blinded now by your disappointment that you can't control your life. Sometimes we're torn by what we *think* we want." She pursed her thin lips, as though to hold back some weighty piece of wisdom, then shrugged and went on in a remembering voice. "I was plenty upset when my father told me that an arrangement had been made with his friend in another village for their children to be wed." Grandmère grinned and winked at Rose as she leaned closer, curved an aged hand to the side of her mouth, and whispered, "I really cut a rusty. I cried and vowed I would hate him. I even threatened to run away from home." Her hands settled calmly on her apron-covered lap.

"Did you really?" Rose was engrossed in the story she had never heard—and was amazed at the sparkle in the old eyes and the mischievous smile playing around the wrinkled mouth.

"It just so happened that my betrothed appeared before I could decide where to run." Grandmère sat up straight and gestured with her hands as she said, "Paul was big and a fine-looking young man, and I couldn't even pretend to hate him; he was so likable! Sometimes my mind rambles back fifty years, and I can see Paul standing in that tall, proud way." Her faded dark eyes seemed to cloud over, focusing on a distant corner while her mind relived treasured memories.

"Did you fall in love with him?" Rose asked, the question returning the old woman to the present.

"Not right away. I was still too busy resenting the forced marriage. But I finally decided that if I had to marry a stranger, a young, good-looking one beat an ugly, old one by a good mile." Cocking her head to one side and smiling now, Grandmère patted Rose's hand. "Wouldn't you agree, child?"

"What happened?" Rose asked, sidestepping the question, too eager to hear the outcome to appear disinterested, as she had originally planned to do.

"Paul was patient and kind, with only a bit of temper, and he set out from our first meeting to win me over. I began to fall in love with him after we married, but I was enjoying his pursuing so much that I wouldn't acknowledge it right away." The old woman licked her lips and smoothed her apron. "I knew I was in love when I began to want him to love me back . . . and to tell me so. I almost played too hard to get, and Paul seemed about ready to give up trying to humor me."

Rose looked serious as Grandmère continued, "But I did what any sensible girl would do—I told him exactly what was on my mind and how I felt in my heart. That conversation began the most beautiful and rewarding years of my life. We were so happy, me and my Paul." Dabbing at a tear sliding down her creased cheek, she smiled at her granddaughter's troubled face.

After a brief silence, Rose said thoughtfully, "Jean Pierre *is* handsome, but we don't have much to say to each other anymore. I loved him as a child, but he's been so *trying* these last few years."

"Maybe that's when he realized he loved you, when he saw you as a beautiful young woman. Some men can't show their love easily, and they hide it behind gruffness." When Rose looked doubtful, her wrinkled hand patted the young, smooth ones. "Rosalind, what you imagine as trying can be the very thing that brings the most happiness. My maman once told me that happiness is much like a butterfly."

"How can that be?"

"Remember how you liked to chase them in the summers . . . and the harder you ran, the faster they flew away?" When Rose's eyes sparkled in agreement, the wise voice went on, "Afterward, when you'd be resting, no longer even thinking of them, one would come and light on your shoulders, yes?"

"Yes, I remember." Grandmère often used little stories to explain life as she saw it, and Rose wondered what she was trying to say. Surely not that marrying Jean Pierre would bring happiness. Ridiculous!

Grandmère lifted her frail body from the chair and started across the room. "Come along, Rosalind, it's time for you to try on Marie's wedding dress so I can alter it. The length should be all right, but I'm sure I'll need to nip in the waist a good bit. You modern girls and your trim figures! In my day, if you didn't have a little flesh on your bones, you'd never get a second look."

Rose smiled at the spry little woman as they left the room arm in arm. Jarrette had been so right. Names meant little. The kind-voiced old woman was her dear grandmère.

With little enthusiasm for the project, but determined not to complain, Rose stood still—or turned first one way and then another as commanded—while Grandmère diligently pinned, basted, and snipped thread as she rambled on and on about those first years with Grandpère Paul, the man she had vowed to hate and then had come to love so deeply.

Rose listened absent-mindedly while she mused about her own situation, wondering if it was truly possible for her to find happiness, as Grandmère had. Honesty made her confess that she felt *something* for Jean Pierre, but she doubted she could ever fall in love with him. Grandmère probably embroidered the part about Jean Pierre's loving her just to lend comfort. The new thought that his harsh ways might be a way of showing love swam around in her mind.

The gown made for Maman over twenty years ago *was* lovely, Rose thought. Of soft white batiste with a banded neckline and long full sleeves, Grandmère had designed and sewn it. Floral motifs of hand-tatted lace encrusted with clusters of seed pearls decorated the voluminous skirt. A billowing chapel-length train with matching appliqués highlighted the back of the gown. A filmy veil cascaded from a wreath of lace petals adorned with seed pearls, the same veil that both Grandmère and Maman had worn at their weddings.

"You look beautiful, Rose," Maman exclaimed as she entered the room. Her eyes misted. "Just like a princess."

"She certainly does," the old woman heartily agreed. "I can't decide which one of you looked prettier in the gown." Soft brown eyes glanced from one to the other, then Grandmère clasped her hands together and let out a chuckle. "That's one decision I'll not have to make, no."

Marie acknowledged her mother's compliments with a pleased smile before turning to say, "You look tired, Rose. Why don't you lie down and rest?" Her expression was gentle, as if she had just noticed the weary droop of Rose's shoulders.

The loving concern in Maman's voice brought quick tears to Rose's eyes, but she blinked them back and left the room. She was exhausted, and bed sounded good.

That afternoon, on the way back from accompanying Robert to see the bird's nest, Rose saw Jean Pierre sitting straight and tall on Traveler, riding along the trail from Attakapas toward home. Except at meals, she had seen little of him all week, and she had never asked where he was. His well-muscled body was silhouetted against the light from the setting sun, and she didn't need to see the expression on his face to know he was in deep thought. Astride Beauty in the way all Cajun girls rode, Yvette followed closely behind.

Yvette left Jean Pierre to lead the horses to the barn and rushed to the kitchen to tell Rose who was at the store and that everyone was excited about the wedding.

Half-listening to Yvette's continuing chatter, Rose confessed new disappointment to herself. How she had longed for someone new and exciting, someone to flirt with, someone to pay court to her. Thinking of Jean Pierre as a man and not as a cousin was scary. After all, there he was in the flesh, familiar yet strange, handsome and attractive in ways she had never dared imagine before. Shivering with expectation and fear, she put aside such thoughts.

It was safer to recall wistfully the thrill of anticipation she had felt on her way to the party at Grenfall. The handsome Louis had fit her hazy vision of that faceless, romantic stranger who would fall in love with her and fulfill her wishes to be cherished and adored.

"Maman's calling me. I'll tell you more later." Yvette ran in the direction of Marie's voice.

"Please open the door for me, Rose." Jean Pierre stood outside holding two saddlebags bulging against their straps.

As she held the door for him, he squeezed past her, brushing her breast with his arm. She stepped back farther, giving him more room, for his touch was disquieting. Her earlier thoughts about viewing him as a husband returned to taunt her. Ever since he had returned from the first trapping season, Jean Pierre had seemed different. Now that she had learned they weren't kin, she admitted he could be called "new." But exciting . . . someone to flirt with . . . to pay court to her? Her thoughts soared and dipped like a kite riding wayward air currents.

Emptying the contents of the bags on the dining table, Jean Pierre said, "Maman sure had a long list." After pulling purchases from the saddlebags, he brought out a small, folded tissue from the bottom and handed it to Rose. His dark eyes searched hers, and he seemed almost hesitant to speak. "I brought you something."

The deep velvety sound of his words seemed to blanket Rose, and she felt herself shiver as if to break a spell. She laid the package on the table, then lifted a fold of tissue. Her eyes fell on shiny blue ribbon lying curled up against the white paper. She glanced up at him, wondering at the vulnerable look about his mouth. There was an air of tension in the quiet kitchen, and she felt threatened in a new, alien way. "Ribbon?"

"Blue ribbon," he corrected, his voice sounding rough, unnatural. He leaned to look over her shoulder. "They say every bride should wear something blue for good luck."

She could hear his breath falling close to her ear and realized her own was as irregular as his. Did the unsettling mood that had hovered over her all week plague him, too? Was he, too, frightened of marriage? "Don't tell me you're superstitious," Rose declared, looking up to see the formerly pleasant face now becoming grim. "You shouldn't have done it."

"Damn! Couldn't you have just said 'thank you'?" His eyes and his voice radiated deep emotion, and his lips stretched into a straight line. A faint reddening showed beneath the dark skin. *Rose Guilbeau, or Winstead, or whatever,* Jean Pierre thought, *I must have you...and your love.* Determination strengthened his resolve, and he moved away from the tempting woman who stood so close. In little more than twenty-four hours, she would be his—all his. He felt his heartbeat quicken at the staggering thought.

The force of Jean Pierre's outburst and hasty retreat stunned Rose. How like her to unknowingly displease him, she agonized. But hadn't that been the character of their relationship over the past two years?

Looking down, she saw the coiled ribbon, now coming unrolled in her hand, one satin end slipping to the wooden floor. Whatever made him buy ribbon for her? Her thoughts again picked up on the idea that the Jean Pierre she would marry in two days was indeed someone new—puzzlingly so.

Her eyes remained on the blue ribbon as she began unfolding it. It *was* pretty, unlike any she had ever owned. Tied around white azaleas and baby's breath, it would add a colorful touch to a bridal bouquet. She sighed.

Chapter Six

Saturday arrived. The warmth of the June sun invaded the bedroom of the Acadian home, drifting around the plainly furnished room, chasing the night's chill from its corners, and rousing the sleeping young woman to face the day ahead—her wedding day.

The Guilbeau home was abuzz. Rose mechanically followed Marie's instructions, with no heart for participating in the sundown ceremony. She and her friends had sometimes discussed what their weddings would be like when they married their true loves, but Rose's girlish daydreams about her wedding were far different from the reality of this one. Contributing to her zombielike state was the revelation about her true parents. So much had happened in such a short time that Rose was forced to draw like an adult upon inner strength to face each passing hour. Harsh reality had strangled the carefree, fantasizing girl she had been. Earlier that week, her seventeenth birthday had come and gone, leaving her feeling far more than one year older.

By mid-afternoon, Papa and Jean Pierre had packed all the food and drink in the wagon. It was time to leave for the church by the time all had bathed and donned their Sunday clothes. Observing Acadian tradition, the bride and groom knelt on the porch before Pierre and received his blessing before starting out. The horses hitched to the family wagon stamped their feet impatiently, wearing white ribbons in their manes and on their tails to honor the bride.

Riding Traveler and leading Beauty and a pack horse, Jean Pierre went on to the church right after Pierre gave his blessing. Earlier in the week, he had paddled to Grenfall to tell Louis that he wouldn't be traveling with him to the North Wilderness but, instead, would meet him at Fort Arkansas after he had settled Rose there. Fort Arkansas, serving as a center for many of the trappers, had a trading post and a few crude houses occupied by trappers and soldiers. While the hunters trapped, the wives remained behind at the fort for protection. It was with these women and soldiers that Jean Pierre would leave Rose while he trapped with Louis.

When the family wagon reached the church, and Pierre handed down the solemn-faced family, Rose looked around at the familiar grounds of the Commons. Shaded by huge water oaks with the familiar moss sweeping almost to the ground, wild azalea bushes and spindly dogwood trees almost hidden under their drooping limbs, the Commons always seemed to welcome people. Rose admired the brilliant pink oleanders and the purple bougainvillea vines trailing in the edges of the shade. The sweet fragrance of honeysuckle rode the peaceful air.

Stopping and taking a deep breath, Rose faced the church, the dominant force in the lives of all these gentle and fun-loving people she would always consider her own. Next to the church was the cemetery with its eerie-looking tombs of stone sitting on top of marshy soil. On the other side, of the church stood the small, unpainted house of Father Sebastian. Of the same gray cypress boards and oak shingles, the school and the large general store on the north side completed the boundaries of Attakapas.

Friendly calls from the Sunday-dressed crowd greeted the Guilbeaus when they neared. It was then that Rose saw Jean Pierre talking with a group of men and noticed that his eyes were riveted on her. She quickly turned her head and made her way toward the church.

Marie and the other women, chattering and gesturing the whole time, set baskets of food on long tables, decorated that morning by the women living nearest the church. Someone's heirloom cut-work cloth of worn linen covered the main table, with a massive arrangement of dark pink roses and baby's breath in its center. Wax-myrtle candles in fat pewter candlesticks surrounded the flowers.

Father Sebastian met Rose at the church entry and ushered her into his private study to freshen up after the hour's ride and to change into her wedding dress. Excited and giggly, Yvette went along to help with the bride's clothes and hair.

"Rose," Yvette said as she was brushing the blond windblown curls, "I've never seen you look so pretty. Maman's dress is just perfect for you." She finished arranging Rose's hair and fussed with the long train at the back of the lovely white gown. "You're so lucky to have such a handsome groom." Stepping back to run appraising eyes over the bride-to-be, Yvette reached to extract the ruby pendant from inside the high neck of the wedding gown, straightening the exquisite chain and centering the gem upon the filmy fabric. She had been flattered that Rose had told her why the wedding was taking place, since only the adult members of the family knew the real reason for the quickly planned ceremony. "I'll bet Jean Pierre meant to ask you to marry him all the time."

"I'm not so sure," Rose replied. She looked at herself in the small mirror Yvette was holding and saw a blush flooding her face. "You know nothing I do pleases Jean Pierre. This marriage is doomed."

"Shush, Rose!" Yvette burst out, catching her breath in horror. She crossed herself, whispering a prayer. "You mustn't speak so."

"It's true, Yvette. Jean Pierre treats you and Robert differently. He sometimes teases you without mercy, but he does it with good humor. You know he's downright ugly with me and has accused me of being a flirt for the past two years."

"Grandmère says that sometimes people do things to hide their true feelings. Have you thought of that?" Yvette went on, "I love Jean Pierre as if he were truly a brother. I think he's the best-looking man I know, other than Jarrette."

A sudden knock at the door kept Rose from having to reply, and she took a final look in the mirror, not pleased with the circles under her eyes and the strange pallor of her skin.

"Are you ready, daughter?" Pierre stood there at the door, tall, still handsome, and nervously pulling at the cravat falling across the front of his black coat.

"As ready as I'll ever be, Papa."

"I love you. Be happy," Pierre whispered as the accordion music started and they began to walk down the church aisle.

Someone had decorated the altar with banks of greenery, tall candles, and pots of pink roses and white jasmine, their aroma filling the high-ceilinged church. Rose felt it was a mockery for people who had not willingly chosen each other to be married in such beautiful and sacred surroundings.

The church was crowded and all turned to watch the bride, though she barely heard the "oh's" and "ah's" and complimentary whispers. Rose looked to the altar, where Father Sebastian waited along with the bridegroom. In contrast to the priest's mottled complexion, Jean Pierre's face was tan and healthy. A dark suit, tailored in New Orleans during one of his trips there, fitted his broad shoulders to perfection, while the soft, white ruffles on his shirtfront created a gentleness on his features that she had not noticed before. Dark brown eyes drew her gaze in a mysterious way as she moved slowly down the aisle on Pierre's arm.

Jean Pierre looked so different in the elegant suit, not at all like the other Acadians in their home-fashioned clothing. For a split second, Rose entertained the startling thought that the young man awaiting her was that someone new she had dreamed of. But he moved his head then, and she saw the curls Jean Pierre despised springing up on his forehead. Obviously the water he usually plastered them down with had dried.

Rose remembered Grandmère's words of yesterday, that marrying a good-looking man was better than marrying an ugly one. Yes, she admitted with reluctance, her groom was handsome; but in her troubled mind, that fact was little compensation for everything else she was giving up. She forced the painful thought away. Jean Pierre's eyes held hers until she lowered her head and marched the rest of the way looking down. She was determined that he not know how close the events of the past week had come to breaking her spirit. As for the people in the church, they whispered that her sudden high color was evidence of the great love only recently discovered by the young couple, the impression that the family had desired when they announced the surprise wedding.

The ceremony was mercifully short. The groom's voice as he repeated his vows was strong and vibrant, while the bride's wavered as she pledged herself to him in a near whisper. As the priest declared them man and wife, a sense of unreality rushed through Rose. This had to be a nightmare; she would soon wake up and life would go on as before—simple, uncomplicated, and filled with promise. When the priest instructed the groom to salute his bride, Jean Pierre lifted her veil, and Rose trembled when his lips gently covered hers for a few seconds. This was no nightmare. It was happening.

The customary musket shots outside the church signaled the end of the wedding. Lively music started up as the crowd, eager to begin the festivities, followed the newly-weds outside, laughing and talking. A young voice called, "Let the good times roll!" The party mood was set.

June was almost over, and the air was warm, even though it was dark enough to see the stars above the Commons. A moon was rising in beautiful splendor over the bayou, so bright as to cause shadows. The pleasing smells of roses and honeysuckle filled the night air. Gay music and warm laughter drowned out the normal songs of cicadas, night birds, and frogs. Caught up in absorbing the surface beauty of the moment, Rose felt her heart flutter. On this perfect, romantic night, she had become Jean Pierre's wife. Forever. In all ways.

"You look exhausted, my darling wife," said Jean Pierre as he guided her to a bench. Stealing a look to see if he was making fun of her, Rose felt better when he smiled and said, "I'll fetch you some punch."

Suddenly shy, Rose moved away from his arm and leaned against the back of the bench, her mind churning from all that had taken place and what was to come in the future. The man beside her was no longer the boy she had admired. He was forceful, handsome . . . and her husband. "I doubt punch can help much."

Jean Pierre leaned down close, his soft breath caressing her ear, and whispered, "That pretty face should be smiling. Maybe a sip or two of punch will perk you up. Uncle Jules must have made it, since it's ninety percent wine." And then he was gone.

Rose remained on the bench talking with everyone who passed by, thankful for the good-natured banter among friends and aware that their wishes for her happiness were sincere. Too soon, Jean Pierre pushed his way through the people around her and handed her a cup of punch. Rose took one swallow. Her eyes flew open, and she struggled for air.

After regaining some control, she said, "You'd better tell Uncle Jules to add a few gallons of fruit juice to his punch. I think he might have forgotten and left it out completely.''

''Well,'' he whispered with a teasing look dancing in his dark eyes, ''I did give Uncle Jules a little help with yours. I thought you might need it.'' He laughed then, low in his throat.

Come to think of it, Rose reflected, she hadn't heard him laugh since the dismal visit to Grenfall. She took another sip of punch, slowly, and cocked her head at him there in the torchlight. If her plan worked as she hoped, Rose mused, he might be fortifying his own punch instead of hers. She couldn't keep back her smile any longer. After watching the transforming effect it had on him, she sipped again from her cup, afraid to look at him for fear she might giggle.

When Jean Pierre saw her smile, his heart expanded. Did she care for him? Could he make her happy? How much pain he could have saved himself had he been able to make his feelings known. And, he confessed in honesty, he could have spared her the pain and humiliation of Grenfall. No wonder she had drawn away from him. Had he ever shown her anything but harshness, harshness caused by his repressed love and the desperate feelings that his desire for her would remain unrequited forever? He watched her eyes sparkle just before she lowered them to drink again and wondered if she could sense his tender passion—the passion that would unite them as lovers in body and soul before the night was over. He emptied his cup and let out a contented sigh.

''My love,'' he said as he leaned toward her. ''The music has started, and we're to begin the first dance.''

An icy, trembling feeling crept over Rose, freezing her thoughts, chilling the earlier look of secret amusement in her eyes. The violins called, but she didn't want to answer. Not yet. She was not yet ready to go to Jean Pierre as his wife. It was too soon. She wanted more of a dream lover first. Jean Pierre took the cup from her and led her to the center of the crowd. His touch was almost too much to bear. Faceless lovers would make no demands. . . .

Everyone was whispering that they made a beautiful

couple: the fair-haired bride with delicate features and big
blue eyes, the top of her head hardly reaching her groom's
chin—a lovely contrast to his rugged good looks, broad
shoulders, and manly grace. Knowing all eyes were on
them, Rose did what was expected. She slipped her small
hand into his large one; and, as Jean Pierre's right hand
moved to her tiny waist, she placed her left hand on his
shoulder. For a second they stood immobile, blue eyes
searching brown ones. With eyes still locked and wondering expressions on their faces, they began to dance around
the Commons.

"How lovely you are tonight," Jean Pierre said softly.
"You exceed all my visions of beautiful brides."

Only then did Rose drop her eyes. His flattery confused
her. Did he think he controlled her now that she was his
wife?

"Thank you, but compliments seem out of character for
you, Jean Pierre." Did he think she was an empty-headed
fool not to know what went on between a man and his wife
in the bedroom? She had grown up on the same farm as he
had. Always the male thought he played the major role,
she reflected moodily. "Just remember I'm not one of
those wanton women you've been trying to entice into
your bed." Inside, a part of her still felt chilled.

"My compliment was sincere," Jean Pierre replied.
Should he have made a move over the past week to tell her
he loved her, that he thought she was the most beautiful
young woman he had ever seen? But she had seemed
cocooned, completely shut off from the events around her,
and he had thought it best to wait until they were wed and
alone. "Let's not quarrel on our wedding night. It's
supposed to be a time of happiness." She scorched him
with a look, squelching that hopeful feeling rising within
him since he had seen her smile earlier.

Jean Pierre drew her body tight against his and whirled
her expertly around and around. Rose pushed against his
chest. She wanted to get away from the feel of his hard
muscles and the heady scent of his nearness that was
making her lightheaded, causing the inner chill to thaw.

On the outside she was beginning to feel as warm as summer sunshine.

The open area was soon crowded with dancers, and Rose changed partners so often that she couldn't keep track of their names. She was glad it was the custom for the bride and groom to dance with each guest and that she hadn't had to see Jean Pierre since the first dance.

Pleading fatigue, Rose walked to the refreshment table for a cup of punch. As she sipped, she saw Uncle Jules's wife nearby and joined her, prepared to do a lot of listening.

"Aunt Alva! I asked Uncle Jules where you were when I danced with him." Rose hugged the smiling woman and kissed her cheek. "How you manage to look so young while raising ten children I'll never know."

"Living the good life," Pierre's sister answered while she glanced over the crowd as though mentally counting her children. She turned back to Rose and said, "I brought you a wedding present, a quilt I pieced for you last year. I'm surprised I needed it this soon. Your and Jean Pierre's decision to marry surely did shock us all. I'm glad you finally reached that seventeenth birthday and learned what we kinfolks always knew about your real parents—not that anybody could ever have loved you more than Marie and Pierre. You are a perfect match, yes? Maybe the reason Cousin Jean Henri handed his two-year-old to Pierre to sail with Marie and him was so that Jean Pierre would meet up with you. Who knows? He might have sensed the ship Mary and he took the next week was headed for disaster. I'm so sorry about all that. . . ." Alva took in a deep breath, then went on, "Anyway, you two make a handsome couple—both of you so spirited, so easy on the eyes, with a real zest for enjoying life. Much happiness to you both, and many pretty babies! Something tells me that yours will be a very happy marriage." With a fond wave, she dashed off, calling to one of her youngsters across the way.

Rose thought how wrong that prediction was—and from Aunt Alva, of all people, who claimed she had a sixth sense!

"Yoo-hoo, Rosalind," called a familiar voice.

"Yes, Grandmère, can I bring you something?" Rose asked. She walked to the benches where Grandmère and most of the older folks were congregated to reminisce about the old days in Nova Scotia before coming to Louisiana. No matter what the occasion, she reflected, they never failed to get together and stir up what seemed to her the same sad memories.

"Yes," the spry old woman replied. "Will you bring us some more of that good blackberry wine Mrs. Landry brought?"

When Rose returned with a full pitcher of wine and began filling each cup, Grandmère asked, "Rosalind, did I ever tell you about the brave and stalwart men our sons, husbands, and fathers were when those tyrants tried to force us to pledge allegiance to Britain?"

"Yes, Grandmère," Rose said with a patient smile. She knew she would have to listen again no matter what her answer.

" 'Never!' they cried as they shook their fists in the face of the officials who had been sent to force us to sign those citizenship papers." Grandmère took a long sip of wine before continuing. Everyone watched her and listened as though they had no idea what she would reveal. "Not even when they burned our houses and barns and forced us into ships leaving our homeland forever did we weaken," she went on. "Men were men in those days and would sacrifice their lives, if necessary, to uphold their belief that no king has the authority to take away a person's God-given right to believe as he chooses."

"Yes," interrupted one of the old women at the far end of the bench, "I left my Charles buried there on the beach, dead from a broken heart. God rest his soul. I reckon it was better to leave him there than to have had him go down with a ship . . . as Jean Pierre's parents did." She made the sign of the cross and blinked her eyes several times in rapid succession before bringing the wine back to her mouth. "They would've been so proud to see him wed tonight."

Mr. Arsoneaux, with a faraway longing in his tired eyes,

said, "Ah, but the most vivid memories are of the beauty
of our village, Grand Pre. I remember her now, lying in
her fruitful valley, with meadows stretching almost as far
as the eye could see. Dikes on the one side to shut out the
turbulent tides, and on the other, fields of corn and flax
spreading as far as you could see over the plain. Then to
the north were those mighty mountains with forests on top
of them. I remember my dear wife as she . . ." His voice
quivering, the old man quieted as he wiped at his eyes
with his shirtsleeve.

Almost in tears herself, Rose quickly planted a kiss on
Grandmère's cheek and hurried to escape.

Seeing the hesitant approach of Hans Mettscher, one of
her classmates who paddled from the German coast down
the Teche to join the Acadian young people for his education, Rose lifted her hand in greeting. "Hello, Hans." Not
often did the German immigrants take part in the activities
at the Commons, and she felt flattered that he had come to
her wedding. Was it only last year that she had found it
fun to smile at him to see him blush?

Hans gave her a courtly bow. "Do you think your
husband would allow me to dance with his bride?" He
seemed a trifle embarrassed.

"He would expect it." Flirting with the blond young
man in the past seemed to have been a part of a dream.
The thought struck her that it must be such innocent games
as Hans and she had played that had led Jean Pierre to
label her a flirt. But such actions were normal, she reassured herself as she let Hans lead her into the open. Even
Jean Pierre couldn't be that dumb or pigheaded! They
melted into the merry crowd, keeping time with their feet
to the strains of an Acadian love song.

"Rose, you broke the hearts of many hopeful suitors by
marrying Jean Pierre today," her partner told her with a
shy smile.

"Oh, I doubt that. I don't see a tear in one eye," Rose
retorted in a teasing voice. She had no desire to get into a
serious discussion, nor to answer any questions about her
marriage.

"Are you happy?" Hans asked.

The flustered bride was trying to decide how to answer him when there came a tap on Hans's shoulder, a wordless signal to change partners. Hans released Rose into the arms of her husband.

"I don't know how I'm going to persuade all these hot bloods to keep their hands off my wife. Isn't that the German boy you were making eyes at last summer?" Jean Pierre asked. His casual tone belied the annoyed expression on his face. "Maybe letting all the guests dance with the bride is a bad idea, yes?"

Jean Pierre was holding Rose much too close for her comfort, and she glared up at him. The punch and vigorous dancing had done a great deal toward warming her, both inside and outside. As angry tears at his remark welled up in her eyes, she tossed back her head and said defiantly, "I can't imagine why you should care. We both know this marriage is a farce. The ceremony is over, and your obligation to the family name ended there. I'm as unhappy about it as you are." Her anger caused her to stiffen and pull away even farther.

"Unhappy? Why would I be unhappy? I married you because I wanted to, and I hope you won't be sad now that we've just begun our life together." Jean Pierre studied her flushed face, wondering how to coerce her into a good mood. Only once before their first dance had she smiled at him. What had she been thinking? He relaxed his hold on her and changed the subject. "Louis and I have already talked about the arrangements for our trapping expedition. He'll get to Fort Arkansas soon after we do."

"Are we to leave in the morning?"

The detachment in her voice cut him, sent his thoughts whirling, even as he replied, "Yes. As soon as we can get our packsacks ready, we'll start toward Natchitoches. I brought Beauty for you to ride. Papa said you've ridden her nearly a year now and can handle her well." Teasingly he added, "For a girl, that is." He wanted to remove the faraway look that had glazed her eyes when he mentioned Louis and their departure. Jealousy tugged at him, but he cast aside the idea that it was the mention of the handsome Creole bringing the closed look to her face. More likely, he reasoned, she was frightened at the thought of being alone with her husband later.

"I can sit a horse as well as you or any other man!"

She was her old conceited self, determined to put him down, Jean Pierre decided with amusement. As cantankerous as she could be during attack, he welcomed the return of a familiar Rose. It was the only one he knew how to deal with.

"Pull in your claws, you wildcat," he warned with a deep laugh, delighted to see her blue eyes flash in that old way. Too many cups of punch and too many visual images of her in his arms later that night made him bold. "I think I first began loving you while you were acting mad as a hornet."

Rose pondered his surprising statement, then discarded it as a further attempt at teasing.

"Last dance, folks," called the lead fiddle player.

Several men had already rushed toward Rose, but turned away at the announcement. Her groom had such a fierce look on his face that none would have dared claim a dance.

It was midnight before the party was over and the last of the revelers were ready to leave the Commons. One of the young couples had gone home with the wife's parents to let the bride and groom borrow their one-room cabin nearby for the night. When all "good-nights" and "best wishes" had been said, each one left for his home.

The bride and groom walked silently in the moonlight to their borrowed bridal suite. A feeling of numbness surrounded Rose as she somehow put one foot down and then the other. After Jean Pierre lit a candle, he went to bed down the horses.

Earlier in the day a neighbor had brought Rose's belongings to the cabin. She undressed hastily, wishing she had accepted that final cup of punch. Pulling on the soft white nightdress Grandmère had hurriedly but beautifully sewn, she admired the neat hemstitching that edged the round yoke and noticed that her hands trembled as they looped the narrow ties. She blew out the candle beside the bed and slipped between the sheets. Through the window in the silvery moonlight she watched the swagging moss on the live oak tree dance threateningly in the night breeze. A whippoorwill called in mournful tones from the surrounding forest. Bullfrogs from the bayou seemed to be competing with all the other night animals in a persistent, haunting chorus of bass sounds.

Tense and aware again of the icy knot in her heart, Rose's thoughts whirled like a windmill on a breezy day. For the hundredth time, she went over how she would react if Jean Pierre made advances to her. She knew a woman was expected to give a man his "husbandly rights," but she was still piqued that the man she must now call "husband" had agreed to marry her out of some misguided sense of duty. She had known from the beginning that she could never be docile.

In fact, she thought as she lay in bed, it would be fine if he would leave her alone permanently. He had such a reputation for charming the women, he would have no trouble finding someone to share his bed. Bits and pieces of her thoughts over the past week floated in and out of her mind. For every argument he might give, she had an answer ready. Then she heard the door open and close, the latch falling with a click of finality.

Snuffing out the candle across the room, Jean Pierre looked at Rose as she lay upon her pillow in a patch of moonlight. He began to undress, aware that she didn't turn away. His heart sped up. Mayhap their union would not be filled with conflict. If she would only smile again. . . .

In big-eyed wonder, Rose watched as Jean Pierre removed his shirt, then unbuttoned his breeches and slipped them down over his lean hips. She squeezed her eyes shut tight, seized by a flash of panic when he sat down on the edge of the bed. Holy mosquito! Was he coming to bed naked? She lay frozen, pretending to have fallen asleep. Strong arms reached out and enfolded her. Before she could protest, his mouth took hers in a long and gentle kiss, a kiss far less demanding than she had expected.

A tingling awareness, having nothing to do with fear or doubt, shot through her. She felt a throbbing in her temples and a weakness in her body that sought to control

her. She wanted to deny her responses, but he gave her no
time. He moved to kiss the top of her shoulder, nibbling
and kissing a spot near her neck, one she had never
suspected could be so sensitive. Raising goosebumps on
her spine, his warm breath reached her ear. Her heart
pumped wildly against her ribs. Unfamiliar sensations
bogged her down; the surprising reaction to Jean Pierre
and his kiss seemed a threat. From parted lips, a small
throaty sound escaped.

Lifting his head, Jean Pierre looked deep into his bride's
eyes. His were softer and warmer now, the eyes of a lover.
They searched her face in the wash of moonlight, drinking
in each of her lovely features, intoxicated by what he saw.
She was his.

Jean Pierre's pausing to look at her interrupted his subtle
seduction, and Rose regained her senses. How had she
gotten into this impossible situation? Things weren't going
as she had planned. *It must be the wine in the punch*, she
thought frantically.

With all her strength she pushed against his bare chest.
Never would she let him sense the disturbing emotions he
had aroused in her. The knowledge that he had any degree
of domination over her would make him more high-handed
than ever. It both surprised and flattered her to learn that
he found her desirable—his actions left no room for doubt.
Wrapping herself in a flimsy covering of bravado, she
coolly assessed the man so near. This was the time to
make her stand while she had some bargaining power. All
at once she felt confident about telling him of the idea that
had plagued her all week.

Untangling their arms and legs, Rose sat up straight in
bed. "Cover yourself and light the candle, Jean Pierre. We
have to talk." Her tone was one of command, revealing
none of the pitterpats of doubt.

"Talk!" Jean Pierre hooted in disbelief. "This is no
time for talking." With the force of a triggered bear trap,
he reached to pull her to him again.

She slapped at his persistent hands. "I insist on talking.
Will you do as I say?" Her voice was low-pitched and her
tone even more demanding.

Mumbling under his breath, Jean Pierre got up and stumbled into his breeches before lighting the candle. He sat down on the edge of the bed and faced Rose as she leaned against the headboard, her eyes fixed on his.

Never had she looked more beautiful, more desirable, he thought. Her hair was tangled, her lips pink and moist from his kisses. How much longer would he have to wait to make her his? "What do you want to talk about?" His voice sounded strained, even to his own ears.

"Us." Just that one word, she noted, and she had pulled his attention from whatever was filling his mind, whatever was creating a soft, puffy look about his mouth.

"What about us?" Seeing that black pinpoints had darkened the blue of her eyes, he realized that she was in no mood to be taken lightly. He took a deep breath and settled back to listen, eager to have the matter done with so that he could get back to more pleasurable pursuits.

"I can't allow you to make love to me this way." Pulling her body up straighter, she never let her eyes waver from their steadfast hold on his.

"You're my wife now, Rose. Can't you understand that?" While his desire to claim her was so strong that its very intensity frightened him, he was desperately trying to show patience, a quality he recognized he was short on. He recalled how all other pretty faces and all other winsome bodies had faded into nothingness the moment he first saw her as a young woman that day two years ago when he had first returned home from trapping. Some part of him longed to blurt the truth—but another warned him the time wasn't right. Let her have her say, then he would have his. He swallowed.

"Yes, but I'll never understand why you married me."

He leaned forward, gambling that he was making the right move, and asked softly, "Have you never suspected that I might be in love with you?"

Determined to pursue her plan, she shook her head in denial. "No! And don't try to cozen me with sweet talk. I want you to hear me out. For once, can't *you* listen to *me*? Will you never admit that I, too, have thoughts? What am I to you—a dumb little girl? A silly flirt? I'm neither!"

She saw his jaw tighten, watched the jump of a muscle in his cheek. Brushing back the hair falling into her face, Rose went on, aware that his breath came in noisy spurts, "I'm Rose Guilbeau, with normal dreams of happiness as wife to a man I can love. If the way young men paid attention to me turned my head and made me giddy, am I to be called a flirt? How else can a girl gain knowledge of young men if she can't talk with them, listen to their compliments, give in to her need to feel desirable?"

The candle sputtered while dark eyes burned into hers as if trying to speak, but the generous lips remained still. Something akin to pain washed over his handsome face.

Rose went on, "You showed great courage to marry me, I suppose, and maybe I should be grateful for it, but I hated being bargained off like a slave." She pulled the sheet up higher over her breasts, her control hanging by a thread—one of well-tempered steel. She would never let him have his way with her out of any warped sense of gratitude. Gratitude! Ha! It was as much his fault as hers that she was in this predicament.

"A slave! My God, woman, you come up with the damnedest notions. I just told you that I married you because I love you." He was angry now, his brown eyes seeming to shoot sparks in the candlelight. So what if some of her remarks did hit a nerve? He had a side, too. To preserve her own identity, she had no right to cut into his. "Anyway, I don't have to *buy* attention!"

"Don't curse at me, you overbearing nincompoop!" Rose shouted back. "Why would I believe you love me?" She yanked aside the sheet and leaned forward on her knees, waving her finger under his nose, glaring up into the face only inches from hers. "You conceited, pompous numbskull, you—" Rose searched her mind for another adjective strong enough to express her feelings while her gaze slid over his bare torso. Her heart lurched crazily. Dark mats of hair covered the broad chest, tapering down to a vee where it disappeared into the band of his breeches. Every time he made the slightest move, muscles bulged on his arms and rippled across his chest. Fascinated at her first closeup view of a mature man's body, she felt her mind spin. Her eyes refused to move to safer subjects.

"Are you quite finished now?" Jean Pierre asked, his controlled voice drawing her attention to his face.

"No, I'm not," she hissed, her cheeks burning as her emotions churned. "Put your shirt on. I'm sick of having to look at your half-naked body!"

For a long moment he ignored her remark and moved his eyes downward from her face. They slipped over her shoulders, lingering on the uptilted breasts pushing brazenly against the filmy cotton of her nightdress, before sliding to her tiny waist and blazing a path down the barely concealed slim hips and shapely legs. His bold inspection complete, he retraced the journey and was looking into her wide blue eyes once again before he spoke. "All right. Calm down and tell me what you have stuck in your craw."

From just outside the window, a mockingbird startled the pair on the bed by adding a midnight aria to the cacophony of night sounds. The high, sweet notes served as a dissolution to the previously raucous serenade. A new mood prevailed.

"I want to be courted," Rose announced with a flip of her hair over her shoulder and a lift of her chin. The shock on his face gave her courage and quelled the threatening spring of tears. Now she had him on the defensive. "I've always looked forward to being wooed and won by the man I married." Her soft, sure voice and her steady look defied him. "You've been declaring the unbelievable fact that you love me. Prove it."

"Unbelievable?" he echoed, pained beyond belief. Did that mean she felt nothing at all for him? What was that bit about courtship? Hell—they were already married!

"You might make me believe it if you pretended we had just met and you wanted to court me."

She wasn't fooling, Jean Pierre realized, his brows shooting up first in puzzlement, then in disbelief. He couldn't decide whether to laugh or to cry. Could those suspiciously bright sparkles be tears forming in the challenging blue depths? The feel of her exquisite body next to his a few moments ago had set him on fire and left his passions smoldering. He thought of her unexpected, burning response to his kiss and his initial wonder at his good fortune. Though he had taken many young woman to his bed, none had excited him as the temperamental blonde studying him. None had aroused this new desire to love, protect, and cherish for a lifetime.

"Do I have a choice?" When he saw her gasp in surprise, he fought down the urge to smile. The little minx. Did she honestly think he would walk away from such a challenge without at least one countermove?

"No." The full upper lip met the bottom one with precision, the little protrusion of the top one more noticeable as she pouted. And more tempting.

"What if I took you back in my arms . . . like this?" Before Rose could guess his intention, he reached out and pulled her delicious softness against his naked chest. In a purring voice of black velvet closer to her ear, he went on, "And kissed you . . . like th—"

The force of Rose's hand on his face shocked Jean Pierre and froze him in place. He battled the impulse to grab her and force her into submission. Who in hell did she think she was? A husband had rights, and by God— His brown eyes fought to subdue her suspiciously bright blue ones . . . and failed.

His cheek smarting, Jean Pierre released her and let her fall back against the pillow. He studied the determined set of her jaw, the scornful lift of delicate eyebrows, and the daring spark in her eyes. Only her mouth revealed a touch of pleading, and it was that small hint of vulnerability that tugged at him somewhere deep inside and brought him to his senses.

His thoughts detoured. He would strive to be the gentle, loving husband she wanted and deserved to have. Filled with an awful tenderness he hadn't known he possessed, Jean Pierre did something very much out of character—he put up no further fight. If courting was what it took to convince her that he loved her and desired her for that reason, he would do his damnedest. Not that he had had much experience in pursuing the fairer sex, he agonized, since conquests had always come easily. He sensed that this blond beauty he loved would be different, that hidden within her lay a spark of love for him, despite her apparent unwillingness to recognize it. To have her in his arms willingly would be worth the chase—about that he had little doubt.

"All right, Rose. I agree to show I love you by courting you and to wait until you say the time is right for us to come together as man and wife." Inhaling deeply, he let out the air in his lungs slowly. "Did you have anything special in mind? Remember that I'm not a patient man." His heart played leapfrog in his chest as he watched her move toward him, feathery lashes half-hiding her sultry eyes, her tempting mouth moving closer. This courting business might be easier than he had anticipated, he thought. He might even manage a short-cut or two. His eager lips parting slightly, he leaned close and asked, his voice deep and soft, "What can I do first to please you?"

She was almost over him now, tendrils of blond hair brushing his shoulders, the sweet smell of her invading his nostrils, setting his blood to racing again. She reached past him to snuff out the candle beside the bed, lay back on her pillow, and said, "Go to sleep."

Chapter Seven

"What is that all about?" Jean Pierre demanded, not even trying to conceal his shock and disapproval of his wife's attire. The sun was barely up. Morning birds twittered and mocked the newlyweds from the moss-laden oaks.

Rose looked down at herself before replying, "Do you mean why am I wearing some of Jarrette's outgrown breeches and shirt?"

"You know what I mean. Don't play games with me."

His voice came out cold, accusing. Having agreed to play the role of suitor was one thing, but to let her have full rein was not a part of the bargain. The dark breeches hugged her hips and failed to hide her femininity. Accentuated by the neat way the belt captured the oversized garment inside the breeches, her breasts fought against the soft blue fabric of the shirt. "No respectable woman wears such garb, and you know it. I won't let my wife be an object of ridicule. Get back inside and put on something decent to ride in. You're not going to wear clothing that calls attention to every curve—and besides, for a woman to wear breeches is unheard of." He turned back to tying rolled tarps of goods onto the pack horse. Was she deliberately trying to vex him?

Rose narrowed her eyes but didn't budge. Would they always end up quarreling over every issue they disagreed on? If she intended to have a say in this marriage, she sensed she had better stand up for herself in more matters than those in the bedroom.

"Jean Pierre, you've often accused me of flirting and liking the attentions of men. I don't deny that I may have unconsciously had such pleasures as a single young woman, but I did *not* take yesterday's wedding vows lightly. I no longer consider myself unmarried, and I intend to try to make the best of our situation. For me to ride like a man for days at a time, I need a man's clothing."

He spun around and glared at her, not believing her obstinance. Where did she get her crazy ideas? First the courtship bit and now this. . . .

Before he could speak, she went on, "My underclothes and stockings are thin and offer little protection from chafing against the saddle. These breeches are soft but thick enough to make me more comfortable. You can stand there and be bullheaded, or you can listen to reason and see that I have no plans to gain the attention of any man." When he shot angry eyes her way, then let them move suggestively over her curves, she added with new venom, "Especially yours."

Jean Pierre huffed, not willing to dignify the situation with an answer. An impatient hand slapped at the curls falling across his forehead before he returned to his task. He hated to admit it, but what she had said made sense.

One more appraising look, though, and he called over his shoulder, "Couldn't you at least wear a jacket or vest to cover your . . . ah, shape?"

A gasp of indignation was Rose's only answer. Jean Pierre watched her whirl around and go back inside, intrigued by the winsome sway of her hips in the breeches. Holy Mother! No wonder she had looked so different all over. Just before she disappeared, he saw twin braids bouncing across her back. He tried not to grin. This trip was going to prove even more of a trial than he had anticipated last night.

Within a short time Rose came back outside. Mounting Beauty and offering her bridegroom a haughty stare, she followed him up the trail away from the house, away from Attakapas, away from the only place she had ever called home. She was relieved that he had made no comment when she reappeared wearing a long, loose vest, another of Jarrette's cast-offs. He didn't need to know that she agreed with his logic and that she did feel more comfortable with the overgarment concealing her feminine form. There was no need to add to his belief that he was always right.

They rode the first miles in silence, Jean Pierre on the spirited black Traveler in front, leading the pack horse. Rose followed easily on Beauty, aware from past remarks that the sorrel's unusual flowing white mane and tail accentuated her own blondness. By the time they paused to water the horses in a narrow stream, the sun was moving westward.

Jean Pierre tossed her a small bundle from his saddle-bags, saying, "There's some jerky in there and some biscuits Maman cooked for us." He studied her face to check for signs of fatigue but saw none. With her hair drawn back severely in the twin braids, the exquisite lines of her face showed up more than usual. Was that dainty nose what one might call patrician? Just looking at her— even in the awful outfit she wore—brought a little skip to his pulse.

"Where will we be stopping for the night?" Rose asked, nibbling at the dried meat and wishing she were sitting at Maman's table with regular food before her. She pushed down painful thoughts of family and home.

"On up the trail there's a clearing beside a bayou that I hope we'll reach," he replied as he tore into his own rations with gusto. "It's a popular camping site for travelers stopping between Attakapas and Natchitoches. Louis and I have camped there several times."

They had not seen anyone, either on the waterways they sometimes followed or on the trail. The farther they went, the narrower the trail and the denser the woods. Occasionally even smaller trails branched off the main one.

"Are we in Indian country?" Rose asked while Jean Pierre was readying the horses. Soft, short hairs about her face and neck had begun to escape from the braids, and she brushed at them in annoyance.

"Sure. We'll nearly always be for the entire trip. There aren't too many around here, though, and they won't bother us unless we bother them. Only farther north will we need to watch out for troublesome Indians." The pale, feathery curls about her face fascinated him.

"What would we do if we met Indians?" Rose had never seen more than a half-dozen or so, and they had been trading at the general store in Attakapas, seemingly uninterested in the other customers. Papa had spoken many times of the way the Indians in the area of the Bayou Teche had accepted the Acadians as peace-loving people and left them to till the soil and hunt in the forests once enjoyed only by them. But the thought of meeting Indians in their own territory put doubts in her mind as to how much they actually approved of white men moving into their homeland. The look she sent him showed her fears.

"Nothing. I know a little about their ways from having been around them the past three years. You should be quiet and let me handle it. And all other such problems which might arise on the trail." His deep voice gave away none of his misgivings that he might not meet the same acceptance from Indians now that he had a beautiful young woman with him. No need to scare her more than her own thoughts had done. To pretend that he was truly in control was the only way to reassure her, he decided. Whether she wanted to admit it or not, he would have to be master on the trail and make the major decisions. The best way to do that, he reasoned, was to keep the upper hand in all matters, so that if an emergency arose, she would be accustomed to taking orders without quibbling. Jean Pierre would have to harden his heart and do what he thought best, no matter how much she tried to fight him.

"Because you're the husband and naturally smarter than the wife?" Rose couldn't help but let his high-handed manner rile her.

"That's right, lady," he replied, teeth flashing white in his tanned face. She might not believe it if he told her, but he admired her spirit. He rode on ahead then.

Even though the sun hadn't gone down all the way, it was almost dark in the forest when they reached the clearing. Jean Pierre watered and fed the horses, then hobbled them before joining Rose in her half-hearted search for twigs to start a fire.

"I don't see why I have to be the one scrounging around for kindling since you're the smart one," she grumbled. The women at the Guilbeau house did not ordinarily fetch their own firewood. The long day in the saddle had tired her far more than she cared to admit.

"Because I'm the one in charge."

Rose glared at him but made no reply. He was dragging a fallen tree limb to the pile of kindling she had found.

"I'll teach you how to make a campfire so that when we make camp, you can be starting one while I tend the horses," Jean Pierre said, not daring to look to see how she might be taking such direct orders. He aimed sparks from his flint onto the pile of shavings he had made.

"No, thank you." She raised her chin. When he seemed uninterested in her reaction and kept at his task, she watched, not missing a movement. He probably would stop at nothing to prove he was master. She would make sure she knew how to start a fire just so she would not have to ask him anything. Why had she thought he would want her in his bed enough to treat her any differently than he always had? As for his claiming he loved her—ha!

He stood and moved to put his arm around her shoulders, but she tried to pull away. Grabbing her then, he said, "You seem to forget we're in this together. One person alone doesn't make a team. Both of us need to work at building a marriage, Rose. You'll have to do your part as I see it while we're on the trail, or else—" His dark eyes were unreadable in the near darkness, but from his tone and painful hold on her, Rose could tell that a powerful emotion prodded him. The grip of his large hands on her shoulders made her feel trapped, and she shivered, feeling a dryness creep into her mouth.

"Or else what?" she flung after him when he released her and moved to fan the small flame beginning to flare beneath the little pile of kindling. Maybe his reasoning did make sense, but she wasn't ready to let him know that she agreed. She was still chafing from his seeming indifference to her desire to be wooed.

"Or else I might have to turn you over my knee and spank you," he responded with a devilish grin.

Rose gasped. "You wouldn't dare!" Inside, she realized he very well could if he chose to, and her blood boiled.

"Why wouldn't I? When you act like a child, I'll treat you like one." Smiling grudgingly to himself at her spunk, he reached into a tarpaulin sack and pulled out a skillet and utensils. "One of the first things you'll need to learn— after you learn to build a fire, of course—is to cook over an open campfire." He could feel her eyes raking his back.

"I'm not quite as stupid as you think! I've helped Maman and Grandmère cook dinner on an open fire when all of us went to the back woods to clear land." Rose raised clenched fists to her hips and tried to put him on the defensive, a gesture that she had learned over the years could sometimes best him. "Get me something to cook and I'll show you."

Still amused at her show of spirit, Jean Pierre left her standing by the fire and strode to the bank of the bayou. Using a hurriedly cut cane pole from a nearby thicket and a piece of jerky for bait, he threw his line into a dark pool. Just as he feared that all the fish had disappeared with the falling darkness, a scrappy catfish tugged at his bait. In a short time he had skinned and cut up the large fish and carried it to her at the campfire.

Despite their edginess with each other, both enjoyed their meal. Rose had lived up to her promise. Jean Pierre became even more fascinated by the half-child, half-woman he had married. Or was she half-wildcat, half-woman, he corrected as he admired her in the dancing light.

Rose wondered what the brooding, black-haired man was thinking. She washed their few utensils and returned them to the packsack, aware of his eyes fixed upon her every move until he disappeared into the darkness.

"I'll put our bedrolls near the fire," Jean Pierre said when he returned carrying two packets of blankets. "You can use your saddle for a pillow if you want to." He looked around for a cleared spot.

"I don't intend to sleep close to you," Rose declared, snatching a set from him and taking it directly across the fire from where he was spreading his own. Several times when Jarrette and she were young and feeling adventurous, they had been allowed to sleep out in the yard on quilts in early summer. She remembered what fun it had been to lie on the ground and talk and look up at the stars until sleep washed over them. Such a long time ago, she reflected. All at once weariness claimed her.

"What is taking you so long over there?" Jean Pierre called. He hadn't watched when she went to the tree where their gear was stacked on the ground, figuring she was tending to the call of nature.

"I'm putting on my nightdress."

"Putting on—my God! You aren't supposed to undress when you're on the trail." He turned then, and wished he hadn't. The white garment was just falling over her nakedness, and in the faint light from the dying fire he saw tempting curves. God! She was beautiful. A flash of fire down low stole his breath.

"Well, I did. I used some of the water left over from

cleaning up after supper to wash myself a bit, and I didn't want to put my clothes back on to sleep in. I always sleep in a nightdress.'' The chill of the night, or something, was sending little goosebumps down her spine.

''Get back in your clothes,'' Jean Pierre snapped in a half-strangled voice. Annoyed at his burning reaction to her body and also at her stubbornness, he cleared his throat before going on. ''What if someone were to join us in the night and there you were in that thing? Or what if it rains and we have to make a dash for cover under a tree? When you're on the trail, you sleep in your clothing—or at least in most of it.'' When she seemed to be ignoring him and going about folding her breeches and shirt as if she hadn't heard, he spoke louder. ''Did you hear what I said?''

''Yes.'' Rose headed for her blankets. He didn't like what she wore on the trail, she fumed, and now he was going to criticize what she slept in. Who could please him!

''Get back over there and put on your clothing.'' The soft fabric clung to her breasts, and when she knelt to pull back the blanket he could see the shape of her bottom.

Rose shot him a look of pure malice and prepared to slip into her blankets. No doubt he was not as interested in wooing her into his bed anytime soon as she had thought, or he would be using a kinder tone. If his actions indicated a courtship, then she was an alligator's uncle. She gave in to a noisy yawn and lay down—but never even stretched out. Jean Pierre was upon her, jerking her to a sitting position and shaking her.

''Listen to me, you hot-tempered little fool,'' he rasped, trying not to notice the way her gown gaped open and revealed her breasts. ''Get your clothes back on, or I'll do it for you. I know a lot more about the rules of traveling in the forest than you do, and until we run into an area where you're the one with experience, I'll call the shots.'' Her eyes bugged, and her mouth dropped open. Whether what he read in her eyes was fear, shock, or anger—or a combination of all three—he couldn't tell. He had no problem in identifying what had gnawed at him below his waist ever since he had glimpsed her nakedness. Only by reminding himself of the promise he had given her the preceding night was he able to refrain from snatching the gown from her body and making love to her. In the forest setting in the glow of the campfire, she was more of a temptation than he had bargained for. He clamped his lips shut to keep from kissing her and telling her of his love, of his desire to possess and protect her.

Rose watched Jean Pierre close his mouth as though he were fighting for control. She trembled from the force of his hold upon her and from the harshness of his words. He was so close that she could feel his erratic breath upon her face. Licking her lips and hating herself for feeling her pulse race—surely she was not that afraid of him?—she retorted, "If keeping one's clothing on is so damned important, why did you wait until now to tell me?"

She twisted beneath his hold and shoved at his hands, surprised that they fell away and that he rose and turned back to his bedroll. With a great show of indignation, she marched to the shadow of the tree, letting out a little oath when her bare foot met a sharp twig. Even though he made no effort to look in her direction, she ordered just before she pulled off the garment, "And you'd best not try to do any peeking." Once more back inside her own blankets, the breeches and shirt on, she glanced across at him, wondering if he was truly asleep as he appeared to be. Why did he think he was right about everything?

Sleep had almost come when she heard Jean Pierre make a sudden movement across the campfire. Rose lifted her head and saw that he had risen to a squatting position. "What's wrong?" she asked, seeing a strained look on his face.

"I believe we're about to have company." As he quickly fastened the sheath holding his large knife around his waist, he kept his head cocked toward the trail.

"Company?" Rose squeaked, sitting up and listening. When she heard what sounded like horses approaching, she grabbed her blankets and ran around to his side, sinking onto the ground just as two horses appeared at the edge of the firelight.

"Howdy, folks," called a deep voice. "Mind if we

share your camp?'' The horses stopped, nearly invisible in the shadows.

Jean Pierre peered at the two horses and riders, saying, ''Nope. That'll be fine. Get down.'' Rose noticed for the first time that his gun lay underneath one edge of his bedroll and that one hand lay near it. Her eyes opened even wider. ''My wife and I just finished our supper and washed up everything or I would offer you coffee and leftovers,'' he continued, eyeing the men as they dismounted and came into stronger light. He was never averse to sharing campsites with strangers, but it was best to stay on guard.

''Where you folks headed?'' asked the first man, the taller one. A full beard covered his face, allowing little to be determined about his features. With a deferential bow toward Rose, he removed his large-brimmed hat. She saw that at his right hip he wore a leather holster holding a large pistol that gleamed in the firelight. Rose swallowed hard.

''Natchitoches,'' replied Jean Pierre. ''My trapping partner should be along any minute.'' He forced a small laugh and said, ''We thought that might be his horse we heard, didn't we, old woman?'' The obvious lie, plus his unflattering name for her, gave Rose a definite clue that everything might not be all right. She nodded, her throat too full for speech. ''Where are you two going?'' Jean Pierre asked, looking then at the other man.

The second man was no more attractive than the first, Rose decided, letting out a small, shuddering sigh. Uncomfortably aware of their scrutiny, she was grateful that she no longer wore only the thin nightdress. The other stranger also sported a gun in a holster, its belt riding high over a round belly and making the gun appear to be too high to reach easily.

It was the second man, the one of average height, who answered Jean Pierre. ''We're cattle buyers from over near Natchitoches.''

''Yeah,'' chimed in the taller one, ''we're on our way to Teche country to get a herd if we can buy up enough.''

''Whereabouts in Teche country?'' Jean Pierre asked,

still in a half-crouch beside his bedroll. He was aware that
Rose kept inching closer to his side.

"Folks at Fort Natchitoches told us to go way on down
to Grenfall. Said it was a big place belonging to a Mr.
Brearde. Are you folks from that part of the country?"

"As a matter of fact, we are," Jean Pierre replied. "The
trapping partner I'm expecting is the son of the owner of
Grenfall." He stood then, and Rose felt more at ease.

"Brearde's son, eh?" asked the fat man, his Adam's
apple bobbing. He turned to his partner and laughed.
"Well, what do you know? We must be among friends."

The strangers seemed as relieved as the young couple to
find the four might have enough in common to spend the
night peacefully in the same clearing. After brief introductions, the men cared for their horses and prepared to sleep
opposite the fire from Rose and Jean Pierre. Rather than
build up the fire and cook, the men announced that they
would chew some jerky and go to sleep.

The day's long ride had already tired Rose, and she
rolled up in her blankets next to her husband, grateful to
have his broad back to cuddle up to. The ground was hard
through the light blankets, but she had little difficulty in
falling asleep, despite the snores from across the way.

The strangers didn't tarry the next morning, riding off
soon after sharing breakfast with Rose and Jean Pierre.

That day the young couple made good time, and before
dark they had left behind the flat, swampy land. Rose
noticed that even though the forests were still dense with
familiar oaks, beeches, and cottonwoods, new trees had
appeared. Jean Pierre told her they were pines, and she
found their straight trunks, needlelike leaves, and brown
cones strange sights. They still saw a few paths branching
off the main trail, but not as frequently as on the first day
out of Attakapas.

An increasing number of birds and small animals and
their sounds astonished Rose, and she was almost as
surprised at Jean Pierre's knowledge about them and their
habits. Her persistent curiosity about their surroundings
both amazed and pleased him. By the time they stopped to
make camp for the night, they had seemingly forgotten

their private war and were talking and laughing easily like old friends.

"Can you start a fire while I take care of the horses?" asked Jean Pierre. Some previous visitor had left a pile of logs and branches nearby in the flat area near a stream.

"Of course," replied Rose, not overlooking that he had asked rather than ordered. Was this the first step in his courtship? She gave him a pleased smile, surprised that approval sparkled in his dark eyes.

Just as she got a blaze started, the nearby boom of a gun sent her screaming toward the bayou, yelling for Jean Pierre.

"I'm here, Rose," he called, propping his musket against the tree hiding him and emerging from behind it just in time to catch her trembling body. The way she clung to him touched him in pleasant ways, and he tried to convince himself that he put his arm around her merely to comfort her. Her head nestled close against his chest, and with a tiny dipping movement his chin rested upon the top of her blond head.

When Rose pulled away and seemed interested in what he carried in his hand, he held up a fat squirrel by its bushy tail. "I saw this rascal while I was watering the horses, and I didn't think about how the shot would scare you." That she had come seeking his protection pleased him more than he would have her know. For a second, she looked so much like a wide-eyed, scared little kid standing there in Jarrette's old breeches and shirt that he couldn't keep down a laugh. A smudge of soot marked one pink cheek.

"Stop laughing at me!" He was back to his old tricks. Tears stung her eyes, and she felt her face flush with embarrassment at having given in to fear and sought him out.

"Don't be mad. I laughed because you looked like a little boy lost in the woods and—"

Rose interpreted his maddening grin and unflattering words as further insult and yelled, "Well, I am not a little boy—as you very well know, you lummox." Braids flying, she turned and ran back to the fire as quickly as she had left it only minutes earlier. Jean Pierre had no respect for her, she agonized, and probably never would. His agreeing to prove he loved her by courting her was nothing but talk. He was having too much fun ordering her about to change his views. It was plain that he didn't see her as a woman worthy of his attentions. Well, she huffed to herself, that was fine with her. The longer he put off consummating their marriage, the better she liked it.

"You're a good cook as well as a good fire builder," said Jean Pierre when she handed him a cup of coffee after their meal. She carefully avoided touching him when she gave it to him, keeping her eyes on the cup. They drank in a silence broken at intervals by the high-pitched calls of night insects and the throaty "be-deeps" of frogs. A far-off scream from a fox sent her blue eyes to scan his contemplative face.

"Wonder if we'll have company tonight," he said. He had seen her reaction to the eerie call of the fox. "We were lucky those were good men last night." She looked into the fire and sipped her coffee as though she hadn't heard. If he was trying to scare her, she was not going to let him succeed. "I noticed you changed your tune about not sleeping close to me after you heard those horses," he added after a long period of staring into the dying fire. Somewhere deep in the forest, a whippoorwill sang its three-note song.

Jean Pierre admired the way the firelight danced across the delicate bones of her face. The strong chin gave it an oval shape; the slight hollows beneath the cheekbones lay in intriguing shadow, calling attention to the generous mouth with its slightly overlapping top lip. He missed seeing the glorious cloud of hair, but realized that for her to wear it in braids while on the trail was sensible. The thought came to his mind that, in more ways than he had realized, his bride was sensible. He recalled the way she had caught on to starting a fire with flint and shavings, no easy task for most beginners. The slight tightening of her full lips was the only sign she showed of having heard any of his remarks. Strange. He had never before noticed the way her mouth tipped up at the corners even when she was solemn.

He couldn't forget how good it had been to hold her for that brief moment when she was frightened, and that same urge to make love to her that had come over him last night plagued him now. He let out a silent sigh. If he was going to coax her into his arms, he reflected, he would do well to get busy with the wooing. To yell at her as he had last night about sleeping in her clothing was not the way to win her. And laughing at her tonight hadn't been wise either. She had said she had a mind of her own, and he was becoming more and more aware that she truly did. Hadn't she demonstrated it clearly on their wedding night? A beauty such as she deserved more than he had offered, he admitted. He had no desire to break her spirit; he loved her just as she was. For some reason, she had seemed not to notice that he had tried all day and night to be especially courteous and attentive. Tomorrow he would try harder.

"It's time for us to turn in," Jean Pierre said after all was cleaned up from their meal. When he had offered to help her wash up, she had refused in martyred tones. He threw her bedroll near where he spread his own and lay down.

From behind lowered lashes, Rose watched him stretch out and remove his boots. He was sly like a fox. All day he had pretended that he was decent just so he could get her twice as upset when he decided he wanted to laugh at her or boss her around. He had little regard for her; that was clear. Remembering her need to run to him this afternoon brought warmth to her face. And his jabbing at her a few minutes ago about her having to scramble to his side last night smarted. Even so, she didn't move her blankets very far from where he had thrown them. Let him think what he wished, she thought. He would anyway.

Near dawn, raindrops on her face awakened Rose. Letting out a little curse she had learned from Jarrette, she grabbed her shoes and bedroll and ran beneath a large, low-limbed pine tree. The raindrops fell onto the thick branches with little sighing sounds, sometimes halting on the tips of verdant needles before sliding down to cling a moment, then plopping to the straw-covered ground. Before she could get her shoes on, a sleepy-eyed Jean Pierre dashed over to join her.

"What will we do about breakfast? How can we keep everything from getting soaked?" she asked, saddened at the thought of having no shelter nearby. Her hands brushed at her untidy hair. Home seemed a million miles behind them. Strange, she thought, that she had never before wondered what travelers did in bad weather.

"I have some treated sailcloth to put over our gear. We can even make a small tent of some of the tarpaulin if the rain doesn't let up soon." Giving in to an urge to stretch and yawn, Jean Pierre seemed unperturbed.

Rose watched the way he moved his long arms and body there in the predawn light, struck by the unselfconscious, animallike way he did so. He had not yet buttoned his shirt, and she saw the matted curls on his chest, fascinated by the way they thinned and formed a narrow path before disappearing inside his waistband. Did he have hair—She twisted her head away and bit her tongue at her thoughts. What was wrong with her, she scolded that wayward part of her. Even though she had never seen a man completely naked, she reminded herself, she had no interest in his body.

When the rain continued, Jean Pierre took sheets of the tarpaulin from the pack and covered their bedrolls before tying them behind their saddles. He then took large squares and cut holes in their middles large enough for their heads. The folds then fell from their shoulders to their hips, giving them good protection. He placed a wide-brimmed hat on Rose's damp head and fished around in his packsack until he pulled out a furry coonskin hat.

Struck by the incongruous picture he made in his garb, Rose burst into laughter. He turned to look at her, causing the hanging coon tail to flop around crazily. "You look like what I always imagined a *loup-garou* looks like," she said between fits of laughter. His look of annoyance fed her amusement. They mounted, ready to move on.

"So now you can laugh at the superstition about evil spirits living in an animal's body? I remember when you were as quick as the other children to tremble at the mention of a *loup-garou*,'' Jean Pierre retorted, more piqued at her reaction than he cared to admit. To have a young woman laugh at him was a new and unwelcome experience; to have the bride he loved do so galled him. He looked at her critically and asked with a hoot, ''And what about you?'' The ill-fitting hat sat low over her ears, and the tentlike covering billowed over her saddle. She had tucked her braids up under the hat, and only when she tilted her face to look up at him, blue eyes crinkling between silky, brown-tipped lashes, could he tell she was not a shabby young boy. Deep laughter joined hers then, and they started down the trail side by side in the rain, still breaking into howls of laughter when their glances happened to meet.

All that day the rain slowed them down and made the horses irritable, but they traveled onward. Making camp in a drizzle and eating jerky and cold biscuits for supper, they talked little. A tarpaulin stretched over two curved saplings kept off the worst of the rain, and Rose was too weary to complain.

She had no conscious knowledge that after she dozed off in her blanket, she snuggled close to the warm body next to hers—or that protective arms hugged her throughout the night.

Chapter Eight

Rose awakened with a start at daylight. Smelling woodsmoke and finding the blankets next to hers empty, she ducked from beneath the tarpaulin and called to Jean Pierre over by the fire, ''Look at that lovely pink sky!'' Her hand raked at her hair and paused. ''Could we stop long enough this morning for me to wash my hair? That rain yesterday made it filthy.''

''I don't know yet. We'll see.'' He was already setting a pan over the fire to cook breakfast.

''Please, Jean Pierre,'' Rose said, once they were back in their saddles, ''can't we stop at the stream here beside the trail? I feel grimy all over, and my hair is smelly from staying wet so long.'' She raked at tendrils about her face.

Jean Pierre looked at Rose fully then. Her blond beauty seemed an extension of the soft radiance of the pink and blue sky glimpsed through overhead branches. The fact that she hadn't even pouted when he'd not agreed earlier came to mind. And even with her second request she hadn't demanded anything or sounded querulous.

''I'll make a deal with you,'' he replied after a few moments. He reined in Traveler, looking back to make sure the pack horse stopped, too.

Rose halted Beauty. Right beside her, dark eyes twinkled with devilment and something mysterious as they gazed at her face and settled on her mouth. For some reason, she sensed that Jean Pierre might be seeing her in a new light. Her pulse quickened, and she could find no reason for that strange occurrence, either. ''What kind of deal?''

''A kiss for my stopping to let you wash your hair.'' The blue eyes seemed to hold as much promise as the new dawning.

She felt her face warm up. ''For a kiss, you should let me take a bath, too.'' He seemed to have no thoughts about anything but her at the moment, and the idea pleased her.

''There's not time enough for a bath.'' He wondered at the magical way the blush of the sky reflected in her cheeks. ''How about it? Do we have a deal?''

''I don't know much about kissing, so you might not like what you win.'' To break their locked gazes seemed the thing to do, but she couldn't. Without her knowing it, her full lips parted.

''I wasn't disappointed in your kiss three nights ago.''

His deep voice wavered a bit, right along with his heartbeat. He squashed the painful thought of what had disappointed him. "What do you say, Rose?" When she continued to look deliciously pink and white and flustered, he
teased, "Your hair really does look a sight . . . and you did
say you wanted to be courted, didn't you?"

"But such a kiss would be more like a bribe than—"

Interrupting, he insisted, "Not to me. We can pretend
we've only just met and that I'm playing the gallant to
escort his lady to repair damage to her hair. Afterward, she
would naturally reward such a kind and thoughtful suitor
with a kiss, wouldn't she?"

Rose smiled then and lowered her eyes. The warmth in
her cheeks spread to her neck, and she shifted in the
saddle. A sideways glance from beneath half-opened lashes
showed her that she was still the center of his attention.
His handsome features seemed to reveal a new admiration
for her, and she wondered if the soft light playing about
his face and smiling lips might be leading her to think wild
thoughts. Not caring what led her, she met his wondering
look and said, "I think you've made an offer I can't pass
up."

Jean Pierre tied their horses upon the banks of the
nearby stream and then walked with Rose down the slight
incline. She had soap and towel in hand and found a
kneeling place clear of underbrush.

"I think I should stay up on the bank with the horses,
since everything we own is up there," he told her as he
climbed back up. "But I'll be close if you need me." By
the time he tethered the animals near a grassy spot and
turned back to check on Rose, she had removed her vest
and shirt and was wetting her hair in the clear water.
Intrigued, he watched her lather the soap in her hands and
work it into her soiled blond hair. He heard a little squeal,
then a muttered oath from where she rested on her knees
and leaned out over the water.

"What's wrong?" he called, already moving from beside the grazing horses back down to the stream. Quickly
he checked for snakes, both in the water and on the banks,
but saw nothing.

"I have soap in my eyes," she complained, with her eyes clamped shut.

"Let me help," Jean Pierre offered, squatting beside her and cupping his hands to scoop up water. When she figured out what he was doing and lifted her face, he doused it. The way she gasped tickled him. "I might as well finish rinsing for you while your eyes clear. We really need to be on our way as soon as possible."

Touching her face had added quivers to Jean Pierre's already uneven heartbeat. Now his big hands worked with gentleness and thoroughness through the long blond hair floating in the water. The sun was chasing away the pink sky, turning the clouds in the east into bursts of rosy gold—not unlike the hair he rinsed, he realized with awe at her closeup loveliness. When Rose could see again, she lifted her hands to help wash away the soap from her head. Their fingers met near the base of her scalp, the contact electric, stopping all motion for a moment.

"If you'll hand me the towel . . ." Rose said in a voice unlike her own. Shut away as she had been during the battle with the smarting soap suds, she had had the eerie feeling, when he knelt beside her and so tenderly cared for her needs, that only the two of them existed in the forest on the new day. Next to her ear she could hear the unsteady pattern of his breathing, then the sound of his stretching to reach behind for the towel. All at once she was blanketed from the world underneath the soft white cloth he draped over her head and face.

After a brisk swipe across her face, Rose tossed back the wet mane and tied the towel at the top of her head. Not ready to look at Jean Pierre as he knelt beside her, she admired the artful changes in the overhead sky. She knew that the sun would come popping above the forest within the next few minutes and dispel all of its colorful prelude. Aware that Jean Pierre seemed to be waiting for her to make the next remark, she said, catching his eye, "Thanks."

Not even a whicker from Traveler up on the bank behind jerked Jean Pierre from the spell holding them kneeling there beside the clear stream and getting lost in each other's eyes. Mesmerized by the perfection of the face lifted now to his, he murmured, after what seemed like a long time, "You're welcome, my lady. Do you plan to reward me?"

Her pink tongue tipping at the underpoint of her full upper lip, Rose watched Jean Pierre's face move closer. She shut her eyes just as his mouth claimed hers in a most delightful way. From the touch of his lips, thrills zinged to secret places. Instinctively she leaned toward him, not minding at all when his arms gathered her close against his broad chest, surprised only when her own arms reached up around his neck in welcome. There was something so right about their honeyed kiss, their warm hug, that her mind clouded; and her heart played a crazy hopscotch beneath the cambric shift. He smelled like soap and water, like saddle leather, like the essence of strong maleness as she might have imagined the faceless stranger of her romantic dreams to smell. Then her thoughts faded in the way the colors of the dawn had. She heard nervous whinnies from the horses.

"What was that?" Rose asked, ending the kiss and leaning back to rest on her heels, her arms falling back to her sides.

"They're probably jealous that we're playing a game and leaving them out," Jean Pierre replied, once he trusted his voice to come out level. *Game?* a part of him chided. *That was no game.* Removing his arms hadn't been easy. The soft firmness of her breasts against his heart had satisfied an old longing. All over he burned with love for his beautiful bride. His mind reeled from the realization that she had responded to his kiss with far more than acceptance of her part in a playful bargain. His heart pounded in joyful anticipation.

Rose stood then, untying the towel and blotting at her damp hair. Game, he had called it. Was that all the kiss meant to him? Or to her? an inner voice demanded.

"I guess I'd better check on the horses while you finish up down here," he remarked. It was plain that the magical moments were gone as surely as the majestic dawn. A new sun spread its clear light now.

Overhead a flock of white herons sailed in the fresh

blue, beginning their day of searching for food. While Rose finished toweling her hair and donned again the shirt and vest down beside the stream, Jean Pierre busied himself up on the bank with routine tightening of the saddle girths and checking his saddlebags. A long journey lay ahead.

"What's that hanging around your neck?" Rose asked late that afternoon. "I've never seen it before." As it had warmed up, Jean Pierre had unbuttoned most of his shirt.

He laughed and reached to pull out the necklace and show her the pale-colored object hanging from a leather thong. "My good-luck piece, my bear's tooth. See the carvings?"

She grimaced. "Why would you wear an animal's tooth?"

"I wear it only when I'm away from home," he explained. "An Indian called Red Fox gave it to me." At her obvious interest, he went on, "Red Fox is the oldest son of Chief Red Bear of the Caddo tribe. He and I became friends last winter. As Louis and I sometimes separate to do, I was trapping alone, and the Indian was hunting away from his party. We both were lying low to avoid a warring mountain tribe, and we happened to choose the same cave. He helped me dress my catch of the day, and I let him take some meat back to his party the next morning."

She studied the strange necklace with its carvings. "This Red Fox also gave you the tooth?"

"Yes. Indians sometimes do that when they claim a white man as a friend or brother. The witch doctor carves messages from the spirits onto bleached animal teeth for the chief's sons to ward off evil. For an Indian to give up his talisman to anyone, especially a white man, is probably the greatest sign of friendship. The snow was pretty deep that day we met up, and he needed meat for his fellow hunters. Having to hole up had kept him from hunting for an entire day, so I guess he and his people were pretty grateful for the meat I gave them."

Rose puzzled at how little she knew about the man she had married, even as she urged Beauty up the trail.

Ahead lay Fort Natchitoches, the post that Jean Pierre told her served some two thousand settlers and merchants on the western edge of what was now called Spanish Louisiana. She had learned from listening to him during his visits at home that nearly all trappers stopped there to make ready for their treks north.

"This Fort Natchitoches seems more than a fort," Rose said when they could see a settlement up ahead in the twilight.

"The citizens dropped the word 'Fort' some time ago," Jean Pierre remarked. Her questioning eyes and animated face led him to explain, "Back in 1714, when the French ruled, they needed an outpost to serve as a buffer between them and the Indians and Spaniards of the Tejas area. Trade routes with Mexico grew, and now Natchitoches is a good-sized place." He watched her eyes widen as they neared the numerous houses and stores. "Especially when compared to Attakapas."

In the deepening dusk, Rose saw that the small town sat on the banks of the large stream Jean Pierre had told her was a bypass loop of the Red River. Before she could take in all the strangeness, Jean Pierre told her they had arrived at the place where he always stayed while there. In the half-light from a lantern near the porch, Rose read the sign: MA DIBERT'S, ROOMS AND FINE MEALS.

Jean Pierre tied their horses to the long hitching rail in front of the large, two-story building of rough-planed cypress. For the first time, he went to assist Rose in dismounting, letting his hands linger just a moment at her small waist. One hand cupping her elbow, he escorted her across a long porch with a swing and several long benches, then to a wide doorway.

The flickering yellow light from a whale-oil lamp inside the entry seemed especially nice to the round-eyed Rose. Until that minute, she hadn't realized how hungry she had become for the familiar comforts of civilization. Tempting smells of freshly baked bread and stewing meat brought rumbles of hunger to her stomach. She glanced down at her muddy, stained clothing, then at her grimy hands. Brushing at the untidy tendrils escaping from her braids, she felt embarrassed that both Jean Pierre and she looked uncouth—but she especially, in Jarrette's old breeches and shirt.

Around the huge rectangular dining table in the room Jean Pierre guided her into were some eight or ten men eating and talking noisily. Their abrupt silence, evidently brought on by the sight of Rose and Jean Pierre, must have summoned the tall, spare woman to the door at the back of the room.

"Howdy," the woman said, edging around the table and squinting to see the couple in the pale light coming from fat candles on the long table. Instead of softening her harsh features, the candlelight seemed to accentuate her long nose and angular face. "You be wanting to eat supper, I reckon?" She glanced with a frown at the nearly empty serving bowls and platters.

"Sakes alive, if'n it ain't that Jean Pierre Guilbeau back here at Ma Dibert's place," she exclaimed, removing her bony hands from the folds of her apron, where she had been drying them surreptitiously. She looked at Rose with none of the friendliness she had shown Jean Pierre, dark eyes raking over the dainty form in the outlandish garb. "Who's this?"

"Ma," Jean Pierre said with a smile, "this is Rose, my bride." He put his arm around Rose's shoulders, hoping no one noticed that she almost flinched at the unexpected gesture.

"Well, boys, slow down long enough to say 'howdy' to one of my favorite boarders," Ma Dibert said after a noticeable pause and an appraising look at Rose. She motioned them toward an empty space on a bench. Introductions were brief and incomplete, but at least everyone had a chance to look over the new arrivals. Rose learned that two of the diners were peddlers, or drummers, while the rest were stockmen and trappers.

"This here's the last bunch to eat tonight. I ain't sure I can offer you a whole lot, but you're welcome to eat up as long as there's vittles afore you," Ma Dibert announced once the couple sat down. Darting one more guarded look at Rose, she disappeared through the doorway through which she had entered.

The dark-suited peddler named Thom Keller sat across from Rose and made no bones about his interest in the newcomers. She hid her eyes from his blatant stare. The next time she looked up, the huge, bushy-headed man at the end of the table—hadn't Ma called him Rufus Bedlow, a trapper?—was taking his turn at studying Jean Pierre and her. Like the peddler, Thom Keller, the big trapper had coolly acknowledged a previous acquaintance with Jean Pierre.

When Rufus Bedlow caught Rose watching him, he grinned. She noticed then that a livid welt curved from the edge of his left eyebrow beside his bulging eye and on down into a thick, black beard. The grin showed that the left side of his mouth sliced upward, as if the scar stretched through the unkempt beard and ended there at the corner of his mouth. A frisson of uneasiness bringing an inward shiver, she cut away her horrified gaze, relieved when Ma returned then with food.

Despite the hugger-mugger glances Rose received from the men around the table, she ate almost as much as Jean Pierre. The stew was tasty, though short on the meat lending its flavor to the vegetables and gravy. The biscuits were cold but soft, and they tasted fresh, unlike the ones they had been eating on the trail. Let them sneak looks at her and wonder why she looked so bedraggled, she thought as she buttered her third biscuit. As long as she was back under a roof that didn't leak and had good food to eat, she didn't care.

Both Rose and Jean Pierre were soon feeling heavy-lidded. Stifling yawns, they climbed to the second-floor room that Ma pointed out. One of her sons, she told them, had deposited their gear in the room and seen to their horses.

"Jean Pierre, do you suppose I could get some water for a bath?" Rose asked while shedding her grimy outer garments. She hated to think of crawling dirty between the snowy white sheets showing beneath the colorful quilt on the tall iron bedstead. A pewter pitcher stood beside a washbasin on a washstand in the small room, but it was empty. Though he hadn't paid any particular attention to her since their kiss beside the stream, she assumed he was still aware that he was supposed to be playing the role of suitor.

"Nobody is going to see you tonight," he replied in a tone of exasperation, forgetting that, no matter how tiring the day, he now had a bride to consider . . . and to woo. Her first time around a bunch of men since leaving home, he reflected irritably, and she wanted to preen. Only that morning, hadn't he stopped to let her wash her hair? Unlike Rose, he was accustomed to going for long periods of time without having a satisfactory bath, and it never occurred to his weary brain that she wanted to bathe for her own pleasure.

"I know that," she hissed, her eyes shooting blue fire. "You may enjoy looking and smelling like an animal, but I don't." Rose tossed her blond mane in a show of temper before picking up her discarded, dirty vest and throwing it at him where he sat on the foot of the bed, taking him by surprise.

The rough fabric hit Jean Pierre in the face, a button scratching his cheek and adding fuel to his smoldering temper. An animal was he . . . and a smelly one at that! Not stopping to think why he was so angry, he lunged and hauled her, struggling and protesting, onto the bed, where he pinned her across his lap and tore at the buttons of her breeches.

"Don't you dare hit me!"

Rose fought wildly and would have let out a yell if he hadn't warned her through clenched teeth, "If you scream, we'll have not only Ma Dibert at our door, but also the other roomers. How would you like them to see you as you are now?"

"Take your damned hands off me, you brute," she berated in a low but heated voice, glad that he hadn't gone ahead with the spanking. She had been wrong to think he wanted to please her, woo her. He obviously thought of her as nothing more than a flighty, subservient girl. "What

gives you the right to threaten me? You're no better than
river trash, you polecat, you—''

Jean Pierre clamped his hand over her mouth until she
bit it. He caught his breath and drew the wounded hand up
to his own mouth, not believing her audacity.

''You're nothing but a bully,'' Rose accused, clutching
the loosened breeches with both hands and scrambling to
the corner of the room on the far side of the bed. ''I don't
know why I was beginning to think you could be nice after
all.'' Right away she saw that she had boxed herself into a
trap.

Sucking at the bite on his hand, but smarting more from
her pointed reminder that he had fallen from grace since
that morning, Jean Pierre fell across the bed toward her,
reaching for her with his free hand. He grabbed at her
unbuttoned shirt and pulled her to him on the bed. Then
with both hands he held her, in spite of her struggles, and
removed the shirt, a one-sided smile on his face. ''Now,
you wildcat, what next?''

He had backed her up against the headrails, and they sat
with only inches between their bodies, both breathing in
ragged gasps from the exertion. Her eyes met his with
fiery, daring looks. The short candle on the washstand was
sputtering and creating soft, undulating light in rhythm
with her heaving breasts. The same thin chemise from that
morning covered those dark-tipped mounds that drew his
fascinated gaze. Her eyes, close and boring into his,
appeared to be all sparkle with no color at all. In the
strange light, her tangled hair seemed to have the same
alluring opalescence as her body. As though drawn by a
magnet, his head moved down toward hers. Those full,
pink lips tempted him and drove away all rational thought.

''If you kiss me, I'll bite you.'' Rose narrowed her eyes
while threatening him. Backed up as she was against the
iron headrails, she had nowhere to go. Her hands pushed
against his hard chest, no more effective than if they were
made of goosedown. She had never before seen that
strange look in his eyes, and something within her fluttered.
Was she afraid of this . . . stranger? This was not the Jean
Pierre she had thought she knew, the one who was all bark

and no bite. Certainly it wasn't the gentle man rinsing her hair, the one thrilling her with his sweet kiss afterward in the pink dawn. She swallowed at the sudden lump in her throat.

"If you do, I'll really spank you . . . and hard." He was so close he could feel her spurts of breath upon his face, could see the little pulse quivering in the hollow in her throat, the pinpoints of black in her eyes. His chest barely touched her breasts, but even so, he felt seared where they quivered against him. A rush of expectancy filled him. His mouth moved to its target. Lightly at first, his lips brushed upon hers, then they opened and pressed against her trembling sweetness. A drumming in his ears set his senses reeling, and he pulled her protesting body close against him while he captured her mouth, glorying in its warm satiny fullness, sending his tongue to outline its shape.

Although she couldn't back farther away, Rose tried to shrink from his kiss, amazed that it was not hard and brutal and wondering why she didn't bite him as she had promised. The first gentle touch of his mouth on hers set off tremors deep inside, and she shivered, no longer as eager to escape but not understanding why, since she'd not granted him permission to kiss her. Keeping her eyes fixed on his, she pondered the intensity she saw in those dark irises and wished she knew what caused it. She had glimpsed it during the morning kiss, she realized. When his mouth opened against hers and she felt his tongue trace across the inside of her lips, she gasped at the onslaught of fire across its path, the movement opening her mouth as though in invitation for more exploration.

"There," Jean Pierre whispered, lifting his mouth enough to talk and bringing his hands to cup her face, "that wasn't so bad, was it?" Her response had both surprised and pleasured him, and he lowered his mouth again, giving in to his body's demand to have more of her.

Rose thought she detected a smug tone in his voice— was this another of his games?—and she recoiled, twisting her face away and causing his lips to miss their goal and land on her cheek. She wasn't about to let him know that his kiss affected her. If he hadn't forced her, maybe . . . "Is this the way you gentle your women?'' she asked. ''First you threaten to beat them, and then you force kisses on them.''

Jean Pierre drew back, releasing his hold on her. ''You seemed to like the last part,'' he accused, shocked at her rebuff. Had he been mistaken about her response? He studied her face in the half-light. There was something different about her, a little pleased look beneath the outward show of scorn. Had she realized how powerfully her body affected him?

''What choice did I have?'' she retorted, motioning to the confining headrail and taking advantage of his relaxing his hold to flip over and leave the bed. ''Is this your idea of a courtship?'' Haughtily she turned to look at him over her shoulder, for some strange reason no longer caring that she wore only a chemise and that her breeches were half falling off. ''I would've thought from your vast experience with women that you would know more about wooing than that.'' When he merely sat and studied her, she went on, ''But then I guess you look upon winning your women to be on the same level with breaking horses. I've watched you do that on more than one occasion. More brawn than anything else.'' Her lips pouted, and her eyes flicked over him with more than challenge before she turned away, taunting, ''Is it only in the mornings that you can play at courting?''

Jean Pierre gritted his teeth, determined not to rise to her bait. What he had suspected was true. She had responded to his kiss even when she hadn't meant to; and now, although he doubted she knew it, she was flirting with him. He thought, *There's untold passion in that curving body,* and it came to him, as it had briefly on their wedding night, that to wait until she surrendered to him willingly would be worth all the trials required. The kiss had told him that to seduce her would be easy and rewarding, but he wanted more than just her body. The thought that he would have all of her or nothing—and that ''all'' was indeed possible—brought a smile to his face, a thunder of anticipation to his heart.

Neither weariness nor anger weighted his voice when he

said with amused resignation, "Mayhap it's time I went to fetch some bath water for my bitchy wife."

"Bitchy?" she asked, whirling around to face him, not noticing that he no longer looked or sounded angry. "What a horrible term. That's even worse than the 'old woman' bit you bandied about when those men came to our camp that night. You really are the vilest of men, aren't you?"

Jean Pierre was closing the door by the time she got out the last words, and she didn't see the huge smile on his face.

Chapter Nine

Long after Rose and Jean Pierre had left the dining room and gone upstairs, a dark-suited man sat on a bench on the front porch with Mimi Dibert, Ma's sixteen-year-old daughter.

"If you hadn't been in your room primping, you would've seen your Cajun honey tonight," said Thom Keller, the peddler who had so brazenly stared at the late-arriving couple in Ma's dining room.

"Who are you talking about?"

"Jean Pierre Guilbeau, that's who."

"He's no 'honey' of mine. He barely gave me a goodbye kiss when he was last here, and that was after I threw myself at him. You're mean, Thom." She swallowed, afraid he might take her to task for her careless accusation. More than once she had seen that he had a cruel streak, and she held her breath.

"Like I been telling you for the past year, I'm trying to take care of you, Mimi. I don't know why you keep thinking I'm up to meanness." His cigar between thumb and forefinger, he took a big puff, checking to see if they

were still alone. Was she making a sly dig about his
slapping her last night?

"If you'd divorce your wife in Natchez, we wouldn't
have to be thinking up all these tricks of yours," Mimi
accused, glad he had chosen to let her remark go by. She
wiggled her sore jaw, wondering why his cuffs left no
bruises. She watched him exhale the pungent smoke. Not
very tall, Thom had dark hair and a slight build. He might
not be as handsome as some, she conceded, but his fancy
suits and flattering tongue made up for his lack of good
looks.

Mimi was a younger, softer version of her mother. A
full, heart-shaped mouth in a boyish but pretty face and a
perpetual look of innocence made men notice her. Tall,
with high, small breasts, she carried herself easily with an
exuberance men seemed to find stimulating. There in the
small settlement, she was like a transplanted flower with
no like species for engendering.

Growing up in her widowed mother's rambling old
boardinghouse, Mimi had decided at an early age that she
would team up with someone worldly and romantic, someone who would take her away to New Orleans. The
peddlers caught her fancy because they came from faraway
places, the kind she longed to see.

Thom Keller had begun staying at the boardinghouse
about three years back, when Mimi was thirteen. He had
found her aloofness and lithe, animal grace strangely
erotic. Each time he returned to Natchitoches, she had
attracted him more. Last year, right after her fifteenth
birthday, Thom made his move. Adroit in seducing young
girls without their mothers' knowledge, he lured Mimi to
his room late one night. A few promises to take her to
New Orleans had won Thom his prize.

Wanting to make a lasting claim on his apt pupil, Thom
cast about in his devious mind for ideas. In Natchez he had
a bona fide wife and two young children. But in Baton
Rouge and Pointe Coupee, he had liaisons with wives of
long-absent trappers. The lonely women provided the peddler with a home away from home, free of obligations.

Once he found Mimi so willing in bed, he decided to marry her off to a trapper and gain another such safe diversion while making his rounds.

Back in the spring at the time of Thom's scheming about how to lay a stronger claim to Mimi, Jean Pierre and Louis were staying at Ma's boardinghouse while on their way home with the season's pelts. Both young men were attentive to Mimi as she waited on the table, but Thom thought he detected a more respectful attitude on Jean Pierre's part.

"That trapper has his eye on you, sweet," Thom had told Mimi that spring night when she slipped into his room. He sat upon the bed, still fully clothed.

"Which one?" she asked, already stripping off her nightdress and posing for him in the way he had taught her.

"Jean Pierre Guilbeau." As the only light came from the moon, he couldn't determine her reaction. The main attraction was her nakedness, and he gave it his full attention. He motioned for her to make the next move in their ritual. What a gem of a pupil she had become!

"He is handsome," Mimi said, unbuttoning his shirt and breeches and letting her hands rove across his chest and then down to his manhood.

"Then why don't you warm up to him?" He closed his eyes in pleasure at what she was doing to him below his waist. Damned if she didn't seem to get as much of a thrill from their coupling as he did. Not many women dared be so free, but then he never before had been sole owner of one so young and pliable.

"What do you mean?" Mimi asked in a low, throaty voice. Swaying to the caresses of his mouth and hands upon her breasts and hips, she said in a pouty voice, "Would you have me do to him what I'm doing to you? I thought you loved me, Thom." In the moonlight she could see what her hands were telling her. He was hard and ready, and she smiled in anticipation as she pushed him down upon the bed and draped her body atop his.

"I do, baby, I do," he groaned, delighting at the way she moved her hips against his, taunting his swollen member. "I'm thinking of a way we can be together every winter when I come this way. Isn't that what you want, too? Didn't you say you hated sneaking behind your mother's back to be with me?" There was no one who could get him as hot as Mimi could. Never could he let her get away from him.

"Yes, but I thought you were going to take me to New Orleans," she said, stopping her writhing against him and trying to see his expression.

"I am, but that might take a while. In the meantime, you could snuggle up to this Cajun and make him think he's the first. Those Cajuns are the marrying kind, take it from me." Thom knew he was treading on dangerous ground here. She seemed his willing pupil in bed, but she tried to do her own thinking outside of it. That her passion equaled his was far more important, though, and he sent his fingers to tease and taunt her thighs and velvety softness, hoping to entice her hips back into their little rhythmic movements above his pulsating shaft.

"But, Thom, you wouldn't want me to let some other man make love to me like this, would you?" Mimi was more than a little angry and not at all responsive to his bold caresses.

Thom turned her to lie beneath him then, no longer interested in talk. He captured her body with his and filled her with his passion, taking them both to the heights they sought. Afterward he was most persuasive, stroking her body and murmuring his plans. Before she sneaked back to her room on that spring night, both her body and mind were satiated. She had agreed to flirt with Jean Pierre.

Mimi's physical charms were not lost on Jean Pierre the next day. He was aware, however, that if he paid too much attention to her, Ma might inquire as to his intentions. So, no matter how flirtatiously Mimi smiled or how piercingly Ma watched and seemed to give approval, he did not succumb.

Mimi walked Jean Pierre to his horse out back on the morning of his departure, and he wished he had waited for Louis. There was something about her that spelled danger. In the barn, when Mimi moved in her seductive way from his side to stand facing him, her charming eyes raised provocatively, he read her blatant invitation.

"You'll not forget me, will you, Jean Pierre?" she whispered, her arms stealing around his neck.

Even away from Ma's scrutiny, he wasn't greatly tempted, settling for a single, quick kiss. By the time Louis arrived, Jean Pierre had saddled both their horses.

"You will come back?" Mimi asked, her eyes still inviting.

"I reckon so. I always come through here on my way north." With those noncommittal words, Jean Pierre waved and rode off with Louis, not even looking back.

Mimi reported to Thom that, though not sure, she might have made Jean Pierre interested enough to pay her more attention upon his return. Thom had moved on soon afterward, hoping she hadn't become pregnant.

Mimi had become realistic, though, and when Thom returned a few days before Jean Pierre and Rose arrived, she refused to visit his room. Even his slapping her the previous night in an attempt to force her to obey him hadn't changed her mind.

"Honey," Thom said, his thoughts back to the present now, his groin burning, "I am going to divorce my wife. That takes time, though, and I can't stand not holding you in my arms." Laying his cigar on a nearby flowerpot, he tried to caress her breasts, but received a slap on his hands. She must know that someone was still awake, he thought angrily, or she wouldn't have taken a chance on his returning the blow.

"Did Jean Pierre even ask Ma about me?" Mimi asked. She had become adept at fending off unwelcome attentions from men, and as far as she was concerned, Thom Keller was no different from the others until he kept some of his promises to her. Except that she loved him. Wildly. Hopelessly.

"Nope. He had a blonde with him that he introduced as his wife." He picked up his discarded cigar and brought it to his mouth, chewing on it in agitation.

"His wife? Then there goes that little plan of yours."

Mimi suddenly felt out of breath. He would never take her away if she didn't do as he said, and now she had lost out on the hoped-for marriage with a handsome trapper. With a husband gone most of the year, she could have seen Thom without sneaking around. And she had planned to beg Jean Pierre to make their home in New Orleans. Just thinking the name of the capital set her imagination on fire. New Orleans.

"I said he 'introduced' her as his wife. I happen to know she's not." His voice sounded smug there on the porch.

"How do you know that?" She wanted to believe him.

"I saw a blond girl in the store at Attakapas a couple of years ago when I was calling. There are no blondes along the Bayou Teche and few that I've ever seen anywhere with hair like hers. It's what some folks call 'strawberry blond.' "

"Couldn't Jean Pierre have gone home and found her grown up and married her?"

"No, because I asked that day about her and was told that she's a Guilbeau and his cousin, reared in the same house."

Mimi turned to stare. "Why would he be passing off his cousin as his wife?"

"I don't know, but it sure as hell puzzles me."

After Mimi allowed him a lingering kiss before going inside, Thom sat with his cigar and his angry thoughts. To lose the Cajun as a prospective husband for Mimi was a setback, for she was too strong-willed to have just any trapper foisted off on her. He detected a restlessness in her and feared he might be losing his hold on her. He would have to move fast to bind her to him, for the thought of never having her in his bed again devastated him, made him almost physically ill.

No arrogant Cajun trapper was going to mess up his plans, Thom vowed beneath his breath. And, he reflected, he wasn't the only one to feel that way about Jean Pierre Guilbeau. Right then, the wily little man let the memory of his recent meeting with Governor Unzaga's nephew surface.

Jesus! If he could have known that Jean Pierre was going to show up in Natchitoches with his cousin . . .

As he did twice yearly, Thom was calling that day some two weeks back at stores on his way northwest toward Natchitoches. At the small store at Acadian Point, the last southern stop on the Bayou Teche before reaching Attakapas, he was preparing to go inside with his packets of goods to sell when a tall young Spaniard with a battered face strode from inside. A conversation that began with talk about their horses tethered underneath the same tree soon grew into one more personal.

"Yep," Thom replied after the two had talked awhile there beside the bayou and found out a bit about each other. "I know Jean Pierre Guilbeau. He's a Cajun from up the bayou, near Attakapas." His unctuous tone and sly smile told far more.

"You and nobody else will know him long if I have my way," Phillip de Cordoza growled. A hand pressed lightly at his half-closed eye, then at a swollen, purplish cheek sliced by an open cut marked with dried blood.

"Don't tell me that trapper did that to you." Thom's curiosity about the Spaniard's badly bruised eye and face had been building as the two men talked. He laughed knowingly before saying, "I hadn't figured that big Cajun for a fool." Though Thom had never met Phillip before, he had heard much about the vile-tempered nephew of Governor Unzaga. "Want to tell me what happened between you two? I guess he must look a sight worse than you do today."

Phillip sent a belligerent stare at the smaller man, then said with obvious hatred, "That damned fool Guilbeau took it upon himself to get between me and something I intend to have. Mark my words. He'll rue the day."

Thom saw the Spaniard's lips twist cruelly, but he waited to learn more.

"Keller," Phillip said, "I see you as someone I can trust. I don't suppose you know anyone who'd like to earn some gold, do you? I've pressing business elsewhere, or I'd tend to this Cajun myself." His good eye reading greed in the face of the peddler, Phillip pulled a leather pouch from inside his coat and cradled it first in one hand, then the other.

Thom gulped at the sight of the bulging pouch arching in the air between Phillip's hands, trying to judge how many Spanish gold pieces might be in it each time it clinked against the obviously soft palms. Jesus! With such a stake, a man could sell when the weather and the mood suited him, not have to wear himself out traveling among the outlying settlements. But then, he reminded himself, if he didn't visit Natchitoches, there would be no chance to get Mimi into his bed; and the itch in his groin wouldn't get scratched the way only she could do it, the way he had become addicted to since seducing her.

"Afraid I don't know anyone to help you out, friend," Thom replied, his voice thick with yearning for both the gold and Mimi's lithe body. Just that fleeting thought of her caused a pulsation between his legs. He needed Jean Pierre alive and well to marry her and open the way for Thom to spend the trapping season with her in his bed. The war within produced an unwelcome discovery. Never before had sexual gratification meant more to him than gold; and the realization shocked him, made him feel like an old fool, when he wasn't much past thirty. "Wish I could, but—"

"Somebody will," Phillip broke in harshly, looking down at the pouch of coins. "I mean to get that dirty trapper and put him where he won't bother me ever again. He needs to learn that I can claim any woman I choose." He hadn't missed the way the peddler's eyes never left the pouch. The little man was obviously a weakling and a coward, incapable of acting to seize what he desired—unlike himself, he thought with a smug smile. "Next time I get ready to spread that little blonde's thighs, I'll make damned sure nobody interferes."

The pulsation in Thom's groin seared his mind then, and he couldn't concentrate on the rest of the conversation. With apologies for not being available, and a promise to be on the lookout for someone who might help Phillip—after all, Thom realized, he himself had no call to antagonize the governor's nephew, from all he'd heard about him—the peddler watched the riled Spaniard head south toward New Orleans.

Maybe, Thom mused after several puffs on his cigar there on the darkened porch of the boardinghouse, there was some scandal within the Guilbeau family, and he could find a way to force Jean Pierre to marry Mimi to keep down talk. Was the blonde pregnant—perhaps by Phillip de Cordoza?—and being transported somewhere to save face? He wished he had listened closer to Phillip's talk about Jean Pierre's interference in his affairs, about what had actually taken place.

The little man's warped thoughts churned long after he went up to his lonely bed.

Chapter Ten

The next morning at breakfast, Thom Keller covertly studied Rose and Jean Pierre, but mostly Rose. Her pinkish blond hair falling down her back in a profusion of curls, she appeared all shining clean. Thom noted how her loveliness was obviously distracting to the mean-eyed Rufus Bedlow, and if she but raised her blue eyes, the unkempt Bedlow was quick to offer to pass her more food or get Mimi to bring her more coffee.

Jean Pierre ate with his eyes on his food, seeming to ignore the attention paid to Rose. He was aware, however, of the piercing looks Mimi shot in his direction each time she entered the dining room. He hadn't seen Ma's daughter or even thought of her since accepting her goodbye kiss during his last visit, and he was a bit surprised to see that the bloom of innocence he had found appealing seemed diminished.

"Didn't you say last night that you're a trapper from Attakapas?" the peddler asked after Jean Pierre had finished eating and only another man and he remained at the table with the newlyweds. "I'm Thom Keller."

"Yes, Mr. Keller," replied Jean Pierre, not unpleasantly. "We met when I was here a few months back."

"Ask him whose traps his partner springs," Rufus Bedlow drawled from the end of the table. A red shirt accentuated the scar running from the edge of his eyebrow down into his black beard.

"Rufus," Jean Pierre said with a level look at the big, bushy-haired man, "I thought we had our differences settled. Louis apologized and gave you the pelt, didn't he? You said yourself that your trap wasn't marked well."

"What Louis and you gave me was a ratty skin with holes in it," Rufus complained. The drawn side of his mouth turned each word into a snarl. "He'd ought'a left my catch alone."

"And you ought to file down the teeth of your traps if you don't want holes in the pelts. Louis made a mistake, but he made up for it by giving you the one he cleaned and stretched from your trap. What else do you want from us? Do you want to step outside and talk about this?"

Rufus glared at Jean Pierre, then let his eyes flit to an assessing Rose as he stood and stalked from the dining room, his big boots clomping loudly on the plank floor.

"You weren't a married man last spring, were you?" Thom asked, an oily smile splitting his face.

"No, Mr. Keller. We married only recently." Jean Pierre looked hard at the little man.

"And you, Mrs. Guilbeau," Thom went on as though unaware of her husband's piercing looks, "are also from Attakapas?"

"Why, yes, I am," Rose answered, startled at being addressed as Mrs. Guilbeau. The tense exchange between Rufus and Jean Pierre had upset her; the big trapper seemed to detest Jean Pierre. And now there was something disagreeable about Thom Keller's smile.

Jean Pierre abruptly shoved back his chair and nodded to Rose. She allowed him to pull out her chair, and he escorted her upstairs in silence.

"Stay in the room while I attend to business today," he said in that same commanding tone he had used on the trail, going to his saddlebags in the corner and taking out his money pouch.

"And pray tell why?" His relenting last night about the spanking and then his fetching water for her bath had seemed signs that he might be willing to treat her with more respect. Obviously she had read him incorrectly . . . again. He was back to ordering her about.

"Because you already have half those men down there panting after you." He looked at her in her simple blouse and dark skirt with the black waist girdle and thought she had never looked more innocent and appealing. It was no wonder to him that the men had feasted their eyes on his bride. Even though none had made any movement he could question, he felt it unwise for her to traipse around alone. Women of any kind were too rare in the area not to attract attention, but one as lovely as she—

"You never could stand it that others might think I'm nice to look at, could you?" Rose asked, interrupting his thoughts. "Why didn't you send me to a convent instead of marrying me? I would have been better off. I despise you!" She plopped down on the bed with a defiant toss of her hair and glared at him.

"Do I have to threaten you to make you do as I ask?" He didn't allow her plea to soften his voice, but inside his heart tugged at him. Seeing the way the quarrelsome Rufus Bedlow had looked at her had reminded him that she knew far too little about the ways of such men. He had to know she was safe or he couldn't attend to his business. The only way to reach her seemed to be through threats. Was it just last night that he had thought he might win her soon? He let out a sigh.

"What is this 'ask'? You never ask, you 'tell.' I know how to act without orders from you."

"You proved that at Grenfall, didn't you?" he shot back in a cutting voice. Why did she have to be so unreasona-

ble? Not proud of the hurt his words brought to her face,
he wheeled about and left.

Rose fell back on the bed and contemplated her lot,
becoming angrier when she relived his roughness of the
previous night. She refused to dwell upon yesterday's
kisses. Seeming to taunt her that she wouldn't be outside
in its warmth, the morning sun streamed through the single
window. He might know how to cut her down, she reflected,
but she couldn't blindly obey Jean Pierre when his orders
made no sense. Nearly all of their clothing had gotten wet
and dirty, and she had no idea how much longer they
would be in Natchitoches. Rising and gathering up their
soiled garments, she went in search of Ma Dibert to ask
about using her laundry facilities. She would show Jean
Pierre that she had a mind and could use it.

Ma pointed Rose toward the wash shed out back near
the stables and sent one of her boys to fetch hot water for
the washtub. Rose had just finished rinsing the clothes and
was stacking them in a basket when she heard someone
approaching.

"Good morning again, Mrs. Guilbeau," said Thom
Keller when she turned to see who had come into the small
room. She merely nodded, keeping her eyes on his in an
effort to determine the reason for his appearance.

"I was curious as to what you're doing," he said. When
she gave him a haughty look, he went on, "And I'm
curious as to why you're passing as the wife of your
cousin." Thom noted the indrawn breath and the increased
swell of firm breasts beneath the white, scoop-necked
blouse. If she was pregnant, he mused, she wasn't showing. The black waist girdle showed off a tiny waist and the
dark skirt fell flat over her small stomach and hips. She
bore an air of aloofness that intrigued him—and he sensed
that she must be the one Phillip de Cordoza had referred
to.

Rose stared at him with instant loathing, her chin raised
defiantly. Who did he think he was to be eyeing her body
in that manner? "I'm the wife of Jean Pierre and I am *not*
his cousin, sir. You're mistaken. I would appreciate your
leaving me alone to my laundry." At breakfast he had

seemed the most polite man at the table. The thought crossed her mind that Phillip de Cordoza had also seemed nice at their first meeting. All at once her heart hammered.

"I saw you in the store at Attakapas a year or so back," Thom continued as though she hadn't spoken, "and I asked who you were. I know you're a Guilbeau." He cocked his head and gave her an evil, knowing smile. "Phillip de Cordoza told me all about you."

"Please let me by," Rose demanded, noting that he still filled the doorway. All at once the air in the laundry room had become stifling. Where had he run into Phillip, and what lies had Phillip told? Her heartbeat tried to run away. "I must hang out my laundry. I have no need to explain anything about my husband or me to anyone." When he made no move to let her by, she added in ominous tones, "I'll report your insolence to Mrs. Dibert."

"You do that, girlie," he sneered, his normally bland face taking on a look of ugliness. "She won't like having an unmarried couple sharing one of her rooms, especially if they're kin. Incest is a mortal sin. Or didn't you know?" He found that her rising color made her even more beautiful. He felt the urge to put his arms around the tiny waist and pull her against him. She would indeed be an armful of soft curves, maybe even more to his liking than the slim, boyish body of the recently uncooperative Mimi. He swallowed the accumulation of spittle in his mouth. "Maybe I'll let you alone if you'll give me a kiss."

His words didn't fool Rose. His insinuation about Jean Pierre's and her relationship being incestuous was humiliating, but the lust she recognized in his eyes was frightening. With her hands behind her, she backed up until she touched the washtub, silent but fixing him with scornful eyes.

Having met Mimi in this same out-of-the-way place several times in the past, Thom grinned to think of the way the morning had turned out. No one would hear her if she screamed. All were busy in the kitchen preparing the noon meal. He figured that she would not want anyone to know her "husband" was actually her cousin and that she wouldn't dare report him for forcing himself on her. Never had he made love to a blonde, and the thought of touching her hair and fair skin set his blood racing. And from the fire in her eyes, he figured she would put up a good fight before he conquered her. Small wonder that the Spaniard had been so vehement in his threats against Jean Pierre. With such a prize at stake, what man wouldn't risk all? He enjoyed the throbbing sensation in his groin and moved toward her, licking his lips.

Without turning, Rose felt on the bench behind her for the big scrub brush she had been using. When her fingers closed over it, she aimed at the bulge now visible in Thom's pants. He stumbled forward with a groan, bent over from pain. Rose tipped the tub of warm suds forward, splattering his head and shoulders with the grimy contents. With a quick turn, she grabbed her basket of laundry and ran up the path to the house, ignoring the quiet curses flung her way by the no-longer-dapper Thom Keller.

When Jean Pierre returned to their room at noon to escort Rose down to eat, he found her surprisingly docile. He wondered at the change in her in such a brief time, but attributed it to his sagacious handling of her prior to his departure and gave it no more thought. To keep a tight rein on her was the only way to handle her.

Rose wanted to tell Jean Pierre what had happened, especially about Phillip's name being brought up, but she felt sure he would only harangue her about not obeying him and then scold her again about her trying to tempt men. She had a pretty good idea that Thom Keller wasn't going to mention their meeting. What she did wonder about was whether Thom would bring up the question of Jean Pierre's and her relationship. Even if Jean Pierre had their marriage papers to show, would they prove anything? She couldn't remember if her real surname had been used. What was the peddler's motive in stirring up all this business that seemed to be no concern of his? She shuddered at the memory of his evil, lustful eyes.

"You're mighty quiet," Jean Pierre said as they strolled toward the main street after their noon meal. She had sat demurely throughout, despite all the appreciative looks sent her way. All morning he had tried to think of ways to make her happy, but he felt stymied. He wondered if he should have paid more attention to Louis's way with women and picked up some pointers. He had figured that to take her to the main street would please her, but she seemed aloof, unaware that he believed himself to be courting. "Is something wrong?"

They were approaching the board sidewalk in the center of the trading area. Stores, saloons, and other places of business opened onto the board walk.

"I guess I'm tired," Rose replied, taking in the long street and buildings so close together. "How much longer will we be here?" She looked up to find the handsome face wearing a contemplative look.

"We might get away in a day or two if the blacksmith finishes repairing my traps. Why?" She seemed withdrawn and anxious.

Rose shot him a sideways glance. "I'd like to go to confession before we get on the trail again." To keep from returning his searching look, she smoothed her hair. A slight breeze ruffled the cloud of pinkish gold about her shoulders.

"There's the church up ahead. You can go on in now and see if the priest is there." He did his best to read her face but found it closed. For some reason she had avoided meeting his eyes ever since his return. Had he crushed her spirit with his heavy-handed remarks? He wanted to guide her in the right way, but he had no desire to squelch her into dull submission.

Rose looked where he pointed and saw the large building with the tall wooden cross over the doorway. The board walk ended before it reached the church, and the mud looked almost as deep as that in the wide street, though it did not have the same numerous ruts, tracks, and mud puddles.

"Now there's a pretty sight," Jean Pierre said with a smile when Rose turned to look at the display in a windowed box of the general store. He saw a black bonnet trimmed with curling egret feathers, a bolt of green calico, and a pair of pink satin slippers. He was hoping she'd tell him which object drew her admiring gaze.

"Yes," Rose agreed. "I never knew stores had windows to show what they had inside." She leaned her forehead against the glass to see beyond the closeup display, liking the way the cool, smooth surface felt against her troubled brow. "The store must be three times as large as the one at Attakapas."

Disappointed that she hadn't voiced a wish for something she saw so that he could buy it and maybe convince her that he was trying his best to woo her, Jean Pierre asked, "Do you want me to walk you over to the church before I go inside to buy supplies?"

"No," she replied. "It's so close, I'll go on and meet you back here."

They parted, Jean Pierre going into the general store after seeing Rose make her way down the deserted board walk. Holding up her skirt, she gingerly picked a path through the mud and reached the portico of the church with gumbo mud stuck all over her shoes. Removing them and leaving them on the brick floor just outside the double doors, she went inside.

After her prayers and confession, Rose felt much better. Her burdens seemed lighter now, even though she hadn't liked telling a strange priest about the unusual twist her life had taken recently. Outside she looked for her shoes, but they weren't where she had left them. Perplexed, she looked down the street and at the board walks on either side. There were a number of people on the walks, and a wagon, as well as several horsemen, moving on the street, but none seemed aware of her standing barefooted on the portico.

"Who could have stolen my shoes?" Rose muttered to herself. She saw hoof tracks in the mud, but couldn't recall if they had been there when she had crossed over to the church. So many curious things had been happening to her that she decided that to expect the unusual was what she should do now. She tried not to think how angry Jean Pierre would be that she had so foolishly lost her shoes.

Planting her feet in the tracks she had made on the way over, she shuddered at the way the mud felt squishing up between her toes, but kept moving toward the board walk, her eyes on the path. Busy with her thoughts, Rose was unaware that a horse had approached until a strong arm scooped her up and held her tightly against a bruising saddle and a hard, masculine body. She tried to scream, but the arm holding her right under her breasts cut off her breath. The horse moved swiftly to the opposite side of the street, splattering mud all over her legs and skirt before halting.

"Look what I have here," said a strangely accented voice above her just as she was dropped unceremoniously onto the sidewalk beneath a sign, THE FIGHTING COCK. The group of men standing nearby laughed raucously as Rose tried to maintain her footing and smooth her clothing at the same time. She looked up then to see who had dared yank her up like some animal and embarrass her.

A broad, friendly face with eyes as blue as her own laughed down at Rose. Blond hair, though not nearly as pale as hers, fell from under a large, light-colored hat. His teeth were dazzlingly white in the afternoon sun, and a dimple in one tanned cheek quivered from his deep laughter. Before she could catch her breath and vent her anger on him, he dismounted, looped his reins around the hitching rail, and bowed before her, his hat in his hand.

"Beau Bradford at your service, my lady," he said in that odd accent, his laughing eyes taking in the details of her clothing and bare feet.

Without hesitation, Rose reared back and slapped him right where the dimple had danced. If he hadn't been in the process of straightening up, she realized, she probably would have had to stand on tiptoe to reach his face. The man was even taller than Jean Pierre.

"You despicable beast! What did you think you were doing? You can't just pick up a lady in the street and ride off with her." Her eyes shot sparks both at him and at the now-growing audience. Glimpsing the grotesque, lopsided grin of Rufus Bedlow as he stood among the men fed her anger. She glanced across the street, trying to locate the general store. She couldn't decide if she longed for Jean Pierre to appear or if she should try to handle the affair herself and avoid a further scene with him. She couldn't be sure he would take her side anyway, she thought angrily.

Jarrette was the only one in the family who had ever done that without first checking all the facts. She bristled anew.

"I never saw a barefooted 'lady' before, and I couldn't resist," said her rescuer, apparently not the least nonplussed by her slap, despite the red now flooding his cheek. The men gathering around them laughed, but with apparent good humor. "You must admit you were having a hard time getting across the street."

An Englishman, Beau Bradford had been taken aback when he rode into town and saw the only true blonde he had laid eyes on since leaving home two years ago. Impulsive by nature as well as good-humored, he had had no qualms about snatching the young woman from the mud to set her on the board walk. His biggest surprise was to find when he set her down that she was as beautiful as she was fair. And even though she called herself a lady and wore a wedding band, she looked more like a young girl to him. She was no bigger than a minute, he thought, but she was perfectly put together. A new smile of appreciation wreathed his large face.

"Not that it's any of your business, but someone stole my shoes while I was at confession. I was on my way to the general store to meet my husband," Rose replied with as much dignity as she could muster. "And I would thank you to get out of my way so that I can cross the street to get there." She eyed the broad expanse of mud and puddles with distaste.

"That'd be one of them half-breed kids from the edge of town snitchin' your shoes," Rufus said. "They'll take anything they see and then try to sell it back to you."

Rose's rescuer flicked a speculative look toward the speaker before turning back to her.

"Allow me to carry you across on my horse," Beau offered, with goodwill in his voice. She appeared flustered by all the commotion his trick had caused, and men were still coming out of the bar to stand grinning at the spectacle of the angry beauty and the huge, smiling man. Though Beau was sorry to have embarrassed her, he was enjoying looking at her.

"No, thank you." With her chin and nose elevated in disdain, Rose picked her way across the street, agonizingly aware of the many eyes on her every squishing step.

Jean Pierre could hardly believe that the dirty, barefooted young woman who entered the store was Rose. Face flushed, she came to stand beside him where he was visiting with some other customers in the back. He gathered up his purchases and guided her from the store in the direction of the boardinghouse.

"What the hell happened to you?" he asked the minute they turned the corner. He hadn't meant to say "hell" and sound so vexed, but he knew no way to take it back. Everything he did around her seemed wrong, he mused.

"Don't curse at me, Jean Pierre Guilbeau. I've had all I can stand from men for one day," Rose said through clenched teeth. Her eyes raked him hotly.

"Where are your shoes? Did you go to church?" To get answers quicker, he decided to ignore her riled temper and speak in a softer and kindlier tone.

Rose hissed, "I don't know where my shoes are. Someone must have stolen them while I was at confession. And yes, I went to church. I'd just as soon not talk about it." Her lips and voice trembled, making her angry at herself.

Jean Pierre knew she was close to tears, and his heart wrenched at the hurt and anger in her blue eyes. She looked so young and indignant that he was tempted to put his arms around her right there on the street. Having learned too well that she would not appreciate being told she looked like a wronged child, he didn't reveal his thoughts.

"You're laughing at me, aren't you?" They were almost at the boardinghouse, and his first look of shock had gradually changed to one of anger and, now, to amusement.

By refusing to answer, Jean Pierre managed to avoid an argument there on the walkway. Though Rose may have looked as ridiculous as she felt, none of the men sprawled upon Ma's porch benches let on that she looked unusual.

At Jean Pierre's request, Ma's sons brought up a tub to their room and filled it with warm water. Rose waited impatiently for Jean Pierre and them to leave so she could strip off her mud-splattered clothing and sink into the tub.

When the boys left and Jean Pierre kept fiddling around with his purchases, she decided she had no choice but to ignore him and undress with him there in the room.

She gathered her hair into a large knot on top of her head and stepped out of her clothing. Jean Pierre watched from where he sat at the small table across the room, his breath catching at the sight of her. She was so slim yet generously curved that he wondered how anyone could ever think she looked like a boy in Jarrette's breeches and shirt. She seemed unaware of him as she stepped into the tub and sat down.

The water came up to the bottoms of her breasts, leaving bobbing, rosy nipples exposed. Each graceful movement she made as she soaped and bathed herself fascinated her audience. He had never before watched a woman in her bath. The warmth he had felt in his loins ever since she had stood unclothed became a burning desire, and he shifted on his chair. He noticed the tiny blond curls springing from the dampness around her face and neck, and was amazed at how even the sight of the nape of her neck heightened his passion. His lips hungered to taste that spot.

When Rose stood, dripping and preparing to step from the tub, Jean Pierre walked to pick up her towel and hold it out, enveloping her in it . . . and his arms.

"Don't, Jean Pierre," she said, twisting to free herself. "I'm tired and in no mood for your games. Don't bother me."

His romantic mood squashed, Jean Pierre remarked, "I've unfinished business to attend to. I'll be back before long."

Even when he tried to approach her in a gentle way, she rebuffed him, Jean Pierre agonized all the way to the main street. He still suspected that hers was a passionate nature, from the way she had responded to his kisses the previous morning and night. What was it about him that repulsed her? Was she so carried away with the idea of being wooed that she would ignore whatever natural attraction seemed to be building between them? That seemed to be the way it was, and he guessed he might as well accept it. He vowed not to approach her again until he was sure she was willing to accept him as her husband—if he could restrain himself.

At the general store, Jean Pierre took care of the business he had in mind when he left Rose in their bedroom. A secretive smile riding his face, he headed back toward Ma Dibert's.

"Pardon me," a big blond man called from down the board walk. "I've asked around and learned you're Jean Pierre Guilbeau," he said when Jean Pierre paused and the stranger caught up with him. "Beau Bradford here."

Noting that the English accent went well with the tall man's blue eyes, even features, and neat clothing, Jean Pierre shook the proffered hand and puzzled. "What can I do for you, Mr. Bradford?"

"No need to stand on ceremony," Beau replied, flashing his easy smile. "We've a mutual friend, Louis Brearde, whom I've met and dined with in New Orleans. I tried to apologize to your lady for embarrassing her earlier this afternoon, and I wanted you to know I truly am sorry." At Jean Pierre's obvious bafflement, the Englishman offered to buy drinks at the bar across the way and explain.

By the time Beau had told about rescuing Rose from the mud, Jean Pierre decided the young man was as likable as he had seemed from the first greeting. He wasn't at all as he had figured Englishmen to be, especially since the older Acadians often recalled how the English had forcibly removed them from their beloved Acadia in Nova Scotia and still painted a grim picture of anything British. Talk between the two became easy and relaxed there at a back table in the bar.

"And you've been away from England two years?" Jean Pierre asked. Though Father Sebastian, teacher for those near Attakapas, had taught his pupils the English language, Jean Pierre knew little of the country's customs. "If your father and you have a law firm together back there, what do you find to do over here, and how does he get in touch with you?"

"I keep a hotel room in New Orleans and go back ever so often to check for letters. Sometimes I search for people who left England a long time ago and whose families want to learn what happened to them. Sometimes there's a legacy needing to be delivered. Finding people over here isn't easy, and not many will hire out to do the job. Many of those still loyal to King George have left the Atlantic colonies to settle along the Mississippi. They don't want to go back home, but they don't want to fight against the British in what is sure to be a real war soon.''

''I kept hearing in New Orleans recently how trouble has been growing ever since the business of dumping the tea shipment in Boston harbor a couple of years back.''

''Yes,'' Beau remarked with a serious look. ''Talk was fierce last time I was there, a few months ago. Heard shots had been exchanged at Concord and Lexington in Massachusetts.'' He swigged at his beer in the companionable silence, and the pleased air once more claimed him. ''I like being in Louisiana, and I'm trying to see as much of the new world as I can. Guess I'm going to have to go home before long, though, and find a wife and settle down, as my father is after me to take over more of the work back there, now that he's getting older.''

Jean Pierre narrowed his eyes in thought after finishing his beer, then asked, ''Could you find out about a family back in England?'' At Beau's puzzled nod, Jean Pierre filled him in on Rose's background. The talk grew excited as the two young men shared information.

''I'll be heading back to New Orleans soon,'' Beau said when they left the bar and walked out to the board walk. ''I feel sure I'll hear from Father before Christmas, especially since the Winsteads live only one county over from us. And I'll be honest with you, Jean Pierre, your wife is going to be mighty pleased that you're finding out about her real family for her. Why don't you want her to know about this?''

''I feel I owe it to her to wait until you have definite information. For her to have living relatives and not know anything about them might cause her grief later on. So far, she hasn't said much about her true kin, but I think one of these days she's going to do a lot of wondering. If I hadn't run into you today—'' Jean Pierre laughed then at Beau's knowing grin, and went on, ''or if you hadn't 'rescued' my wife and tracked me down, I might never have thought of hiring a lawyer to look into this matter of the Winsteads. I'll appreciate anything you can find out, Beau.''

''I'm heading toward New Orleans now, and I'll write my father,'' Beau said. ''If I learn anything, I'll leave a message with your folks as you suggested. From your description, I won't have any trouble finding Attakapas.''

A firm handshake between the tall black-haired Cajun and the taller blond Englishman signaled the end of their conversation. Each man walked away feeling that he had made a friend for life.

Chapter Eleven

That night there were only a few boarders eating when Jean Pierre and Rose came downstairs. She wore a fresh blouse and skirt. The varying shades of their blues set off the fiery red of her ruby necklace. She had tied up the front half of her hair with a long length of the ribbon Jean Pierre had given her before their wedding. From under the shiny ribbon, a little cluster of golden curls cascaded down the back of her head, the remainder tumbling down her back. Invigorated by her bath, Rose decided she had never felt better. Little did she realize that her sense of well-being was reflected on the outside by a decidedly becoming flush and that the blue of her blouse deepened the color of her eyes, causing them to sparkle provocatively.

Mimi was replenishing a platter of fried catfish when she noticed Thom sending sidelong looks at Rose. Jean Pierre seemed as unable to keep his eyes off his wife as the other men were, and she noticed that he was eating little. Not having seen Thom all day, Mimi wondered if he had been able to find out anything about the couple's relationship. The only good thing about the evening was that the surly Rufus Bedlow and some other trappers had left early to watch a cockfight.

"Mr. Guilbeau," Thom said when Mimi had served coffee after the plum pudding, "may I have a word with you?" At Rose's hard look in his direction, he added, "Alone, of course."

"I can think of nothing you could have to say to me alone," Jean Pierre replied. He had noticed the peddler's seemingly prurient glances at Rose. Once he thought he had detected her hurtling a chilling glance of condemnation across the table at the dapper salesman. She usually seemed to pretend innocence when men clamored for her attention, he reflected, and he wondered about the malevolent look he felt sure he had seen. The old demon jealousy swelled within him.

"I would like you to meet me on the porch, as I wouldn't care to embarrass you or your lovely wife by talking here," Thom said threateningly, his eyes fixed on Jean Pierre.

Deciding he might as well find out what the obnoxious man wanted, Jean Pierre escorted a now solemn-faced Rose to the stairway. She had been right to object to his previously heavy-handed manner, he told himself in a burst of clarity. No longer was she the unattainable young woman filling him with repressed love and desire; she was his bride needing reassurance, trying in her way to make their marriage work. He reminded himself not to order her to wait upstairs for him, but to act as a man courting the woman he loves.

"I'll be up soon, Rose," he said gently, liking the way the blue eyes shone beneath silky lashes. He pressed her hand and smiled encouragingly when she seemed troubled, almost fearful. He turned and went to the porch.

"Now, what is this all about?" Jean Pierre asked when he reached the peddler standing at a far corner of the large porch.

"As I told your wife this morning—"

"When did you speak with her?" Jean Pierre broke in,

studying the man's smug countenance there in the pale light. What else was he to learn? That Rose hadn't told him about her innocent encounter with Beau Bradford still troubled him. Was she afraid of him?

"She didn't tell you?" When he saw the immobile features in the face above his, Thom realized that Rose hadn't confided in her husband. He was curious about her reasons for that.

"Get to the point," Jean Pierre ordered in a gruff voice.

"As I told her and am now telling you, I know that she is Rose Guilbeau, your cousin—not your wife." Spurred on by the Cajun's indrawn breath, Thom went on, "I think it's only fair to tell you that I met up with Phillip de Cordoza down at Acadian Point a couple of weeks ago, and we had a nice, long talk." His beady eyes scanned the scowling face above him, and he congratulated himself on having shocked the big trapper. He carefully removed a cigar from his coat pocket, a malicious smile spreading his lips. "Have one on me while we have ourselves a little chat," Thom said, preparing to hand it to Jean Pierre.

But Thom Keller didn't get the cigar very far from his pocket. Jean Pierre grabbed the peddler's coat with one hand and lifted him up, while the other became a fist pounding his jaw with enough force to knock the groaning man sailing off the porch. Thom lay sprawled on his back in a muddy bare spot between the porch and the path to the stables. Before the surprised peddler could recapture his breath, Jean Pierre was astride him, a fist in his face and the other hand grasping the lapels of his coat up around his neck like a noose.

"The lady with me is my wife and not my cousin. You are mistaken, sir," Jean Pierre said with a sarcastic accent on the final word. "Not that it's yours or anyone's business, but my wife's parents were English, not Acadian. As for Phillip de Cordoza, he can go to hell as far as I'm concerned. If you ever mention his name to my wife or me again, you'll look worse than he probably did when you saw him." He leaned nearer to the cowering, walleyed man, still aiming a fist at his stunned face. "Do we have more to discuss?"

All that Thom could muster were an emphatic shake of his head against the muddy ground and a gutteral sound meant to be "No." The tall Cajun rose slowly, still staring down at him. When Jean Pierre glimpsed the still-unlit cigar lying near-by in a pile of horse droppings, he plucked it out of the muck and jammed it, filth and all, into Thom's half-opened mouth.

"Here," he said with quiet force. "Have one on me." Turning and stepping lightly up on the porch, he went back inside and climbed the stairs.

Thom Keller's words to Jean Pierre had upset Rose, and as she left to go upstairs she wished she had confessed about her encounter in the washroom with the peddler. Something about the final look her husband had given her touched her heart. He was going to be twice as mad to hear it from Thom, she agonized as she removed her clothing and put on her nightdress. She didn't have to wait long to find out what happened.

"What about that Thom Keller? What happened this morning?" Jean Pierre asked as he burst into the room. He had mud on his shoes, and his lips were set in a straight line.

"He's a horrible man," Rose said with more composure than she felt. Her heart kicked around and almost took away her breath. "What happened down there?" She didn't believe she had ever seen him angrier, and she tried to back away.

"I asked first." He put his hands on her forearms, gripping tighter than he intended. "Tell me," he commanded.

"You're such a bully! Take your hands off me," Rose replied angrily. "I wish you and all the other men were smaller than I am just so I could boss all of you around for a change and make you do what *I* want. I'm sick of being treated like a pawn!" Although she had not raised her voice, it was strong, and her eyes fired blue missiles.

Jean Pierre could feel her trembling with indignation. He dropped his hands and watched her move to sit on the bed, not missing the way the white nightdress revealed more than it hid. He pulled the chair from the table up close, awed by her innate ability to draw composure about herself like a cloak. Her eyes never faltering from his, she lay back against her pillow and folded her hands across her middle, prepared for what she viewed as an inquisition. Guided by his surprisingly calm questions and comments, Rose related the details of her morning, omitting the mention of Phillip, but explaining the reasons why she had considered doing their laundry more important than obeying what had seemed to her his unreasonable demand that she stay in the room.

Concealing the fact that Thom had not even alluded to the attempted attack on Rose or her retaliation, Jean Pierre found it hard not to burst from the room to seek the man out and beat him senseless. Her expressed need for the approval of society and of God as to the sanctity of their marriage both shocked and pleased him. Only then did he realize why she had sought out the priest.

Jean Pierre found that he too had felt unclean at the salesman's implication of theirs being an incestuous relationship. He had had no idea that the lovely young woman before him possessed the many-faceted qualities she was revealing each day he was with her. He felt as if he might be seeing her for the first time. As she continued in that soft voice he had come to love, he was aware of long-buried beliefs of his own—some only half-formed—being called to the surface by a kindred spirit.

Love and respect for his bride exploded into even grander proportions as he turned away and took off his shoes, shirt, and breeches. Heart thumping and hands damp—like a gawky schoolboy, Jean Pierre realized—he padded in his under-breeches over to his saddlebags piled in the corner and picked up a paper-wrapped package.

From where she lay propped up against a pillow on the bed, wearing the nightdress made by Grandmère, Rose watched her handsome groom come closer. Each time she saw him in the short white breeches, she was tempted to stare. The way his muscles, at the tiniest movement, rippled so rhythmically under the olive-toned skin fascinated her.

"I bought these for you when I went back to the store." He laid the package beside her, not pleased that his voice revealed his nervousness. He cleared his throat in the silence, still standing and looking down at her in the candlelight. His heartbeat drummed a new rhythm. If he had ever seen her look more beautiful, he couldn't recall when. The fair skin of her face and shoulders had that rosy tone that seemed to go so well with her hair. And the blue of the eyes lifted to his reminded him of yesterday's morning sky when he had kissed her: fresh, clear, full of promise.

"How thoughtful, Jean Pierre." An unreadable expression in his dark eyes baffled her. Was that a flush beneath the tanned skin?

The sound of the brown paper crackling as she unwrapped the gift filled the room. A scent of something brand new added its subtle fragrance to that of the wax-myrtle candles. Both kept their gazes on her noisy opening of the package.

She gasped and held up the surprise, letting the paper slide from the bed to the wooden floor with a dry rustle. Blue eyes met pleading brown ones in the dancing candlelight. Rose smiled.

"Pink satin slippers? For me?" Her cheeks deepened to a matching hue. A mysterious glow in the watching dark eyes warmed her all over. Tucking away some of her pleasure in a secret corner of her heart, she hid behind lowered lashes before murmuring, "Thank you, Jean Pierre. They're the most beautiful shoes I ever saw." A testing forefinger caressed the dainty toes, creating an invisible pattern of circles on the silken threads. She wondered if she would ever forget the delicious smell of new, closely woven fabric teasing her nose, would ever again feel so special. A shy peek up at him from half-opened eyes showed how much he had pleased her, that she knew he was wooing her in the only way he knew. Never would she reveal that the satin shoes were utterly useless in their world, that they were no suitable replacement for the leather ones stolen from the church porch. Her smile widened.

A sigh of relief whooshing from his mouth, Jean Pierre sank heavily onto the foot of the tall bed, smiling both

inside and out—but not for long. A resounding *"whop!
bang!"* filled the room. A worn slat had given way. The
foot of the bed had crashed to the floor, jolting the two on
it, causing Jean Pierre to sprawl backward instantly on the
dropped-down end of the mattress, his knees angling
across the siderails, his feet dangling in mid-air.

The sudden dropping of the lower part of the bed flipped
a squealing Rose forward at the same time that it deposited
a thunderstruck Jean Pierre on the fallen portion. Dainty
pink shoes and voluminous nightdress joined in the little
melee, the first landing on his head, the second ending up
around her waist when she tumbled head first across his
middle.

Peeking from behind a jumble of blond curls, Rose
began giggling before she met Jean Pierre's disgruntled
gaze. One pink slipper sat squarely on his forehead amid
black curls, the other nestled beside his neck. Beneath her
belly she could feel his naked one tighten and then quiver.
Bass rumbles burst out and joined her rich, high peals of
laughter. Between spasms, Jean Pierre noticed that Rose's
exposed rear curved over his middle. Figuring the alert Ma
Dibert would surely come to investigate the god-awful
crash, he reluctantly pulled down her nightdress. And just
in time.

"Jean Pierre!" came an excited feminine voice, accompanied by a rapid knock on the door. "Jean Pierre! Did
that old bed fall down again?" Not waiting any longer for
a reply, Ma rapped again and entered, her gawking son
behind her. "Oh, my," she exclaimed when she saw the
collapsed bed holding the laughing couple, "are you all
right?" A bit shocked, she verified the source of the
sounds she had heard in the hall. "I guess anybody that
can laugh like that can't be hurt very bad." Embarrassed at
the sight of the couple's intimate but unorthodox contact,
as well as what appeared to be Jean Pierre's nakedness and
a daring display of Rose's thighs and legs, the older
woman blushed and jerked her head away, motioning her
son to leave. How could she explain to a youngster how a
great hunk of a man like Jean Pierre Guilbeau came to be

lying naked, with his bride draped across his middle—and with pink satin slippers about his head and face?

After the newlyweds had sobered and righted their appearances, they allowed Ma and her son to help Jean Pierre replace the broken slat. Throughout the task, neither Rose nor Jean Pierre could look at the other without breaking into huge smiles. More than once, she suspected those daring, half-veiled looks bordered on being outright flirtatious. Once more alone, Jean Pierre put out the candle, and the exhausted couple almost fell into the bed there in the dark.

He turned and gathered her close, relieved that she made no protest. Savoring the feel of her softness next to him, he found her lips in the darkness. Tenderness flavored the kiss, along with all those earlier feelings of awe and admiration for her coming to terms with all that beset her. Her lips answered sweetly, noticeably more schooled at responding than when he had first kissed her on their wedding night. The way her heart pounded beneath his reassured him that she was feeling something special.

Not realizing that she was kissing him back with equal ardor, Rose floated in a new kind of ecstasy as he held her in his strong arms. This Jean Pierre who had listened attentively to what troubled her mind, given her a lovely but impractical gift, joined in her helpless laughter over their ridiculous situation, then flirted with her in front of Ma and her son—and was now kissing her breathless— who was he? Her arms hugged him closer.

With great effort, Jean Pierre managed to recall his vow not to pressure Rose, not to mention his love for her as an inducement. He wanted her to love him as fiercely as he loved her, not merely to give in to aroused passion. When he ended the kiss and felt her arms slide from around his neck, he almost reneged on that vow. Instead, he whispered unsteadily, ''I'd like it if you'd snuggle up to my back. We've both had a tiring day and we need to get to sleep.''

His body protested that sleep wasn't what he needed, even after he turned away and she silently did as he asked.

Lying close to her husband's back, Rose found she was

weary but not sleepy. Every part of her seemed wide awake.

Heartfelt thoughts from both spewed unvoiced into the dark bedroom.

Wonder why he made no attempt to make love to me?

Wonder what she would have done if I had tried to make love to her?

He looked so . . . so different while we talked, and then later when he gave me the package. Could I be falling in love with him . . . just a little?

She never before has talked so openly with me. And she looked so pleased when she saw the pink slippers. Is she beginning to care for me . . . maybe a little?

Jean Pierre's thoughts kept him awake long after he heard regular breathing behind him. The encounter with Thom Keller didn't bother him, though to learn that Phillip was mouthing off was not good news. Surely the Spaniard wasn't fool enough to attempt retaliation for a beating he had deserved. True, Jean Pierre mused, he had decided it was best for him to get Rose away from the bayou country right after the wedding so that she wouldn't be so visible in case the arrogant Phillip chose to try to get even, as he had promised. As for himself, he longed for the day he could face Phillip one on one, man to man. But to imagine that even the governor's wily nephew would attempt to carry out his threat in the remote areas of Natchitoches or Fort Arkansas was ridiculous. He shelved thoughts of Phillip de Cordoza and Thom Keller for more immediate matters.

What filled Jean Pierre's mind were the perplexities of personal relationships, something that had never concerned him until he had admitted to himself that he loved Rose. To live the carefree life of a runner-of-the-woods, with delicious samplings from varied females while he accumulated enough money to purchase and maintain his own land, had been his primary goal. He thought back over his homecomings and the way in which he had become more aware of the budding of the beautiful young Rose each time he saw her.

And he had wanted her to be perfect. It was as if he could accept shortcomings in anyone except her. Her vanity had actually been no greater than that of any beauty living in a close-knit community, he reflected with new wisdom. He realized now that her innocence was genuine, that only his jealousy made him read calculated temptation into the way she carried herself. An inchoate longing to know Rose, to share her innermost thoughts, and to gain her approval bubbled up as he thought of how he had wronged her. He could force her to yield her body to him because, as she had pointed out, he was bigger and stronger than she. He could even seduce her, if the events of the previous night were any indication. But he knew he could never reach her inner self through such means, could never earn her love. More smitten by his bride than ever, Jean Pierre puzzled over ways he might change Rose's attitude toward him.

Thom Keller wasn't wasting time puzzling any longer about what action he should take. His jaw aching as if it might be broken, he waited on the dark porch of the boardinghouse for Rufus Bedlow to return from the cock-fight. Pain or no pain, he couldn't keep from spitting every once in a while. Relieved to see that the rough-talking trapper was alone, he went to meet him beneath a tree out front. Quickly Thom explained his plan, pressing a gold coin into the smelly, rough hand when he learned that what he had suspected was true: Rufus had no scruples and no love for Jean Pierre Guilbeau.

"You ain't got no traps to be tampered with. How come you got such a grudge against that Cajun?" Rufus asked, watching the little peddler's face while he brought the coin up to his disfigured mouth. His teeth met the metal, and he smiled in his crooked way.

"That's for me to know and for you not to think about." He was glad they were in shadows and that the big man couldn't see his jaw and get nosy. Wondering if his mouth would ever again have a decent taste in it, he spat twice before going on, "Just make sure you do what you've agreed to do, and I'll give you a mate to that gold piece next spring here at Ma's place." Lying to a man as stupid as Rufus seemed didn't even rank as a lie, he told himself—not that he had a conscience.

"Appears to me it's worth more'n one piece aforehand."

"Not when you're going to enjoy your work."

Stepping toward the porch, the two conspirators went inside the dimly lighted hallway, deserted at that late hour. Thom hung back until the evil-eyed Rufus had gone to his room at the rear of the first floor. He then rushed up to his own room, counting on Mimi to be there waiting for him as she had promised.

It had taken a little scheming, Thom mused just before opening his door, but he now had everything going his way. When his regular route landed him back in New Orleans around Christmastime, the first call he would make would be to Phillip de Cordoza to collect the bag of gold. Despite the pain it caused to his jaw, he smiled.

When Rose awoke late the next morning, Jean Pierre had already gone. Surprised that he had not wakened her to "give her the day's orders," she dressed in the blue blouse and skirt she had worn the night before. Was this leaving her on her own another step in his "courtship"? The sight of the pink satin slippers brought a little smile, and the memory of the crashing bed turned it into a smothered giggle. Recalling their kiss transformed the giggle into a smile of grander proportions. The thought that they might be nearing some kind of understanding cheered her, brought a lightness to her feet. Maybe she was falling in love with him, and maybe he had meant it when he told her on their wedding night that he loved her—though he hadn't told her since, she mused with a slight frown. Using a length of the blue ribbon he had given her to tie back her hair at the base of her neck, she went downstairs in search of breakfast.

Just as Rose reached the bottom stair, she heard the voices of Jean Pierre and Ma Dibert coming from the dining room. She was crossing the entry hall to join them when their words froze her in place.

"But I never even hinted to Mimi that I was going to return and marry her, Ma," came Jean Pierre's deep voice.

Rose peeked around the doorframe and saw the room was empty except for the two standing with their backs to her.

"She told me you were," Ma said. Her voice sounded muffled, as though she had been crying. "And I remembered how you were always teasing her...."

Rose tiptoed out of earshot back across the hall and halfway up the stairs. No longer were her steps springy. She had no desire to hear about one of Jean Pierre's exploits and, obviously, a breach of promise as well. Why else was he having to explain to Mimi's mother? After he had seemed so human last night, almost like a caring groom, she felt betrayed. How could she have entertained the foolish notion that he truly loved her, that she was falling in love with him? Tears burned behind her eyelids, but she ordered them to cease.

Then with deliberate noise Rose retraced her path and entered the dining room, her face composed in a polite smile. "Good morning," she called as she entered the dining room, conquering the dryness in her mouth and speaking normally. "I hope I'm not too late for breakfast." She looked around at the empty benches.

Ma and Jean Pierre turned toward her, the woman's eyes showing signs of recent tears. "No," she said. "I'll have some food out in a shake." She headed for the kitchen.

"What's wrong with her?" Rose asked when Jean Pierre joined her on the bench. She managed not to show that she knew more than she was telling and that something inside her was withering.

"Mimi, her daughter, ran off in the night with that peddler, Thom Keller."

"Why would she do that?" Rose was truly surprised that the shallow Thom had fooled the vibrant Mimi. "Was she trying to get back at somebody?" Watching him from behind half-lowered lashes, she tried to appear disinterested.

"Her note to Ma said she was in love with him and that she was going with him on his route, that they'd settle in New Orleans. Ma's shocked, since she had no inkling that Keller was paying Mimi any attention."

Jean Pierre was still a bit shaken by his confrontation with Ma. It had never occurred to him that Ma might have thought he was seriously interested in her daughter. He had inquired about Keller at breakfast only because he meant to beat the hell out of him for his actions against Rose, and he had been unprepared for Ma's tale. Deciding that he had had enough of Natchitoches, he left a sober-eyed Rose to eat her breakfast while he made plans for them to leave right after noon.

Rose wished she could know for sure what had Jean Pierre so deep in thought, but she figured it had to be his relationship with Mimi. Was he regretting his having to marry her instead of the tall, vivacious beauty? And, she fumed, hadn't Mimi and he been clever to have avoided letting her see them reunited, as they must surely have been since their arrival? Did knowing that Mimi was with another lover now pain him? Was that why he had made no advances toward her last night? How wrong she had been to think that he was truly courting her, that they might be becoming closer! The gift of last night, even the searing kiss, now seemed a mockery. When Ma brought her food, Rose found that she had lost her appetite.

"Somebody found these on the front porch with your name on them," Ma said when Rose pushed back her chair to leave the dining room.

Startled, she took the shoes that the sad-featured woman was offering. Had the big blond man retrieved them from the thief, cleaned them, and brought them to the boarding house? She had too much to ponder to give the matter of everyday shoes further thought. Pink satin slippers held far more weight.

After going to their room and packing, Rose decided to write a letter to Maman and Papa as promised. She knew that any kind of letter delivery was slow and uncertain between settlements, but that even late news would be welcomed. When the troubled young woman read over her brief account of their experiences during the four days since the wedding, she longed to tell of all the confusing things that had happened, but she realized that such might upset them. Both Maman and Papa had done their best to prepare her for the world. If Rose let them know how inadequate she felt to cope with her new life, they might feel they had failed her in some way, and she would never want them to think that. Somehow, she would bear up under every surprise that Fate dealt her. She might have to bend—hadn't she already?—but she promised herself that she would never break.

That Rose made such a strong resolution was probably what enabled her to face the biggest blow yet, the one that would befall the newlyweds before they reached their destination.

Chapter Twelve

The weather cooperated, and Jean Pierre and Rose made good time after they left Natchitoches. They watched the forests change even more drastically than on the trail from Attakapas. Soon, Rose noted, there was no hanging moss, not even in the trees along the sheltered banks of the streams. The oaks became straight, with less girth and height and with broader leaves. Pines became more numerous, their towering trunks capped up high by branches of shorter, thicker needles. Elm, ash, hickory, cottonwood, and a few cedar trees joined the several varieties of oak as they traveled north. The trail changed from the black gumbo of the subtropical part of Spanish Louisiana to the red sand deposited over the years by the flooding Red River.

Fewer trails branched off into the backwoods the farther they rode. On the second day, when they came to a ford in the Red River, Rose stared in wonder at the sluggish water she had first seen at Natchitoches. And after they had swum their horses across, she looked with distaste at the heavy red deposits of mud on everything—the horses, their clothing, the tarps protecting their bedrolls and packsacks.

Aware that the muddy river offered no pleasant campsites, Jean Pierre led them on until after dark to reach a cleaner stream. Even in the falling darkness Rose noticed that their path was changing from tightly packed red dirt to light, sandy soil dotted with small rocks. The sobering thought that with each mile she was leaving far behind all she had ever known gnawed at her, set her to eyeing the tall figure up ahead in a new light.

Too dirty and weary to do much more than build a fire and eat cold rations, both Rose and Jean Pierre crept exhaustedly into their bedrolls before the campfire had had time to reach its peak. She had made no protest on the previous three nights, or on this one, when he spread their bedrolls side by side. Surprised that since leaving Natchitoches he had made no move to touch her, she was far too relieved to dwell upon the reasons. She felt sure that the loss of Mimi was the major one.

Though the days on the trail were tiring and they talked little, Rose felt better than she had since leaving home. Riding Beauty in the quiet woods, she experienced a kind of release, her mind freed to skip and jump at random. An expert equestrienne and completely relaxed, she found the forest exhilarating and conducive to all kinds of mental pleasures. Sometimes she drank in the changing landscape, and at others she sought out signs of animals: their nests and holes, their droppings, and sometimes the sight of their scurrying to hide from the trespassers. Ably Jean Pierre led the way, never covering much ground without looking back to check on Rose and the pack horse.

Could she ever know how much her very presence meant to him? Jean Pierre mused more than once after turning back from looking at her. He hated that the business with Thom Keller had taken place, that it had forced Rose to endure a degree of shame and hurt. On the other hand, he reasoned, she had seemed far less flighty and smoother-tempered since the incident. She appeared to be deep in some private conversation with herself while they rode, and he fought down a little feeling of jealousy that he had no way to find out what she was thinking.

Rose found that the old daydreams sometimes attempted

to surface. But somehow the pretty images of a faultlessly
gowned and coiffed Rose being wooed ardently by a
handsome, well-dressed young stranger no longer offered
her pleasant escape. Rather than muddle through the reasons for the puzzling development, she refused to give
credence to such thoughts when they nagged at her, reminding
herself that all yesterdays were gone and that the todays
and tomorrows were what counted. Often the path led into
deep woods where green shadows lay cool and inviting,
and the sounds of birds and small creatures called to her
above the groans of leather and the clip-clop of horses'
hooves. And sometimes the trail zagged across open,
grassy areas or zigged alongside a river or small stream,
presenting her with one more new scene. Always the
travelers seemed to be climbing.

Upon awakening that morning after crossing the Red
River, Rose found Jean Pierre's blanket already rolled and
tied behind his saddle. For the first time, she saw their
campsite in adequate light and was surprised to see the
many large rocks lying about the grassy spot. Some were
as large as her head. When she stood after putting on her
shoes, she could see him kneeling beside the rushing
stream. The water appeared to be clear and green, and she
hurried down the bank, eager to see one more new side of
nature.

"Jean Pierre," she called, picking her way among
rocks, "I never saw rocks so big, and I never knew water
could be this clear." She saw their coffeepot in his hands
when he turned toward her and realized what he had been
about. "I'll bet we'll have the best coffee ever." She
tipped her head back and sighed in anticipation. The
morning was glorious, and she couldn't remember when
she had felt so alive. Neither was aware that it was the first
time she had declared that anything so far from Attakapas
might be superior.

Jean Pierre nodded, smiling to see her exuberance. This
was the Rose he had dreamed of. "You like the mountain
streams, yes?" His eyes moved caressingly across her
face.

"Mountains? Are we in the mountains?" Blue eyes

sparkled as she turned to look up and down the stream and then toward the horizon. "They look like hills to me."

"We're in the foothills. They'll lead us to the high country and the mountains," he replied. Tearing his gaze from the gold of her hair, he turned back to dip the coffeepot full of water and went up the slight rise to start a fire.

Figuring that Jean Pierre would call her if he needed help, Rose stayed to drink in the sights. Behind her she heard him breaking kindling, then the crackling of the first blaze. Woodsmoke teased her nostrils, and she took a deep breath. She felt a compulsion to rid her clothing and herself of the red mud and dust in the clear water with its graveled bed. Determined to ignore the morning chill, she removed her shoes and waded fully clothed, with teeth chattering, out to the middle of what looked like a shallow dip. But the clear water deceived her, and before she could do more than let out a small "yip," she lost her footing on the slippery rocks and went all the way under, hair and vest floating around her. From the shock of the cold water more than from fear, she let out a yell while struggling to her feet. The water seemed warmer than the air, she noticed, and she lowered her shaking body back beneath its surface.

Busy with the fire and the placing of the coffeepot, Jean Pierre was unaware that Rose had gone into the water until he heard her cry out. Tearing down the bank, he saw her sputtering and floundering out in the middle as though in trouble. He didn't wait to shed shoes or clothing; he splashed his way toward her, calling her name loudly.

Rose heard Jean Pierre before he reached her and turned her laughing face in his direction, astonished at the look of fear on his countenance.

"Are you all right?" he asked, grabbing her shoulders and pulling her toward him. Water streamed down her face, matting her lashes. Small teeth gleamed between smiling, full lips. Wet now, her hair lay in pale wisps about her face and in large ropes down her back.

"Of course, silly," she retorted playfully. "I didn't mean to yell, but then I didn't plan to get wet all over quite so soon." She gained her footing and stood in water reaching to her breasts. "It's warmer in the water," she said, shrugging off his grip on her arm. That he had showed such concern over her safety touched her, and that he still looked so solemn even now that he realized there was no danger triggered a spark of mischief. "You're already wet, so come on under." With those words, she grabbed his protesting hands and sank up to her chin in the water.

Caught off kilter by Rose's pull, Jean Pierre lost his footing and fell face-down alongside her with a great shout and a noisy splash. Attempting to regain his balance, he grabbed her hips on his way down and pulled her under with him. Her shirt slipped out of her pants and joined her vest and hair in floating around her. She thrashed about, managing to right herself just as he fixed his slippery shoes on the rocky bed and rose to full height, bringing her with him.

"You pulled me under, you wench!" Before she could dart away, he captured her hands and pulled her close. The pink of dawn bathed her face, causing him to catch his breath at her beauty . . . or was it at her nearness? Close enough to kiss with no more than a ducking of his head, she dared him with eyes peeking from beneath spikes of brown.

"I did not!" she denied impishly, shaking the water from her face like a frisky puppy. "You're just a clumsy ox." There was that strange, softened look about his mouth again, she thought, the one she had first noticed on their wedding night when he had kissed her. Something more than his grip on her hands seemed to hold her in place, and she wondered if it was those compelling dark eyes. They were almost black, and she could see her image caught in the pupils. Her pulse skipped. Now those eyes were staring at her mouth.

Getting a hold on himself, Jean Pierre broke the spell. He pushed her backward with a laugh and tried to run when she surfaced, reaching for him and making threats. But his shoes and the weight of his sodden clothing slowed him. Rose grabbed his wet shirt and toppled him again. By the time he came up, spitting water and laughing at her cunning, she had moved out of reach a few feet downstream where it was shallow. She flung the oversized vest toward the bank, heedless of the way her shirt clung to her heaving breasts. He grinned to see the way her breeches draped upon her hips, the waist button no doubt loosened when he had grabbed at her during that first ducking. God! She was beautiful. His arms ached to hold her.

"A clumsy ox, huh?" Jean Pierre called, working hard to control his voice. "You'll eat those words, little Cajun." He felt for firm footing before moving toward her.

Through the trees, the sun's rays lifted enough to point out the scene. Wonderingly, Rose watched a shaft single him out for one shining instant there in the gurgling stream. Black hair lay plastered to his well-shaped head, a mass of curls dripping water upon his forehead. His clothes hung in wet folds upon his rangy frame, leaving no doubt as to the breadth of the shoulders, the trimness of his waist and hips, lending him an alien air of ineptitude and vulnerability. She could not recall a time when he had looked so appealing, so much like a devilish boy full of himself—and yet unmistakably virile. Blaming her trancelike state on the tantalizing smell of woodsmoke blending with the clean scent of the water, she stood staring at the young man she had married as though she had never seen him before.

Jean Pierre's splashes and taunts jarred her then, and she took off. Like truant children, they played chase, a game acted out in slow motion due to the difficulty of maneuvering on the rocky bed in rushing water. Calling out insults, tripping, coming up laughing and sputtering, and throwing huge rocks near each other so as to splash the victim just when he thought he had eluded his pursuer, they created their own world of fun.

The sun edged up over the trees until its golden warmth claimed them, drying their hair and upper clothing as they ran about clumsily in the shallows, intent on besting each other. Their shouts of dares and hoots of laughter, together with their noisy pursuit in the water, could have been heard for a great distance . . . had there been human ears to receive. But they were alone. Only their horses and the wild animals wondered at the sounds.

Small fish darted around them, making blue and silver streaks in their wild attempts to avoid contact with the intruders. While Jean Pierre leaned to rest against the trunk of a willow reaching over the stream, he spied two large fish hovering in a hollow beneath an outcropping of rock. He put his finger to his lips to shush Rose and pointed. At first she suspected trickery, but when he remained motionless, she moved quietly to his side and leaned her head next to his, letting her eyes follow the path of his.

As soon as the eddies she had created dispersed, Rose too saw the fish. They looked almost transparent and unreal there in the shadowy hiding place, lying as if suspended in the clear water, barely perceptible undulations from tail fins their only movements. Mouthing and gesturing instructions, Jean Pierre eased toward them, beckoning Rose to follow. With wild, frantic grabs, they forced the fish to retreat toward the far bank, where he scooped up one and flung it out on the dry rocks. Rose's hand closed over the one she was after, but the feel of it, or the fear of it—she never knew which—caused her to hold back long enough for it to scoot away.

"You got one! Oh, Jean Pierre, you got the biggest one. Look at it flop." They both rushed to where it lay protesting its rude removal to the rocky beach. "It's beautiful. What kind is it?" She was familiar only with bayou fish.

"A speckled trout," he replied, pointing out the mottled markings and symmetrical jaws. He broke off a willow limb and removed all its leaves and protrusions except for the lowest branch. Deftly he slid the peeled limb through a gill and held up his squirming catch. A pleased grin brought a twinkle to his eyes, and he said, "I'll bet he weighs more than two pounds. He'll make us a fine breakfast. Do you know how to clean it?"

"No, and I don't care to learn," she replied with a touch of her old defiance. She tried to read his face, but he seemed more interested in the fish than in her words.

"Come on and I'll show you." He rolled up his shirtsleeves past his elbows and knelt by a large flat rock near the water's edge. "I know Maman and Papa both think cleaning fish and game are jobs for men and boys, but you never know when you might need to know how." He paid no attention to her negative attitude and expertly prepared the large fish, explaining the skinning and the cutting away of head and bones. It was hard to ignore the effect her nearness had on him, despite his activities. Rose smelled like sunshine and water—and delectable woman. When he asked her to fetch a pan to hold the white fillets, he watched her hips and buttocks in the clinging damp pants as she moved away and felt a flaring of that heat he had nursed in his groin ever since he married her.

In spite of her pretended indifference, Rose knelt and watched every move Jean Pierre made, secretly admiring his skill with the hunting knife he nearly always wore in a sheath around his waist. She found herself examining Jean Pierre's large hands and long fingers while they worked— would they be gentle when he made love to her? Her face flaming at the unbidden thought, she noticed the dark hairs covering the tanned skin of his wrists and forearms, then the play of muscle in his upper arms, plainly visible through the wet, clinging shirt. Her fingers crept up to her ruby pendant to play it against the gold chain, her thoughts sliding back and forth in like rhythm. What did she really know about this man she had married? Never had she doubted that he could and would take care of her, but all at once a deep sense of her dependency on him washed over her, and she felt almost humbled. Impatient at such ruminations, she lifted her hair to the sun to speed its drying.

The tempting odor of brewing coffee met Jean Pierre and Rose when they came up from the stream. With good humor and huge appetites, they cooked and ate the trout fillets. The heat from the rising sun and the campfire soon dried their wet clothing. As they broke camp and prepared to continue toward Fort Arkansas, they laughed about their accidental discovery of the way to launder clothes while wearing them. Rose couldn't resist one backward look from the last bend in the path leading to the main trail.

All day they climbed, and the horses required more

frequent rests and water. Late in the afternoon when they halted for a brief time, Rose saw in the distance the purplish mounds which she knew must be the mountains.

"They look like low, thick clouds," she said. A slight breeze played in her blond curls. "Do they have a name?"

"They're called the Washita Mountains after the Washita Indians who live in the area. Most of them live near a big river that heads up in the higher mountains farther north."

"We've come a long way, haven't we?" Rose asked in a musing little voice, blue eyes fixed on the horizon with its mysterious humps. Excitement over actually seeing and traveling in the mountains, when until today they had been mere words in her geography book, brought new color to her cheeks and awe to her voice. She glanced at Jean Pierre and wondered at the pensive look he was giving her.

"And we've a sight more to go," he replied, his deep voice thoughtful, as if he had answered a weighty question instead of her casual one. Spying a patch of little blue flowers nearby, he snapped one at its base and carried it back to her where she still gazed at the view. When she took it and lifted wide, questioning eyes, he felt blood rush to his face. "It looked so pretty, I thought—"

"Thank you, Jean Pierre," Rose broke in, letting her surprise show more than her pleasure. Why was he flushed? And that look hovered about his mouth again. Bringing the full-petaled blossom to her nose, she sniffed and said, "It looks like a miniature of Maman's irises." A sideways glance told her he still watched her. Was he wooing her? The startling thought brought a deeper pink to her face and an alarming skip to her heartbeat, and she wondered if she dared meet his eyes. She dared—and she liked what she saw.

Without further talk, they mounted and continued the journey. Keeping to the valleys and the open areas along the rushing streams, they came to a sharp turn in a small river, the abrupt change in its direction caused by a steep mountain rising straight from the floor of the valley. Rose had noted how the gravel and pebbles of the previous day had become rocks and boulders as they moved northward, both along the banks of the little waterways and in the beds. The clear water had seemed to run swifter at each new stream. For some time now she had heard the singing noise made by the river's swift movements over the rocks, audible even above the slipping and sliding of the horses' hooves along the bank.

"This must be the most beautiful spot on earth," Rose exclaimed, reining Beauty to a halt for a longer look. Now she could hear the songs of birds blending with that of the river. In the angle of the sharp bend, the water collected in a circular green pool some thirty feet across before continuing in its race along the rocky bed. Jutting from the edges of the deep pool, huge rock formations sat as though on guard, their gray, irregular surfaces dotted here and there with patches of velvety green moss and dark gray lichen.

"Would you like to camp here?" Jean Pierre asked, his voice strangely quiet. He had watched the play of emotions on her face as she took in the idyllic scene. Her lips had parted in a semblance of awe, and his own hungered to taste their sweetness.

"Could we?" Happiness bubbled in her throat. Excitement sped up her pulse. Everything seemed new. Here in this place of pristine beauty, there were no reminders of their former lives. Her thoughts seemed to have sprung from a secret place never before tapped, and they startled her. The force of his gaze, from where he sat upon Traveler looking back at her, brought a touch of unaccustomed shyness.

A clearing on the bank behind the cottonwoods, and elevated several feet, seemed perfect for a campsite. A towering pine and several gum and oak trees offered shelter. Downstream, but within sight, Jean Pierre found a grassy spot beneath low willows to tether the horses. Their biggest task was moving stones to make flat places for their bedrolls. Once they managed to clear enough area, Rose padded them with layers of pine straw and sheets of tarpaulin while Jean Pierre brought up firewood. Giving in to a feeling of languor, she stretched out on her blankets to watch the twilight fall. Nearby she could hear the comforting sounds of the fire she had started as it ate at the fallen tree limbs Jean Pierre was adding.

"Do you plan to sleep through supper?" came that bass voice not far from her ears.

Rose opened her eyes, shocked that she had fallen asleep and that overhead stretched a canopy of stars. She would have scrambled up, but he was kneeling beside her and she would have had to bump into him to rise. In the glow of the campfire she saw that vulnerable look riding his mouth, saw his eyes fixed upon her face. Her throat felt full, and she swallowed. Not that it eased the constriction. She sensed that she was surrounded by some invisible force more powerful than her will, one she was unprepared for. A noticeable tremor feathered her spine and set her heart racing.

"May I collect a small token as payment for the flower this afternoon?" Jean Pierre asked, reaching to pull her to a sitting position, hoping that she was not trembling from fear of him. His voice came soft and low, like the sudden, throaty call of a mourning dove somewhere in the woods behind them. Taking her silence as consent, he pressed his mouth against hers and gathered her into his arms, cradling her against him as he sat upon the blanket, glorying in the feel of her unresisting body against his. She was warm from sleep and seemed not fully awake. He kissed her into submission, then moved his lips away to let her head with its tousled curls fall back on his arm. There in the firelight as she met his gaze, he glimpsed a telling spark of flame in her eyes, no larger or longer-lasting than one from his flint. Her fuller top lip glistened from their kiss, and he smiled at the picture she made there in his arms.

The song of the river below seemed to echo the pulsing Rose heard in her ears. Almost like the face of someone she had just met, Jean Pierre's loomed before her eyes. Had the lean cheeks always seemed so manly? And why the sudden impulse to smooth the unruly eyebrows, to let her fingers brush back the curls falling upon the broad forehead? The touch of his mouth on hers had shaken her far more than at any previous time, and she knew somehow that his kiss promised a mysterious ecstasy. A flash of teeth triggered an answering smile from Rose, and for the first time, husband and wife exchanged looks of raw recognition.

"I loved the flower. You do know how to court a woman, don't you?" Rose teased with a flirtatious look from beneath half-lowered lashes. Everywhere his body touched hers, she tingled. Some secret rhythm, which she suspected had gotten its start that morning as they cavorted in the water, seemed off and running. Was it love that sang in her heart?

"Give me credit for choosing the right time," he murmured in a curiously hoarse voice. "We've been pretty busy ever since we married." That she seemed willing to accept his attentions made him feel light-headed and as frisky as a colt. He wished he could think of some way to impress her with whatever qualities he might have which would appeal to young women. But, he reflected, he had never before had to *try* to win a young woman, and he'd had no need to look closer at himself. As long as she continued to let him hold her, kiss her, and did not retreat, he thought he might be on the right track. And the way she was smiling and looking at him—God! He loved her. Before she could have a lightning change of mood, he pulled her to him and kissed her again. The honey of her mouth almost made him forget his resolve to wait to claim her until she felt something for him. "And now," he announced with a firmness he didn't feel, "we need to cook and then get a good night's sleep." He stood and pulled her to stand beside him before moving off toward the fire.

"Do we have to leave at the crack of dawn tomorrow?" Rose asked after they had eaten. She was surprised to find that while she slept, Jean Pierre had trapped a rabbit in a hollow log during his wood-gathering mission and cleaned it. Something about the site by the river appealed to her, and she wished she had done more exploring instead of falling asleep. Even since he had held her and kissed her, he had worn a pleased smile. She didn't know that the same kind of smile graced her own face. Sitting cross-legged on the ground, their knees almost touching, they found all kinds of excuses for looking at each other, sometimes secretly and sometimes openly.

"We could stay another night if you'd like." He felt powerful, in charge. If he could have, he would have given her the entire mountain and the river as well . . . and thrown in all the rocks. Each time he turned to admire her, she seemed to be studying him. Was she regretting the kisses? The way she had of letting her gaze rest upon his mouth made him think not.

Not admitting that she had felt cheated when Jean Pierre had ended his caresses, Rose prepared for the night. Longingly she looked at the nightdress in her bag, but after recalling the fit he had thrown that first night on the trail, she let it fall from her hands. She dawdled as long as she could over brushing her hair and slipping into her blankets, but Jean Pierre made no effort to leave his position before the dying campfire, and she finally snuggled down.

The memory of the near-perfect day swam at the surface of her thoughts, and, almost submerged, a tiny one begged for recognition: all day, a smile had replaced Jean Pierre's usual contemplative look. Once she peeked to see what he was doing, puzzled to see that he still sat staring into the dying fire as though searching for the answer to some problem of worldwide importance. The serious look once more claimed him.

Chapter Thirteen

Not until midday did Jean Pierre and Rose awaken and start their day. Both felt a bit foolish to have slept so long, but neither had fallen asleep until far past midnight.

"What now?" Rose asked when Jean Pierre walked

down the bank with purpose. When she saw him cutting long branches, she guessed out loud, "We're going fishing."

"I like to watch the fish chase the bait in these clear streams," he confessed when he had fetched line and hooks from his gear and rigged up two poles. "That's one thing we can't do on the bayou."

"Don't be downing the fishing back home, though. Sometimes it's more fun to be surprised at what you catch." Unbidden, the thought rushed to mind that she was indeed falling in love with her husband, that she need no longer pine for someone to love. He was there beside her.

Jean Pierre fixed her with a thoughtful look, wondering if she realized that her words held double meaning. Laughing at the antics of the fish in the clear water, they fished until mid-afternoon, then decided to stash their catch downstream and cool off by wading in the shallows.

"Look at the way these boulders lie beside each other," Rose exclaimed, motioning for him to join her out in midstream. The bed widened there, spreading the water into depths no higher than her knees. The water narrowed and raced for several feet through the space she pointed out. "It looks like a natural bathtub."

"We'll have to try it out, won't we?" He watched to see her reaction, pleased to see a blush race up her neck and face. The mental picture of her naked in the water tantalized him.

Rose didn't reply. Instead she climbed up on one of the boulders and stretched out on her back, using her hands as a pillow. She heard him splash away toward their campsite. Fascinated by her discovery that she was more than a little in love with her husband, she gazed up at the steep mountain forming the opposite bank. A few trees defied gravity and grew straight up the sides, becoming smaller the closer they grew to the top. Now covered with leaves, they hid from plain view the large rock formations she glimpsed here and there all the way to the top.

"Are you sleeping again?" came Jean Pierre's voice.

He had announced his coming by tossing a rock in the river just beyond where she lay. At the interruption, she sat up and turned, only to explode in laughter. Obviously prepared to bathe, Jean Pierre had removed all his clothing except his breeches and was miserably jumping barefooted from one hot rock to another, as though performing some grotesque dance. Each time his foot landed on a sun-baked stone, he leaped sideways or forward with jerky movements and increasing speed until he was in a dead run by the time he reached the water.

"Damn! My feet are blistered and my wife does nothing but laugh," he said with wry amusement while wading out toward where she sat on one of her "bathtub" rocks.

Still tickled at his loss of dignity during his flight to the river, Rose watched him remove his breeches in the edge of the river. The necessary intimacies of being constantly together as they traveled had eroded most of their initial shyness at undressing in view of each other. Still, she couldn't remember his having stripped before her so boldly, and her eyes rushed over the lean body with unabashed curiosity. Each ripple of muscle captivated her. He waded out to plop down on the sunlit boulder near her, his exaggerated yelp of pain so loud it echoed. She glimpsed red spots on his lean buttocks before he sank into the cold water, letting out another yell at the quick change of temperature.

Like a self-conscious boy, he cut his eyes her way then. At the sight of her doubled up with laughter, he had to smile. Without a word, he splashed over to her, picked her up, and carried her, squealing and kicking, upstream to the deep pool in the bend and dumped her.

"No fair," Rose taunted when she surfaced. "I didn't even have a warning." Treading water, she removed her shoes and threw them onto the bank. The pool was deep enough to swim in, and she wouldn't need them to protect her feet from rocks. "I'm going to dunk you, you Cajun bully!"

Blue eyes sparkled with devilment as she pursued him around the pool. Realizing that her wet clothing gave her a tremendous disadvantage, she stripped to her chemise and took up the chase in earnest. And once when Rose slipped from Jean Pierre's grasp, leaving part of the thin garment in his hands, she didn't notice when the remaining part floated downstream, leaving her as naked as he. Like some mythical white and gold nymph and bronzed, black-haired deity, they cavorted in the river until the sun began to slip toward the west, no longer warming their playground.

Their frolic had erased the tension between them, allowing them to forget its existence. Like children let out of school early, they had seized the gift of time and reveled in its bounty. But when the sun ducked behind the mountain above them, throwing the green pool into shade, both became aware that they were not truly water sprites without human frailties or passions. They were man and woman, young and beautiful—and suddenly aware of their nakedness.

Jean Pierre gathered Rose to him there in the water where they floated and kissed her. To his delight, she didn't push him away. And when he reached to pull her nakedness closer to his, he felt a tremble attack both bodies. Holding her hand, he floated with her to the far edge of the green pool, his eyes questing, her own sending out encouraging answers. He led her behind the huge boulders to stand with him on a bed of velvety moss. He leaned to kiss the bee-stung fullness of her lips again. When she returned the kiss, his enveloping arms closed the small gap between them.

His lips molded hers into pliable acceptance, and when his tongue flicked at her own, Rose scuttled her earlier denials of its demands. Arms at first awkward and unversed moved to embrace his shoulders, slipping on up around the corded neck. As Jean Pierre's mouth and tongue moved hungrily against hers, her hands crept into his hair, the fingers exploring the forest of crisp black. Her heart drummed a sizzling beat throughout her body, signaling to a secret part of her she had only suspected existed, startling it awake. Even though his hands trailed webs of fire across her back and ribcage, she was unprepared for their touch upon her breasts. A little cry back in her throat stilled him.

"This loving is good between us, yes?" Jean Pierre asked, adoring her face with his eyes, lowering his arms to the smallness of her waist. Could he bear it if she wasn't ready?

"I . . . I think so." All kinds of emotions transformed his face, and she wondered what her own face revealed. Could she confess now that she loved him, that being with him day and night was the most exciting part of her life? "Jean Pierre, I . . ." Her voice drowned. Her eyes hid.

"You're afraid, aren't you?" he asked, his words tender yet overladen with passion. He hooked a forefinger beneath her chin, urging her to look at him. "I promise to be gentle." The swirling pinpoints of black in the blue irises begged for more reassurance. "If you ask me to stop, I will." But inside he agonized over the truth of his words. As if finding what they sought in his eyes, the blue ones flared with that same spark he had glimpsed before. He lowered himself to the moss, pulling on her hands for her to join him.

Rose found herself sitting across his lap as he leaned against the boulder, a willing prisoner in strong arms cradling her to his chest. His mouth captured hers, and she arched her head over his arm in surrender. An exploring hand found her breasts again, and she fought back the moan of pleasure nipping at her throat, finding that it settled into a barely audible purr. No longer were her breasts mere outward signs of her womanhood. An entity of their own, they throbbed in tune to that primitive inner rhythm he had set up, seeming to swell beneath his caressing palm, as if seeking to entice and meet his tantalizing fingers. A spasm of ecstasy tore at her deep inside when his thumb teased the pulsating knobs that she barely recognized as her nipples.

"You're beautiful," Jean Pierre whispered when he lifted his mouth from hers. His eyes adored her, skipping from the silk-fringed eyes beneath curving brows to the small nose, then to the honeyed lips, on down to the satiny mounds of her breasts with their rosy tips tilted and inviting. When she gazed at him with a doubting look, he asked, "Haven't I ever told you before?" He couldn't resist touching the baby curls springing from her still-damp hair. The softness of her skin and the silkiness of her hair satisfied some hidden longing and he sent her a new smile. At last he held his love in his arms.

"No." Her voice sounded strange to her ears. She felt his heart beating against her breasts, felt her own thudding along with it. His mysterious smile added to the warmth already spreading to secret spots inside. Rose felt as if she might be a ripe peach, all soft, juicy, and ready to be consumed. A forefinger lifted to trace the little laugh indentation in his lean cheek. "If you'd been a girl, everyone would have called that a dimple," she teased, peeking through her lashes at him.

"I think," he quipped, "that we both know I'm no girl. And I, for one, am damned glad of it, yes." Pulling her closer, he felt her flinch from the warmth of his arousal. "Is this the right time?" he whispered against her mouth, exulting in the way the exquisite body curved against his, the way the golden hair fanned across his arm. "Tell me it is."

Rose's mind welcomed the question, but yielded control to her overheated senses. The drumbeats of her heart sped up. Her arms pulled his mouth back to cover hers, and she murmured "I love you" so low in her throat that the words got lost. The taste of him, the smell of him, the feel of him attacked her every nerve and cell. To exist as a ripe, molten mass of rapture in his arms became her single goal. The way he kissed her neck and her breasts seared her, both inside and out, bringing little cries of pleasure. While he cupped her face and gazed at her with unfathomable looks, her hands discovered each patch of the handsome face, traced the shape of the wide, sensuous mouth, then lingered at the eyebrows long enough to smooth them into submission before going on up to rearrange the curls drying across his forehead. The man she had come to love, the one transforming her from green girl to wise woman, from innocent to knowing, was indeed handsome, she conceded in a lucid instant.

Never holding back from the promise of Jean Pierre's caresses for fear that the raging fire would continue to taunt her, Rose yielded to his further, bolder caresses. He shaped her with knowing hands and mouth into a soft vessel of desire, moist and warm and inviting. She met his unspoken demand for entry with unremitting eagerness, yearning for the unknown, yet sensing that he held the key to squelching the fire burning out of control inside her.

Firm hot flesh seared velvety flesh already burning from the magic, slashing at her with a tearing pain, almost tempting her to deny that excruciating need for him to claim her in whatever way he chose. His arms cradled her with tenderness, his breathless endearments encouraged her, and then a great wave of fervor consumed her when he touched her center. Rose cried out and hugged him closer, her body joining with his rhythmic movements. The ensuing explosion of radiance seemed to include him, some part of her noted, and for some reason she felt even more exhilarated at the jagged thought that he was finding pleasure in their coming together.

An ever-changing pattern of searing emotions floated the man and woman becoming one into a celestial world they had created, one they left behind with fleeting pangs of feeling too intense to define. Back to reality, though neither one could ever again view it in the same way as before, they clutched each other in mind-boggling awe. A delicious languor washed over them there on the shadowed bed of moss.

"My Cajun Rose," Jean Pierre whispered in a ragged voice, his head resting upon hers. When their breathing settled a bit, he rolled to his side and guided her head to rest against his shoulder. Would there be condemnation in her eyes? His gaze plumbed their blue depths. A warm recognition glowed there. He breathed deeply and leaned to kiss the love-swollen mouth. "I'm a lucky man to have you to love as my wife." If he told her he was madly in love with her, he agonized, she might not believe the declaration came from more than spent passion. Later. He would confess later, so she would believe him.

"Maybe I'm the lucky one to have a husband like you to love," she whispered, too satiated to say more.

Ah, thought Jean Pierre, at least this was a start. She had spoken the word *love*. Maybe soon she would come to love him as he desperately needed her to do.

They slept then, not stirring from their secret bower until the shadows deepened at the foot of the mountain. With haste and secretive, pleased looks, they swam across the icy water to find their clothing and get a fire going before twilight faded.

Having started a fire while Jean Pierre cleaned their fish and tended the horses down on the rocky beach, Rose wandered into the woods behind the campsite in search of firewood. For some strange reason, she was glad that her trail breeches and shirt were sodden and that she'd had to pull more feminine garments from her packsack. She felt womanly, in tune with some mysterious force reserved for females. Uppermost in her mind was the realization that she was in love. Completely. Wildly. Her half-dazed state blinded her to all but that mind-boggling thought.

In the fading light, which was even dimmer in the forest, she could see movement in the branches of a tree up ahead. Maybe it was a squirrel. She quickened her steps. If she could spot it, perhaps Jean Pierre could bring the gun and shoot it for their breakfast.

When Jean Pierre returned to the campsite and saw Rose in the distance, he picked up his musket and headed that way. He slowed when he saw her pause and look up. Aware of her knowledge of the trees and animals, he figured she might have spotted game. Quietly he prepared a load of shot and readied the weapon. He tried to concentrate on the tree up ahead, aware of movement but as unsure as she as to what caused it. Just as he saw the black tail flip through a space in the leaves, he realized that what lay in wait for some unsuspecting animal on its way to the river was a panther. The increased trembling of the leaves in the overhanging limb told him that the killer was preparing to spring.

"Come back, Rose," he warned in a quiet voice, moving near her in long, silent strides.

Rose turned to see him, gun pointed, hurrying toward her in the near darkness. Before she could question his strange behavior, an ear-splitting scream rent the quiet woods. The musket added its deafening roar to the commotion going on over her head. She thought she heard a yell, but she couldn't be sure whether it came from Jean Pierre or herself. The animal she had wondered about was suddenly on the ground at her feet, rolling and tumbling and snarling. A black monster with flashing, pointed teeth.

Trying to run, she backed into a large tree but couldn't seem to find her way around it. Jean Pierre dived onto the angry, wounded animal just before it pounced on the terrified Rose. With his knife he searched for its throat, but the panther clawed and scratched its assailant as though aware that Jean Pierre was the one who had shot it through its shoulder. Whether it was from revenge or fear or hunger or just plain wildness, the panther rolled and fought noisily with Jean Pierre for what seemed to Rose and him like hours.

At last Jean Pierre's viselike hold on the animal's throat gave him the chance to plunge in his knife. He didn't have strength enough left to roll out from under the blood spurting from the animal's jugular vein. As though the jugular had been all that was holding it together, the panther collapsed all at once on top of its foe, pinning Jean Pierre down and leading Rose to fear that he, too, was dead.

The night sounds increased in volume, echoing her pounding heart. For what seemed like minutes, but must have been seconds, she stood as though transfixed by the sight of the motionless forms on the ground near her feet. Waves of nausea attacked her, and her hands became cold and wet. She could see the campfire blazing up in the distance and realized she must get Jean Pierre and herself near it before some other night animal discovered them.

Choosing to forget all notions of what she might or might not be capable of doing, Rose eased to where Jean Pierre lay beneath the still-bleeding animal. Holding her trembling lips between her teeth, she gingerly touched its black form with her foot. When it made no move, she grabbed its hind legs and pulled with a superhuman strength until she had rolled it from atop Jean Pierre. Trembling, she stooped to feel for his pulse, calling his name, declaring her newfound love. He stirred but made no response. At first her thoughts were wishful ones: *If only Papa or*

Jarrette were here to help; if only God would send a miracle. Recognizing the folly of her wishes, she breathed a hasty prayer for strength and set to work.

She removed Jean Pierre's belt, ignoring the blood smeared over his clothing and body, and then tore her skirt into two large strips, making a sort of harness, which she slipped around his shoulders and under his armpits. Moving slowly like a horse pulling a slide, she threw his musket ahead in the direction of the campfire. With gritted teeth she went to the panther and felt for the knife she had watched sink into its throat. She slipped it into the waistband of her skirt, unmindful of the blood dripping from both handle and blade. Once she began dragging the inert form, she never stopped except to pick up the musket when she reached it and throw it in front of her, aiming it at last to land beside the saddles near the campfire.

By the time Jean Pierre had regained consciousness, Rose had stripped away his bloody, torn clothing and burned it in the huge fire she had built. She had tied a cold cloth on the lump on the side of his head, which must have popped up during the furious battle with the enraged animal. With a clean cloth, she rebathed the raw spots on his back and shoulder where its claws had raked deeply and torn the flesh.

"Rose," he said, trying to turn over and sit up. He could do little more than flounder on the blanket of his bedroll. "Are you all right? What happened to the panther?"

She folded the cloth over one of the deepest gashes and leaned down close where he lay belly-down. Looking into his eyes, she smiled in relief to see lucidity there. Her fingers lightly brushed at some superficial scratches on his neck while she explained what had happened.

"My God!" he groaned, lifting his head to stare at her pale face. "That panther outweighed you. You could have been killed." That either of them was still alive filled him with wonder.

"But you could have been, too, mighty hunter," she said, returning to the task of stanching the flow of blood from the deep cuts on his shoulders. "Are there many more where that came from?'' She looked anxiously toward the dark forest, hoping her light tone hid her fear.

''Not many,'' he assured her. ''They usually stay up higher in the hills. Our next problem will be to fend off the scavengers who'll be along shortly to feast on its carcass.'' A brassy taste filled her mouth.

''I wondered how we'd get rid of that monster.'' She couldn't let him know how afraid she had been, not when he was so weary and battered. In fact, she hadn't allowed herself to admit fear until now. Tears welled. She knew she couldn't speak any more without breaking down.

''If we're lucky, a timber wolf will scent the kill and drag him off to his cave before daylight.'' He cocked an ear toward the loudest sounds from without the circle of their campfire. ''Have you heard a howl . . . like that of a dog?''

Rose shivered involuntarily, fighting down the tears, struggling for a steady voice. ''Yes, but it was far away.''

Urging him to rest, Rose bandaged his wounds as best she could and fetched clean clothing from his packsack. When she handed him underwear and breeches and helped him slip into them, Jean Pierre was overcome with embarrassment at the thought of Rose's having had to strip and bathe him like a helpless child. But she treated him no differently than he had seen her treat Robert when the little boy had been put to bed with a childhood illness. Her hands were deft and gentle; her expression revealed tender concern.

They had finished their cups of the tasty potato soup that Rose had earlier set on the coals, he half-propped on an elbow in order to drink, she sitting beside his blankets, when they heard yelps and other doglike noises nearing.

''Do you know how to load a musket?'' Jean Pierre asked.

''I'm not sure,'' Rose confessed. ''Jarrette taught me how to shoot, but he always did the loading.'' To reassure him as well as herself, she added, ''Last year I went hunting with Papa and Jarrette and killed a deer at some sixty paces.''

''No wonder I've loved you for a long time. You're a

good girl,'' he replied. ''Hand me the powder horn and the gun.''

She flinched at his casual declaration of love, as if it were no more than one made about a family member. She could read no more passion in his voice than at the few other times he had professed love for her. If he was truly in love—as she was—wouldn't his words ring with excitement? Sighing at what was likely never to be, she did as he asked and listened to his instructions, setting about the task with compressed lips. In a short time Rose mastered the art of measuring the fine gray grains from the powder horn and filling the hole.

As she worked diligently there beside where he lay, Jean Pierre became aware of her bloodstained clothing and her tousled hair. She still wore the remnants of her skirt, and her petticoat was stained and ripped. In the light from the roaring blaze, she bore little resemblance to the teasing coquette he remembered from the night of the Brearde party. He knew his present state was a bit shaky, but he realized how much worse off he could have been had she not taken charge as she had. In his befogged state of mind, he wondered how many more facets of this girl-woman he had married would surface before he felt he truly knew her. Remembrance of their lovemaking episode of the afternoon coursed through his veins and warmed his heart.

The animal sounds came louder and closer. Jean Pierre cautioned, ''We'll stay close to the fire. Sounds like several are out there after the carcass, and it's unlikely they'll even venture this way. Spilled blood is what they're after, and perhaps they'll not scent the horses down on the beach.'' He listened again. ''They'll probably tear at the food and drag it off to their dens.''

Rose nodded in understanding, her eyes fixed in the direction of the angry snarls, her hands resting on the musket lying across her lap.

''They're going away now,'' he said in a weary voice after a nerve-racking hour of their listening in silence. ''Go to the edge of the firelight and shoot in their direction. Maybe that will hurry them on their way, so they won't be hanging around all night fighting over the spoils.''

Rose did as she was told, recoiling only a little when the musket kicked painfully against her shoulder despite the folded jacket she had thrown over it. "Did you hear a yip?" she asked with a nervous giggle. "I believe I hit one."

Both listened and heard the yipping become fainter. The angry noises had ceased, and before he willed it, the exhausted Jean Pierre sank into a deep sleep. Rose kept the fire blazing all through the night and periodically checked his wounds for hemorrhaging. Occasionally she dozed as she sat huddled near the fire.

Jean Pierre slept as if in a coma until just before dawn. The bullfrogs in the river had begun to tire of their bass complaints, bellowing now only at intervals. The numerous other night callers were also becoming less raucous. Rose wearily thought to herself that had they been at home, the cocks would already have begun to crow. She searched the sky for signs of dawn, but the stars were still visible. She moved to lay her hand on the now-restless Jean Pierre's forehead, sucking in her breath at its warmth.

Knowing no better way to reduce a fever, she scrambled to the rocky beach and fetched cold water before she could worry about how many night crawlers she might encounter.

By the time the sky did brighten and signal a sunny day, she had sponged her husband's face and cooled his fever. She checked his bandages and replaced the soaked ones before allowing him to sink back into a deep sleep. Even in her confused state, she realized then that she would have to get some rest, but first a cleansing bath in the cold, clear water seemed a logical step.

Wearing only her chemise, Rose waded out into the shallow water right below their campsite, goosebumps popping up all over. Periodically glancing up to note Jean Pierre's stillness, she washed the blood from her hair and body, quickly because she was turning blue in the morning chill.

When Rose finally slipped into her bedroll near the still-sleeping Jean Pierre, she hoped to rest an hour or so. To her surprise, she didn't wake up until the sun was far past the meridian. Jean Pierre was moving fitfully, and the fire had almost gone out.

"Rose?" Jean Pierre called, keeping his eyes half-shut against the bright sunlight. He could hear her putting wood on the fire.

"Are you feeling better?" she asked, hurrying to kneel at his side. "I've been so worried about you."

"I believe so." He struggled to lean on an elbow and look up at her. She wore a clean skirt and blouse and her eyes seemed to match the sky.

"Don't move around too much," she cautioned. He was trying hard to sit up.

She touched his forehead. "Your fever is back up."

Rose lay a cool cloth on his forehead, then hurried down to see if the poles she had set out had fish on them. Only one did, but the wriggling rascal was a beauty. She put on more bait and reset the pole before she cleaned the fish and prepared it the way Jean Pierre had showed her. While it cooked, she made fresh coffee and replaced the bandages on his wounds. She tried to remember what Grandmère used to make tea that would cure infections and chase fever.

All that afternoon Rose scurried up and down the bank, replenishing her supply of water and pulling in several fish, which she stashed downstream on a long cord. Before dark she collected a huge pile of tree limbs and stacked them close by. While gathering wood, Rose spotted several sassafras bushes and a bay tree. And when she saw a bed of yellowish green moss at the base of a squatty oak, she recalled the ingredients for Grandmère's medicinal tea.

Cutting down to get the roots of the sassafras bushes was difficult due to the rocky soil, but she finally managed to get enough. Once while she was scraping off the bark of the roots after giving them a bath in the river, Jean Pierre roused long enough to question her frenzied activity on the other side of the campfire. When she told him, he managed a crooked grin before dropping his head. For some unexplained reason, Rose felt her heart lift.

The brew resulting from Rose's simmering of bay leaves, bark from sassafras root, and club moss smelled better than it tasted. But Jean Pierre grimaced and sipped anyway that night when he awoke with rigors.

"Now you'll get better," Rose assured him with far more confidence than she felt. It had been over twenty-four hours since his battle with the panther, and she prayed the fever might break before dawn.

It had never occurred to Rose that Jean Pierre could remain feverish for so long. He had always appeared to be so much in command of everything that it seemed impossible for an illness to incapacitate him. She sat looking into his face, closed now to all but the raging fever inside. How was it that she had been able to get him to go along with her plan of the courtship? And he had tried, she confessed, not liking to recall her earlier rebuffs and his acceptance of them. A mental picture of the pink satin slippers, tucked now in her saddlebag along with the blue flower, teased her questing heart.

For the first time, Rose let the memory of their lovemaking surface. She recalled her eager responses to his caresses, musing that he was a gentle lover. Her body remembered the way his hands had memorized it, her breasts tingling at the recollection. But he was a passionate, demanding lover as well, she reflected with a pleased smile. Thoughts of the way he had claimed her rocked her mind and led her to recall the overpowering climax of their joining. The knowledge that he couldn't have become such a lover had he not experienced other women pained her ego a bit and forced her to admit that some other woman's body had demanded passionate response from his. Had she given in to him too soon to earn his respect? No matter. Love for him ruled her now.

Fragments of whispered talk over the years about Jean Pierre's ways with the ladies rode her mind and stirred up a wave of something akin to jealousy. Pursing her lips and working her ruby pendant across its chain with unusual force, she stared hard into the fire, not wanting to imagine his arms around someone else. Mimi's face came to mind, and she shook her head in annoyance, blotting out the image. *You never thought you'd be jealous of Jean Pierre, did you? He may say that he loves you, but is it the same as being "in love"? He turned his back on you when you were younger, causing you pain. Has the situation truly changed? Aren't you once more vulnerable?*

When Jean Pierre mumbled and tossed his head fretfully, she buried her troubling thoughts and hurried to place her hands on his cheeks, hoping to quiet him. Unmindful of the prickly stubble, she stroked his cheeks and crooned those comforting sounds she had learned to make for Robert when he was feverish. She brushed back the black curls with light fingers and found herself saying prayers aloud for his recovery.

"I love you, Jean Pierre," she whispered raggedly. "I probably always have. Do you hear me? I love you."

And then the dam, which she had built long ago to hold in her feeling, broke. Waves of scalding questions washed over her. Tears flowed unchecked, unheeded. In the same desperate way that she wanted him to live, Rose realized as she continued the vigil at his side, she wanted Jean Pierre to love her in the abandoned way she loved him—and to tell her so.

Rose welcomed the chilly night breeze that began about midnight because it helped to cool Jean Pierre's burning skin. Morning found them asleep near the smoldering fire. The birds and small animals started their day without them.

"Jean Pierre, are you feeling better?" she asked when she heard him stir beside her.

"I think so. My head doesn't feel quite so fuzzy, but my brain seems to be still in a coma." He kept thinking that in the night he had heard her weeping, praying for his recovery and telling him over and over that she was in love with him. Prayers, maybe. The other had to be hallucinations.

"How far are we from the main trail?"

"Several miles," he replied, moving slowly to a sitting position and shaking his head groggily. "After you seemed to like the mountain streams so much, I decided to detour and follow them instead of sticking with the regular trail. I guess that wasn't such a smart thing to do." A pained

expression came over his face as he relived the episode
with the panther.

"The idea wasn't bad," she consoled. She set about
making breakfast.

Now that Jean Pierre's fever had broken, he was ravenous. To Rose's delight, he ate fish and potatoes and asked
for more coffee. When she inspected his wounds, she
happily reported that they were healing and no longer
seemed infected. She heard herself laughing at his slightest
remark. By mid-afternoon he was insisting that he was
strong enough to bathe in the river.

From their camp upon the rise, Rose saw him stand
naked for a moment before he waded toward the deep pool
in the bend, and she smiled at the ludicrous figure he
made. His broad shoulders were still wrapped in white
bandages, while his lean buttocks and muscular legs caught
the waning sunlight. It was as if he had covered his
shoulders in a misguided gesture of modesty.

Jean Pierre reveled in the feel of the refreshing water.
He grinned a bit when he felt his manhood shrivel from the
icy water, wondering devilishly what Rose would do if he
invited her to join him. His thoughts turning to more
serious matters, he wondered if she would willingly return
to his arms now that they had made love that first afternoon after their arrival here. He glanced at the boulders,
picturing the way she had looked there on the mossy bed.
Everything about her had thrilled him, pleased him, made
him know for certain that she was the only woman he
could ever love. He found himself wishing that the halluci-
nation from his feverish night had been real, that she had
indeed come to love him in some fashion.

The exertion of the bath, followed by a visit to the
horses, forced Jean Pierre to admit he was weaker than he
had thought at first. After he stretched out on his bedroll,
Rose picked up the musket.

"I'm going to find us some meat," she said, tucking his
knife into her skirt band and thinking how good it felt not
to be wearing breeches. Having rested while Jean Pierre
bathed, she looked fresh and bright-eyed.

"And get jumped by a panther, Miss Rosalind?" He

couldn't resist teasing her, plus he was concerned for her safety.

"It's broad daylight, silly," she retorted, flipping her think blond braid in agitation. "I have a little sense, even if I am a mere woman." She glared at him, bringing her free hand to rest on her hip.

He ignored the barb, deciding against telling her of his earlier thoughts about her remarkable achievements during his fever. She wouldn't believe him now that she was riled. It struck him, and not for the first time, that to have fallen in love with such a spirited woman kept him on guard. "You'll not go far, will you? I don't like the idea of your going alone. We could eat fish again."

"Just because the wife tries to go out and kill meat for supper, you have to get in a temper."

"For God's sake," he replied, rolling his eyes in surrender. "Go ahead. Do what you please. You usually do."

Rose marched into the shade of the forest, her chin high, the musket resting on a narrow shoulder. She wouldn't have believed how genuinely he fretted over her when he lost sight of her. When he heard the blast of the gun, he could barely restrain himself from trying to dash to see if all was well. Soon she came running back, grasping a fat brown rabbit in her small hand and grinning like a pleased child.

"Look what I shot," she called, her bad mood gone. "He's a pretty sight, yes?" Her eyes twinkled at him, setting his heart to a more rapid pace.

Agreeing with her and even bragging about her prowess, Jean Pierre privately thought that she was the "pretty sight." Her cheeks were a delicious pink, and the blue of her eyes shone with fierce pride. Her lips were moist and terribly tempting, especially where the fuller upper one met the lower in the center.

Rose refused his offer to skin and clean the rabbit for her. But after she botched up the knife slits and began pulling off the skin and leaving fur on the meat, she called up to him to join her down by the river. "I've never watched skinning close enough to know what I did wrong," she admitted, hoping her defense was good enough to keep his jeers to a minimum.

Jean Pierre managed to straighten out her amateurish attempt and showed her how to roll the furred side under and against itself as the skin came off, avoiding in that way all contact with the white meat. An apt pupil, Rose kept her gaze on his skillful maneuvers with the big knife. Was there anything he couldn't do well? Not that she planned to tell him, not when his mouth wore that negative look. With a shrug, she blamed his silence on his wounded male ego.

Again Rose worked some of Grandmère's magic in cooking. She made dumplings from flour and water and laid them in the rich sauce formed from the slow simmering of the rabbit. The smell of mixed herbs blended with the woodsmoke and sent out a delicious aroma. While the meat and dumplings bubbled and before complete darkness fell, she rebandaged Jean Pierre's back, insisting that he drink the remainder of the tea she'd made the night before. A coziness cloaked the little scene.

"What's in this vile concoction?" he asked after taking a few sips. He cocked his head and sent her an accusing look. "You're trying to poison me, yes?"

"I would wait till I got you back to civilization if I were going to do that," Rose assured him with a mischievous grin. He looked just like Robert always did when she made him take medicine, she thought. How could a grown man sometimes look and act exactly like a cantankerous, but lovable, little boy? She added with a solemn look, "I thought you were a mighty hunter who wouldn't mind a touch of horse droppings."

Jean Pierre threw the cup and the remaining liquid across at the fire, grabbing her arms and laughing when he saw from the devilish gleam in her eyes that she was joking. He ran his finger down her ribs, rewarded by the burst of laughter he wanted to hear. Delighted at the way she kept him feeling so alive and happy nearly all the time, he reached to tickle her again. But this time she swerved her torso to avoid him, and his hand landed on a tantalizing breast.

Her laughter ceased. The song of the rushing river seemed to be echoing in her pulse. Her eyes darkened in the firelight. Before she could protest, he gathered her into both arms and pulled her from where she sat beside him to lean against his chest. He could feel her heart beating beneath his. The brush of her breasts through the thin blouse against his bare skin set him afire. He claimed the full lips so near his own, trying to ignore the sharp pains in his shoulder from all the exertion of the past few moments.

Rose gloried in the sweet kiss, closed her eyes in new gratitude for his being himself again. Somehow she felt that to have her handsome husband kissing her and stirring up those strange, hot feelings inside her was the surest sign that he would soon be completely well.

"It's time to eat," she said, a bit disappointed when he freed her without complaint.

The next morning, they started out to the main trail leading to Fort Arkansas. The rocky, narrow paths up the sides of mountains and down into shaded valleys made the ride difficult and left little opportunity for talk.

Before the sun hid late that afternoon behind a rain cloud hovering over a nearby mountain, they stopped beside a narrow creek. Finally having to ask Rose to help him for fear of breaking open his wounds, Jean Pierre made a slanting shelter in a niche between two tall rocks backed up to the mountain. By the time the shower broke, they had eaten and prepared for the night. At the drum of rainfall rushing down the mountainside toward them, he grabbed a tarp and draped it over their heads, running with his arm around her to their little shelter. The patter of raindrops on the tarpaulin made their bedrolls seem more snug than they really were. "Thanks for keeping off the rain just now," she said when they settled down, dry and protected.

"You're welcome." His voice sounded gentle . . . but weary.

"I was glad to find your back and shoulders better tonight." Rose fought down the memory of her hands caressing those parts of him behind the boulders that afternoon, when they were smooth and muscular and . . . She erased such thoughts from her mind and scolded her pattering heart. Loving him in secret was doing crazy things to her.

"Yep, so was I," he replied with a yawn. The feel of her in his arms for just that brief time as they ran to the tent had thrown him off balance. All day he had been thinking how much he loved her, how good it would be to hold her.

"How much farther to Fort Arkansas?" She sensed that she would go anywhere he took her . . . and be glad.

"With good luck, we should be there before tomorrow night." *And with a little more good luck, I'll be able to coax her back into my arms.*

"I'll bet we'll wish for all the wedding gifts that we left behind." She couldn't keep the wistfulness out of her voice. Material things were safer topics of conversation. The nearness of his warm body within the blanket next to hers kept leading her into elusive mind-wandering. And she had a wild urge to throw her arms around that broad back and lean up to whisper that she loved him.

"Don't worry, Rose. We can buy enough kitchen goods to get by on at the post, and the Spanish government furnishes the cabins with essentials. We'll manage." *Tomorrow night,* he promised that threatening warmth down low. Tomorrow night he would be strong enough to make love to her again. And maybe, just maybe, the time would be right for him to confess how he really felt about her. He reached behind and threw an arm across her in a protective way.

Snuggling closer into the intimate embrace, Rose admitted silently that she was ready to trade the wearisome traveling for a normal life. Had she known there was to be so little of that for her at Fort Arkansas, she would not have allowed the steady rhythm of Jean Pierre's breathing and the softly falling raindrops to lull her into sleep so easily.

PART
* TWO *

Chapter Fourteen

Late the following afternoon when the weary Rose and Jean Pierre first glimpsed Fort Arkansas near the banks of the sprawling Arkansas River, they urged their horses down the last rise with renewed energy. She cast one more look backward to the purple mountains they had left behind before following him down into the valley.

In the crepuscular light, Rose and Jean Pierre looked at the cabin assigned to them. Made of crude, hand-hewn logs chinked with clay, it had a chimney made of the same clay mixed with straw. The roof was formed by overlapping, uneven cedar shakes.

Pushing open the heavy door, Jean Pierre turned to Rose and said in a teasing tone, "Well, Miss Rosalind, our first home." One of the first true smiles she had seen him give since he was hurt spread across his face and lit up his eyes. Gesturing toward the wounds still on his back and shoulders, he quipped, "Seeing as how I'm incapacitated, why don't you carry me over the threshold?"

The wry question formed ludicrous images in the minds of the couple, and they entered the cabin laughing. Rose's heart sank and she sighed with disappointment as she viewed the place. The cabin was one big room with rough wooden floors. She grimaced as she saw the crude fireplace for heating and cooking. There was one long table holding a water bucket and gourd dipper, plus a few blackened cooking utensils hanging on the wall. A small table and four chairs sat beneath the window. On the other side of the room was a big, homemade bed. She wished for someone near with Papa's extraordinary talent for making furniture.

"Don't fret, Rose," Jean Pierre said, noticing her woebegone expression. "It's not that bad. I'm relieved you'll have a roof of any kind while I'm gone scouting and trapping. At least you'll no longer be sleeping on a blanket with a saddle for a pillow."

"I'm just tired from the weeks on the trail," she replied.

Rose threw back her shoulders, set her jaw, and swept the cabin floor with the worn straw broom. After putting the linens she had brought with them on the bed, she decided all else could wait until tomorrow. Jean Pierre brought in all their belongings and together they stowed them.

A knock at the door surprised Rose. She opened the door to a shocking sight.

"Hello, I'm Lela Rodriguez. I live in the cabin yonder across the parade grounds."

Rose gaped at the woman. Almost as tall as Jean Pierre, her big hips and bust accentuated her small waistline. Her hair was an unnaturally bright red, piled on top of her head in frizzy curls, and she wore a green satin dress so tight it looked impossible for her to walk in it, the neckline cut so low that Rose feared her generous bosom would fall out if she leaned over. She had never before seen anyone with paint on her face. The woman's cheeks and lips were as red as the inside of a watermelon, with a black mole painted high on one cheek.

"Well, honey, ain't you going to ask me in?" Lela asked with a wide friendly grin. Her voice was coarse and low-pitched.

"Oh, forgive my rudeness. Come on in," Rose said, holding the door open wide and standing back so the uninvited guest could enter. "I'm Rose Guilbeau and this is my husband, Jean Pierre," she said, nodding in his direction.

Jean Pierre held out his hand. "Hello, Lela."

Lela ignored the hand and heartily slapped Jean Pierre on the back, almost knocking him off his feet. "My, my, you are a hunk of a man. I'll bet you have a contented wife, big boy."

Jean Pierre laughed self-consciously. He looked at Rose and saw her blush.

"Rose, honey, don't pay me no mind. I don't mean nothing by the things I say. It just ain't my nature to even try to act like a lady," Lela said, wriggling her dress down over her hips with bejeweled hands. "I just come over to ask you both to our house for supper tonight. I know ya'll are tuckered out, but me and Juan would be plumb tickled to have your company."

Rose and Jean Pierre exchanged glances. Sensing the woman's sincerity, and realizing how nice it would be not to have to prepare a meal, Rose quickly said, "We'd love to." She wasn't sure Jean Pierre approved of her acceptance, but the thought of a good hot supper cooked by the friendly Lela was too tempting. "What time?"

"Come over right away. We'll have time to wet our whistle before we eat."

Rose walked Lela to the door and watched as she returned across the grounds to her cabin, swaying her hips in a seemingly natural, seductive way.

Closing the door, Rose turned to face Jean Pierre. "That was nice of her to invite strangers for supper." Astonishment played around her face, widening her eyes and leaving her slightly breathless. "Lela looks . . . different," she said.

Placing both big hands on his wife's shoulders, Jean Pierre said, "Lela *is* different from women you've known. Here at the fort you'll meet all kinds." Bending down stiffly and smothering a knowing smile, Jean Pierre kissed her forehead. "I wonder if she can cook."

"I hope so. I'm starving for a good hot meal."

Without further conversation they freshened up and walked to Lela's cabin. With a warm smile, Lela welcomed them and introduced her husband, Lieutenant Juan Rodriguez, a small, dapper Spaniard. A pencil-thin mustache sliced his narrow face, and he wore a haughty military expression along with his full-dress uniform. Looking from man to wife, Rose thought she had never seen such a mismatched couple.

Lela had decorated their cabin in much the same showy way as she adorned her body. As though ostentatious ruffles and bows in evidence everywhere weren't enough, gaudy paper flowers in empty wine bottles sat upon every table. On the bed in the corner, a red satin counterpane overpowered the room.

A gracious host, Lieutenant Rodriguez offered them drinks as his wife made small talk. Rose accepted a glass of wine while Lela joined the men in a glass of whiskey. They sipped their drinks and discussed the life and conditions at the fort before sitting down for the meal.

"Lela, this food is delicious." Rose ate greedily, savoring each mouthful.

"Thanks, honey. Juan likes his Spanish food best, but I've used up the seasoning we brought. We'll be eating plain grub until our supplies get here from N'Orleans."

"Everything tastes good, Lela," Jean Pierre added in barely disguised surprise. He turned to Juan and asked, "Have you had any trouble with the Indians?"

"Very little," Juan answered. He sat very erect in his chair as he ate, ever the proud career soldier. "Our scout, Slash Crowe, came back today. He said the Indians are still miles away, but they are headed this way. They usually camp near the fort in the winter for protection and ready supplies. They tell me they don't have a great deal of trouble with the Indians until then."

Jean Pierre said, "I've not seen you around the fort before, Lieutenant Rodriguez."

"That's right. We arrived here six weeks ago. For years I was stationed in New Orleans."

"Then you know the capital well?" asked Rose.

"As well as any Spanish soldier is allowed to know it, señora," he answered with a rueful smile. "The French settlers—and I hope neither of you take offense—have not welcomed us Spaniards and still consider themselves French.''

''Along our bayous in the Acadian settlements, we have so little contact with any government that we scarcely realize there is one,'' Jean Pierre said. The image of Phillip de Cordoza as the Spaniard now in charge of approving land titles loomed to mind. He refused to let it linger. Then with a laugh he added, ''But I hope the Spanish don't demand a blood oath of allegiance, or all of our people might flee as they did from Nova Scotia to get out from under the redcoats.''

''*Sí*, the spirit of the Acadian is well known,'' agreed Juan affably. ''And speaking of the British, have you heard news about their problems with the colonies?''

''In Natchitoches I heard there had been some recent fire exchange in Massachusetts,'' Jean Pierre answered.

''At Concord and Lexington,'' Juan commented. ''We've been expecting trouble there ever since we heard of the quarrels about British laws and taxes being forced on the colonists.''

''We're too far away for that to affect us, ain't we, honey?'' asked Lela, leaning to pat his hand affectionately.

''Unless the Louisianans get ideas to overthrow us,'' Juan replied. Then with pride tempered by tolerance, he said, ''I doubt there would be such a problem. As Jean Pierre pointed out, we Spanish don't impose many rules on our subjects.''

Easily Juan played the role of host and brought the conversation back to pleasantries.

''Sweetiekins, would you and Jean Pierre like a refill on your drinks?'' Lela asked, not waiting for permission to fill their glasses. ''Food ain't fit to eat unless there's plenty of good wine to wash it down.''

''Thank you, *querida*.'' Lieutenant Rodriguez looked at Lela with adoring eyes, as if seeing something about her that wasn't visible on the outside.

''Tell me, how many men are stationed here at Fort Arkansas? I met Captain Alveraz back in the spring, and there weren't many soldiers then.'' Not for the first time, Jean Pierre pondered his decision to bring Rose to this wilderness fort with so few soldiers to protect her and the other women staying there. But, he reminded himself, at least she was safe from Phillip.

"A dozen, not counting the scouts that are in and out," Lieutenant Rodriguez answered. "We have others coming in every few weeks with supplies from New Orleans. They stay a day or so before returning."

"Which reminds me, Rose," Lela said. "I've ordered two pieces of silk to make dresses. I can't stand that homespun stuff touching my body. I'll keep the red and I'll make a dress just like mine for you out of the pink."

"I appreciate it, but I wouldn't dream of taking your cloth." Rose shuddered mentally to think what she would look like in one of Lela's creations. "We Cajuns find no need for elaborate clothing."

"I done made up my mind, honey. You're made for pretty things." She cut her eyes at Jean Pierre, asking, "Don't you agreed she'd knock your eyes out in some fancy gowns, like them I bet you've gawked at in N'Orleans?"

Jean Pierre glanced at Rose and, remembering how lovely she'd looked at Grenfall, nodded. "Yes, my wife would be beautiful in anything."

She turned back to Rose then. "The pink is yours." Lela began passing food around the table. "Eat up, everybody."

All refused her offer, insisting they had already eaten and drunk so much that they were beginning to feel sleepy. Soon after the meal ended, Jean Pierre and Rose excused themselves, truthfully pleading exhaustion, and began the walk across the parade grounds to their cabin.

"Mercy, it's hot tonight." Rose wiped perspiration from her neck as she released a button on her blouse. "Lela told me there's a creek that runs behind our cabin. Let's go for a swim."

"Someone could see you."

"Who's to see? Look around. All the windows are dark, yes?" She gestured energetically and moved closer to look into his face. She had already learned that as gruffly as Jean Pierre sometimes talked, he seldom refused her requests.

"I swear, Rose, you'll drive me crazy," he teased, slapping both hands dramatically to the sides of his head and moaning in mock misery.

They hurried, both eager to reach the cool water welcoming them in the pale moonlight. Jean Pierre insisted Rose swim in her chemise, but he shucked all his clothes.

She touched a toe in the water and jerked her foot back, squealing, "That's cold!"

"As if you didn't know how cold mountain streams are. You wanted to cool off, so jump in."

"In a minute. I have to get up my courage."

Before she finished her statement, he picked her up, threw her in the creek, and jumped in behind her.

"That was a dirty trick!" Even though she was spitting out water and shivering from the cold, she slapped water toward him with enthusiasm.

Jean Pierre watched, mesmerized, as she swam away gracefully, her slender body, with the high, beautifully formed breasts, cutting a path through the cool water sparkling in the moonlight. Every fiber of his being ached to hold and caress her until the love she obviously was holding in reserve became his. The abundance of food and wine seemed to have healed his wounds and soreness miraculously. "Let's go, Rose. I must get up early to buy and pack things for the first trip out to scout the woods. Louis should be here tomorrow or the next day."

"You'll go so soon?" When he nodded, she lost her appetite for swimming.

Painful thoughts of leaving her behind plagued him, and he caught Rose's arm and pulled her to him, his mouth crushing hers in a fiery, demanding kiss. His tongue explored her mouth as his hands pushed down her chemise. He carried her from the water and placed her on a grassy spot underneath a small tree, his body covering hers.

"Let's go to our cabin now," Rose whispered breathlessly between his kissing first her lips and then her neck and breasts. She had no desire to fight against the tingling ache in the pit of her stomach and the warmth claiming her body. The touch of his mouth and hands seemed to reach deeper than her skin, seemed to be searing her very soul. With longing, she remembered their afternoon by the river and his sweet gentleness when he had taught her the meaning of love between husband and wife. Her pulse sped up.

Rose was shocked to realize that they had entered the cabin; she couldn't remember walking there. He was leaning closer to kiss her gently on the mouth, not bothering to light a candle. From above, a half-moon spread its meager light and bathed the cabin in shadowy beauty.

As Jean Pierre's kiss deepened to a turbulence that sent the room spinning around her, Rose pushed away from him to look into his eyes. The mystery she saw reflected there called to some identical part of herself, erasing all rational thought. It was not the time to ponder if he loved her, she reminded herself. Arms pulling his head down, she lifted parted lips to his waiting ones.

Stirred by her surrender, Jean Pierre hugged her closer, holding her tightly against him as their lips met. The feel of her wet, warm body against his brought an embracing warmth and stepped up his need to rediscover her charms. His tongue explored the inner sweetness of her mouth; his hands scorched new paths down her back, over the shape of her, following curves of satiny perfection.

Loving what his caresses were doing to her, Rose fondled his bare chest and shoulders. Her hands stopped short when they slipped under his arms and touched the bandages on his back. Sliding them away quickly before she could cause him pain, she tracked a slow route to his head, trailing her fingers down his neck and across his shoulders, delighting to feel his muscles ripple beneath her touch.

Reaching the bed now, she lay down, never losing contact with the lean, hard body that enfolded her, that inflamed her, that caused her brain to malfunction. His mouth left hers and brushed her face and throat with a warm shower of kisses while he pulled her hips close against his eager arousal. Thistledown kisses followed the curve of her throat; his lips then sought the unfastened opening where her damp chemise revealed the cleavage of her full breasts. He pushed away the offending garment to reveal the smooth, creamy mounds inviting his ravaging hands and mouth.

She held his head to her, reeling with delight while his tongue circled one hardened peak and then the other. With a low, husky moan, he drew her closer to him. Rose buried her face in his neck and inhaled the heady, masculine scent of him, her logic entangled in softly murmured love words escaping his mouth as he caressed every secret, sensitive spot. Rose fell captive to the spell his experienced hands and teasing mouth cast upon her, letting it fan her desire into uncontrolled yearning. His skillful hands removed their clothing so subtly that she hardly knew when it happened.

Need, and something she couldn't identify, echoed in his voice as he whispered softly, "My Cajun Rose . . . you are so beautiful . . . so lovable. . . ." His words trailed off, leaving her to wonder what he had uttered.

Jean Pierre moved to cover her mouth with his own, cover her body with his, and then, with a velvety moan from him and a throaty gasp from her, he buried himself deep within her. Feeling delirious and beautiful, she surrendered completely. Unimaginable heights of pleasure, of pure ecstasy, engulfed her; and her love for the man capable of leading her there was bouncing her inner self around and spinning her reasoning into a web of fairyland fantasies. They soared together, sailing across edges of darkness, catching glimpses of heavenly lights, and melding together as one in a distant world before gradually returning to reality, exhausted and contented.

In the shadowy moonlight from the window, Rose watched his smile flash. For one precious moment there was an understanding between them. Their union had been special— swelling with tenderness, overflowing with passion, ending in fulfillment. It had lacked nothing . . . including love, though as yet unvoiced.

Rose woke the next morning to a delicious aroma filling the room. From the bed she could see Jean Pierre squatting in front of the fireplace stirring the coals.

"That coffee smells good," she said, lazily pushing back her tousled hair and propping herself on an elbow.

Jean Pierre turned to look at her, amazed as he had been each morning of their few weeks of marriage to find her as beautiful in disarray as when well groomed. "Well, lazybones, you've slept away half the morning." He brought a cup of coffee to her, placing it on the table beside the bed. When she reached for it, he pushed away her hand. "No, not until I've been properly rewarded."

"And what might you consider fair payment?" A devilishness spiced her tone, and she gloried in her new-found power that could cause his eyes to glaze, his voice to soften, and his resistance to weaken.

"This," he said, lying down across her, his fingers weaving through her silky tresses as he covered her sweet lips with his.

Knowing from experience how his lips and hands could manipulate her, she moved away before they were able to push her past the point of no return. "The barter I had in mind was cooking your breakfast." Her smile was impish.

"I can't accept those terms." Jean Pierre grinned, his eyes scanning her face, lingering on her mouth for a time before catching her gaze again.

"Why not?" Rose studied the face before her. Didn't he know how devastating those slow smiles of his were? She was better able to cope with her emotions when he was his usual cocky self.

"I can cook my own breakfast." Holding her face between his hands, his lips came down on hers, branding her with the strength of his feelings for her.

When he wanted to charm, she had no defense against him, and had no wish for any, she realized with a start. *If he prefers to cook his own breakfast instead*, she thought, *let him*. She raised both arms to encircle his neck and willingly bowed to the inevitable.

A half-eaten stack of pancakes lay on the plate before Rose. She watched Jean Pierre wolf down his breakfast, seemingly oblivious to the fact that he had left out the leavening in the pancakes and they were as hard as a board. Between bites he glanced across the table at her plate and asked, "What's wrong? Aren't you hungry?"

"No." Her voice betrayed none of her real thoughts. At least not hungry enough to eat the heavy, leathery discs that fell to her stomach with the thud of a rock, she mused. She felt her husband must have an iron stomach, not only to clean his plate with gusto, but to finish the pancakes she had left. Suppressing a grin—and it was no easy task—she sipped her coffee.

After breakfast Rose changed his bandages and happily reported that healing pink skin had replaced the angry red infection.

"Would you like to come with me to see the fort? We need to stop by the trading post and lay in some food, and I want to see if Louis has arrived, though I feel sure he would come directly to our cabin if he had. I'll introduce you to Captain Alveraz. I'll feel better knowing he'll look after you. He's the one in charge here."

"I'd love it," Rose said with the enthusiasm of a child. "I'll act like a prim and proper little old lady."

"That'll be the day!" He grinned at the thought.

As they walked around inside the small fort, Jean Pierre pointed out the few cabins for married couples, the barracks for the soldiers, and the stables. All were made of logs; even the wall surrounding the fort was of logs standing on end. When they came to the headquarters building, the largest on the grounds, with the red, white, and gold Spanish flag rippling in the late summer breeze, Jean Pierre escorted her inside and asked the sergeant at the desk if Louis had arrived.

Before they received an answer, the door behind the sergeant opened and a man came through it. Old for a soldier and with a body gone to fat, he wore a wrinkled uniform with missing buttons.

"Good day, Señor Guilbeau. You're early this year, aren't you?" the old soldier asked. Pendulous lips sprayed saliva as he talked. "None of the other trappers have arrived yet."

"Yes, sir, we came early to scout some new areas. The

better animals are getting scarce hereabouts. I'd like you to meet my wife, Rose.''

The captain turned to her, his interest and animation increasing noticeably. He made an exaggerated bow and kissed her hand with his wet lips.

''My pleasure, señora.''

Captain Alveraz talked to Jean Pierre then, but his small eyes stayed on Rose, undressing her mentally, it seemed to her.

''This is a real pleasure to see you again, Señor Guilbeau. I insist you and your lovely wife be my guests for dinner tonight, unless you are previously committed.''

''We'd like that very much, Captain Alveraz,'' Jean Pierre said, preparing to exit and not looking at Rose as he guided her in front of him. ''See you then. I want to get my wife settled in before I have to leave.''

''Why did you accept an invitation from that horrible man without asking what I thought?'' Rose hissed as soon as they were outside. ''You could have talked it over with me.''

''He's the commandant and he'll be able to look after you while I'm gone.''

''Ha! I'd be better off with no help if I'm to depend on him. Didn't you see the way he looked at me?'' She shrugged off his hand from her arm.

''All men look at you that way. I thought you liked it.''

''They do not! And I hate you for your crudeness.'' She glared at him as he tried to take her arm again.

''You accepted Lela's invitation without asking me what I thought,'' he countered, his own anger rising.

They had reached the trading post and from necessity dropped the conversation, but both still fumed inwardly. With carefully guarded talk, they bought the supplies they would need. Jean Pierre left a credit for her to use if she needed anything else in his absence.

Rose spent the rest of the day putting away their purchases and getting the cabin in order while Jean Pierre cut and stacked firewood at the back door. To provide a place to hang laundry, he trimmed straight saplings and suspended them between low limbs of cottonwoods.

When they arrived at the captain's quarters for dinner, an Indian opened the door. The young woman might have been pretty, Rose thought, except for her wide, flat nose.

"Welcome, Señor and Señora Guilbeau." Captain Alveraz shook Jean Pierre's hand, and Rose again endured his slobbering kiss on her hand.

Rose saw that the captain's quarters were crude, but larger and somewhat better furnished than their own, with a few items of luxury in evidence. Not until after that first quick look around the room did she notice another guest.

"Hello, Mr. and Mrs. Guilbeau," Louis called from one of the comfortable chairs. A smile on his face, he stood and shook Jean Pierre's hand, then addressed Rose. "The long trip on the trail didn't damage your beauty, Rose. The tan on your face is becoming."

"Thank you, Louis. When did you arrive?" She lowered her eyes to conceal anything he might read in them. Had it really been only a few weeks since she had last seen him that awful night at Grenfall?

"Late this afternoon. I didn't look you up, having found out from the commandant that you were also expected here for dinner." How had she accepted her marriage to Jean Pierre? he wondered. She seemed edgy, but Louis could see no sign of sullenness or misery. In fact, she had become even lovelier.

Over drinks, the men talked about their weeks on the trail from Attakapas while Rose listened. Surprisingly, seeing Louis had not brought back painful memories of some unfulfilled yearning. Instead she felt her newfound love for Jean Pierre growing stronger.

The Indian girl came and announced in broken English that dinner was served. The captain was seated at the head of the table, with Jean Pierre on his left, Rose on his right, and Louis across from him.

"I must apologize for the food here at the fort. It's impossible in this almost deserted area to acquire anything but the most primitive supplies, hardly fit for human consumption," the captain said as he piled his plate high.

"It is very good to me," said Rose, moving her leg farther away from her host's. It was the third time since they had been seated that she had had to escape the unwelcome pressure from his leg.

"I admire you greatly señora. May I call you Rose? My wife would not consider coming with me to this uncultured place among all these savages. Your husband is a very lucky man," Captain Alveraz said, again moving his knee to seek hers, but without success this time.

Rose fidgeted and picked at her food. Having to keep out of the captain's reach distracted and annoyed her. But that wasn't as bad as having to endure the way he looked at her. She found him repulsive and fought against the thought that something about him reminded her of Phillip de Cordoza.

"Captain, I'll depend on you to look out for Rose while Louis and I are gone," Jean Pierre said, ignoring the desperate look she shot him. The captain's invitation to dinner had flattered him, and he seemed oblivious to her plight.

"I'd be delighted to." The captain smiled with wet lips at Rose as if he had just won a victory.

"That's not necessary, sir. I'm capable of taking care of myself," Rose replied with noticeable spirit. She made herself look him in the eyes. "I've met Lieutenant Rodriguez and his wife, and both of them offered to help with anything I need."

The captain filled his mouth with food before he said, "Rose, you shouldn't spend your time with the lieutenant's wife. She's common and below your station. Lieutenant Rodriguez may be the only other officer stationed here, but, as you may have noticed, they are not at my table tonight." He paused to chew vigorously and noisily before going on in his condescending manner, "I fear he's ruined his military career by marrying that woman out of Belle's, a place in New Orleans young ladies like you would not know about, señora."

Noting her shock, the captain added as he boldly touched Rose's hand where it toyed with her glass, "Pardon my straightforwardness, but it's to your advantage to know who and what she is."

Rose pulled her hand away from his pudgy grasp but

said nothing. Realizing that she liked the good-natured Lela in spite of her brash ways, she felt disloyal for not offering a word in her defense. Louis and Jean Pierre seemed to be having a good time planning their trip and were so engrossed with themselves that their behavior bordered on rudeness. From time to time she had tried to pull them into general conversation, but by now she was too upset to try anymore. She had become accustomed to her bridegroom's full attention, but now he seemed blind to her needs, and even blinder to the sly glances and overtures from the repugnant captain. Feeling distressed, she longed for the evening to be over.

Just then Captain Alveraz said, "I've heard recently from headquarters in New Orleans that Fort Arkansas will have a doctor soon, a Dr. Morgan from Mobile."

Accustomed to the Acadians' ministering to their own and sometimes needing professional help that was not available, Rose remarked, "How fortunate for everyone."

"I'll feel better about leaving you here with a doctor about," Jean Pierre turned to her to say.

Louis made a comment then to their host, and Rose said to Jean Pierre in a low voice, "From the way Louis and you seem to be having such a good time talking about your scouting trip, I figured you'd not need anything to make you feel better about leaving."

Jean Pierre studied her face, puzzled at what seemed to be an angry look. Before he could do more than wonder at its cause, the two men pulled him back into conversation.

Little Beaver, the Indian girl, who had served them throughout the long dinner, brought coffee then. When she leaned over Rose's shoulder to set down her cup, the hot liquid splashed onto Rose's lap. Everyone at the table jumped up.

"Let me help," Jean Pierre said, taking his napkin and joining her in her attempts to blot up the hot liquid.

Rose glanced at the stony-faced serving girl and whispered, "I don't think she's a bit sorry to have soiled my gown."

"Of course she is," he assured her in a private voice. "What's wrong with you? You've been touchy all day. Don't make a scene."

She stiffened at the order. All at once, the inner doubts and fears about being brought to such a strange place and being left alone for the coming winter washed over Rose. Close to Jean Pierre's ear she hissed, "You've no feelings at all."

Jean Pierre stared and straightened up, but made no reply. Everything he had said since their meeting that morning with Captain Alveraz seemed to have angered her. She knew so little of the world outside the Acadian settlement that he felt he must appear in control in order to keep her safe. Maybe he should have explained more about . . .

"Captain Alveraz," Rose said, moving toward the door. "Thank you for having us over for dinner. I'm going now to attend to my wet gown."

From the corner of her eye, Rose watched Jean Pierre's eyes narrow and his mouth become grim. Without another word, she ran from the room, then across the parade grounds to their cabin. In her fury she slammed the heavy door and locked it. Leaning against it, her chest heaving both from her flight and her anger at Jean Pierre, she ignored the frenzied banging.

"Go away, damn you!" Rose yelled.

"Don't be ridiculous," Jean Pierre called. "Let me in so we can talk."

"Why should I?"

"Because I'm your husband."

"You didn't act like one tonight."

"Let me in, Rose, or I'll break down the damned door."

Figuring he meant it, she released the wooden latch and moved away. She heard a click and he was inside, prepared to explain all the intricacies of getting along with the people at the fort. The incongruous thought that Rose and he needed first to learn to get along better almost took away his breath!

Rose, dabbing at tears, turned to Jean Pierre and said in a low voice, "I'll never forgive you. It was bad enough to have to accept that awful man's invitation, but for you to ignore me all evening and make me feel so . . . so alone— that was too much!" She struggled to hold back more tears. "I had no idea you'd be leaving tomorrow or the next day. Go on now to that precious wilderness Louis and you can't seem to wait to return to!"

Jean Pierre stared at her, angered anew by her words. "You don't understand about my work or life here and—"

"And no wonder!" she broke in. "You've not tried to explain anything." A sudden rumble from an overhead cloud startled her, fitting right in with her mood.

"I'm trying now." As nonplussed now as he had been by her demands to take a bath that first night at Ma Dibert's, he watched her sink upon the bed and lift a pouting face. "Captain Alveraz isn't the most admirable of soldiers, but he's the one who rules this place. When people come here, they're actually under his jurisdiction."

"So?"

"We have to get along with him."

"Am I supposed to let him take liberties?" Blue eyes flamed up at him. Where was the easygoing man she had fallen in love with on the trail, the one who had seemed concerned only with her needs? Had she been wrong about him?

Jean Pierre scoffed, "Of course not. He's an old man and means no harm. Just ignore him and stay too busy to be around him." Whatever was she talking about? The captain had done no more than fawn over her in a kindly way, as far as he could tell.

"Doing what?"

"Whatever women do while their men are trapping." He felt stymied at her questions and less sure with each one that he had done the right thing to bring her here. "I wish—"

"That I weren't such a burden," she snapped.

"No," he denied, moving to stand beside the bed. Damn! Just when he had thought she was gentling, he was learning that he was no closer to understanding her. His voice softening with love and compassion for whatever brought the pain visible in her eyes, he said, "I wish you understood that I'm trying to make things easier for you."

For some reason, Rose read pity into his words, and pity from the husband she had come to love wasn't what she

wanted. A great wave of indignation flooded her. "Then
go ahead and leave now on the scouting trip Louis and you
talked of all night. To have you out of my' sight will make
things easier!"

"You don't mean that." Her apparent disdain cut him,
let loose a boiling anger. How absurd that he had hung on
to the memory of half-heard declarations of love for him.
There was no doubt now that he had indeed been halluci-
nating in his feverish state. It seemed clear that she didn't
love him, might never love him. "Anyway, it's raining."

"I do mean it, and I don't care if you get wet. Go on.
Leave. I'll be fine." Now she would see how much he had
meant those earlier declarations that he loved her. If he
did, then he'd take her in his arms and tell her again so she
could believe him, tease her into good humor with kisses ...

His lips compressed, Jean Pierre grabbed his still-packed
knapsack and saddlebags from the corner and stalked into
the night.

Stunned, disbelieving, Rose stared at his retreating back,
heard the slam of the door. Her breath rasped in her throat,
and her heart pumped wildly in her chest. She stood at the
window watching the rain slanting across, tapping against
the panes. Even when she pressed her forehead against the
glass, she could see no movement through the downpour.
Rose felt lost, angry—but mostly she felt sad and empty.

What had come over them?

Chapter Fifteen

Where was Jean Pierre now? Rose wondered. Had he left
for the North Wilderness with Louis as planned? She had
not seen him since he stormed out of the cabin the night
after they ate with Captain Alveraz. As she had learned in

the past twenty-four hours, rehashing the events solved nothing. Two hot tempers had bumped head-on, and she could see only her side.

Glancing around where she stood in front of the cabin, Rose noticed for the first time the rank growth around it. From her Acadian upbringing, she knew hard work busied the mind as well as the body, and she began pulling weeds and cleaning the area around the cabin. By dark she had transplanted flowering bushes and ferns, brought one at a time from the edge of the woods. Wearied both mentally and physically, she had no trouble falling asleep that night.

Rose spent the next days scrubbing the inside of the cabin. Within a week she had it shining, with scrim curtains at the windows and Aunt Alva's patchwork quilt covering the bed. Potted ferns and fresh wildflowers brightened the room. Seeing the cabin so pretty and sparkling lifted her spirits somewhat, but the last few days had been long and arduous and the nights dark agony. The bed seemed too big without Jean Pierre's large, virile body snuggled up close to her. How was she to survive the loneliness?

To ease the ache within, Rose reminded herself that Jean Pierre was the cause of her misery. She was the injured party, she told herself. He had ignored her all during that horrible meal with Captain Alveraz. She promised herself that she wouldn't think of her maddening husband again, knowing it was a vow she couldn't keep.

Thankful for all of Grandmère's teachings in the arts of handicraft, Rose was busy a few days later braiding a rag rug when she heard Lela calling to her. The two had visited back and forth often since Jean Pierre's departure.

"Come in, Lela. It's good to see you." The troubled look on her face softened.

Lela came into the room dressed in her finery and said, "You're shore hard to reach. I've been over here a half-dozen times the past few days and could never find you."

Rose didn't tell her that she had been at home and hadn't answered the door, not wanting to see anyone, even Lela, the only one at the fort to treat her kindly.

"Sorry, but I've been busy trying to get this place

cleaned up," she managed to say. She couldn't look at her friend just then; lies did not come easily.

"Well, you shore have it fresh and clean." She looked around, holding back further comment.

Rose liked her for not saying more. She felt sure that anyone with Lela's tastes wouldn't find the place appealing, and she respected her new friend for her honesty.

"I'm braiding a rug for this bare floor. It won't be very big because I couldn't find much cloth at the trading post, but it'll improve the looks of this room some, anyway."

With a brief "Be back in a minute," Lela left, returning soon with her arms full of colorful silk and satin garments. She dropped her load of clothes on the floor and began to tear strips.

"All right, honey, you look like death warmed over. Let's talk. I saw that drawn look around your eyes when I come in."

"There's nothing to talk about." She joined her guest in the ripping of the garments, keeping her voice light and her eyes on what she was doing. She would have to guard her words around the discerning woman, Rose thought.

"Look," Lela said after a spell, "I've seen about every kind of trouble there is, and you got trouble. Now unload on me. I got broad shoulders and sense enough to keep secrets." She reached across and patted the younger woman's shoulder, her compassion showing plainly.

Rose could no longer hold back, and she poured out her burdens. She had never told anyone her feelings in such depth, not even Father Sebastian. It was a relief to tell someone, so she began with the party at Grenfall and completed her story with her ordering Jean Pierre to leave the cabin. When she finished, she felt as if a heavy weight had been lifted.

Lela listened intently and watched Rose with sympathy in her eyes. "You really have had a rough time lately, haven't you? But, honey, you give me the impression of being a lady with spunk. True, thangs look purty bad to you now, I daresay, but, sweetie, they ain't no hills a'tall for a stepper like you. Now, you just gotta understand men like I do. Lord knows, I guess I've seen ever' kind there is."

"I don't want to understand men, Lela, not even Jean Pierre. I just want to forget it," Rose said. "I'd rather not talk about it anymore."

"All right, we won't talk about it today," Lela said. "But you ain't as smart as I took you to be if you don't get things straight with that man of your'n."

The two women spent the next few days together working on the rug, both apparently enjoying their blossoming friendship. Rose had never met anyone more giving of herself than Lela.

"Sure," Lela replied one day to Rose's questions, "I've met those other women here who've called on you—Mrs. Barlow, Mrs. Linder, and Mrs. Ferrare—but they look down their noses at the likes of me, so I just pretend they ain't even here. What do you think of them?"

"I didn't seem to have much to talk about with them," Rose admitted. "They seemed nice enough, but their cabins are close together on the other side of the trading post, and I got the feeling they spend nearly all their time together."

"They made you feel you didn't belong, didn't they?"

"Maybe so." Looking Lela in the eyes, Rose said, "I sometimes feel I don't belong anywhere."

By the time the two women completed the rug over the next several afternoons, Lela had become a closer friend than any Rose had ever had outside her family. Without any formal education at all, Lela was an amazing person. Rose learned that she had done much traveling, visiting places most people only dreamed about. She loved museums, operas, and life in general, and talked to Rose for hours at a time about them. But mostly, the older woman was wise in the ways of the world and men.

Rose listened. She knew that some of the things Lela talked about were for her benefit. Her not-too-subtle hints about how to manage husbands and make them happy didn't convince Rose that life with Jean Pierre could be any different.

"Well, Lela, we finally finished this rug. Let's put it on

the floor and see how it looks.'' Smiles came easier now than when they had first begun to work together.

They spread the rug and stood back to see their handiwork. It was beautiful! Even Lela said it was the finishing touch the room needed.

Smiling down at the rug, Rose said, ''Your brightly colored silks and satins made the difference.''

Once the work on the cabin was finished and Rose could find nothing else to do, she became restless. She had borrowed books from Juan Rodriguez and read them all. Occasionally both Juan and Lela would go horseback riding with her in the surrounding woods, but the plump Lela didn't truly enjoy riding and Rose hesitated to request more frequent outings. A few visits to the three wives who were such close friends left her feeling she had intruded.

Captain Alveraz continued to send invitations for her to dine with him, but she always found excuses. Several times when he had knocked on her door, she had refused to answer it, not caring that he might suspect she was inside. The few times she had run into him at the trading post, she managed to move away from his overtures and pinches without attracting the attention of others. She felt relieved when he apparently gave up his obvious attempts to seduce her.

Some six weeks after Jean Pierre and Louis had headed north, Rose was in the trading post for supplies when a tall figure filled the doorway. She glanced up and saw Louis Brearde. Her heart leaping into her throat, she looked around, but the handsome Creole was alone. Where was Jean Pierre?

''Rose,'' Louis exclaimed, his face lighting at the sight of her. ''It's so good to see you again. You look wonderful.'' His broad smile exposed dazzlingly white teeth, and his good-looking face made believable his reputation as a conqueror of the fairer sex.

Flushed with pleasure to see a familiar face, Rose was glad to know that she looked nice in a blue blouse embroidered with pastel flowers and a black full skirt. ''You look well yourself.'' Rose decided the outdoor life had been kind to Louis. He was tanned even darker than she remembered and looked very dashing in buckskin shirt and pants. "Have you begun trapping?" Maybe he would tell her about Jean Pierre, and she wouldn't have to ask.

"Not yet, but we have found new territory where the animals are plentiful, and Jean Pierre explored one valley while I took on another. We should have a big year." Louis spoke without the usual happy face. His eyes searched hers.

"I'm happy for you. Are you staying with Captain Alveraz again tonight?" She refused to give in to the urge to voice the question about Jean Pierre.

"No, he only asked me the last time because of a message I delivered from my father. I prefer to stay in the barracks." He lowered his voice. "I don't care for that man."

"Neither do I. In fact, I find him repulsive. Imagine a married man acting like he does," Rose replied in a whisper. She blushed to recall some of his crude overtures to her.

"He really was enamored of you. I'm surprised Jean Pierre didn't notice it," Louis said. "Being married doesn't stop men from being attracted to you, Rose." He attempted a flirting tone, but his eyes revealed a sincere respect for her. "Jean Pierre is a lucky man."

"Louis, you do know how to turn a woman's head, but I'm not available. Nor are you, for that matter." Two could play that game, though she had no heart for it.

"Wisdom from the lips of a woman," Louis teased. His finely etched brows rose slightly, diverting her attention from any hidden meaning in his eyes.

Rose laughed to ease the tension, her blue eyes sparkling. In spite of everything, it was good to see someone from home.

"You haven't asked about Jean Pierre." His face once more took on that serious look she had noted earlier. "He ought to be coming in soon, for we weren't that far apart."

"I didn't ask because I don't care." Her heart seemed to be thumping in erratic skips at her lie. She fought against the memories clouding her mind. "I don't want to talk about him." She tossed her head and raised her chin in that proud, captivating way Louis had first noticed that day on the pier when he had surprised her after her bath.

"By the way, I've been invited to supper at Lieutenant Rodriguez's tonight. Will you be there?" Louis asked. He saw that she looked more mature with her hair caught high in a chignon.

"Yes, Lela asked me to come, but she didn't say she had invited other guests as well."

"Good, then I'll stop by your cabin and walk you over."

"Be prepared for a shock then." Rose laughed as she added, "Lela made me a dress like one of hers a few days ago, and I'm afraid if I don't wear it tonight I'll disappoint her. She's a very good friend, and I wouldn't hurt her for anything in the world."

Louis burst out laughing. "I can't wait to see that sight. It should be a real show. However, I agree that as soon as I met her, I knew she was a jewel. Too bad no one else here seems to see that, except Juan and us. I'll come by later to walk you over, if that's agreeable." He looked down at her as he spoke, a lazy smile playing at the corners of his mouth.

When she opened the door that evening, Rose looked like a picture with the door facing as the frame. But it wasn't Louis Brearde who stood tall and handsome before her, staring with open-mouthed wonder at her in the new dress Lela had made.

"Are you all dressed up for me?" Jean Pierre asked, his eyes rushing over the lovely vision in pale pink silk. The bodice of her gown dipped so low that he could see her breasts rising from the neckline in spectacular mounds, her ruby necklace almost hidden in the seductive valley between. The dress fitted her body like a glove from bosom to knees, with ruffles from the knees to halfway down her beautifully shaped calves. He was disappointed to see that she wasn't wearing the satin slippers he had given her.

"Jean Pierre!" Rose exclaimed, happiness welling up inside like a spring trying to surface in a shadowed forest. She stepped back to let him come inside, not sure what to say or do. Gone was her pretense that she could get along without him. Her love for him set her heart dancing in jig time, and she could feel her face flushing. Why didn't he kiss her, or at least hug her? Was he still angry? "Louis told me you might be coming in soon."

He dropped his packsack and saddlebags then with a loud thump. "Is it Louis you're all fancied up for?"

Rose shot him a wounded look. "No. Lela made this gown for me and asked me to wear it tonight to have supper with Juan and her. You don't have to think it's pretty."

"I never said it isn't pretty. I just wondered if you were expecting Louis. I saw his horse in the stable."

"Not the way you're suggesting," she managed. His dark eyes were crucifying her, when what she wanted was their approval. "He offered to come by and walk me over to Lela's, that's all."

"That's all?" He was close to yelling. "You're my wife and that Creole damned well knows it."

"You're right, my friend," came Louis's soft drawl from the still-opened doorway. "Glad to hear you appreciate my offering to keep your wife from having to walk across the parade grounds alone." At Jean Pierre's startled turn, he added, "It's good to see you made it in all right, partner. I hope you've good news to go with mine when we meet in the morning. The valley I scouted is heavily populated with both beaver and fox." Then, his eyes obviously reveling in the sight of her in the revealing gown, he asked the pink-faced Rose, "Shall I tell Lela and Juan you'll not make it to supper tonight?"

"Please do," she murmured.

After Louis closed the door and his nonchalant whistle floated behind him, Rose gave her full attention to her husband. She didn't think she had ever seen him more furious. Something about the way he held his head reminded her of an angry bull ready to charge.

"I should've punched that Creole. If he comes near you again, I'll do just that." His tone was menacing, the words spilling from a white-rimmed mouth.

"You have a warped sense of truth, and the worst

temper I've ever seen. Can't you tell there's nothing between Louis and me except friendship, that he knows well I'm the wife of his partner and that he has a wife of his own? If you've no more faith in him or in me than that, you might as well turn around and leave again.'' She nervously worked the ruby pendant back and forth on its chain, suddenly so drained that she gave up caring whether he understood.

''Hell no! I'm not leaving this time just because you've got me spooked. Maybe I let the way things looked make me jump to wrong conclusions, Rose.'' He turned to where she sat upon the bed, an unusual look of frustration clouding his features. ''I've thought so much about the way it would be when I came home that I guess seeing you dressed up so pretty . . .'' His gaze drank her in from head to toe. Even he could tell that the satin slippers would have gone with the pink gown. Didn't they fit? Or had she merely pretended to like them?

''Do you really think I look pretty?'' She heard some new note in his resonant voice. Why was he staring at her feet?

''You're perfection,'' he replied with noticeable huskiness. ''But why aren't you wearing the slippers I gave you?''

She felt her cheeks warm up again, then hid her eyes behind lowered lashes. Should she be honest? ''I couldn't . . . I didn't want to wear them for the first time . . . without your being with me.'' Her voice had sunk to little more than a whisper. There. Let him laugh and call her a romantic fool. Her pulse pounded in her ears. Why was it so hard to open her heart to him?

Not reading the truth behind her hesitant words, but feeling himself moved by them in some heartrending way, he pulled her up from the bed into his arms and kissed her trembling mouth until it calmed and met his own with the same desperate hunger.

''Why did we quarrel?'' he asked when he lifted his mouth and reached to tip up her chin and make her look at him. ''And why did I rush off earlier than I had to? God! I hated every miserable night, knowing we had parted in anger.'' Those black-flecked pools of sapphire were mesmerizing him. He hadn't remembered that her gently arching eyebrows were no more than a few silken brown hairs against her pale skin. And he hadn't remembered how sweet she smelled up close. All at once he was doubly glad that he had stopped to strip and bathe in a rushing stream just beyond the fort and had changed into clean clothing.

"I hated the days as well," she confessed with a tremulous smile. There was a manly fragrance about him of soap and water and saddle leather, one she had tried but failed to recall in moments of loneliness. "But you're back now, and we can get everything settled."

"The first thing I want to settle is this need to make love to my bride," he whispered, eyes drowning in hers without a struggle. "How do I get you out of that ruffled affair?"

And she showed him there in their cabin on that early fall night. Both of them naked then, and hungry for loving, they snuffed out the candles and made a claim on their bed.

Jean Pierre hugged her nakedness close to his, delighting in the small softness of her body molding to his. He felt lightheaded, despite the powerful feeling of virility her surrendering mouth and body gave him. His stepped-up heartbeat acted like a bellows to the fire in his loins. Or was it the way her mouth opened to his, the way her tongue welcomed his, the way her little throaty moans rewarded his ears? The crazy thought that he couldn't have felt more masterful had he been one of his traps ensnaring some exotic creature clicked to mind, and he forced the frenetic search of his hands upon her back and buttocks to one of soothing caresses. Like a distant bell, the knowledge that he already held a claim on the one he was trying to capture so completely softened the edge of his raging desire, and his arms became those of a gentle lover.

During their two other bouts of lovemaking, Rose hadn't detected such fierceness in her husband as she sensed when he first grabbed her to him there on the bed and fixed his mouth on hers. To have him back safe and to

have him creating the magic she had longed for were all
that mattered. A soft purring in her throat echoed her
glory in tasting his warm, sweet lips and mouth, smelling
the wondrous, masculine fragrance of his skin, hearing his
frenzied breathing match up with her own, feeling his heart
thudding against her crushed breasts and his manhood
pulsating against her below her waist. A headiness at
the way he seemed intent on making her his captive joined
with her insistent heartbeat and made her feel more of a
woman, and more attuned to the primitive, than ever
before. When his tight hold lessened and his hands grew
gentle, she was as much a prisoner as before and exulted
in her status.

"I dreamed of kissing and holding you like this," he
told her when he freed her lips. Peering at her in the
darkened room, he lifted a finger to trace the downy
hairline from her temple to her forehead. "And I swear, I
believe you've become more beautiful." With his fingers
he combed out pale silken tresses to fan behind on the
pillow.

"Jean Pierre, you don't have to pretend to woo me any
longer." Even if he were still playing at that game, she
loved hearing his compliments, and wanted even more,
she realized as she watched a warm sparkle in the dark
eyes washing over her face, then her breasts. Her body
seemed to be waiting, and she wondered how long she
could ignore its inner purring. Somehow, she reflected, the
way his hands moved so gently upon her face and hair
seemed as much a part of lovemaking as the actual coming
together. All at once she had the need to touch him, and
sent a hand wandering across a broad shoulder with a soft
laziness. "You'll think I'm terrible, but I must say I love
it." *And you,* an inner voice added. *Tell him.*

"And I love it when you flirt with me and cut your eyes
like that." As he spoke, he knew it was true, knew then
that for him to suspect that she did it to others was
unreasoning, ugly jealousy of the notice she might be
gaining from others. His own arousal was demanding more
attention, and he admitted that he wanted to capture
everything about her for himself.

The hand playing in the hair at his neck suddenly became a weapon forcing his head down until their lips met. It was the first kiss she had ever initiated, and his response pleased her, led her to tease with her tongue in little shy forays.

"Hmm," he said when she loosened her hold on his neck and smiled up at him, "I think I might keep up the courting, if I'm going to gain such rewards."

Her dark-tipped breasts caught his eye in the dim light reflecting from the sky through the window, and he gave in to the hunger to taste their honey. Trailing kisses from her silken neck on down to the delicious swells, he let his tongue flick the hardening nipples into sweet little rose-buds before filling his starving mouth with firm, yielding flesh. His hands were already memorizing the flat belly and the outward curves of her hips, even as his mouth savored her breasts in a way that set her into some private rhythm of restless movement as she lay on her back with him half-leaning over her. Her fingers convulsively clutching at his back told him that he was feeding her inner needs as well as his own, and he swelled with double pleasure. Begging hands stroked his shoulders, igniting tiny fires at each touch, then slid on down the taut muscles to find the smooth spot below his waist, lingered there for a tantaliz-ing moment before going on to explore his flat buttocks. His breath caught in his throat at the exhilarating waves of desire washing over him from the feast of her breasts and from the play of her small hands.

That primitive part of her that Jean Pierre had earlier aroused with his forceful embrace seemed to control Rose as he made love to her. Caught up in some whirling need never before recognized, she writhed in ecstasy at the way his tongue and mouth worshiped at her breasts, giving in to the primeval longing to know his body as well as he was learning hers. Her fingertips became her eyes, her mouth, her every sense as they caressed his smooth flesh: his neck, his shoulders, his back, his flat buttocks—as firm, she noted with wonder, as the rest of him. She was achingly aware of his swollen manhood throbbing hotly against her thighs; in fact, she realized with a start, she seemed to be directed by its pulsations and gave her hands freedom to touch that part of him designed for loving. Deep inside she could feel a matching throb, could feel it becoming more than just a part of her down below, could feel it becoming her entire being, one she had already learned would continue to pound and burn until it ensnared that searing shaft already sending out signals that it would soon master, not by trapping, but by entering. Unable to be quiet and still during the agony of wanting and waiting, she moaned and writhed with love for the man working his special brand of mastery.

"Kiss me," Rose begged, no longer able to bear losing his mouth to her breasts, no longer able to stand the way his hands were gently building raging fires in secret, velvety places, no longer able to content herself with the outward feel of him. Her heartbeat and breathing had long been out of control.

And he did kiss her then, thoroughly, tenderly, then voraciously. Thrilled at her eager responses to his love-making and at the loss of her earlier shyness, encouraged by the flashes of wanting in her eyes, he asked against her moist lips, "Do you want me to capture you, my Cajun Rose?"

For answer she whispered, "Yes," and moved her hips with a wisdom she hadn't known she possessed, thrilled anew to find his tumescence against her begging entry, losing her breath at the promising touch of his warm firmness against her fiery gateway.

When he claimed her, it wasn't an entrapment in the purest sense, not on his part or hers. Rather, it was a giving from one fierce lover to the other. She opened to him with wild welcome, took his firm length as if it were a coveted gift.

He gave himself over to savage delirium at the way she seemed to know that the center of her was his goal and wrapped her legs about his hips to make the capture easier. Frenzied rhythm directed their mating. Both animalistic cries and wondering endearments marked the reunion of bride and groom as they strove to seize again the remembered joy of perfect oneness. Faster their senses climbed.

More intensely burned their passion. Higher than before, they scaled an unknown peak at the perfect instant before crying out in mutual celebration. Still awed, they let the magic taking them there have the task of relegating them back to the roles of mere man and woman.

Satiated and terribly content to clasp an equally languorous Rose against him as he lay on his back in their bed, Jean Pierre wondered at his cowardice to confess his love. He hadn't forgotten the pain of her apparent indifference toward his previous attempts to declare that he loved her. So few things had baffled him as the young woman in his arms had done over the past few years—and especially since their marriage—that he found it hard to believe how much she still puzzled him. Rose had always seemed such a vital part of his life; yet he sensed that ever since their marriage, he had been dealing with someone he had never before known. While one side of his mind told him over and over that she was unlike any other woman, he had continued to treat her in the way that most men seemed to treat their wives, the only way he knew.

Surely, before he had to leave on the morrow to return to the woods and get on with the serious business of setting traps in the places located, he could find the time to sit and talk with her in broad daylight, learn what caused her to be so easily riled, figure out a way to quell those pained looks he glimpsed too often in her eyes. Did she still view her marriage to him as a kind of entrapment? His hand fondled her face, even as his thoughts about his spirited wife whirled.

Rose wondered at her doubts about admitting to Jean Pierre that she had been wrong to think their marriage wasn't meant to be. She had thought that once he came back to her, she would spit it out, tell him she loved him even if he didn't love her. But she was tongue-tied. Now that he was back for a spell, she would have time to feel her way, she assured herself, to pick just the right time— and not one following such a tempestuous lovemaking as they had just had. She didn't want him to think she was caught up in pure emotion; she wanted him to see that she had given the matter mature consideration.

Her thoughts drifted to little remembrances of the ways
he had thrilled her only moments ago, and she smiled and
hugged him closer, wondering if she hadn't been a bit
wanton in her overpowering need to know every inch of
him, to offer her all to his loving hands and mouth. A
delicious fatigue wafted away all thought then, and she
nestled in the encircling arms of her trapper husband and
slept, more contented than at any other time in her seventeen years.

The morning flew, one starting on a perfect note: At
dawn, both awakened and found the fires they had quenched
in the darkness had once more flared. With more exquisite
tenderness and less of the ferociousness of their earlier
lovemaking, Rose and Jean Pierre again came together as
one and parted with a similar sense of fulfillment, of
wonder at the joys each brought to their union.

He fetched water and heated it in the coals of the
fireplace, then went with her down to the clear stream
behind their cabin to wash his garments. Together they
hung them on the saplings he had placed down low for her
on that day he had worked about the place cutting wood
and getting things in order. And all the time they talked—
but never about what gnawed at their hearts. It was as if
each dreaded to mar the magical spell they seemed caught
up in with anything that might send it sailing away as
quickly as it had appeared.

"Jean Pierre, are you about ready to set out?" Louis
called from outside the cabin soon after the noon meal.

Rose's troubled gaze flew to her husband's suddenly
pained eyes. Not yet! He couldn't be leaving yet. He had
just come home the night before.

Jean Pierre went to the door and spoke with Louis, but
Rose could hear every heart-singeing word. Within the
hour, he would be ready to leave. Within the hour, she
would once more be alone. For some reason, she felt
betrayed and more than a little angry that he had let her
believe he was staying for a day or so. Would he never
take her into his confidence, truly share his life with her?

"Why do you treat me with so little respect?" she

demanded once Louis had gone and Jean Pierre turned again to her.

"What do you mean?"

"I thought you were going to be home for a few days."

"Did I tell you that?"

"No, you never tell me anything, except 'Do this; don't do that,'" she hissed, slapping away the hand trying to touch her hair and brush back a stray curl. She backed out of his reach. Now she wouldn't get the chance to cuddle up with him before the fireplace tonight and tell him she loved him, that he was the handsome stranger she had dreamed of wooing her someday and teaching her the ways of love. Oh, she had planned it all so beautifully! Her heart squeezed painfully, and hot tears attacked her eyes.

Frowning at what seemed an unfounded accusation, Jean Pierre watched the opportunity to face her in cold daylight and tell her that he had married her because he loved her, and that he had fallen more in love with her every day since, dash away on the wings of unreasoning hot temper that matched her own. She was so upset now that nobody would be able to reason with her until her anger had abated. Not that he was fool enough to try, he reminded himself as he turned and went to gather his clean clothing from the saplings.

"How long will you be gone, or can't you honor me with such information?" Rose asked after she had silently watched him pack and place his things near the doorway.

"Rose, if I knew, I'd tell you." He was calm by then, but his heart was encased in hurt.

"Would you really?"

"Yes. I wish you understood that trapping is something that requires a man to give it his full attention during the season, that he can't make promises hinged to calendars."

"Or wives."

"I'm trying to get enough skins this winter so that I'll never have to come back, so that we can live comfortably on our own land down on the bayou. I know I've told you that."

She nodded; he had. But she hadn't known how hard it

would be to wait while he was gone, she reflected. "Do you think you'll be back for your birthday in November?"

He shook his head. "A big snowstorm must be coming in from the west and north now, for the Indians are gathering outside the fort and making winter camp for their families."

"Maybe by Christmas?"

"I'll work to make it in by Christmas," he promised. It was time to go then, and he went to her with purpose. This time he didn't intend to leave without a kiss and some kind of smile. "Will you wear the pretty pink hussy dress for me . . . and the satin slippers if I do?"

Louis called from outside just then and knocked on the door.

Rose swallowed at the searing knot in her throat and smiled in a way Jean Pierre didn't think he'd ever forget before she nodded her head, sending clouds of pinkish blond to tumble about her face in lovely profusion.

"Then come give your loving husband a kiss to last him till he comes back at Christmas."

She was already on her way and threw her arms up to pull his head to hers. The kiss held so much promise and longing that she wondered if she would ever live long enough to see all of the unspoken messages become reality. "Oh, Jean Pierre," she murmured brokenly, not caring that tears salted the sweet kiss. "I want to be the kind of wife you want."

"You already are," he assured her.

Louis pounded on the door and called, "Come on, Jean Pierre. Time's awasting and the snow clouds are forming."

Rose walked outside and watched the two partners head toward the stable, their backs burdened with packsacks and saddlebags, their strides long and easy. Only once did the taller figure, the more handsome face, turn back to reward her with one more look. Her husband was gone again.

Rose busied herself the next morning with cleaning the cabin, then baked a syrup pie to take to Lela as a peace offering for not showing up at dinner the night before. Despite her attempts to put away troubling thoughts, she kept scolding herself for losing her temper during Jean Pierre's final hour at home. But she could see plainly that when all she wanted was for him to love her and to tell her so weighed her mind in that depressing way, rational thought had no chance to rule her in his presence. Surely, the next time he came—at Christmas, he had said—she wouldn't even let him kiss her hello without first telling him she loved him and finding out how he truly felt about her. *Well*, she confessed when an inner voice snickered, *maybe just one kiss.*

Brushing aside such thoughts because they did nothing to comfort her, she got her shopping sack and went to the trading post to replace the cornmeal, coffee, and dried meat Jean Pierre had taken with him. Her spirits lifted under a clear blue sky, and she looked at the mountains in the distance, noting their purplish beauty. And not for the first time, she thought of how the tall pines and rushing mountain streams of the area were direct contrasts to the big-topped oaks with their hanging moss beside the sluggish swamps and bayous of Cajun country.

Entering the trading post and seeing a stranger in conversation with the storekeeper, she stood back awaiting her turn. The man was of average height and size, she noted idly, with light brown hair beginning to gray at the temples. When the storekeeper called Rose by name, she joined the men at the counter.

"Mrs. Guilbeau, this is Dr. David Morgan."

"Hello, Dr. Morgan, and welcome. Captain Alveraz told my husband and me a while back that you'd be coming to Fort Arkansas."

"Thank you, Mrs. Guilbeau. I only arrived this morning. I threw my belongings in an empty cabin and came here for supplies."

Rose noted that the doctor had a smooth, melodious voice, much higher-pitched than Jean Pierre's, but still manly. His accent was far different from the ones she had heard lately from the Spanish at the fort, and even more different from the distinctive inflections of the Acadians.

"Oh, then you'll be staying right here at the fort?" she asked.

"Yes. I was talking earlier to the captain about needing someone to help out in my office. He told me there are few women here, but he mentioned your name as one of the most capable. Would you be interested?"

"No, thank you. I don't plan to be here after trapping season, and I've no training, anyway." Rose picked up the packages the storekeeper had collected for her from the list she had given him. "I hope you'll like it here."

"Thank you. May I walk along with you?" Dr. Morgan asked. Once outside, he said, "I believe, Mrs. Guilbeau, that my assigned cabin is the large one next to yours."

"Please call me Rose."

"That's a pretty name and it suits you, too," the doctor said thoughtfully. "Most folks call me Dr. David."

Rose wished then that she hadn't asked him to call her by her first name, for he seemed to have felt obligated to return the compliment. He must be close to forty! Back home, she wouldn't feel at ease calling a man almost Papa's age by his first name, even with the title "Doctor" in front of it.

However, she enjoyed the short walk. Dr. Morgan was obviously a well-educated man and an interesting conversationalist. From her speech and name, he had surmised that she was Acadian, and she liked exchanging casual information with him. Running into him seemed the antidote to her gloomy mood.

"Well, I'm home and I guess you are, too." Rose peered toward the two-room cabin next to hers, but saw no movement from within. "Why don't you and your wife eat with me? I know you're still unsettled."

"That would be too much bother and—"

"No bother," she insisted, liking the idea of having company and getting her mind off missing Jean Pierre. "By the time you go inside and get Mrs. Morgan, I'll have it on the table. Actually, I'm lonely today."

"What I was trying to say was that I'd enjoy eating with you, but that there is no Mrs. Morgan and it might not seem—"

Rose couldn't figure out a way to get out of this embarrassing situation without making it more so and insisted that she didn't mind that he'd be coming alone. Dr. David arrived just as she had finished placing cold chicken and cheese on the table.

"Would you like a glass of wine with your meal?"

When Dr. David said that he would, she filled a glass for him, trying not to show her doubts as to the wisdom of having insisted that the two of them share a meal.

"Why don't we take our plates and sit underneath the tree separating our cabins?" he asked.

Rose's smile showed her relief and pleasure. "That's a great idea."

Soon the doctor had carried two chairs to the spot, moving them near the patch of sunshine. "It might be a bit nippy in the shade." he remarked.

"Everyone at the fort will be relieved to have a doctor," Rose said after they had begun to eat from the plates on their laps. "People have said that one has been needed all along, but that with so few living here at the fort, the Superior Council didn't think the place rated one till now."

"Actually, I'll be doctoring at two forts, traveling between Fort Outpost to the north, and here, though I plan to spend the majority of my time here."

Rose and Dr. David continued to eat leisurely. They sometimes watched an occasional passerby across the parade grounds, and if she knew the person she would pass on tidbits of information. Their conversation was light, and they seemed comfortable in each other's company.

"The captain told me your husband is a trapper. I've heard that can be a very profitable business."

"Yes, he and his partner do well. They also buy furs from other trappers who don't care to haul theirs to New Orleans, where the prices are better."

"Sounds as if your husband is a smart man," Dr. David said, his gray eyes holding hers. "Would you consider working a few hours a day? When I'm away at the other fort, you'd be much help to others. I'll be working out of the extra room in my cabin, and it would be convenient for both of us."

"I know nothing about your kind of medicine. I'm afraid I'd not be much help."

"I'll be happy to teach you. I'll have to train anyone I hire, so you'd not be an extra burden."

Rose studied the man sitting across from her, an empty plate resting on one knee, a wineglass in his hand. His demeanor was calm, exuding confidence in his abilities. She heard herself say, "I accept your offer. When do I begin?"

"Is tomorrow too soon? The captain sent his Indian servant to clean the place earlier this morning. It's shining now, and I'm ready to set up my equipment. We'll discuss your wages then."

"Tomorrow's fine," she answered, her excitement showing on her face. There would be something worthwhile to do to fill the lonely days ahead, and she would be earning money. In an area so remote, women could do things unheard of in settled areas such as the bayou country, she realized.

Rose smiled to think what Maman and Papa might say. What would Jean Pierre say? She quickly erased the thought, telling herself that he would have to understand in that way he seemed to expect her to understand everything he did.

"I'm curious," Rose said after they had talked a bit about his plans for his office. "It's obvious you're an educated man and probably a very good doctor. Could I ask what you're doing in this out-of-the-way fort?" A faraway look filled the gray eyes, and she wondered if she might have hit upon a painful subject. "It's none of my business," she added quickly. "I'm sorry I asked."

"Don't apologize, please. I don't mind telling you. My wife died six months ago, and I had to get away for a while, make myself useful somewhere. I plan to go back to Mobile someday, when I can face my former world."

"I'm sorry. I'm sure losing someone you love is a painful experience." Standing then, she headed back to the cabin.

Dr. David again showed his thoughtfulness by taking the chairs inside while she carried the plates and glasses. "You're a charming hostess, and I hope I've not taken up too much of your time. I'll see you in the morning."

"I've enjoyed talking with you, Dr. David, and I had nothing of importance to do."

He left then, leaving Rose to ponder her final words. But after today, she exulted, she would have something important to do while she waited for Jean Pierre to return.

Chapter Sixteen

"Come on in, honey," Lela said later that afternoon when she answered a knock at her door. She smiled when she saw Rose standing there holding out a dish. "Whatcha got?"

"I baked you a syrup pie this morning, but as you can see there are two pieces missing. Dr. Morgan and I each had a slice at lunch." Rose saw Lela's eyebrows arch slightly.

"Dr. Morgan?"

"Yes, he came this morning and will practice at this fort and Fort Outpost. He asked me to help him in his office awhile each day, and I'm going to try it. Can't you see me as a nurse?" Rose minced around the room, pretending great dignity until they both broke into giggles.

"Why in the world would you go to work?" Lela asked after they settled down. She frowned as she tugged at her tight dress, something she always did when she was nervous.

"Jean Pierre won't be here, and it'll only be for a few weeks. I'll go crazy if I don't do something." Rose could tell that her announcement about helping Dr. Morgan had upset her friend.

"What will that husband of yours think about it?"

"He's not here to ask, and he seems to have no qualms about making decisions without talking with me."

"Well, I hope you know what you're doing."

"I believe I do, and I must be going. I've much that needs doing at the cabin if I plan to start working tomorrow. It's about time for Juan to come home anyway. I'd hate for him to think I monopolized all your time."

"Juan wouldn't think nothing like that, sugar, and anyway, he promised Jean Pierre he'd look out for you. We both think you're something special with your cute way of talking, your hands and eyes going as fast as your mouth. Juan says he knows a lady when he sees one and he thinks you're a real lady." A wide smile backed up her sincere flattery.

"Thank you, that's a compliment. Both Juan and you are special friends to me. You're lucky, Lela, to have a husband who loves you." Rose heard the wistfulness in her voice and glanced away from Lela, who was watching her intently.

"I know it. I give thanks for him every day, just like I bet you do for yours, 'cause that Jean Pierre is crazy about you."

Rose watched the colorful sunset on her walk home, not eager to ponder Lela's well-meant assurance. Pleasing Jean Pierre in bed didn't mean that he loved her.

Late afternoons often reminded her of home. She recalled some of the sounds she had grown up hearing, especially the tinkling bells on the necks of the lead cows in the distance becoming louder and faster-paced as they neared the barn for their evening milking. She visualized Maman feeding the squawking chickens, using her apron to hold the grain until she scattered it around on the ground.

A deep longing for the day they could return to the bayou country where she had felt loved and wanted claimed Rose. For the first time, a curiosity about the place her true parents had come from surfaced. She had wondered what they had looked like, how they had sounded, but never before had she faced the fact that their beginnings had taken place across the Atlantic. *In England,* she reflected. *Wonder what part of England?* All at once, the world seemed bigger and lonelier than ever.

Reluctantly, the thoughtful young woman entered her

cabin. Lighting a candle, she ate her supper of cold pork and bread with little appetite. Until she was too sleepy to stay awake any longer, she read, for the second time, a book borrowed from Juan.

The next morning Rose took her time with her toilette. She brushed her hair until it was a gleaming frame for her small face, then folded the ends under and over until they formed a round ball, which she tied with a black ribbon at the nape of her neck. She chose a plain, pink-striped blouse to wear with her second-best black skirt and tightly laced her black stomacher. As an afterthought, Rose pulled out a simple white demibonnet such as most Acadian women wore for everyday outings and set it atop her smooth crown. She decided she looked as a doctor's helper should and, winking at herself in the small mirror on the wall for courage, headed for the cabin next door.

When Dr. Morgan greeted her and invited her inside, she saw that his cabin consisted of two rooms. He already had the room nearest her cabin arranged as an office, his medical instruments neatly placed on a table against a wall. A crude desk and a few chairs lined another wall. She could see a bed through the door connecting the rooms.

"Are you ready to begin?" Dr. David asked, convinced that he had done the right thing in securing her assistance even before seeing her so neatly groomed this first day.

Dr. David showed her all the instruments and explained their uses, instructing her in her new duties of keeping records, pausing to answer her questions in the kindest of ways. He also added to Rose's excitement over the new turn of events in her life by naming what seemed to her the generous wage he would pay her at the end of each week. She barely recognized him as the man with whom she had shared a meal beneath the tree yesterday. Somehow, Dr. Morgan in his office and Dr. David outside of it seemed to be two separate people. Dr. Morgan was in complete control, definitely his own master, whereas Dr. David had seemed as subject to human frailty as she or anyone else.

From the very first day, Rose enjoyed her work. By the end of the first few weeks, she had learned many things

about medicine—and her employer. Dr. David sometimes
left the fort to attend patients in the nearby wilderness
where a few trappers and frontiersmen had settled with
their families; however, most of them had built their cabins
within a few miles of the fort for the protection it offered
and could come to his office when necessary. During Dr.
David's absences, Rose sometimes treated minor cuts and
illnesses herself.

She and Dr. David often chatted about various patients
and their illnesses when the office was empty. One afternoon after they had gotten to know each other in the weeks
of working closely and had become good friends, Dr.
David offered Rose a glass of wine at the end of the day.

"Dr. David," Rose said, her blue eyes smiling along
with her lips, "it's good to see that you appear much
happier than when you first arrived." Sitting in one of the
chairs reserved for waiting patients, she sipped at the red
wine he had poured.

"That's because I am much happier. In fact, these last
few weeks have been some of the nicest I can remember."
It wasn't quite dark, but he had lighted the whale-oil lamp
on his desk and was leaning back in his chair behind it.
His soft gray eyes wandered over his young assistant's
pretty face.

"My grandmère always said that time heals most
wounds. I know things must be bad for you, having lost a
wife you loved." When she was with him, she realized,
she always felt wise and mature. The peaceful twilight and
the wine made her feel cozy and relaxed. In the fireplace,
fresh logs blazed and warmed the small office.

"You embarrass me with your concern. I'll confess my
unhappiness was caused by guilt, not by the loss of a loved
one. I never loved my wife, Rachel . . . nor did she love
me. Our marriage was arranged by our parents. I loved
another. Rachel was a good woman, and when she died, I
couldn't forget that my not being able to love her might
have contributed to it." He paused before he continued,
"You see, she killed herself." Dr. David sat holding his
glass, a distant look in his gray eyes.

Rose looked down at her wedding ring gleaming in the

flickering light and said, "It would be a sad thing to live your life with someone who didn't love you . . . or whom you didn't love." Thinking of her own arranged marriage, she wondered if Dr. David and she had more in common than just their work. Except that in her marriage, the wife loved.

"What happened to the woman you truly loved?" she asked. Talking with him was as easy and natural as breathing.

"After my marriage to Rachel years ago, she left Mobile, and I haven't heard from her since." David leaned forward to light a cigar, then leaned back in his chair. "Now you've heard my life story, let me hear yours."

"There's little to tell. I've led a routine, maybe dull life—at least it was before my marriage." For an instant a line creased her pretty forehead, and her blue eyes darkened a bit as she thought of her experiences over the past few months.

"It's none of my business, but why is it that you never speak of your husband? I know by what others say that he's well liked and respected, but I get the impression that there's something amiss." Without being downright rude, he had done his best to find out from others but had not received any answers.

"I guess Jean Pierre and I got started off all wrong," Rose said with an eloquent shrug and a careless toss of her hand. "I'm beginning to think he's too used to being free to run loose in the wilderness to give much thought to the needs of a wife." She hadn't realized she had come to that conclusion until she said the words, and she glanced from her wineglass across to the attentive listener, wondering if he, too, recognized the newness of the idea. Briefly, then, Rose told David about Jean Pierre's and her earlier lives, without going into the details of their marriage and the reason for it.

David listened with interest, aware that he still hadn't learned the major reason why she seemed unhappy. "You're a wonderful young woman and you deserve to be happy. I hope things work out for you. Trust your grandmère's saying about time being a master healer, Rose. I'll be here if I can help you anytime, in any way." Long, slender fingers tapped the glass he was holding with the same gentle touch as when he examined patients.

Glancing at the clock on the mantel above the burning logs, Rose said, "It's late, and I must go. I enjoyed the wine and our visit, Dr. David. Thank you."

Stepping outside in the cold night to watch Rose reach her cabin door and go inside, Dr. David pondered what kind of damned fool was this Jean Pierre Guilbeau. If he had to spend the winters trapping, why didn't he erase the doubt and uncertainty in his wife's incredibly beautiful eyes before leaving?

The supply troops were expected at the fort, and Rose hurriedly dressed that morning in a bright multicolored skirt and white blouse. She looked forward to their arrival every two weeks or so to see if there were letters from home, though she admitted to herself that since she had begun to work with Dr. David, she felt more content. Helping others seemed to fulfill some vacancy in her, an emptiness growing since her adolescence, but only recently acknowledged.

To ward off the chill of the morning, Rose threw a shawl around her shoulders. The crispness of the sweet-smelling air and the beauty of the purpled mountains in the distance occupied her thoughts.

At the trading post, Rose asked for her mail and smiled when the shopkeeper handed her a letter from Maman. She had received only two others since her arrival and was so eager to read it that she tore it open in the store. Hungry for news from home, she read the letter hurriedly, glad to learn that all were well. A wave of homesickness rushed over her as, through misty eyes, she reread Maman's words. A familiar voice calling her name startled her.

"Rose? Rose?"

Looking around, she saw Jarrette coming toward her with long strides, his arms outstretched and his handsome face breaking into a wide grin. Rose squealed with joy and met him halfway, laughing as the one she would always think of as her twin brother caught her up in a bear hug.

"Jarrette, I'm so happy to see you. I was just—"

He broke in, "I thought I'd never get a chance to come see you here at the fort." He was still holding her at the waist, leaning down to look into her face with the remembered, soft brown eyes probing hers.

"Let's go to the cabin. There's so much for us to catch up on. I just got a letter from Maman," she said, urging him away from the trading post.

Jarrette linked his arm in Rose's as they walked the short distance. He had hardly gotten inside before turning to her. "Now tell me, little sister, how are things with Jean Pierre and you? Has he been in at all from the woods?"

"Only once, but I'm hoping he'll make it back for a visit at Christmas. Sit down, Jarrette, and I'll get some coffee." Rose filled cups for them then and joined him at the table.

"That doesn't sound to me like a bride unhappy with her groom," he teased, eyes sparkling across at her as she blushed. "Have things worked out better than you thought they would that day we talked in the swing?"

She glanced at her wedding band as she said, "Yes, they have, and I've—"

"And you've found Jean Pierre is a decent man," he completed her thought in that old way.

"Actually," Rose confided after a moment of companionable silence, "I've found I love him."

"You always did, little sister."

"No, not that way, Jarrette." His brown eyes squinted at her with attempted understanding, and she went on, "I'm *in love* with Jean Pierre, in love with him as if he were some good-looking stranger riding out of nowhere, someone I'd never seen before we married. It sounds like a fairy tale, doesn't it?"

Jarrette smiled his approval and satisfaction and said, "In a way, but I can't think of any two I'd rather see have such a happy ending to a stormy beginning. Your news is worth riding so far to hear."

And then Rose turned the talk to news from Maman's letters and to questions about Jarrette's trapping with Arlee Simpson, for she had no wish for Jarrette to question her further. What if he were to ask if Jean Pierre was in love with her and she had to tell him ''no''? It was far better to let him think the loving was mutual.

''What about your life, Jarrette? The one outside this season's trapping?''

''I'm making plans,'' he answered with a secretive smile. ''In time, maybe they'll materialize.''

She couldn't stand his keeping anything back. ''I saw the way Celeste and you seemed to be pairing off that night at Grenfall. Does Celeste figure in your plans?''

''I had just picked up two letters from her and read them before I saw you.'' A flush stained his fine features, gave him a more boyish look than when she had first run to hug him.

Rose laughed and clapped her hands. ''Oh, Jarrette, she is so nice! Do you think—''

''I'm keeping my fingers crossed that in a year or two, when I've enough saved to start my own place, she'll still be waiting and I can ask for her.''

''Do you think Mr. Brearde will consent to her marrying one of our kind?'' Her eyes rounded at the devastating thought that some Creole families looked upon Acadians as inferiors.

''I suspect Mr. Brearde mightn't be so quick to deny Celeste's wishes to marry for love since Arlene's death.''

''Arlene's?—do you mean Louis's wife is dead? When? What happened?'' Those thoughts that had punished her that night at Grenfall when she had first heard of Arlene Duhon brought a smidgen of guilt.

''I figured Maman might've told you about it in her letter. Celeste wrote that Arlene had a miscarriage in early fall and died soon afterward.''

''Maman must not have heard. Does Louis know?'' Even if Louis and Arlene hadn't found happiness in their marriage, she sensed that beneath his façade of rakishness, Louis possessed a warm, caring side. Such news would bring sorrow and pain, and she grieved for him.

''I'm not sure. Unless he's been back lately to get letters, he might not. How long has it been since he and Jean Pierre left?''

Rose answered without having to stop and count, "Five weeks and two days. They plan to come in for a rest at Christmas. Poor Louis. He's going to feel awful."

They found more pleasant topics and, with pride adding to her smiles, she took him to meet Dr. David, then walked with him arm-in-arm across the parade grounds to show him off to Lela and Juan. Afterward, Rose and Jarrette talked away the day, savoring their reunion, delighting in the hopeful futures of each.

"You'll be sure to come back in two weeks for Christmas, won't you?" Rose asked when Jarrette told her he'd have to leave and meet Arlee north of the fort at the designated spot. "You saw how sincere Lela's and Juan's invitation was for all of us to join them."

"You bet! Arlee promised. And anyway, he sent me in for our mail and a few supplies just because he knew I was dying to find out about you. He's been counting on Christmas as a time to load up on goods and store our catch at the fort while we go back out afterward."

Remembering the anguish of watching Jean Pierre leave after that too-brief visit, Rose bucked up and sent Jarrette off with a cheerful wave and a pasted-on smile. It was a slow process, she reflected, but she was learning that trappers could pursue the game with far more success and ease when the snow covered the ground in the North Wilderness. Their families had to learn to be patient.

That night Rose found the bed felt harder and colder than usual. Tossing restlessly, she slipped her hand across the sheet to the empty spot where Jean Pierre should have been sleeping. No warmth greeted her there, and she flipped over to lie on her back. How could she bear to wait much longer to see him, hear his deep voice, touch him—and get up enough nerve to tell him she loved him? No moon or stars shone through the window to reassure her. The normal sounds of barking dogs and calling nocturnal creatures were strangely missing. The darkness and silence of the night lent no comfort. Exhaustion finally won out, and she fell into a fitful slumber, one troubled by dreams of snarling wild animals with giant teeth, of mysterious flickering lights, and of white flowers scattered about.

"You look like something the dogs drug up," Lela said after opening her door the next Saturday afternoon for a solemn-faced Rose. "What are circles doing under them pretty blue eyes?"

Going to the fireplace, Lela lifted the ever-present coffeepot and poured two cups of the fragrant brew, lacing it with whiskey and a dollop of thick whipped cream. She handed Rose a cup. "Here, drink up. You gonna need it to talk and I'm gonna need it to listen." Her low-pitched voice and uneducated way of speaking might have seemed harsh to some, but Rose had already found Lela to be sympathetic and loving and paid no heed.

"I love him, Lela." Her eyes filled with tears, and the hurt look on her face tore at the older woman's heart. Even Rose was surprised at her unsolicited, obviously startling confession. Before having told of her love out loud to Jarrette that week, she had thought the secret might have to die with her. Now that was all she wanted to talk about or think about.

"Well, of course you do. Has there ever been any doubt?"

"Not since we camped by the little river in the mountains where he saved me from the panther." She couldn't admit even to Lela how often the memories of that first lovemaking haunted her and made her ache for Jean Pierre's return.

"So what's the problem?"

Staring out the window, she pursed her lips to keep them from trembling. "The problem is that Jean Pierre said he loved me when we married, but he never told me he was *in* love with me. He doesn't come to the fort as often as some of the married trappers. It has to be because he doesn't feel for me what I feel for him. I've disappointed him by picking a quarrel every time he leaves." Rose dabbed at her eyes and sipped her coffee, unable to decide if she felt better or worse for having verbalized her feelings. "Why can't we get along? Why can't I learn to accept his ways?"

"Honey, you two hardheads jest gotta talk and straighten this here thing out." Lela reached across the table and patted one of Rose's pale hands with understanding. "Take it from me, nothing beats two people talking over their problems."

"For a while I thought he was beginning to see me as more than just someone he grew up with." Picking up the cup of fragrant brew, Rose drank half of it. "He could be so gentle, so understanding when we were on the trail, almost loving at times. Did I tell you how he stopped one morning just to let me wash my hair? Or about the flower he picked for me in the mountains, that I pressed and keep in the shoes he gave me?"

Lela shook her head, knowing no answer was needed, and wouldn't be heard if given.

A remembering look glazed Rose's blue eyes before the expression on her face changed, along with the tone of her voice. "Then when we got here and he kept making decisions and never caring if I agreed or understood—" A hiccup escaped from her throat, interrupting her statement.

Lela got up to fetch more coffee, her flowing purple robe trailing across the rough plank floor. As she refilled their cups, she said, "The way I see it, honey, Jean Pierre is ever' bit as smart as he is good-looking. He ain't used to thinking about what might make a pretty wife happy, but he'll come around. You two have had it rough, having to be separated so much right after your marriage. Couples have to have time together to learn to live with each other."

Rose drained her cup and wiped the cream from her upper lip. "May I have more, please?" In thoughtful silence she waited for another serving of the tasty concoction, thinking how she was beginning to feel better already. Talking with Lela always seemed to revitalize her. "I don't know how I can convince that mulehead I love him." Her tongue felt heavy and the words were hard to form.

"Have you tried telling him?" Lela placed the nearly empty coffeepot on the table and returned to her chair.

"Yes, but he never heard or let on. He probably would've laughed if he had," Rose said indignantly, her cheeks flushing at the thought. "Let's talk about something else."

"Have you wondered if that might be why he acts so ornery? Maybe he needs to hear you say how much you love him." Lela knew her young friend was feeling pretty low to drink anything stronger than wine.

Rose straightened her back and regained her composure as Lela refilled her cup, again lacing it with whiskey. They sipped the strong brew and changed the conversation to lighter subjects. Rose began slurring her words, but her depression had lifted.

With a childlike face and a thick tongue, Rose said, "My friend, do you know it's only two weeks until Christmas? I'm making Jean Pierre a blue robe with white piping and his monogram. I may just give it to Juan instead. My husband probably won't be here. His birthday present is still wrapped up." She sobered when she recalled how disappointed she'd been that he hadn't made it to the fort for his birthday. He was twenty-four now, she realized.

"Never mind. I'm making Juan a robe, too, honey. Besides, he wouldn't like his robe with a 'J.P.G.' on the pocket." Lela laughed. She had never before seen Rose drink so much, and to see her carrying on over her husband just as men in their cups so often did over their women amused her. She got up and put the bottle away.

"Well," Rose added, "if you hear of someone with those initials, let me know."

Lela filled their cups with plain coffee. "Drink this, honey, and I'll take you home. I'd hate to have that Cajun's wrath falling on my ears for getting his wife drunk."

In a short time, Lela walked her visitor home and helped her add logs to the fireplace. Before leaving, she insisted that Rose lie down for a nap.

Rose awakened to see eerie shadows from the dying fire dancing on the ceiling. She wondered if her chance at happiness with Jean Pierre was to be destroyed from lack of fuel in the same way as the fire was being denied. He probably wouldn't return from his trapping until the end of the season. Giving in to a tad of feeling sorry for herself, she pictured her first Christmas away from home as a bleak, lonely affair.

A small piece of wood in the fireplace flared and crackled briefly, in the same way as hope suddenly dispelled Rose's moment of self-pity. Hadn't she brought much of her heartache on herself? She had been like a child in her refusal to accept Jean Pierre as her equal in some things but wiser than she in many more ways. Only now could she admit that her ready anger came from her overpowering need for him to love her. How could she expect him to love her as a wife if she continued to act like a foolish girl? For the mature, she scolded the wayward part of her, love and respect transcended such pettiness. When she finally closed her eyes again, the flame in the fireplace had gone out, but the resolution in her heart to change had taken on a new life.

Chapter Seventeen

The early winter snow that had fallen through the night covered Fort Arkansas like a crystalline veil. Then, to cap it off, the morning sun bathed the snow with new, sparkling pristine beauty. Just outside Rose's window a robin huddled on the lowest limb of a tree. His ruffled feathers and lowered head were a natural thermometer for gauging the temperature.

Her first sight of the fluffy white flakes all about fascinated Rose. Feeling like a child on Christmas morning, she scampered about inside the fort, running unnecessary errands until wet feet and a chapped face forced her inside. She yearned for Jean Pierre to be there to share her excitement. Eager to tell him she loved him, still she was apprehensive about his reaction to her revelation. She had heard that there was no hunger more gnawing, no thirst more unquenchable than the human desire to experience love. She could vouch for it.

With Juan's sentries along for protection, Rose and Lela went to the woods and cut down Christmas trees. Together they made decorations. They popped and strung popcorn, then covered sweetgum balls in colorful paper to hang on their trees. Boughs of pine and red berries decorated the mantels over their fireplaces. With much laughing and joking, they hung bunches of mistletoe over their doors.

Content to stay inside the next afternoon, Rose sat in front of her fireplace enjoying its warmth while she wrapped the last of the Christmas presents she had made from the goods ordered from a drummer. He had been an old, gaunt man, and she had wondered, with a shudder, if he had been a threatening rascal in his younger days, like that Thom Keller back in Natchitoches.

It was almost dark, and she was humming a snatch of an old Acadian song, when Rose heard a commotion outside her door. Were those bells tinkling?

"Hello and merry Christmas! Anyone home?" a familiar voice called happily.

Her heart dipping and diving, she jumped up as the door burst open and Jean Pierre came in, dropping his gear in the middle of the floor. He hurried across the room and hugged Rose close, swinging her around.

"Merry Christmas, little wife." His deep laughter rang out and Rose realized that she had hungered for so long to hear it. He let her feet touch the floor again and crushed her mouth with his, stifling any reply she might have made. He kissed her then with lingering gentleness that left her senseless and out of breath.

Too full of love for him and of joy at having him back to be coherent, Rose melted against the cold of his coat, returning eager kiss for eager kiss. Reluctantly she pulled her mouth from his to ask, "Aren't you going to take off your coat?"

Both broke into laughter, whether from her inane question or from overflowing emotion they didn't know. And when he shed his outer garments and opened his arms, she returned to what she remembered and longed for: the reassuring feel of his firm chest against her breasts, his muscular arms around her, and his tall length serving as a nestling place for her smallness. For a long moment Rose clung, her arms around his neck, her face so close against his chest that she could hear his strong heartbeat rushing in tune with her own.

There in front of the warming fireplace, Jean Pierre savored the feel of his wife in his arms. His hand stroked the golden head, each movement a kind of thanksgiving for having found her well and safe . . . and waiting for him. His weeks away from Rose had given him more time than he needed to get his thoughts together. No longer would he concern himself with "what if's." His pulse labored, and his tongue tried to dry up on him, but he made himself speak. "Rose, I love you so. I was in love with you before we married."

Her heart raced. Had she heard him right? She was the one who was going to speak of love. Nothing was going as planned—and she wondered if she was fantasizing. She lifted her head then, and he kissed her. When she was able to catch her breath, Rose asked, "What did you say?"

"I'm in love with you. Please believe me. What must I do to prove it?" He kissed her eyes, her nose, her neck.

Rose moaned and gave an involuntary shiver as his lips moved down to her throat, lingering there before going down to the swell of her breasts. Surely she was dreaming!

"I think I've always loved you. I need you more than anything in the world. Do you think you could learn to love me?" his voice pleaded with naked emotion.

Her blue eyes reflecting her fathomless love, Rose replied hoarsely, "Jean Pierre, I already love you with all my heart, forever and ever, yes." She pulled his head to meet hers and verified her answer with a kiss. "I knew I was in love with you before we first made love."

Wonderingly, they sank to lie on the braided rug before the cozy fire, their lips and bodies clinging in fiery contact. They separated long enough to rid themselves of garments, flinging them in sundry directions, laughing low in anticipation and teasing in the way of lovers. Rose slipped off her shoes, feeling the warmth of the flames on her feet, but feeling far more warmth from her beloved's gentle kisses on the newly exposed skin of her thighs and legs as his hands eased her stockings down and off.

"I'm a man who likes to work his way up from the bottom," he teased with a flirty wink that brought the breathy giggle he wanted to hear. And then, rewarding her with knowing smiles between the kisses, he kissed the top of each toe until she shivered with excitement and longing. His warm lips began the slow upward journey, stopping only for an exquisite torture on her breasts. Trailing tremor-causing kisses along her neck and jaw, his mouth captured hers in a kiss that sparked into a sensuous fire.

Lying back on the rug, Rose saw familiar, dancing sparks in his dark eyes as he flirted with her and seared her flesh from her toes on up—why hadn't she earlier suspected they came from love? As his head moved upward, her hands reached to feel again the springy black curls, to marvel at the manly shape of his ears, to feel the texture of the dark skin on the handsome face now so close. She could feel his warm, sweet breath on her face, could hear him crooning endearments beside her ear. *Beloved*. Had she always loved him without realizing it? Her heart near to bursting, she welcomed his lips on hers, welcomed the tongue seeking inside her mouth, welcomed the maelstrom of emotions rocking her body and soul.

Rose yearned for his possession, pleaded for it with her hands, her lips, her eyes, but he lifted his mouth from hers, ignoring her groan of complaint

"Tell me you love me, my darling. I must hear it from your lips again." Begging for confirmation, his eyes burned into hers.

"I love you." Her arms tightened around his neck. "Never doubt it."

Jean Pierre whispered, "I've waited so long."

Murmuring words of love and scattering searing kisses, the pace became frantic as their bodies touched, flesh to flesh at last. Her hands caressed their way across his curl-matted chest and eased under his arms to his back.

With gentle fingertips she touched the scar on his shoulder, and then the magical soft hand slipped down, down.

One way or another, the beautiful young woman in his arms would slowly drive him crazy, Jean Pierre mused. *Let it always be this way,* he prayed. He placed a kiss upon an erect nipple, and she sighed. When his mouth closed over the pointed breast, she moved her body in that sensuous way that fed inner fires.

"You make me know the meaning of the word *love,*" Rose whispered while his fingers lazily followed the curves of her jaw and her cheek, the arch of her eyebrows, the shape of her eyes after he closed them with butterfly kisses. Inside she trembled with ecstasy.

"That's because you yourself are love . . . *my* love." Pleasuring her and watching her beautiful face glow for him fed all those hungerings that had plagued him in the weeks of trapping in the cold wilderness. The silkiness of her pinkish blond curls in his stroking hands brought a look of adoring wonder to his face. How could such loveliness belong to him? With sudden gratitude for his good fortune, Jean Pierre lay down and hugged her close again. His manhood throbbed with increasing intensity at the touch of her silken thighs. The need to send that hardness into the remembered softness became his sole desire, and they came together in compelling passion, each murmuring during the blissful joining that seemed a proof of their newly announced love.

There on the rug Rose had braided herself, the blissful rhythm of his motion carried the lovers into a world beyond reality, one lovelier than springtime, sweeter than nectar, higher than the heavens . . . a spot in space defying human description. And it was there that their urgent passion merged them as soul mates and jolted them back into the everyday world.

Their lovemaking had been complete, and they both knew it as they lay locked in an embrace, their pulses and breathing returning to normal. There had been tenderness— there had been fulfillment. It had been perfect. There had been nothing lacking—because they had voiced their love.

Rose lay like a contented kitten on Jean Pierre's arm. "I

love you," she whispered. "It scares me to think how close I came never to experiencing this moment." She talked drowsily as she rubbed her hand lovingly across his muscled chest and arms, delighting in the feel of his hardness and toying idly with the bear tooth hanging from his neck. "I'm glad your talisman kept you safe so that you could come back to me."

"So am I." Jean Pierre lay with one arm under his head and the other under Rose. Only the fire in the fireplace lighted the cabin, for complete darkness had fallen now. "If only I could make time stand still and this moment last forever." He gathered her to him and kissed her convincingly.

Jean Pierre propped up on one elbow and smoked a cigar, feeling completely at peace with the world and himself for the first time in a long while. What a damned fool he had been! He had almost lost the most precious woman in existence. Growing weary, he enfolded the sleeping Rose in his arms and vowed to himself that he would never again be so unreasonable. If he'd had a guardian angel, she probably would have appeared instantly to chide him for making such a vow, one a person with Jean Pierre's fiery temperament would be sorely pressed to keep.

The reunited Rose and Jean Pierre were happy during the following days and nights—happier than either had thought a human could be. They kissed beneath the mistletoe she had hung over the door . . . and other places as well. All the misunderstandings and disagreements of a lifetime were discussed, laughed about, and forgotten. Because they were lovers as well as man and wife, there was no question of forgiveness.

When she told him about working with Dr. David, he brushed aside his initial unreasonable jealousy and declared that he didn't mind. And then when she took him to meet the doctor and to show him where she worked, Jean Pierre was proud that he'd not shown disapproval. Dr. David won him with his easy charm, and he obviously respected Rose.

Christmas Eve dawned bright and clear. Rose woke to

see Jean Pierre staring out the window. Absorbing every beloved detail of his appearance, she watched him in silence. He stood with folded arms, his legs spread apart, confident and proud. She marveled that the characteristics she so admired now in him, she had at one time thought of as arrogance.

At the sound of her uncontrolled yawn, Jean Pierre turned toward her there in the bed, a smile replacing the thoughtful expression she had secretly been watching.

"It's high time you woke up." Each morning since they had been married and awakened together, he had been entranced anew with her beauty. He halted now to gaze at the luxurious mass of hair and her provocative smile.

"What fun to wake up and find you here," Rose said, inviting him into her outstretched arms and raising her lips for a kiss.

"Is this the place to get a free meal?" a familiar voice called from outside, followed by a brisk rapping on the door.

"It's Jarrette!" Rose exclaimed, her eyes sparkling.

"Well, it's about time that brother of ours showed up," Jean Pierre replied with a smile as pleased as hers. Tossing her robe to her, he made for the door.

Reunion was sweet all around, and the three Guilbeaus spent the day exchanging letters and news from home and bits of information gleaned from other sources.

"Arlee and I had a strange visitor one night upon the King River," Jarrette told Jean Pierre that night after they had eaten and gathered around the fireplace for coffee. "A big, mean-looking cuss, he said he knew Louis and you and wondered where you were trapping."

"Did he have a name, little brother?" Jean Pierre drawled with little interest.

"Rufus Bedlow. Do you know him?"

"Yep, 'bout as well a I care to, at that."

"After he left the next morning, Arlee said that he was a loner and a hell-raiser when crossed."

"I believe it," Rose chimed in. "I saw him in Natchitoches, and he looks like he's too mean for anybody to want to be around him. Lela said Slash Crowe, the main scout for the captain, and Rufus had a horrible fight last year and cut up each other badly.'' She shuddered at the thought and begged, ''Please, let's not talk about such things tonight.''

''Wonder why he wanted to know where Louis and I were,'' Jean Pierre said, darting a look at Rose to see if she was going to protest at his ignoring her plea. The three were sitting on the rug before the fire, Rose in the middle. He covered her hand with his in silent apology.

''Beats me. Arlee wondered if he might be meaning to poach.''

Jean Pierre laughed then, dismissing the preposterous idea with the remark, ''Rufus may be big and mean, but he's too smart to tangle with Louis and me. Besides, he's got no quarrel with us.''

''But Louis and you don't always stay together,'' Rose reminded him. ''You've told me—''

''Don't worry your pretty head,'' Jarrette broke in. ''Jean Pierre can take care of himself. We'll not talk about Rufus anymore. I'm sorry I brought it up.''

Before long, Jarrette stood and yawned, announcing it was time to go to sleep in the barracks where Arlee and others spent the night when at the fort.

''You'll not forget to bring Arlee and Louis to eat with all of us at Lela's and Juan's tomorrow, will you?'' Rose reminded him as he hugged her good-night at the doorway.

His twinkling brown eyes darting from one happy face to the other, Jarrette reached then to hug Jean Pierre and said, ''A pack of she-wolves couldn't keep us away.''

The next morning Jean Pierre helped Rose with the stuffing for the turkey he had shot in the nearby forest only two days ago. Having roasted in the edge of the coals in the fireplace the night before, the big bird would be their main contribution to the dinner. To the basket of food she added fresh sprays of red-berried holly Jean Pierre had brought from the woods and announced they were ready to go when the time came.

During the afternoon Lela brought over her Christmas gift to Rose, insisting she should wear it to the party that night.

After her bath in the wooden tub Jean Pierre placed

before the fireplace and filled with warm water, Rose opened Lela's present to find a ruby-red gown, the exact shade of her necklace. It had a snug-fitting bodice with long, narrow sleeves. The neckline plunged, as it did on all the gowns Lela made, but for once she had made one with no trimming at all.

"I love seeing you in fancy clothes," Jean Pierre said. "Will the pink satin slippers go with it?"

"Yes," she answered, not at all sure, but determined to wear them for him anyway. His pleased smile added to her holiday mood.

Rose arranged her golden hair the way her husband said he liked it. Under his admiring gaze, she brushed it away from her face into a cluster of curls at the crown with long ringlets hanging down her back. Earlier Lela had given her some silk roses she had made, and Rose placed some pink and ruby ones on each side of the curls.

Jean Pierre came to stand behind her where she stood in front of the small mirror. His face revealed his proud approval of her appearance. "You're so special, Rose. How did I ever get this lucky? Marrying you was the best move I ever made." His arms moved from behind to hold her close against his tall body. "You always smell so good. I need and want you all the time."

"Get control of yourself." She cocked her head playfully at their images. "And look in the mirror. You're gorgeous. I'm the lucky one, my husband. From what I heard, you left a string of broken hearts reaching from New Orleans to Fort Arkansas and even farther north."

"They never even had a chance after my first trip home from trapping when I found you turning into such a beauty. You know, honey, I felt guilty about my feeling for you then. Thank goodness for the outcome." His eyes sparkled mischievously as he looked into hers. "I love you, but you were truly a spoiled 'little sister.'"

"You're horrid." Rose tiptoed to reach his lips, curving her body to his as she eased her arms around his neck and kissed him soundly. A knock at the door ended the embrace.

"Merry Christmas," Jarrette said when Jean Pierre opened the door to find Louis with him. "Louis and I decided that if you two plan to stay in each other's arms all the time, you should close the curtains. People passing by might think you're in love or something. We came by to see if you needed help getting things over to Juan's and Lela's.''

Rose felt a blush on her face, but turned housewifely and said, ''We took the food over an hour ago, but you can help take the packages.'' She glanced around to see if they had overlooked anything. With their arms full, the four walked the familiar path to the Rodriguez cabin.

Dr. David and Arlee Simpson had already arrived, their greetings blending with those of Lela and Juan.

''A real feast here,'' Dr. David told Lela after all took seats at the table and filled their plates from the bowls and platters of vegetables and roasted meats.

''Ham from a wild pig has never tasted so good,'' Jean Pierre said.

''Juan has saved this here champagne all fall for today,'' Lela announced, sending her husband a doting look.

Everyone especially liked the cake Lela had baked, and each found a small favor she had baked in it. Rose received a small brooch with emerald-colored stones. The men discovered appropriate gifts in their pieces of cake: jade stickpins, silver four-leaf clovers, and a gold toothpick for Juan. Rose marveled at Lela's cleverness and wondered how she knew which piece of cake to serve each guest.

After the leisurely supper, the hosts and their guests gathered about the fireplace and sipped brandy while they sang Christmas songs. Arlee accompanied them on a fiddle he had borrowed from one of the soldiers. Lela asked Jean Pierre to read the Christmas story from the Bible, and Rose grew sentimental at the thought that he would be reading those words in his deep velvety voice to their children some day. Tears of pure joy surfaced.

Then Lela took the packages from under the gaudily decorated tree and handed them to Juan to distribute. All expressed surprise and pleasure over their gifts.

The last present to be opened was the one Jean Pierre had wrapped for Rose. She hurriedly untied the ribbon, wondering what he had chosen from the limited selection at the trading post. She looked at the strange object.

"It's beautiful, Jean Pierre, but what is it?"

"It's a dulcimer I bought off an old trapper earlier this fall." He took the musical instrument from her. "I found playing it helped while away the nights. You pluck the strings and make the chords by sliding this piece of wood along the frets." He demonstrated. The notes flowing forth were hauntingly beautiful.

"Sing a song for us, Jean Pierre," Lela said.

Playing random chords on the dulcimer, Jean Pierre said, "I'd like to sing this song for Rose. While I was gone this last time, I wrote it for her after I learned to play this contraption." Then he began singing in a rich, mellow bass:

> "Well, dry your eyes and rest your mind.
> Whatever tomorrow brings just won't matter
> anymore.
> The past is all behind us now;
> The lessons have been learned.
> And it's time to live like we've never
> done before.
> 'Cause loving you is such an easy thing
> to do.
>
> So I'll hold you in my arms until the
> light of day.
> A blue moon is rising across the sky;
> The stars all shine so bright,
> But all I see is the magic in your eyes.
> And holding you so close to me,
> The world just fades away.
> And I wonder if you realize
> That loving you is an easy thing to do."

There was a hushed silence in the room as Jean Pierre finished his song. Each one seemed touched, both by the beautiful song and by the depth of feeling apparent on the faces of the singer and the lovely woman to whom he sang.

Finally Jarrette broke the silence. "Rose sings pretty, too. Why don't you two sing a duet?"

After a whispered conference, the couple sang an old Acadian love song. Their voices blended in perfect harmony; their eyes were only for each other, oblivious to everyone else in the room.

"Encore! Encore!" everyone shouted.

Reluctantly taking his eyes from Rose, Jean Pierre replied, "That's enough for now. I want to hear Lela sing." He turned to their hostess. "Juan says you have a pretty voice, Lela. Come on. Arlee and I'll both accompany you."

Lela took the stage after talking to the musicians. Tugging her dress down over her hips and sending a flirting wink in Jean Pierre's direction, she said, "Hit it, honey."

In a surprisingly beautiful contralto voice, Lela burst into one of the less bawdy tunes that she had sung at Belle's. She moved with a provocative, gentle sway of hips to the rhythm of the two instruments. She finished the song sitting on Juan's lap, looking into his smiling face.

Lela stood and bowed when the guests clapped. "Man, that felt good. I aint' sung in years. I'm glad y'all liked it."

Lela couldn't be persuaded to sing another number, however. She suggested instead that they listen while Arlee played the fiddle.

It was late when Dr. David stood up to leave. "I don't know when I've enjoyed anything more. Thank you for inviting me, Lela and Juan. I've had a wonderful Christmas with you." He bade everyone good-night and, with one last pleased look at the radiant Rose, left.

It was long past midnight, and the tired but happy group followed the doctor's lead, trudging slowly through newly fallen snow to their beds. Each confessed it had been one of the best Christmases ever, even of those that had been spent with family.

Long after all the candles were out and the fort had settled down for the night, the young couple lay entwined, content to be still. Their eyelids drooped, and their whispering voices faltered.

"Grandmère was right," Rose mused drowsily. "You can't chase butterflies."

A deep chuckle sounded near her ear. "She told me that story, too." Soft kisses began on her ears and trailed a shivering path to creamy shoulders. "Our grandmère knows a lot about happiness."

Chapter Eighteen

The day after Christmas, Rose and Jean Pierre were sitting in their favorite place, on the rug before the fireplace. His head on her lap, they reveled in their newfound closeness. She tweaked his ear one time too many, and he playfully pushed her back on the rug. With his lips only inches from hers, he whispered, "I need a kiss."

Taking his face between her hands, Rose said, "If kisses were sugar, we both would have gained ten pounds the last few days. But I wouldn't miss one opportunity." She drew his mouth to hers, kissing him with her recently acquired expertise. "I love you so, my husband. I don't ever want you out of my sight again."

Staying close, Jean Pierre said, "I've been thinking this week how good it is to know this will be my last season to trap. Now that I've found you, I never intend to leave you again." They rolled over, now lying on their backs, her head on his arm, her blond hair appearing almost white where it touched the black of his. "I wouldn't let you do without anything. I've money in the bank in New Orleans to buy many arpents of land, even if Governor Unzaga won't deed us an allotment. I've had good seasons of my own, plus I have the furs Louis and I bought from other trappers for our company. I'll take you with me when I go to New Orleans to sell.

"You'll like New Orleans, Rose," he went on in his deep, pleasant voice. "Nearly three thousand people of many nationalities live there. Ships from all over the world sail in every few days bringing all kinds of goods and exotic fruits. You'll love the fancy eating places with the best food you ever put in your mouth. I'll take you to dressmakers and buy you the prettiest clothes you've ever dreamed of and ruby earrings to match your necklace. Your beauty will make all other women hide behind closed doors in shame." He turned toward her, throwing an arm across her.

"I don't need such things," Rose told him. "Give me a house on the bayou and lots of babies—and you beside me—that's all I dream about."

"Can't a Cajun want such extras for his beautiful wife?"

"He can, yes, but you might not be able to afford them. I can't believe you've made that much money in three years."

Smiling at her with that grin she had come to adore, he said, "Well, I'm a pretty fair poker player, too. On my trips to New Orleans I've been lucky at cards and banked a sum from the winnings."

"Jean Pierre! You haven't gambled!" Her shocked expression reminded him of what an innocent he had married.

"Yes. But I'm glad I did. Soon I'll build you a house close to Papa's on the bayou that'll rival Grenfall."

Rose smiled at his exaggeration. "I don't need anything but to be wife to the best-looking Cajun on the Bayou Teche. Promise me you won't gamble again."

He rolled over to face Rose, a sensuous tone replacing the serious one. "My little tiger," he said as he nibbled at her ear, "I'll agree to almost anything to keep you happy."

They cuddled in each other's arms and watched the fire. The faint blues and greens danced around, intermingling with the taller, bolder yellows and oranges, making a rainbow of colors.

"This reminds me of the good days on the trail. Only much better, yes?" She snuggled closer.

The faint scent of her perfume and her soft body touching his aroused his ever-present desire for her. Holding her closer, he quipped lovingly, "Come to think of it, you don't smell the same now as you did on the trail."

Pulling away only far enough to look into his face, she retorted, "If I remember correctly, my smell didn't keep you away." Her eyes twinkled. "Oh, had I known then what I know now! I was a fool, wasn't I?"

The words were barely out of her mouth before he leaned over her and held her face between his hands. His gaze swept her upturned face. "No, I was the fool. I wasted so much precious time. I was foolish to try to tame you right off. I should've known better because I've been in the woods too long to think man can conquer every wild thing. Some, like you, my impetuous darling, need to be gentled, not broken. I'll never forgive myself."

In a mock reprimand she tapped his nose lightly with her forefinger and said, "I won't allow you to hold a grudge against the man I love. This week has truly made up for everything. And anyway, haven't we always heard Papa say that anything worth having is worth fighting for? Hold me close, my darling," she said drowsily.

Locked in an embrace, they drifted into dreams that were separate, yet followed the same shining path into tomorrow.

Even though Rose slept fitfully at night, thinking of Jean Pierre's leaving soon, her eyes each morning were clear and bright. Her pink-flowered dress seemed to make her cheeks and lips even more colorful upon that final day as they ate breakfast.

"I don't think I can stand your leaving me tomorrow," Rose told Jean Pierre. She gave up trying to eat. "I feel as if my life ends when you ride off." She looked down at her hand where it rested on the wooden table in his, pale against the tanned, larger one. How could she bear not to touch him whenever it pleased her?

"I feel the same way, Rose. Only a few more months and then we'll never be separated again. April will be here before you know it.'' His brown eyes searched hers, pleading for her to understand that even he didn't believe the time would fly, but that they must pretend and hope.

Struck with an inspiration, she lifted her blond curls and unfastened the gold chain. She opened his hand and closed it over her necklace, still warm from where it had nestled in the swell of her breasts.

''I want you to carry this with you.'' Her fingers forced his to accept her offering.

''I can't take your necklace. It's your most prized possession. It's the only thing you have that belonged to your real parents.'' He looked down at the red stone in its unusual filigree mounting of green and pink gold, touched more deeply than he would have her know.

''Nothing and no one means as much as you do. Please take it and think of me every time you look upon it.'' Her blue eyes compelled him to accede to her wish. ''I'll feel that we have a stronger link if I know you carry it with you.''

Jean Pierre took the jewelry, placed it in his shirt pocket, and then patted the fabric. ''I'll always carry it over my heart, but I don't need it to remind me of my sweet wife.'' He knew he would never forget the picture of her blond beauty set off so well by her pink dress and hair ribbon.

They stood together and embraced for a long and tender moment, each busy worrying about the next few months they would have to face. Their bodies finally separated, and Rose began to clear the table.

Deliberately lightening her tone in a way she was far from feeling, Rose said, ''I'm being silly. Of course you'll rush back with wings on your feet, sweep me up on your white horse, and take me to live happily forever in our beloved Cajun country.''

With a heavy heart, Jean Pierre watched her eyes brighten and a forced smile appear on her face. The image stayed with him as he left to work at the stable with the other trappers in preparing for their departure the next day. Rose spent the afternoon cooking his favorite meal and trying to erase the unhappy thoughts about his leaving.

Jean Pierre returned, bringing Jarrette, Arlee, and Louis for supper as planned. They were seated at the table, eating and discussing their hunting expedition, when Rose interrupted. "Louis, you've been unusually quiet. Aren't you feeling well?"

The day after Christmas, while Jean Pierre and Jarrette engaged in hand wrestling at the table by the window, Rose had found time to talk with Louis in front of the fireplace about the loss of Arlene and their unborn child. She had detected a new solemnity in his handsome face and wondered if a bit of the formerly carefree, flirty-eyed Creole might also have died.

"I'm fine, Rose," Louis replied. "I guess I've just had a lot on my mind, worrying about the busy months ahead." Louis met her concerned gaze head-on, then flashed a facsimile of the old charming smile . . . without it quite reaching his eyes. They finished eating their meal, the gaiety of the holidays at the fort dampened by the knowledge that departure was only hours away. Soon after supper, the three men bade Rose and Jean Pierre good-night and went to the barracks.

After carefully closing the curtains, Rose and Jean Pierre lay together on the rug before the fireplace watching the flames, absorbing these last special moments together, storing them in their memories to be recalled at some later, needed time. With no candles and no moon, the fire roaring in the fireplace served to illuminate the two as well as to warm them. Jean Pierre's dark skin glowed shiny and olive against Rose's paleness. Tenderly she caressed the now-healed welts on his shoulders, hugging him closer to her naked breasts at the memory of his brush with death in his heroic efforts to save her from the panther. When his dark curls touched her blond cloud of hair, the picture was one of contrasts blending to make a new entity. Brown eyes smoldered with deep, abiding passion as they gazed into the blue ones darkening with their answering messages.

Jean Pierre whispered, "I love you." Their mouths met in loving, strength-giving kisses. Their bodies clung together as they again declared their undying love in words innocently believed to be as new and unique as their love,

words which have been serving lovers since time began.
Their lovemaking quickly developed into a towering inferno, quenched only when they lay spent, locked in each
other's arms, fascinated with and youthfully smug in the
knowledge that their love and life together was only
beginning.

Dreams disturbed Rose during the few hours she and
Jean Pierre slept. Once, upon awakening, she smiled to
recall the just-revealed conclusion of a frightening dream
that had visited her before Christmas, one in which she
had been isolated in endless water. How simple! All she
had had to do was look behind her to see Jean Pierre, his
arms reaching out for her. Why hadn't she had the sense to
do that before?

Lifting her head from this shoulder, she peered lovingly
at him in the faint light of dawn, struck by the thought that
her pale hair spilling onto his dark head could be a part of
the old woman's forecast of her future: "White on black."
Wide awake then, she eased her head back to its place on
his shoulder, disturbing Jean Pierre's deep sleep a bit as
she gently disengaged a strand of her hair from where it
had curled around the strange talisman he always wore.
Like a mysterious carved piece of ivory, the bear tooth lay
for a moment in her hand, warmed by her beloved's body
and thus made special. Returning it to its accustomed place
among the dark hair curled on his chest, Rose examined
his features as though memorizing them before letting her
mind wander again to the old woman's prediction.

Certainly Jean Pierre would fit the "someone close,"
and their lives seemed destined to make the third part
come true: "A lifetime of love." She recalled the last
phrases—"search for the fang; white flowers under the
flame; world of water"—and tried to find clues to their
meaning. Could the attacking panther's teeth be called
fangs? But no search had been involved. The "white
flowers" could be the mistletoe still hanging above their
door—but it had no flowers and there was no flame above.
She allowed herself a derisive smile at her foolish thoughts,
giving in to the delicious drowsiness taking her over as

gently and completely as the arms that held her safe and warm.

The next morning Rose stood in her pink-flowered dress on the steps of the cabin waving to Jean Pierre until he turned the corner and was out of sight. She shivered as she turned to go into the house, an unfamiliar feeling of foreboding creeping over her. She felt as empty as the room looked without Jean Pierre's presence.

Dressed for bed in her warmest gown and robe, Rose walked that first night to the back window and threw it open to gaze at the sky. Twinkling stars and a pale moon shone on the whiteness of the undisturbed snow stretching down toward the creek. Shivering, she wondered if Jean Pierre might be watching a similar scene and thinking of her, even as she thought of him. The soft rippling of the unfrozen section of the stream behind the cabin seemed to echo her loneliness. The distant howls of dogs—or were they wolves?—sounded like a melancholy refrain. Sighing heavily, Rose closed the window, turned from the desolate beauty outside, and went to her lonely and suddenly too-large bed.

The days of January dragged by for Rose. The weather was unpleasant and the sun seemed to have disappeared forever behind gray, rainy skies. Only the friendship of Dr. David, Lela, and Juan kept her life bearable to any degree. They seldom allowed her to be alone during the days and early evenings, always thinking of something to keep her busy or to cheer her up. But she spent the long nights alone with her memories, dreams, and hopes of happier times with Jean Pierre.

Rose was eating breakfast one morning in early March when a frantic beating on the door startled her. She opened the door to admit an ashen-faced Louis, feeling her heart leap at the sight of him: His clothes were filthy, and he looked as if he hadn't slept in days. *And he was alone*.

"Oh, Louis! Where's Jean Pierre?" Rose anxiously looked out the door but saw no one. "What's wrong? You look strange." A feeling of panic crept over her.

Louis sank onto the chair by the table. He removed his fur hat and ran his fingers through his hair, then looked at Rose's wide eyes and anxious face. "Sit down. I have bad news."

She almost collapsed on the chair opposite Louis, too dumbfounded to question him and too afraid to hear his answer.

"Jean Pierre is dead." Louis watched as the color left Rose's face, her blue eyes staring blankly at him. She sat as rigid as an ice statue, seeming not to breathe.

"I'm so sorry," Louis said, his voice breaking. He had never had a harder task. "I've already sent a runner to fetch Jarrette. Rose, Rose? Are you all right?" Louis caught her before she slipped from her chair in a dead faint.

She came to with the feel of cold cloths on her face. She prayed she had been having a nightmare. Jean Pierre couldn't be dead. She would have known it inside. She opened her eyes to see Louis, his face and eyes reflecting her anguish. "Louis?"

"Yes?" He searched her eyes and saw nothing but pain.

"Are you positive about Jean Pierre's being dead? Did you see him—"

"You know I wouldn't tell you something like that if I weren't sure." He wished he could say something to erase the agony from her features.

"How did it happen?" Rose asked in a strained voice.

After letting out a harsh sigh, Louis replied, "Jean Pierre and I separated one week to follow different trails and then meet again in a few days. But instead of his showing up, a trapper we knew came to find me. He had found Jean Pierre's canoe broken in half. It looked as if he had crashed against a big rock in some flooding water. Two mountain men found his body a few hundred yards downstream and buried him."

"I'm going to go talk to those men. They buried some-one else," Rose said. The determination in her voice left no doubt of her intentions. "Jean Pierre can't be dead, Louis, or I would have sensed it. He just can't be dead. When will Jarrette get here?"

"He shouldn't be far behind me, but, Rose, dear, there's no need for anyone to go. His body is buried. You'd freeze out there in the wilderness with all the snow and ice. The distance is too great."

"I'm going," Rose stated emphatically. She got out of bed and began to rummage for suitable clothing. "As soon as Jarrette comes, we'll leave."

Louis knew his arguments were in vain. He had learned from Jean Pierre that when Rose made up her mind, she wouldn't change it without good cause. Maybe when Jarrette came, he could—

But Jarrette burst into the cabin just then, halting Louis's thought, and he listened with disbelief to Jarrette's willingness to believe Rose's need to search for Jean Pierre.

"All right," Louis said after the two who had grown up as twins had made their plans. "You're not going off without me. At least I know the site, and I've traveled that way several times." He turned to Rose. "I'll see what I have in my pack that you can wear to keep from freezing." Then to Jarrette, who seemed as grief-stricken and helpless as Rose, he said, "Got tell Lela and Dr. David what's going on, then get supplies from the trading post and saddle Rose's horse. We'll leave within the hour."

After Jarrette went to do as directed, Louis went outside and came back with his pack, followed by a concerned Dr. David. Louis took out some of his buckskin clothing, a fur coat and hat, and finally a pair of small fur-lined boots he had purchased from an Indian as a gift for Celeste. Rose was lost in the big clothes, but she seemed not to notice.

At a tearful Lela's suggestion, Rose packed all the cooked food in the cabin to go with all that Lela had brought. Within an hour she was ready to go, bidding farewell to her upset friends.

The somber-faced trio rode out of the fort and turned northwest. Jarrette wore a savage look of sorrow; Rose's face showed shock and grim determination; Louis would have felt better if she had cried.

Chapter Nineteen

Riding at a mad pace for days, with stops only at darkness, the trio finally reached their destination—the cabin by the lake belonging to the mountain men who had found the body in the river. Both big and brawny with bushy beards, they introduced themselves as John Greer and Jeremiah Mullins.

Rose, Louis, and Jarrette sat around the crude table and listened as John and Jerimiah answered their questions about Jean Pierre. As they talked, Rose's initial glimmer of hope faded. Their story was identical to the one Louis had told her as he had heard it from the trapper. Their description of the mutilated man they had buried matched Jean Pierre's.

"Yes," Louis assured Rose when she questioned, "both Jean Pierre and I let our beards grow while trapping."

John Greer went to the far side of the room, rummaged around in a chest, then came back to Rose. When she saw her necklace lying in his big rough hand, she gasped.

"We found this in the pocket of his breeches, but nothing else on him," the man said in a sad voice. "Everything must have washed downstream."

With a giant lump in her throat, Rose held out a trembling hand and took the piece of jewelry. The radiance of the stone seemed diminished. She lay her head in her arms; her body heaved in uncontrollable sobs. No longer could she hope that the man they had buried was someone else.

She was vaguely aware of Jarrette's guiding her to one of the bunks near the fireplace and tenderly removing her

262

wet boots. When he covered her with a soft bearskin and then sat holding her hand until the sobs no longer racked her body, she longed to tell him of her gratitude for his being with her, but found the blackness washing over her too welcome to dispel with her voice.

That night, as well as the long journey back to Fort Arkansas, was a nightmare. Rose was emotionally empty, having lost the will to live. She ate only at Jarrette's and Louis's persistence, often unaware of the time of day. When they finally reached her cabin, she somehow remembered, before the men left to bed down the horses, to thank them for taking her to the North Wilderness. Denying the need for further company, or help, she crept wearily into bed.

As soon as the news of Rose's return reached her friends at the fort, they came to call, but none could encourage her to eat, to talk, or even to get out of bed. Even Captain Alveraz, who had ignored her after she rebuffed him so effectively during her first weeks there, came to see her and offer condolences, while Jarrette and Lela looked on. The wives of the three other trappers came together more than once, their faces showing private fears as their voices strove to offer comfort.

Lela forced her to drink water, but even she was unable to persuade Rose to allow her to brush her hair or make her more comfortable. Sometimes in sleep and sometimes in a trancelike state, she lay with her eyes closed. The few times she did open her eyes, the pupils narrowed into pinpoints, seemingly afloat in the blue pools of pain.

On the third day of Rose's self-imposed isolation, Lela came over earlier than usual. She came directly to the bed and sat down.

"Honey, the supply soldiers come in yesterday. Jarrette asked me to bring this letter to you. You're being awful mean to your brother, not to let him do any more than keep water in the cabin and the fireplace going."

At first Rose seemed not to have heard. Then, as if with a great effort, she opened her eyes. Slowly the pupils grew, and, with difficulty, Rose turned toward Lela and focused on the beloved face. Still almost as pale as her face, her parched lips moved, but made no intelligible sound. Only after Lela had given her a few sips of water could she speak.

"Oh, Lela, I'm no good to anybody," Rose said hoarsely. "I think of how I never realized what a fine man I married until his last time here. And then I dream the most horrible dreams—an old witch cackles and points her finger, and then snarling animals chase me. When I look back, I see only their teeth—big old teeth before a fire. I'm screaming for Jean Pierre, but he can't reach me for the walls of thick flowers. Sometimes I think I'm losing my mind."

"Why don't you open your letter?" Lela asked, her eyes bright with sympathy. She held up the letter from Maman.

Rose took it, surprised that she seemed to gain strength from its touch. Eagerly she read: Marie wrote that everyone was well and that they had missed their grown children at Christmas. When would they be coming home?

Rose sat up and reached for her robe, knowing what she had to do. "Lela, could you find Jarrette and tell him I want to see him?" At Lela's dubious expression, she added, "I'm all right now. I've gotten a hold on myself."

Jarrette smiled to see Rose sitting before the fireplace and pulled a chair close to hers.

"Can you take me home?" she asked. "Lela says the supply train came yesterday, and they usually return within a few days. Couldn't we travel along with them, even in the snow?"

"We surely can, little sister. I've already asked a scout to let Arlee know I'd not be back because I needed to look after you. He'll understand."

Within a short time, they made plans.

Soon after Jarrette left, Lela came. She was crestfallen to hear that Rose would be leaving so soon. "Family is what you need, though," she soothed. "You're lucky to have one to go to."

Early the next morning, Louis came to tell her that he was leaving to go to the various pickup stations to collect

Jean Pierre's and his pelts before he returned to bayou country.

"I'll stop by when I do come home. Godspeed, Rose," Louis said. "I share your grief . . . because I loved him, too. I know Jean Pierre and you shared a special love."

"We did, yes," she agreed in a husky voice. "I guess we must have loved each other from childhood, but we had a lot to overcome because of it. Not until Christmas did we really express our love. I'll cherish those times with him forever—they were the finest—and will be the finest of all my life."

"Perhaps as you told me when you learned of Arlene's—"

"No," Rose broke in, shaking her head. "Nothing you or anyone can say will help, and I have no faith that even time will ease my ache. Don't say any more, please."

His face sober, Louis left.

The next few days were filled with hurried activity. Rose packed her clothing and personal belongings, weeping as she lovingly folded Jean Pierre's clothes, occasionally lifting them to her face to catch the manly scent that still lingered.

"Rose, may I come in?" a familiar voice called.

"Please do, Dr. David." She held open the door and stepped back for him to enter. "Sit down and have some coffee."

She filled two mugs from the pot sitting at the edge of the fireplace. Ever since Maman's letter had jolted Rose back into reality, she had returned to her old habits. The unsettling dreams hadn't stopped, but she no longer let them weigh her down so heavily. Her hair shone and was arranged becomingly in a low chignon. Although she had chosen to wear nothing but the dark skirts and simple blouses brought from Louisiana, she appeared clean and neat. The simplicity of her attire and hairstyle enhanced her fragile beauty.

"Rose, I want to say goodbye to you alone." He looked at her with serene gray eyes half-hidden behind his long lashes as they sat at the table to drink their coffee. "Things won't be the same here without you. I've been thinking about returning to Mobile when the snow melts. I feel it's time for me to get on with my former life."

"That's good news, though heaven only knows what this area will do without you. You're a good doctor."

"It was easy; I had a good assistant. There'll be someone coming to take my place." He stared into his mug for several minutes, then raised his eyes to meet hers. He saw how the strain of the past weeks had caused faint smudges to appear underneath the blue eyes with their bottled-up grief. Her lips still lacked their usual pinkness. "I wish your leaving was for a happier reason."

"Thank you, Dr. David. You've been a dear friend to me, and I'll remember you always for your kindness."

Abruptly he got up from his chair. "You'll always be special to me, too. Let me know if I can help you in any way." Then he was gone.

Not long afterward, Jarrette rapped on the door and came inside. "Can you be ready to leave at dawn with the soldiers?"

"I'm all packed," Rose assured him.

The three close friends stood outside Rose's cabin in the predawn hush the next morning, waving to Jarrette and Rose as they rode out of the fort. Jarrette led two pack horses loaded with his furs and Rose's belonging. She waved to Lela, Juan, and Dr. David until tears filled her eyes and she could no longer see.

She turned in the saddle and urged Beauty to follow the soldiers southward. With a heart that felt full and yet strangely empty at the same time, she lifted her chin and headed home. Even Rose was aware that the young woman who had made the journey up was not the same one making the return trip. She longed only to reach Maman and Papa and the others and steep herself in their quiet, loving care. Thoughts beyond that need refused to form, seemed unimportant. She prayed that life would create its own pattern for her once she reached home.

The first week on the trail became a clouded memory when Rose tried to recall it later. She remembered the snow that reached to the knees of the horses and the leafless trees covered in ice, creating crystal chandeliers as the bright sun splashed golden beams across the mountains. Seeing no beauty in the surroundings, she compared the frigid desolation to the empty feelings in her heart.

The soldiers were respectful and Jarrette was always near, kind and considerate. Even with his half-hearted attempts to tease, he was unable to bring her out of the doldrums for any length of time.

The weather became warmer as they traveled farther south; soon they were able to remove their heavy coats in the middle of the days. As they came nearer Natchitoches, they saw dogwood trees and early wildflowers in full bloom. They rested a full day in the bustling town that held so many memories for her. The streets and the buildings were the same, but new faces greeted Rose. Ma Dibert was the only person whom she knew and talked to. In response to Rose's questions, Ma told her that Mimi was still in New Orleans, not planning to return to Fort Natchitoches.

"That no-good Thom Keller will never marry her," Ma said with feeling. "She wrote me not long ago that she's pregnant. She sounded so pitiful and alone, I could've died." Tears welled in her sad eyes.

"I'm sorry—for all of you," said Rose, her own grief enabling her to share that of the distraught mother.

"She works at a hotel, and it sounds as if he no longer travels. He's been telling her he's expecting to get rich just any day, and the poor child seems to believe him. Lord only knows what'll happen to her."

Ma's expressions of sorrow at hearing of Jean Pierre's death were sincere. Rose accepted her tributes silently, her grief too new to handle easily.

After their short rest, the party left on the final leg of their trip. Although Rose and Jarrette were eager to get home, they dreaded what must be told.

Her first sight of Attakapas stirred Rose. Her heart was pounding as they rounded a curve in the levee road and came upon the familiar Commons. The tall steeple of the church pointing toward the feathery clouds seemed to promise a peace that was unobtainable elsewhere. The memories of the Saturday-night gatherings and Mardi Gras, and even the now-nostalgic memories of her marriage, crowded her thoughts. What a foolish girl she'd been not to have seen then that what gnawed at both Jean Pierre and her was repressed love. Tears filled her eyes as they rode by slowly.

From the path following the Bayou Teche, Rose saw friends and neighbors in the fields planting the spring crops. She confided to Jarrette that she was glad they were all too far away to recognize them, as she wasn't yet ready to face them. Now that she was so close, Rose became impatient to reach home and coaxed Beauty to move faster.

"Jarrette," she said, "I dread facing Maman and Papa, don't you? Telling them about Jean Pierre's death will be a hard thing, yes? They loved him so much." Jarrette nodded.

The Guilbeau farm lay ahead, and Rose strained to see if some of the family might be outside. Making out a figure near a pile of burning brush at the back of the fields, she wondered if it might be Papa clearing new ground for future use. Some crops had already been planted, for sparse vegetation was visible, causing the fields in the distance to appear green. Cattle grazed in the pasture near the house. She saw a thin spiral of smoke coming from the chimney but didn't see anyone outside. Her pulse raced as they turned their horses off the levee road, slipping and sliding down the embankment.

Before Rose had time to dismount, Robert came running around the house yelling, "Jarrette, Rose!" He ran to her first, almost pulling her from the saddle. By the time her feet touched the ground, he was in her arms. "Where's Jean Pierre?"

"Robert," Rose said in a choked voice. She held him tightly. Her heart almost skipped a beat when she saw how much he resembled Jean Pierre. "It's so good to see you again. Where's Maman?"

At that moment she saw Marie and Yvette running toward her. Grandmère hurried from the porch with a tremulous smile. Rose ran to meet them, grabbing first one, then another, hugging and kissing them amid tears of joy and fresh sorrow.

"Oh, it's been so long since I've seen you. I missed you all so."

Only after Rose's trembling had ceased did Marie pull away from her grasp. With a reassuring pat on Rose's shoulder and a slap at the tears on her own cheeks, Marie walked to meet Jarrette and hug him close. "Where's Jean Pierre?"

Jarrette turned then to thank the soldiers and offer them food, but they refused, obviously eager to leave the upcoming scene, and rode toward New Orleans.

After Pierre saw the travelers and joined his family there in the yard, the entire story was told in bits and pieces. Rose talked and cried; Jarrette took over then, until he too choked up.

"I'm sorry, my child. I'm sorry for everything, but it's good to see you," Pierre said when all was told and digested. He gently patted Rose's hair. "Go ahead and cry."

Pierre released Rose only when Marie blew her nose and announced with a semblance of her old self, "Let's go inside and have a cup of coffee."

Obeying without a word, all trudged inside. They sat around the big table in their customary chairs with mugs of coffee laced with hot milk. As Rose glanced around the familiar room, Jean Pierre's vacant spot across the table loomed big and oppressive. She averted her eyes from its emptiness as she answered new, coherent questions about his death in a detached manner. Her tears seemed to have spent themselves. She told them of her trip northwest with Jarrette and Louis to talk to the mountain men who had found the body crushed against the rocks and then buried it. Their eyes fell on her necklace as she recounted its role in the tragedy; Rose explained how she had insisted he take it with him that last day. When they seemed satisfied that they had heard all the unpleasant facts, Marie stood up, her face wan and strained.

"We'll have more coffee, yes?" she asked.

"Yes, I will, Maman." Rose held up her mug for Marie

to refill from the large pot. "I've missed your Cajun coffee."

"Here, Rose." Marie poured hot milk into a cup and pushed the sugar bowl toward her. "You've gotten too thin. I'll have to fatten you up and get that pretty color back in your cheeks. Drink that, and then you should go take a nap. You look tired."

"Yes, I am. I've slept in a bed only a few nights this last month." She didn't add that each night brought the nightmarish dream filled with fierce, gnashing teeth and flames that tried to sear her. Had it been only a month since the news of Jean Pierre's death? It seemed an eternity.

Rose emptied her mug and went to the bedroom she had shared with Yvette. She bathed in the water that someone had poured into the wooden tub, then donned a nightdress and lay down on her bed. Although she felt bone weary, memories of the cabin at Fort Arkansas and all she had shared there with Jean Pierre raced through her mind. Their wonderful week at Christmas haunted her anew. How could she live without him? Exhausting herself with her thoughts, she fell into fitful slumber. That afternoon, the recurring dream was less frightening, with a single large tooth coming to life and chasing her into a flower bush. But the old witch was still in the shadows, pointing her finger and mumbling.

Easing back into the routine at home, Rose set the table that night for supper. Tearfully, she returned to the cupboard a plate meant for Jean Pierre. She had taken it out without thinking, her body feeling as dull and drained as her mind. After the meal was finished and the dishes were cleaned and put away, the family sat and talked in hushed voices.

Rose and Jarrette caught up on all the happenings of the relatives and neighbors. Yvette and Robert sat by Rose's side, hanging on her every word, until Robert fell asleep with his head in her lap. It was late when Grandmère bade all good-night and asked Jarrette to take the sleeping Robert to bed. Soon afterward, Yvette, her young face much too sad, announced that she was going to her room to say special prayers.

Before long, all except two had made their way to their beds. Rose and Pierre sat alone in the big kitchen.

"I guess I'll turn in also, Papa." Leaving her chair, she walked to his rocker. She bent to kiss him, her hand ruffling his hair just a bit, as had always been her custom.

"Could I talk with you awhile longer?" Pierre asked in a weary voice. He still held his pipe, though it had long been out. She saw that he looked far older than when she had left him eleven months ago and realized he had been unusually quiet since Jarrette and she had come home that morning. Jean Pierre's death had taken its toll on him already, Rose thought. He had been loved by so many.

"Certainly, Papa." She sat back down, pulling her chair closer and facing him.

Pierre fidgeted in his chair, his eyes fixed on his pipe. "I'm sorry that what I ordered has burdened you with the grief you've had this year. I may have made the decision for you and Jean Pierre to marry in too much haste."

"You didn't force me to marry. I could have refused." Her heart wrenched to see his once straight and proud carriage slumped now like that of an old man.

"No, you've always been an obedient daughter. You wouldn't have refused me. I suspected from your letters, even though you never wrote it, that you weren't happy. I'm truly sorry, my child." Papa put his head in his hands.

Rose knelt on the floor and took his gnarled hands in hers. She looked into his eyes. "You gave me the happiest moments of my life by setting up my marriage to Jean Pierre. It didn't begin that way, but that was mostly my fault. I finally found out that Jean Pierre was the good and gentle man that you told me he was. I realized I loved him dearly, and I thank you for that." For a minute the remembered joy of being his wife flooded her face and brought a sparkle to her eyes. In her heart, she would always be Jean Pierre's wife.

Pierre took her head between his hands and kissed her on the forehead, reassured by the look that had illumined her features. "A heavy weight has been lifted from my shoulders by hearing you speak those words." A half-hearted smile replaced some of the agony on his face.

"Good-night, Papa. Sleep well." She moved away.

"And the same for you, daughter." The weight of guilt had lifted, even though the loss of the one he would always consider his first child must be endured.

The next few weeks demanded much from Rose. One day while making herself go through Jean Pierre's papers and belongings left at the cabin, she came upon the song he had composed for her. At first she dropped it as though it were hot, but she couldn't leave it alone. It was the next day before she could bear to read it without choking up. By the third day, she could not only read it, but could sing it without her eyes tearing. She found the dulcimer and began hunting for the right notes, gaining some measure of comfort as she slowly made progress.

To help pass her spare time she had begun to read from the bookshelf in the kitchen. She wrote letters to Lela at Fort Arkansas, hoping the soldiers would keep their promise to stop by Opelousas, farther up-bayou from Attakapas, on all the treks north to pick them up and deliver them. After persuading Marie to help her get Pierre's approval, Rose finally gained a day alone in her old pirogue. With her letters to those at Fort Arkansas and Marie's shopping list in her pocket, she set out for Attakapas. After depositing the letters at the trading post for relay to Opelousas, she planned to visit with the kindly Father Sebastian. On several occasions he had offered her the use of his library, and she had read everything at home more than once.

That morning, for the first time since Jean Pierre's death, Rose had taken pains with her toilette. She wore the pink-flowered dress in which Jean Pierre had last seen her. A matching ribbon caught the sides of her shining hair in a cluster of curls at her crown, while a second ribbon held the long hair in the back away from her face. The deep violet circles around her eyes had slowly receded, and Marie's tempting dishes had brought back some of the flush to her cheeks, even though she was still too pale and thin to suit her family.

Father Sebastian seemed surprised yet hospitable when

she knocked on his door after concluding her business at the post.

"Strange that you should ask about books today," he said after they had exchanged pleasantries and she had told him why she had come. "I was reading just yesterday in my volumes of English history about some of your ancestors."

"My ancestors?" Rose asked, puzzled at first. Then she remembered and laughed. "Oh, yes, I'm not truly a Gilbeau, am I? You know, Father, I never think of myself any other way."

"I can see why, child. You have become such a vital part of a large and loving family that you don't feel any insecurity." With compassion he added, "And you've had a great shock. Of course I grieve with you over the loss of Jean Pierre." When she made no reply but seemed receptive, he continued, "You're young and healthy, my child. Your life is not over, though the grief over the past few weeks might make you think it is. Have patience. The Lord does not forget those who wait."

When she made no comment, he removed several thick volumes from his well-stocked shelves and Rose eagerly looked over the titles.

"I think I'll like reading about England," she said. "Papa says I should learn about my real father."

"I agree, Rose. Pierre told me your grandfather is Lord Elgin Winstead, Earl of Wanington. I don't know if he's still alive. The Winstead family is mentioned several times in sections on the War of the Roses and even earlier. The title and land came from Edward the First in the thirteenth century." He smiled at the interest gleaming in her blue eyes. "I don't know anything about your mother's people, nor does Pierre. Keep the books as long as you like," he said as he laid them in her arms and bade her farewell.

The next day as Rose sat on the back porch engrossed in one of Father Sebastian's history books, she glimpsed a pirogue loaded with furs easing into the private slip. Her heart leaped into her throat as she jumped out of her chair, letting the book fall to the floor. She was halfway across the yard before she remembered it couldn't be Jean Pierre.

She slowed her pace to a fast walk, slowing even more when she saw Louis leap from the pirogue and pull it onto the bank.

"Louis! You made it back safely."

"Yes, Rose. How are you?"

They looked at each other with mutual uneasiness, then smiled. On their way to the house to visit with the family, Louis caught her up on news from Fort Arkansas. "Lela and Juan have left by now for his new assignment in Mexico City. They sent their best wishes," Louis said. He saw a faint glimmer of happiness on her face. "And Dr. David will leave for Mobile as soon as his replacement gets there."

"I miss them all so. I'm glad Lela and Juan will be in Mexico City. That's a place she longed to see. And I'm happy to learn that Dr. David will be going back to his home and friends in Mobile. Those days at Fort Arkansas were some of the happiest of my life. Nothing will ever be the same again."

"I'm here now," he teased. As he looked into her sad face, his heart tugged at him. "You know I would give my arm to make you happy, don't you?"

"Thank you, Louis." She noted his somber eyes. "Nobody will ever fill Jean Pierre's place in my heart."

"I understand," he replied. They were almost to the porch when he said, "Celeste's birthday is in a couple of weeks. Will you be coming down with Jarrette? I'm sure he's already been calling and knows all about whatever is planned."

"You're right about that. Jarrette and Celeste seem to find all kinds of reasons to get together. But . . ." Her eyes clouded and her lips pursed. "But as for me, I'm not ready for a party."

"Actually," Louis said with honesty, "I need to discuss business with you, the business concerning Jean Pierre's and my pelts. By the time of the party, I'll have all my facts and figures together." When she still hesitated, he added, "We need to get everything settled; you know that."

Rose sighed, then agreed. She would go to Grenfall

with Jarrette within a couple of weeks. Memories of that visit nearly a year ago tried to haunt her, even as Louis followed her inside the house to visit with everyone before going down-bayou to his home.

Chapter Twenty

On a sunny June afternoon, Rose sat in the porch swing reading the books on England that Father Sebastian had loaned her. It was quiet time for the Guilbeau household, but she had no desire to nap; the unsettling dreams had a way of coming to her even in daytime sleep.

At the sound of an approaching horse, she looked up from her book. Whoever it was, she mused, was too well dressed to be one of the neighbors.

"Mrs. Rose Guilbeau, may I join you?" a booming, accented voice called as the horse headed toward the porch.

Jarrette came from the side of the house then, his eyes measuring the big man. "Get down, sir," he invited, going to help the stranger tether his horse. "What can I do for you?"

They introduced themselves and spoke privately for a few minutes before Jarrette walked with him to the porch.

"Rose," Jarrette said, "this is Beau Bradford, a lawyer from England who has come to see you on business. He says you might remember him from Natchitoches."

By this time Beau had removed his hat, and Rose recognized the blond giant of a man who had grabbed her up from the muddy street and carried her on his horse to the board walk. With a polite nod, she watched him sit upon a chair Jarrette pulled near the swing.

After Jarrette joined her in the swing, she asked, "What business do you have with me, Mr. Bradford?"

"I came to meet your family and to talk to you," Beau said. "I met your husband in Natchitoches, and we became friends." He smiled across at her.

"He never mentioned meeting you." A puzzled look claimed her face. "What would we have to talk about?" She turned to Jarrette for reassurance. "As for meeting the family, everyone except my brother and me is either working in the fields or resting."

Beau's tone was solemn when he answered, "I'm a friend of Louis's and I stopped by Grenfall on the way here to get directions to your father's house. Louis told me about Jean Pierre's death. I'm terribly sorry. I took a liking to him the minute we met."

That Jean Pierre hadn't mentioned meeting Beau puzzled her. But so much had happened in Natchitoches, she recalled—that dreadful encounter with Thom Keller and . . . She cast aside bad memories. "Thank you for your condolences."

"I'll get straight to the point, Mrs. Guilbeau. As Jarrette told you, I'm a barrister by profession." She nodded as Beau continued. "Your husband hired me to find out all I could about your family still living in England, and, since my father and I have a law firm back home not far from where the Winsteads live, he sent me a world of information." He watched a spark of interest jump in the pretty blue eyes and saw Jarrette's earlier wariness subside.

"My husband really was a most remarkable man, wasn't he?" Her face glowed with pleasure. "I wonder why he didn't tell me he was asking you to find out about my family. He knew I had no wish to be anything more than a Cajun."

"He told me he thought you'd want to know someday, but I guess he didn't want to disappoint you if I couldn't learn anything. He seemed to think you'd want to meet them, see where your family came from. Guess he wanted to make sure you stayed in Louisiana because you chose to."

Rose hugged Jean Pierre's thoughtfulness to her heart

for a while as Jarrette and she swung back and forth lazily there on the porch. "I don't care to go there and meet them." Her heart ached anew at the thought that she'd taken too long to recognize what a fine young man she'd married.

"But you'd like to hear what the man has learned, wouldn't you?" Jarrette asked.

"Of course," she replied. "Tell me, Mr. Bradford."

"It seems that my father served as barrister to your aunt Rosalinde over the years, before I left the Inns of Court and joined him. When she died, there was a letter from Pierre Guilbeau telling of the birth of Rosalind Margaret Winstead in Baltimore, Maryland, in June of 1757. Also there were the reports of the deaths of your mother, father, and brother. By the time the aunt responded, no Guilbeaus could be found around Baltimore, and no one seemed to know where they had gone. Only when your aunt died did all this come to light, for she left you a legacy. It seems she was the only family member remaining loyal to your father after he married your mother and came to the colonies. My father was planning to have me locate the missing heiress—and here you were all the time. There are funds to pay your passage to England, and I'm to escort you—if you'll agree to come."

"Missing heiress!" Rose exclaimed, turning to share her surprise with Jarrette. "Why would I receive a legacy from any of the Winsteads? I never heard of my real father until a year ago, and I understood he had been disinherited."

"I don't have all the details, but I do know you have an inheritance waiting in England."

"What sort of inheritance?" Rose asked, darting looks of disbelief from Jarrette to the Englishman.

"There's some valuable jewelry for you that has been in the Winstead family for generations," he told her.

Rose mused in silence. Turning finally to Beau, she said, "I'm not interested in the jewelry. I never knew my Winstead relatives. I had a happy childhood as a Guilbeau and have no desire to see a family who would disown a son because he chose to marry for love."

Beau said patiently, "We English have our ways of

handling our affairs, and just because they differ from your ways doesn't make them wrong. The property belongs to you, and this matter needs to be cleared up for the records, if for no other reason. Since there was plenty of money advanced for your expenses to make the trip and I'm planning to return home anyway, why don't you consider going to England and at least seeing it before making up your mind?'' To see someone so unaffected by her birthright and fortune as to show no selfish interest made Beau's admiration for her soar. No doubt she knew who she was and accepted that knowledge without qualms.

Long after Rose and Jarrette had ushered Beau inside to meet the others, he lingered. He explained his mission to the entire family, beginning with his initial meeting with Jean Pierre. Rose listened attentively to Beau's persuasive arguments concerning the importance of making the trip to England before signing away her legacy there. Pierre and Marie, as well as Jarrette, asked pertinent questions but were noncommittal about their views concerning Rose's visit to England.

Beau leaned back in his chair and said, ''Mr. Guilbeau, as a barrister, I advise you to encourage Rose to make this trip. I've had no luck doing so, and I hate to see her lose something of value now and regret it later. I promise to take very good care of her, and I invite Jarrette to come along.''

''If Jean Pierre trusted you, Beau,'' Jarrette said, ''then I've no qualms about doing the same, do you, Papa?''

Pierre knocked the cold ashes from the pipe he had been holding, then noted the apprehensive look on Marie's face before agreeing with Jarrette. ''I feel sure you'd look out for her, Beau. Rose is an adult now and has proven since her return to be capable of making her own decisions. We wish her only happiness, but we're selfish enough to hope that it's found here with us.''

Beau nodded. ''I understand.'' He glanced at Rose as he continued, ''I've made arrangements to sail on the *Talisman* leaving New Orleans in a few weeks for Portsmouth. Mr. Brearde has business in the capital this week and says

there'll be room in his carriage." His gaze lingered on
Rose. "There would be plenty of room for another."

Rose looked thoughtful, then turned to him. "I'm refusing your kind offer. My happiness is here with my family."
She saw the concerned expressions on the loving faces
relax and smooth into those of satisfaction.

The Guilbeaus walked outside to bid Beau farewell,
then went inside to eat gumbo and talk about the strange
ways of Fate.

On the day of Celeste's party, Jarrette and Rose placed
their portmanteaux in his pirogue and left for the Breardes's
plantation. They reached Grenfall in record time and were
soon walking the smooth graveled path at the side of the
carefully tended gardens leading to the side door. Rose
was glad they were not using the front walk; she had no
desire to get close to the pergola where Phillip had attacked
her. She admired the beautiful roses in bloom, the neatly
trimmed boxwood, and the graceful azaleas. Her mind
wandered back to the weekend of Celeste's other birthday
party. Had it been just a year ago? So much had happened
since then that it seemed almost a lifetime ago, and the
arrival at Grenfall had been the beginning. A tiny shiver
rushed over her. She scolded herself for ever having given
the old woman's prophecy a second thought. Certainly the
part about the "lifetime of love" had been a lie. And the
rest of it made no more sense.

Louis welcomed them at the door and gave instructions
to a young black woman to place their belongings in the
bedrooms they would occupy. The three stood talking in
the front foyer.

"Jarrette!" Celeste ran down the curved staircase, holding up the front of her pale green skirt to free her feet, the
back trailing several steps behind her. Rose turned to see
Jarrette watching the young woman descend the stairs. He
stood as if transfixed, his eyes wide and staring, his mouth
not quite closed. Jarrette took a step in Celeste's direction
as she reached the foyer and raced to him with outstretched
arms. She ignored the hand Jarrette extended and threw
her arms around his neck and kissed his cheek.

"Celeste," Louis said, with a knowing smile at Rose, "kindly remember you're supposed to be a young lady. Plus you have another guest to welcome. Papa would be very upset."

"Papa's not here just now, Louis." Her eyes danced up at Jarrette, and her full lips seemed poised for a kiss.

When they saw Jarrette encircle Celeste with his arms and place his lips on hers, Louis and Rose turned toward the sitting room. Before they had time to be seated in the beautifully appointed room, Celeste rushed in, followed closely by Jarrette. She ran to Rose and embraced her.

"Rose, I was so sorry to hear about Jean Pierre. Will you forgive me for being selfish just now? I was so happy to see Jarrette again after not seeing him for a whole week that I just clean forgot my manners." Celeste released Rose and took her hand. Her beautiful dark eyes held genuine concern.

"Oh, think nothing of it, Celeste." She let a faint smile of remembering light her face. "I don't think my brother could have waited any longer."

Obviously relieved to have the serious part of the greeting behind her, Celeste moved to the ornate bell pull near the double doors and gave it a yank, talking animatedly to the visitors until the tinkling brass bell summoned a parlor slave. As casually as she would have requested a drink of water, Celeste asked that high tea be served.

"And bring some man-sized sandwiches, too," she added with a gracious smile toward Jarrette and Louis.

By the time the foursome had reduced the once lovely tray to a wasteland of crumbs and soiled cups and saucers, Jarrette and Celeste were deep in conversation on the apricot brocade sofa with its arched back edged by carved rosewood. They seemed to have forgotten that others were present. From their comfortable velvet armchairs placed side by side at one end of the tea table, Louis and Rose found a stopping place in their own conversation about Fort Arkansas.

Louis stood and said, "Jarrette, Rose and I are going to

my office now to discuss the sale of Jean Pierre's and my furs. If you'd care to join us——"

"Not unless you need me to, Rose," Jarrette replied, watching her face carefully.

"No, no," Rose insisted. "I can send for you if I have questions Louis can't answer."

Sending a wink at his sister, Louis said to Jarrette, "I gather Celeste and you will keep each other entertained."

"Fine, Louis." Jarrette scarcely looked up as he answered, having eyes only for the vivacious Celeste.

Rose followed Louis down the long hall and into a handsomely appointed office. Before walking around to his own chair behind the desk, he seated her in a comfortable leather chair drawn up close. She watched him take some papers from the drawer and place them on top of the desk. He glanced over one of the pages and held it out to her.

"This is your receipt for the fur sale," Louis said.

After reading over the figures, Rose looked at Louis in surprise, her eyebrows raised. "So much money. I wasn't expecting half that amount."

"I got a good price for them this year." Louis looked down at the papers, shuffling them busily. He extracted an envelope and gave it to her. "This statement is from the bank. It lists prior amounts as well as the last deposit. The trust officer asked me to give it to you."

Rose broke the seal on the envelope and took out the letter. The size of the account shocked her. She knew she wasn't rich by most standards, but the amount seemed adequate for all necessities during her lifetime! Tears formed. Jean Pierre seemed to have thought of everything.

"Thank you for handling the sale, Louis," Rose said when she was certain she could speak without crying. "And for getting the statement for me. Jean Pierre would have been pleased that you've looked out for me."

"I was happy to do it." Louis scrutinized the lovely face before him. "Will you consider taking Jean Pierre's place as my partner? The future looks good for the company we formed a couple of years back."

Amazed at his question, Rose asked, "Your partner? Why would you want me as a partner?"

He paused, wondering how long he would have to wait to tell her what he felt. Putting away the answer he would have liked to give, he said, "You're an intelligent young woman, and I think the arrangement would be beneficial to us both. If you disagree, I'll buy out Jean Pierre's interest."

As her thoughts raced, Rose considered his offer. At length, she questioned all that was involved in buying furs from distant trappers and transporting them to New Orleans. When he told her of the ready markets there, she realized that such a venture might lead to growth. The more they talked, the more she realized that she wanted to hang on to that part of Jean Pierre's world. Dr. David's frequent talks with her and his belief in her ability lent her confidence. There would be no need for her to leave Attakapas, either.

"Louis, if the pelts could be stored in New Orleans, they wouldn't have to be sold as soon as they reached there, would they?" she asked. "They could sit until the demand was higher and the prices went up, couldn't they?"

"A good point," Louis replied. He had known she was quick, but her grasp of the situation intrigued him. "Jean Pierre and I hadn't anticipated the market we found each time we went to sell. Several times this past winter around the campfire, we discussed opening a warehouse."

Rose felt confident that she could learn about the fur trade—and it could be the answer to the dilemma about her future. Smiling now, she stood and held out a hand. "I accept your offer . . . partner."

Louis stood and, ignoring the extended hand, placed his arms around her and held her lightly for a few seconds. "I don't shake hands with pretty associates. I hug them."

As they separated, Rose noticed that the smile on his face was echoed in his dark eyes. How could she have endured the weeks after Jean Pierre's death without Jarrette's and his help?

The contemplative look on Rose's face lent Louis courage. Before the seemingly intimate moment faded, he said, "I'll wait a year before I ask you to marry—"

"No," she interrupted, stepping back, her eyes stormy.

"We're friends and partners, that's all. I can picture no other man in my life but Jean Pierre."

"You once told me that time can heal," he countered.

"I was wrong, Louis. It can't for me."

With an attempt to recapture their earlier closeness, he said, "I know you must be tired and want to freshen up for dinner. We'll dine early and then have entertainment in honor of Celeste's seventeenth birthday." His heart heavy, he summoned Portia and asked her to show Rose to her room.

The room to which Portia escorted Rose was larger and even more beautiful than the one she had stayed in on her first visit to Grenfall. She pushed away hateful memories and lay down on the big bed. Unable to fall asleep, Rose got up and found her dulcimer, plucking and singing softly until she lulled herself into a kind of peace long before it was time to get dressed.

Telling herself that she would manage to get through the evening, Rose put on the elegant black gown Lela had made for her just before she left the fort, its fitted bodice and demure neckline accentuating her diminutive waist. The ruby necklace hung at its accustomed place above her breasts, the rich red stone gleaming against her fair skin. Leaving the fringe of wispy curls springing around her face, she arranged her golden hair in a French twist at the back of her head. She tucked an ornate black comb at the side of the twist, a trick learned from Lela. Before going downstairs, she looked in the mirror and approved the image there: a young woman in mourning for a beloved husband. Jean Pierre's spirit seemed to be with her, to be approving her brave smile.

For some mysterious reason, she no longer dreaded the evening's festivities. With a heart curiously lighter than at any time since receiving the news of Jean Pierre's death, Rose descended the curving staircase.

The huge ballroom at Grenfall was the perfect setting for the large gathering that night, she mused from where she paused in the entry hall. When she saw how beautifully the women were gowned and coiffed, she wondered if they hadn't all taken special measures to appear especially fashionable for this party. Candlelight from the chandeliers danced on lovely necklaces, bracelets, and earrings as the guests mingled and visited before dinner.

Not until Rose and the others were on their way back to the ballroom after dinner, which didn't drag as much as Rose had feared, did she look up to see azalea blooms adorning the crystal chandelier in the entry hall. The sight held her spellbound for a moment, and she couldn't figure out why. Tearing away her gaze when Louis appeared by her side and made some comment, she thought it must be because she had never before seen such a combination of flowers and candles. Everything about Grenfall was impressive, she told herself as she saw the way the gilt-framed mirrors in the ballroom reflected the chandeliers there and seemed to multiply their number. When a startling shiver rushed over her, she wondered why the scene before her affected her so keenly.

Seated beside an attentive Louis across from one of the tall gilt-framed mirrors, Rose could see some of the guests reflected there while they lingered in the entry hall, chattering before coming into the ballroom to find chairs for the upcoming entertainment. She nudged Louis to join her in watching Jarrette and Celeste in the mirror as they paused in the doorway. Engrossed in conversation, they seemed unaware of the striking picture they made. Just as they entered the ballroom, their eyes caught those of the couple watching them in the ornate mirror. All four waved then at those reflections, laughing at their childishness. Soon Jarrette was pulling up chairs for Celeste and himself beside Louis and Rose.

When all were seated, a visiting string quartet performed and won an easy encore, the three sisters and their brother revealing with pleased smiles their obvious delight in having readied an extra number. Then Celeste played a Bach fugue quite admirably on the harpsichord, but demurred when asked for another.

Waiting for the applause to end, Mr. Brearde busied himself behind the harpsichord before walking over to stand near Rose, one hand holding something behind his back.

His hand raised for silence, he said to his guests, "We've been blessed to have such splendid entertainment. Your applause has been generous." When Rose smiled and nodded earnestly to show her agreement, he continued, "As you all may know, I'm a strange old man, and I confess I've done my share of eavesdropping. Contrary to what you've always heard, the vulgar habit can sometimes pay dividends."

Noting the puzzled looks and polite smiles, Mr. Brearde went on, "My reward is that I know Rose Guilbeau has a lovely voice and plays an unusual instrument. I've taken the liberty of having it brought down from her bedroom, and I now request that she honor us with a sample of her talents."

Rose gasped at his words, her face turning a becoming pink at the enthusiastic applause.

"Sit right where you are, my dear," said Mr. Brearde, laying the polished instrument in her hands. "Will you tell us about the song you sing so well—behind closed doors?" With twinkling eyes he included the group in his sly joke at his own eavesdropping and was rewarded with indulgent laughter.

"Rose, would you prefer not to do this?" whispered Louis, concern for her showing in his searching gaze. He was relieved to see her shake her head.

"The instrument is called a dulcimer," Rose began in a small voice. Her hands caressed it, and she seemed to draw strength from the simple movement. In a stronger voice, she went on, "My . . . my husband gave it to me last year at Christmas." All at once, she wanted to share her treasured memory. "He composed the song for me as a part of the gift. It's my greatest treasure." The proud lift of her head heightened her intensity.

All the guests had become silent. As they looked at the lovely girl and digested her words, a dramatic hush fell over the room, and they sat as though bewitched, their eyes riveted on the blond performer. The depth of feeling and the surprising skill with which she sang and played brought tears to quite a few eyes and lumps to several throats:

''Well, dry your eyes and rest your mind.
Whatever tomorrow brings just won't matter
    anymore.
The past is all behind us now;
The lessons have been learned.
And it's time to live like we've never
    done before.
'Cause loving you is such an easy thing
    to do.''

As Rose began the final verse, she lifted her eyes to the mirror across the ballroom, vaguely aware that singing the song had lifted her spirits and made her feel as though Jean Pierre were with her once again. The very air seemed to vibrate with something more than song. As if in a dream, she watched herself in the mirror and then saw, in another part of it, the chandelier reflected from the entry hall. The candles and their flames were not what caught her eye: it was the white blossoms hanging beneath.

How could she sing and play when her mind was being flooded with memories? a part of her wondered. The old woman's prediction—''white flowers under the flame''—had manifested itself! For a moment she glanced at Louis's mirrored image as he sat in profile watching her intently, but for him to be by her side seemed wrong, and she dropped her eyes to the dulcimer. And when she looked again to see the flowers and candles in the mirror, she felt she must be having a recurrence of her haunting dreams. Light reflected off what looked like a tooth high in the shadows of the entry hall, an animal tooth. Part of her mind tried to run away with her thoughts. Could a tooth and a fang be the same? ''Search for the fang,'' went the prophecy. Only this fang she was glimpsing was a single one hanging from a— She snatched her mind back from fantasy.

Then the song ended, and she forced her eyes away from the mirror to acknowledge the warm applause. She had never felt so alive, so vibrant. As though pulled by a magnet, her eyes returned to the mirror, and this time, with lips parted in disbelief, she saw a movement and a full image materialize therein. The dulcimer fell to the floor, and she gasped, afraid to look away, afraid the mirror was playing tricks.

Reflected in the mirror, a handsome, smiling Jean Pierre stood in the wide doorway, his bear-tooth talisman gleaming against his dark sweater, his eyes holding hers with overwhelming intensity. Her hand holding back the cry of love rushing forth, Rose turned her head, eyes wide, questioning, still doubting. And then she was running toward the doorway.

Jean Pierre was real! Those were his arms pulling her close, she exulted, tears streaming unheeded. That was his voice calling her name, all husky and tinged with what sounded like unshed tears. Only his lips could touch hers in that sweet, melting way; only his skin had that delicious scent and warmth. Whose briny tears she tasted mattered not at all. A million prayers balled up into one massive, fervent message of thanks to God. Her beloved was alive. The nightmare of the last few months evaporated in one fleeting instant. Her world was again perfect.

Almost as shaken as Rose, Jean Pierre tightened his arms around her small figure, starving for the feel of her pressed against him, the taste of her honeyed lips with the tangy trace of moist salt. Ending the kiss only because of the gaily chattering audience moving toward them, he rested his cheek on top of the blond curls. With his eyes closed in thanksgiving, he lifted her and swung her slightly, savoring the joyous laughter, the very moment, and filing it in the back of his memory to be recalled as one of the happiest of his life.

Who knew when the well-wishers stepped aside and ushered the near-delirious couple upstairs? So much excited laughter and talk filled the ballroom that two fewer voices chiming in were hardly missed, now that Jean Pierre had given a brief explanation of how he happened to be alive.

Rose turned to Jean Pierre the moment the door clicked shut. Not yet fully believing, she leaned into the welcoming arms and raised her hands to cup the beloved, handsome face, to feel the texture of his olive skin beneath hungry fingertips, to trace the long laugh indentation on his right cheek with a forefinger, and to end up outlining the adoring smile on his well-shaped mouth. When he playfully nipped her finger and held it between his teeth to suck upon it gently, she heard the whisper of her indrawn breath. It was as if she might be absorbing him through the sensitive pores of her fingers.

She could hear her heartbeat singing in her ears and their breaths mingling in the small space between their faces. So close, so real, his dark-brown eyes impaled her on their wondering, worshipful messages. Like some flower wrenched from its life-giving stem and miraculously restored, Rose glowed and blossomed anew in Jean Pierre's arms. Their bodies clung with such tantalizing fierceness that she wondered if they might not already have become one again, even before their lips met there in the privacy of the bedroom.

Jean Pierre sensed Rose's need to drink him in with more than her eyes. After all, he reminded himself, she had believed him dead. As agonizing as it had been for him to recuperate enough from his broken leg to begin the journey back to civilization, he'd not had the double pain of suspecting she was dead. The delicious feel of her curves in his arms and the slow play of her soft fingers about his face created an awesome flurry of sensations dancing inward, downward, throughout each begging cell. His eyes feasted on the upturned face he had sometimes feared he might never live to see again, and his heart and mind recorded that she was more beautiful than he had dared recall.

The bee-stung lips, the top one curving outward in the center in that intriguing way belonging only to Rose, parted into a dazzling smile as Jean Pierre studied his wife. Her eyes bathed his face with heavenly blue adoration. He saw the whirling, tiny black dots within the sapphire depths and heard a little sigh of contentment. When her hands veered to his ears, then on through his hair to his neck, he bent and closed the brief space between their lips.

Achingly hungry, pathetically trembling lips met first in tender explorations. That first kiss in privacy set off a kind of mutual frenzy. Loving lips pressed, retreated, pressed again, nibbled, their ministrations echoing in secretive places within both. And then their lips parted and evolved into voracious, consuming mouths. Tongues came into delicious play, their reclaiming of velvety recesses throwing more fuel on those inner fires begun downstairs when they first saw each other after those grueling months of separation. Arms clutched bodies even closer, though neither had believed such a feat possible. He groaned. She moaned.

"To hell with this," Jean Pierre growled, his mouth moving just enough to speak against love-swollen lips. "I want to rip that black rag off you and see all of you, kiss every spot."

Never letting his eyes waver from those starred, blue orbs, he swooped her up into his arms and carried her to the canopied bed. The steady flame of the candle beside it paled beside the fire of their locked gazes. A mood of exultation swept them up the moment Jean Pierre sat on the bed and fell back with Rose in his arms. Laughing like excited children on a holiday, they sat up.

"Tell me again what you were telling downstairs about how you weren't the one dead in the stream," she begged.

"Later," he replied, letting his eyes rake her with a teasing leer. "I've far better things in mind than to talk."

"Like what, kind sir?" she quipped, fluttering her lashes mockingly and sliding down one shoulder of the black gown.

"No one thinking she's a widow has the right to look so tempting," he muttered, reaching to ease down the other shoulder of the black silk dress and admiring the new expanse of exposed creamy skin. "I've got to get rid of that black." He reached for the back of her gown, but she twisted from his grasp.

"A pox on shirts, is what I say," Rose declared, slipping the buttons from the holes and sliding the garment over his broad shoulders, down his muscled arms. At each uncovered spot, she placed a spate of moist kisses, each action flowing from the flames living down low inside her.

Once his top half was bare, she asked, "Why hide such a magnificent view?"

"Magnificent?" he hooted. "You want to see magnificent?" He was laughing in that gurgling way back in his throat that thrilled her while he turned her and unfastened her gown, then tossed it over the side of the bed without a glance at its destination, saying, "No more black for you." And when the stockings, shoes, underdrawers, and shift met the same fate, he held her at arm's length for a tension-laced moment for a pretended, objective perusal before whispering in a husky bass tone, "There's magnificence!"

"Jean Pierre," she said tremulously, overcome with the need to say the words piling up in her pounding heart, "can you ever know how much I love you . . . how much I longed—"

"Only because I love you and longed in the same way," he cut in to say in a humbled voice. With a deft step down from the bed, he shed the remainder of his clothing, loving the way she watched him, the way her eyes swept his nakedness and stamped each part with worshipful approval.

"Come to me," she murmured, surprised that a swelling in her throat kept growing, even now that they were alone and she could actually believe he was alive. Alive! *Oh, God,* she breathed, *he's truly alive.* Her eyes invited, revealed what burned inside; her arms reached out.

Jean Pierre didn't know if he trembled on the outside, but he knew he was a quivering mass on the inside when he accepted Rose's invitation. Mesmerized by her loveliness, exalted by her open show of love and desire for him, he enfolded her in his arms there on the bed, losing his breath in a flurry of heartbeats at the remembered feel of her softness melding up and down against his flesh. A sound pulsated in his throat when he once more laid claim to her mellifluous mouth and began the dreamed-of rediscovery of her enticing body. There were the twin mounds of luscious flesh, he exulted, his hands worshipful, his groin swelling with need too long denied.

With her heartbeat roaring in her ears, Rose kissed him back with answering passion, gifted her hands with license to rove over the powerful, muscled form belonging to her man, the one she had feared lost to her forever. Were there any heavenly bodies in the sky that sailed about only half-alive, as she had done the past months? She felt she had been an entity suddenly cut in two upon learning of Jean Pierre's death. But now, she rejoiced as his hands caressed her belly and hips with the mark of ownership, teased her willing thighs and threatened to invade the burning core of her womanhood, she sensed that she was soon to become whole again. Every pore celebrated and begged at the same time.

Endearments half-spoken fell sweetly in the bedroom, washing out and floating back like waves on a gentle seashore. The candle sputtered a time or two, then went out, as if it might have known its glow added nothing to the scene of the reunited husband and wife and so went ahead and died from pure shame. A night breeze whispered through the open windows and caressed the curtains, the sound as intimate as the lovers' soft sighs of reunion. Only the moonlight dared remain and rejoice with the two lost in a passionate embrace.

And when Jean Pierre could no longer refrain from coming home to Rose in that way of loving man and wife, he returned to her masterfully, boldly, almost fiercely, somewhat like the separated celestial bodies she had earlier wondered about might have done had they sighted their severed parts whizzing by and dared not pass up the chance to become whole again. The grieving half of a being had been sundered from its weeping other half and was now being welcomed back in pulsating rhythm. Laboring from the wonder of it all, Jean Pierre's heart poured great floods of joy through every vein, floods inundating his mind and senses as never before.

The glory of their rejoining fully warmed Rose's heart and soul with majesty and awe. She opened to receive him with equal torrents of violent need, welcoming him in the way he desired, clinging to his broad back in appreciation for his return. Only now, she realized as they moved as one to culminate their wild reunion, only now was she herself again.

Both Rose's and Jean Pierre's thoughts skipped upon a visiting moonbeam then, leaving only their senses to continue the dizzying journey far beyond the source of that soft light. A tingling burst of pure joy caught them up high in the heavens, quivered for an exalted moment in perfect ecstasy, then hurled them with exquisite agony back to the real world of moist, weak bodies, of languorous arms, legs, lips, of panting breaths.

"I've come home to you, my Cajun Rose," he whispered in a soft velvety tone, long after they were spent but still joined. His head had found its favored resting spot against her shoulder, while a hand at her satiny breast recorded her rapid heartbeat.

"I know," she replied, her breath feathering across the top of his ear beside her, her hands marveling at the muscles on his back, her heart overflowing with love. "I'll never need another blessing."

Satiated, still clasped intimately in each other's arms, they welcomed the unrequested benediction of sleep.

Long afterward—sometime before dawn—the lovers roused, eager to learn all about each other's activities since their dismal separation. When Jean Pierre told Rose what she had done in the ballroom the night before when she realized he was truly alive and there at Grenfall, she laughed but questioned his account. She couldn't remember screaming and jumping from her chair and meeting him halfway into the ballroom. What she did remember was how glorious it felt to know he was alive and to be in his arms, and she figured it was unimportant how she had reached that haven.

"Mr. Brearde showed uncommon good sense when he announced right away that he thought we might prefer to come up to our room to be alone," Jean Pierre said, a hand smoothing the pale cloud of hair, his lips planting warm kisses along her temple. Her fragrance seeped into his very soul, satisfying a longing he hadn't identified before that moment. In the half-light, her eyes appeared dark, mysterious—utterly captivating, he realized. Intriguing shadows brushed the gentle slopes of her silken cheeks, the sides of her straight little nose, the upturned corners of her mouth. He felt his heart speeding up.

"Isn't he a nice man?" How heavenly to wake up and find she hadn't dreamed their joyful reunion, she mused.

"Yeah, he is, but what in hell was Louis doing sitting by you and watching you sing as though he owned you?" His voice deepened with strong feeling. Holding her there in the bed seemed, all at once, not enough to convince him that she was still all his. He refused to acknowledge that jealousy led him.

"Don't start off being obstinate, Jean Pierre," she said, amused just a little at his quick-rising jealousy. "Louis is my friend as well as yours. And I was singing the song you wrote for me, wasn't I?"

"I may be a dumb Cajun, but I know the looks he—"

"What difference does it make now? You're here, and you know I love only you. Please believe me when I say Louis has been a dear and good friend to me, but that's all." Soft fingers caressed his solemn face, tracking up to the heavy eyebrows and smoothing them into natural lines with a loving touch. Not until she crooned and marked his cheek and nose with butterfly kisses did she feel his body relax again.

"Jean Pierre," she said, hoping to divert his thinking, but truly wanting to talk things over with him, "I kept having these disturbing dreams, and I know now they were trying to tell me you were alive."

"You don't believe that!"

"I do too." Propping herself up on one arm to rest her head in her hand, she didn't notice that the sheet slid down to their middles. "Always there was an animal tooth or sometimes lots of animal teeth. That was trying to show me that if the dead trapper had really been you, the men would've found the bear tooth on you as well as my necklace. How could I have been so dense as not to have figured that out? I should've known you would have had that crazy amulet around your neck in Indian country." She reached for the carved tooth and cradled it in her hand, reassured by its warmth borrowed from his body.

"It did help save my life." Now that her head was

elevated, he could see blue in her eyes. And the bared breasts, areolae dark without traces of pink now, beckoned to him at each lift and fall of her breathing. ''The Indians might have left me to die if I hadn't been wearing it.''

''Tell me again what happened.'' The heat of his gaze brought a tingling to her breasts, a warm rushing of blood through her veins. Instinctively she leaned closer. ''I listened as you told all of us downstairs, but I don't think much of it made sense to me.'' Rose gave in willingly as he pulled her against his furred chest and nestled her breasts to let a nipple cover one of his. The contact shot electricity to secret places, the thrill stealing her breath and creating new sparkles in her eyes.

''I had made camp on a ledge near the Swallow River to get out of the wind,'' Jean Pierre said, as eager as she to get the telling done so that loving could commence in earnest. The current jolting her was also sizzling within him. ''This lone trapper came looking for shelter about dark, and when I recognized him as Rufus Bedlow, I agreed he could share my fire. You remember meeting him at Ma Dibert's, don't you?''

Rose nodded slowly, saying, ''I remember he looked fierce and extra seedy-looking—and then Lela told me how the Indian scout at the fort had a horrible fight with him last year.''

''Yeah, well, I should have been leery, but I guess I was too tired. Anyway, he jumped me when I was asleep. He must have used a pole ten feet long.''

''And Rufus robbed you? Oh, I had a feeling from the start that that man was evil.''

''Took everything he could find,'' Jean Pierre went on. ''Then he must've thought I was dead and rolled me off the ledge, because the first thing I knew, I was wedged between two big boulders on the bank of the river, with my legs doubled under me, and suffering from a monstrous headache. From what I could learn, the next morning Rufus snitched the canoe I'd borrowed from the mountain men to use while trapping along the river; he must have gotten swamped by a tree coming down the rapids and ended up in it, crushed almost beyond recognition. I guess because I don't shave when I'm in the wilderness and we were about the same size, the mountain men would've had every reason to believe Rufus's body was mine, and they made no further search.''

''Poor darling,'' Rose murmured, caressing his shoulder and arms. Desire was simmering, turning her voice into a sultry contralto. ''How did the Indians happen to find you?''

''I never found out. Probably they were hunting near the river the day after I came to. When I heard horses, I started yelling and they came to me.'' His fingers outlined her mouth, then found an ear to fondle with equal tenderness.

''Weren't you frightened?'' Admiration for his bravery laced her words. His touch on her ear was adding new magic.

''Not as much as I was hurting, no,'' he said with a laugh. He suspected it was childish, but he loved the way she seemed impressed by his actions. He tucked a strand of pinkish gold behind the ear he was exploring, liking the way it revealed her flawless cheekbone. ''I found out they were Black Pawnees and fairly peaceable.''

''Then that awful Rufus went downriver in the canoe with all your gear, yes?'' She shook her hair free from behind her ear, watching the pale cloud reach down and brush his shoulder. Now his hands moved at the base of her skull, and she leaned into them, seeking more of his fondling.

''When the mountain men found the wrecked canoe, they started looking for a body and found him drowned far downstream. No doubt he was nigh unrecognizable.'' Now that her hand was lost in his hair and her little tongue tipped at the underside of her upper lip, he was finding it harder to care whether the whole story got told right away.

''And when they gave me my necklace and said it was in the man's pocket, I, too, thought it was you.'' She clung to him then with both arms around his neck and shuddered. He was lying on his back with her upper torso resting across his, and she moved a leg across his. Evidence of his growing desire whipped up her own.

''I was miserable. The Indian camp was in an isolated

area, and no trappers came through for me to send word that I was alive. The Indians told me that for days I was delirious with fever. After my fever disappeared, I thought my broken leg would never heal so I could come home to you.''

Rose ran a lingering hand along the length of his injured thigh, smiling into his worshipful gaze when the hand took a detour on a titillating path, a very warm and firm one. ''Everything feels good as new.'' At his indrawn breath, she laughed and snuggled closer, teasing his hardening nipples with her own. ''Wouldn't you agree?''

His own hands made a foray down satiny curves as he asked in a husky whisper, ''Now how can I tell you what happened when you lie so close and—?''

Passion took over then, and the rest of the story had to wait. He pulled her to lie on top of his nakedness and gave free rein to his wish to stroke each inch of her loveliness. Mouths and tongues sampled at leisure, setting off new searing flames in those original blazes within. This time their caresses were less frenzied, their kisses less fierce, their embraces less violent. A remarkable tenderness, almost a reverence, underlay their deliberately drawn-out movements, as though each was an extension of the words of love whispered often and with abiding, intense emotion.

Rolling to place Rose beneath him, Jean Pierre claimed all that was his. A purring deep in her throat told him as surely as did her clinging arms and legs that she shared his ecstasy. She was like a tender vine clinging to a stalwart tree, seeking support and sustenance, even as the tree absorbed strength-giving nourishment from the ever-embracing vine. Those final moments were an echo of something forever beautiful, something joined for an elusive, pulsating time in the reality of two communing souls, yet joined for an eternity in that illusory sphere of glory frequented only by lovers.

Rose and Jean Pierre slept again, their bodies curved together as naturally as one's left hand fits into one's right.

PART

✳ **THREE** ✳

Chapter Twenty-one

"Tell me again how much you missed me," Rose said, leaning against Jean Pierre's arm in the Brearde carriage. He had told her they were nearing the outskirts of New Orleans, and she felt an odd sense of uneasiness. She was still awed at the newness of having him returned from what she had believed was his death, but the warmth of his arm reassured her.

Jean Pierre first answered with a kiss. "I thought I showed you last night . . . and that you wouldn't need to be told," he replied when he released her with a knowing smile. The way her lashes fanned across her fair skin fascinated him.

"You're a conceited rascal," she shot back, ruffling the dark curls until they covered his forehead. When he continued to send flagrant looks all over her face and body, she pushed at him in pretended annoyance. His reference to their lovemaking of last night brought little flashes of remembered ecstasy to mind—and rushes of pink to her face. She tossed her unbound hair and asked in mock derision, "Is nothing sacred to you?"

"I figured that behind all your sweetness there still lurked some of that familiar spice," he teased, reaching with a forefinger to trace her pouting upper lip and fashion it into a smile.

"You told me once you wouldn't have me be any other way." Her voice was cocky, self-satisfied. She took his finger and bit it lightly, giggling when he snatched it away. Could she bear to have him out of her sight again?

"And I meant it," he replied with a sudden solemnity. The softening of his mouth told her he was feeling something deep, something too powerful to be put into words. "You suit me just as you are." Some shadow flitted across his mind, and he leaned to whisper in her ear, his breath invading the little pinkish shell and bringing skips to her heartbeat. "Promise me you won't ever change, my Cajun Rose."

The driver, Mark, turned the carriage down the slope leading to the ferry then, and Rose became enamored of the sights and smells of Louisiana's capital, as Louis had predicted she would.

"Please use Papa's apartment on Bourbon Street while you're getting title to your land. Rose will love the sights," Louis had said as he escorted them to the carriage that morning, handing a brass key to Jean Pierre. "Papa and I stay there when we have business, and Celeste uses it when she shops, but it's empty far too often—except for old Maria, of course, who vows she'll die if ever forced to leave New Orleans. She'll be there to see to your needs." He gestured then to the young black driver. "And Mark will stay with the carriage as long as you need him to."

"We'll be ever so grateful," Rose had replied, giving Louis a light hug. Even though the handsome Creole seemed pleased, he cut his eyes toward Jean Pierre as though to gauge his reaction. "Don't be concerned about Jean Pierre's previous jealousy," she whispered. "He knows now that we've never been more than friends." As though to give credence to her words, Jean Pierre moved behind the carriage to supervise Mark's loading of their belongings, paying special attention to the bundles of pelts he had brought back with him.

Ever dashing and daring, Louis shocked her by whispering back, "But does he know that I would have swapped that category for the one of husband or lover if you would have given the right answer?'' He brought her hand up to kiss discreetly. His expressive eyes held hers, seeming to hint that the offer still held.

"You're no doubt the world's biggest flirt," Rose told him, happy to see that only a trace of sadness over the loss of Arlene and their unborn child lingered within the dark eyes.

Only when Jean Pierre returned did Louis end his frankly admiring appraisal. Accepting their thanks for the loan of both carriage and townhouse, a smiling Louis had waved them off, calling out that he would be joining them soon to spend some time in New Orleans.

And now they were here, Rose kept reminding herself, looking out first one window and then the other. Jean Pierre pointed out the fort at the west end of the seven-by-eleven-block town when they rolled past it. The streets were narrow, and she noticed that most of the buildings, some with three stories, such as she had never seen, touched one another and screened out the late afternoon sun. Painted in yellows, pinks, and creamy whites, the homes reached almost to the streets, set back only far enough to allow room for small courtyards behind tall fences of ornate iron grillwork. Street signs lettered in blue and gold on white tiles were attached up high on the buildings at each corner. Her eyes widened at each new sight, and she clutched at Jean Pierre's arm, exclaiming, "I feel I must be dreaming."

"Tonight I'll take you to the grandest hotel and feed you like a princess," he promised. To have her all to himself again seemed the best reward possible. Once he secured title to the land next to Papa's and they returned to clear it and build their home, they could look forward to having children. Her radiant smile flooded his heart.

Rose peered out the window at a carriage they were meeting. Like the Breardes', it was of handsome black leather. But it was open, and sitting upon the velvet-covered seat were two of the loveliest women Rose had ever seen. Their hats and gowns were elaborate, the gowns

much like the elegant one Celeste had worn last night at
her birthday party.

For a moment she smiled at the thought that Celeste
obviously favored Jarrette over her other suitors. What
Jarrette had told her back at Fort Arkansas, and again since
their return, about his planning to ask for her hand next
year seemed destined for success, for she had watched
carefully to note Mr. Brearde's reaction to the handsome
young Cajun and had found nothing but apparent liking
and approval. She didn't want to seem like a matchmaker,
she had confessed to Jean Pierre on the ride into the capital
while telling him the latest developments in the budding
love affair, but Jarrette and Celeste seemed perfect for each
other. Overjoyed that he agreed, she had found an excuse
to give him an extra kiss.

"Did you see those gowns?" Jean Pierre asked just
then, well aware that she had and that her face had grown
pensive afterward. When she nodded, he went on, "I want
to take you shopping right away and buy you some even
prettier gowns." The adoring look she gave him tugged at
his emotions.

"This is beautiful," Rose said when Mark pulled up
before a two-story building of yellow stucco with four
separate entries. She heard the iron gate close behind her
and rushed to see the open area behind an arched doorway.
The sight of the small fountain in the center of the bricked
area took her breath away. "Our very own courtyard," she
exclaimed, turning to Jean Pierre following behind on the
smooth brick. A curving staircase of wrought iron caught
her eyes then, and she brushed past tall, lush plants to look
up. "Are those the bedrooms up there?" She indicated the
rooms opening off the balcony running across the inside of
the second floor. When he nodded, she climbed up to see,
turning to make sure he wasn't far behind.

By the time Maria came to welcome them, a huge smile
on her black face, Rose had fallen in love with the
Breardes' townhouse. She was surprised but pleased to
find that even though other owners shared the building, the
separate entries and courtyards created privacy. Jean Pierre

went out back to meet Mark at the combination stable and carriage house and tell him where to bring their belongings.

Pleading fatigue, but actually wanting to keep her handsome husband behind closed doors, Rose persuaded Jean Pierre to accept Maria's offer to prepare them a light meal. He cocked his head at her as if reading her greedy appetite for lovemaking and gave in, the laugh wrinkle creasing his lean cheek, a spark in his eyes leaping to meet the one in hers. He scribbled a message for Mark to take to Governor Unzaga's office at the Cabildo, hoping that an orderly might be able to get it into the list of audiences for the following day.

After eating and bidding Maria good-night, the couple retired to the spacious bedroom upstairs. In the glow of candlelight, they kissed and whispered buried longings until the hour was late and their bodies were flaming with desire.

"Make love to me as if there'll be no tomorrow," Rose begged, her nakedness spread over his. Could she ever get enough of him? Only the anticipation of his advances had kept her from hurrying their love. From where she lay across him, she could feel his tumescence throbbing against her thighs, could feel her own inner rhythm pulsating in moist readiness. Her tongue played lazy chase with his while he molded her breasts to fit the beloved shape of his hands.

"Is there any other way to make love, my darling?" His words were graveled bits of velvet, and her entire body heard the worship in them. He kissed her cheeks, touched the inside of her ear with his tongue, then laughed when she moaned and moved restlessly atop him. His hands went to cup the soft round buttocks, to sway them against his manhood, the great wave of desire racing over him bringing a sound low in his throat. Rushing pulses and heartbeats had been building ever since they undressed and fell across the bed, and now his threatened to drown out all other sound and thought. How many times had he dreamt of holding her like this when he was struggling to hang on to life? Maybe such thoughts had been what pulled him through, he realized. Her mouth moved against his nipples, tautening the already firm knobs. And then her hands slid to shape his waist, his thighs, to move their bodies even closer. Convulsively he squeezed her to him and turned her to lie beneath him, no longer able to postpone his need to be inside her.

Rose sighed, arms reaching to receive him, legs opening to speed his entry, mouth and tongue moving against his in wild urgency. The delectably warm feel of him moving inside her was what she had thought of all day in a secret part of her mind, she realized as she lifted her hips to receive the hot length of him. Inside, she felt like a torch flaring out of control, with flames licking higher and searing with exquisite agony all those wanton, begging parts of her womanhood. And just when she thought she could bear no further extension of his shaft, something within seemed to burst open to clutch and smother, to seek to bury him inside, to contain him forever. Frenzied, captivated, suspended in the splendor of their union, Rose trembled in age-old surrender, finding that to feel him collapse against her and drop his head beside hers was a disappointing surprise. Back to earth, back to reality. Breathless, hearts laboring to slow down, they kissed, murmured love words, and fell into exhausted sleep, naked, still holding each other in a tender embrace.

"What is this about the governor's not receiving anyone today?" Jean Pierre asked the next morning when the sentry gave him the unwelcome message. He glanced around the receiving office in the Cabildo, noting that others also waited, then spotted an officer just inside the door to the back office. "I'll speak to the man in charge of the governor's office during his absence, then." His commanding voice rang out.

"I am Lieutenant Don Charles Leyoso, sir," the man said when he approached the angry-faced Acadian. "May I be of assistance to you until Governor Unzaga has recovered from his illness and once more hears petitions?"

"Tell me where I might find the man in charge of land titles and assignations," Jean Pierre responded, liking the direct way the Spanish soldier eyed him. Here was no dishonest laggard, he surmised. "I believe his name is Mr. Phillip de Cordoza, nephew to the governor." His lips curled at having to pronounce the despised name.

Lieutenant Leyoso studied the man before him in the identical way he himself had been scrutinized, reaching the same conclusion that had been formed about him. Here was a man to be reckoned with, to be accorded respect. "Mr. Cordoza returned to Spain last August, Mr.—may I have your name, please?"

Jean Pierre breathed a little easier at the news that a business meeting with Phillip was not to be. He gave not only his name but the mission he was fulfilling, not caring that his deep voice carried easily to all ears in the room. The officer heard him out and made a few notes before saying, "There's no replacement for Mr. Cordoza as yet in the office of land management. Perhaps if you return tomorrow, the governor will be here to speak with you. If, as you say, you petitioned two years ago, the papers are probably in order, requiring only the formality of handing them over to you."

Partially mollified, Jean Pierre returned to the Brearde's apartment with a plan in mind that he hoped would please Rose.

Rose could hardly keep in step with Jean Pierre, he moved so rapidly up the narrow streets. As soon as he had returned from his morning's brief outing, he had hurried her to go shopping with him. "Surely the dress shop won't close before we get there," she complained when he took her arm and almost lifted her around a corner. He could be so impatient at times that it made her want to scream—and this was one of those times.

"I want to get your order in so that the gowns will be finished before we leave," her husband told her, not slowing his pace at all. "We'll not be here more than a week."

They reached a shop with an ornate gown displayed on a dressmaker's form in a small, cantilevered window and went in the green-painted door, causing a silver bell to jingle and dance above their heads. Rose had read the sign outside, so she was not surprised to be meeting Madame de Pointerre. Madame was tall and thin with undeniably dyed hair, much the same shade as Lela's, Rose thought with a pang of homesickness for her good friend. And then the thought came that Lela would be delighted to see Jean Pierre offering to buy her everything in the obviously exclusive apparel shop, and she smiled.

Madame took the smile and twinkling look as being aimed at her and she bridled, lifting the skirt and ruffles of the sample garment in the window to show the quality of her workmanship. She dashed about to lay upon the table her very best voiles, cottons, and silks, sliding from view the second-best she had at first considered. Such a handsome couple deserved the best, her altered manner seemed to suggest.

Jean Pierre argued with Rose, though politely, over whether each selection should be some shade of blue. When Madame turned her back for a second, he whispered, "Blue is your color. You shouldn't even consider another."

She hissed back, "I know what I want to wear. I love *all* colors, and if you don't like what I choose, you can look somewhere else." When he grinned at her and winked in good-natured surrender, Rose returned to her selections.

Having chosen all that she thought she needed, and then noticing that most of the bolts laid aside were indeed shades of blue, Rose shot him a questing look in case he might be planning some cute comment, but Jean Pierre seemed entirely satisfied. In fact, she reflected, she hadn't seen such a pleased look on his face all that morning. She went behind the curtain for Madame to take her measurements, squelching her earlier suspicion that after being back only two days he was already trying to boss her around. Gratitude for his safe return drowned any silly rise of temper. To have her love back was all that mattered. Perhaps she should have let him have more say about her choices, she thought.

Rose could hear Jean Pierre prowling around restlessly in the small shop out front. Wondering what Madame and Jean Pierre were talking about in low tones after the seamstress left her alone to dress, Rose took her time. He really was a wonderful husband. Her smile was that of a young woman secure in her power over her beloved.

That evening after they had bathed and were dressing for dinner at the hotel, Rose heard Maria at the door and Jean Pierre's answering voice. She stuck her head out of the dressing alcove to ask, "What was that all about?"

"It seems that a package has arrived for Mrs. Guilbeau." Jean Pierre held out the large, flat box. When she took a hesitant step toward him, his heart sped up at the beauty of her breasts almost spilling over the top of the form-fitting chemise. Her body had ripened since he had last gazed upon her from a distance, he realized with a start, suddenly jealous of the ruby pendant's claim to its spot at the place where the pale, firm mounds met.

Rose squealed low in her throat, her eyes dancing from the box to Jean Pierre's deliberately closed countenance. "What is it?" she asked, trying not to sound too eager. Her heart thudded in a ridiculous way. She well remembered the pink satin slippers. Her hands reached hungrily for the string.

Her eyes widened and sparkled as she hesitantly pulled out the elaborate gown that had adorned the dressmaker's dummy in the window of her shop. What could she say to her husband, who had obviously worked some kind of magic to snare the only ready-made gown the shop owner had? That it was beautiful? It was, and she had been open in her praise of its workmanship that morning.

A double flounce edged in luscious lace rode the off-the-shoulder neckline, and the sleeves widened at the elbow to end in similar, smaller flounces. The skirt, with lace trailing numerous circles centered with rosettes of matching ribbon bows all around its width, billowed over the included petticoats, its silken sheen rich and stunning. She held her breath a second longer before saying, "Jean Pierre, it's lovely. Thank you."

But even after he took her in his arms and kissed her shoulders and the tops of her breasts until she was breathless, her mind kept echoing that first crashing thought: *Orange?* Why had he bought her a dress of such a hideous,

unflattering color as orange? She swallowed at a suddenly
unpleasant taste in her mouth, one decidedly orange.

On the arm of her proud husband, Rose entered the
plush dining room of the elegant Maison de Charles that
evening, her head high, her cheeks flaming, her blond
curls arranged defiantly about her face and shoulders. If
Jean Pierre suspected that the open stares from the numerous conservatively dressed diners had to do with her
beauty, Rose knew better. She sensed that the glaring
combination of her pink and white blondness with the
garish orange gown suitable for a harlot quite set their
teeth on edge. The normally glowing ruby lay dull and
lifeless, as if it tried to hide from shame. It seemed to
Rose that the dignified waiter who led them to a table in
the back corner near the kitchen flashed looks of disbelief
at her, even as he walked in black-garbed splendor ahead
of them. Never again would she tell Jean Pierre that she
could wear any and all colors, Rose assured herself for
perhaps the tenth time that evening.

The little wash of whispers subsided once they were
seated and studying their menus. Jean Pierre looked over
his to see her eyes hiding behind those incredible lashes.
"Have you decided what you would like to eat, Rose?"

"I've never seen so many things to choose from, never
even heard of most of them." She lifted puzzled eyes to
his, wondering at the dancing splashes of fire there. And
what caused the secretive smile? Surely he wouldn't have
bought the dress knowing that . . . Of course he had! Her
mouth parted in surprise—and a touch of admiration for
his devilishness. "Will you order for me?" *There* her tone
plainly told him. Blue eyes gave in to brown; they had
won, fair and square.

"Are you sure you don't want to trust your own judgment?" He read the knowledge in her eyes. His heart sank
a bit at the slight tremble of her lifted chin. The fuller top
lip seemed to be having trouble keeping still. Holy Mother! She was beautiful. Even in the god-awful orange gown.
Fighting down the laugh he had harbored ever since she
recoiled upon first glimpsing the contents of the box, he
admitted to himself that he loved everything about her,

even her wide streak of stubbornness. She was a game one, his wife.

"I'm sure." Her words came out smooth and warm like butter. He wasn't going to catch her up again in her own hardheadedness, she vowed. Not this soon.

With an ease that Rose admired in secret, but would never confess on this night, Jean Pierre told the waiter in those compelling bass tones what they would eat. Rose knew she shouldn't, but she felt pampered, spoiled, and very, very special. Carefully refraining from looking at his wife, he ordered the final course: "Perhaps oranges with sauce for our dessert." He heard her little indrawn breath and added, "And please bring champagne now."

The waiter, not the one who had ushered them in, sneaked a startled glance at Rose's gown before giving a smart click of his heels and leaving. The brand-new sound reached Rose's ears and her tickle box at about the same time, and she broke into helpless laughter. The world was glorious, and she was the center of it, with the only audience she desired.

"Tell me what's funny," Jean Pierre urged, leaning across to cover her small hand with his. When had she ever looked more kissable, more desirable? She gasped for breath, looked into his eyes, and leaned back against her chair.

Before she could do much more than gulp for air and get out the word *waiter,* the solemn-faced young man returned with the champagne. After he had poured the crystal glasses full of the bubbling liquid and given a second click of heels upon leaving, Jean Pierre realized what had set her off. He smiled in baffled approval of the mysterious ways of the fairer sex and asked, "May I toast my lovely wife?"

With lighthearted indulgence for her beloved, who had bested her so cleverly, Rose lifted her glass, letting him bring his to meet it with a faint bell-like tone. Her eyes adored him.

"May she ever look at me with eyes of love," Jean Pierre said. They sipped solemnly, looks meeting with enough warmth to shame the flickering flame of the candle on their table. "And may she ever be as beautiful as she is this night,"

Rose could fight her inner battle no longer, and she let out a tiny ripple of laughter before moving her glass to touch his again. "And may my husband ever show the perfect taste he showed today in his desire to make me beautiful."

The little crystal note pealed again when the delicate stems met. Both Jean Pierre and Rose tossed their heads in great bursts of laughter then, causing the other diners to examine the young couple again. But all they saw that time were lovers holding hands across their table in the candlelit corner near the kitchen, making toasts and drinking champagne, lost to all that smacked of the everyday world, interested in nothing and no one except each other.

But through a slightly opened door from the kitchen, one of the cook's helpers marked Rose and Jean Pierre, in fact stared in disbelief—and not because of the gaudy orange gown.

"Didn't I tell you that was a sight not to miss?" her fellow worker Dora whispered before they closed the door and returned to washing and drying pots and pans. "Have you ever seen such a pretty little blonde a-wearin' anythin' so tacky? And one just married, judgin' by what George reports ever' time he comes back from waitin' on their table. I swear, if'n I didn't know he's not bright enough to make up anythin', I'd think she was a new whore in town."

Mimi Dibert made some kind of remark that hushed Dora, then let her mind work while the two continued their chores. Jesus! Thom would be fit to be tied upon learning that his source had been wrong about Jean Pierre being dead. Ever since they had left Natchitoches, he had been telling her that once they reached New Orleans, he'd be rich and would divorce his wife and marry her. Not until he got drunk enough one night six weeks ago to confide in her about how the governor's nephew Phillip de Cordoza had tried to hire him last summer to kill Jean Pierre had

Mimi put together the bits and pieces of what he had been telling her ever since she ran off with him.

"You can't mean you hired Rufus Bedlow to kill him for you, Thom. Please, tell me you're lying," she had pleaded after hearing about Thom's plan to pay the big trapper a coin and then collect many times over that amount from Phillip once they got to New Orleans. "Then that's why you got to drinking and carrying on like a crazy man when we got here and you found the governor's nephew had returned to Spain. I just now figured out why you hardly ever peddle and made me get a job. Thom, you can't act this way; it's not right. Jean Pierre never harmed you, and you know it. It probably never would have worked for us to be together during trapping season, even if I could've tricked him into marrying me. I came away with you because I loved you—and because I thought you loved me. I never thought you were evil before now." Tears streamed down her thin face, and she reached out to him for reassurance.

"Shut up, you stupid girl!" Thom shouted, grabbing her roughly. He slapped her face and ran his eyes to her belly. "I don't need to hear preaching from you. Now that you're going to be swelling up before long, you're going to lose your job at the hotel, and when I get that money from Phillip, you're going to be just as happy to see it as I am."

"What makes you think he'll even answer your letter demanding payment?" she retorted, not feeling the pain of his cruel grip on her arms there in the sordid room opening onto the alley behind the kitchen of the hotel. From necessity during the time she had been with him, she had become insensitive to his meanness.

"He did answer it, but the arrogant bastard said he'd not send any money until he heard Jean Pierre was dead. By then, I'd learned from the soldiers making up the supply train to Fort Arkansas that not only was Jean Pierre dead, Rose was already back home. I wrote him about it and also about my learning from the storekeeper at Attakapas that she's the granddaughter of the Earl of Wanington in

England, and that rumor has it she'll go over for a visit. He'll send the gold."

"Blood money, Thom," Mimi accused. "How could you?"

Thom hit her again and flung her from him, laughing drunkenly when she stumbled over a stool and landed squarely atop it on her stomach. "How dare you criticize me, you . . . you whore! I've a good mind to leave you and go back to my wife and young'uns in Natchez. You've gone to seed, and you're still nothing but a green girl."

Mimi retched from the pain cutting her insides. "Help me, Thom," she begged. "I'm hurt bad and may be losing the baby."

"That's the best news I've had all day," he snarled, slamming the door with muttered curses as he left.

Mimi stuck her hands deep into the warm sudsy water in the big dishpan there in the hotel kitchen, not liking to recall the ugliness of their numerous quarrels, but especially not liking the memory of that night some six weeks ago when she had lain sobbing on the floor of their miserable room and writhed alone throughout the miscarriage. It was on that night that she had come to hate Thom Keller.

Mimi would have been even more overwrought had she known that out in the hotel lobby, Thom was lurching from the bar when he spied the laughing, black-haired Cajun and his blond wife sitting at the table in the back corner of the dining room. A murderous set to his small face, he managed to get to the back alley leading to their room before he gave in to the powerful rage inside. He leaned over a barrel behind the hotel and retched, feeling that what boiled forth was his very life.

Not until after noon the next day did Governor Unzaga receive Jean Pierre. That the elderly man had actually been ill was apparent from the pallor of his skin, and Jean Pierre tried to hold back his temper when the governor seemed not to believe his claim wasn't filed, ready to be picked up.

"How is it that your complaint hasn't been resolved?" the frail man asked when Jean Pierre listed his grievances.

"I well remember your impatience last year when the title was withheld until inspection could be made, but I assumed everything had been taken care of. Surely I would have heard had there been further problems."

"For one thing, sir, I've been away trapping. And for another, I would suggest that mayhap your nephew conveniently misplaced my request and kept it from the proper channels." To accuse the governor's kinsman of wrongdoing was risky, but what else could he do? He wanted that piece of bayou land adjacent to Pierre's, and as far as he was concerned, he had taken all the necessary steps to secure title to it.

"Pray tell, sir, why you make such an accusation." A pained look upon his face, the governor stared at his caller.

Jean Pierre studied his own clenched fist, fighting for control. How honest dared he be? "I attended a party at Antoine Brearde's Grenfall with Phillip early last summer. He was on his way to survey other Acadian petitions for land as well as my own, and he told me that the final decision rested with him. As we didn't see eye to eye on several issues discussed that night, I thought he might have wished to slight me." He cleared his throat of a sudden thickness. Damn! Why was it necessary to lie? But the thought of losing the land weighed more heavily than that of reporting Phillip's attack on Rose. "Sir, I see no legitimate reason why my petition isn't here waiting for me."

"This meeting is ended, Mr. Guilbeau," Governor Unzaga said in an icy voice. Evidencing his anger, a mottled red suffused the thin skin of his face. "My advice to you is to make out a new application for the plot you desire, since we no longer have one. I haven't yet named a replacement to fill my nephew's position, so speak with Lieutenant Leyoso in the outer office about how to reapply. Then when the Superior Council meets again in October, your request will be considered again." He rose then, apparently upset. "Good day, sir."

Lieutenant Leyoso ushered the fiery-eyed Acadian across the hall to his own office and invited him to sit. When Jean Pierre repeated his unrewarding conversation with the governor, Lieutenant Leyoso replied in a cool, professional tone, ''Often Governor Unzaga is short-tempered because he isn't well. We who know and respect him fear that he'll be replaced soon unless his health improves. To add to his problems, his eyesight seems to be fading. He's a just man, that much I know from having served him most of the seven years of his governorship.''

''I wonder how it is that his nephew inherited none of his sterling qualities,'' Jean Pierre shot back, his hand rubbing at the back of his neck. Inside he was boiling.

''Ah,'' the lieutenant said knowingly, ''then you've had personal dealings with Phillip.'' His hand fondled his goatee while his eyes studied the young man before him. Rumor had it that as first assistant to the governor, he himself might soon be taking up Phillip de Cordoza's former title. If that was true, to have the friendship of such a stalwart as Jean Pierre Guilbeau could prove very helpful in the remote bayou country. In many instances, such men could settle local disputes over land boundaries and claims without having to bother the Spanish with petty squabbles. He leaned across the desk to say in a lower tone, ''If all of Phillip's enemies were to line up, I daresay the end would be across the parade ground. You aren't alone in your judgment of him, Mr. Guilbeau, but I assure you he still has contacts here who might be beholden to him.''

''What would you suggest?'' Jean Pierre asked, sensing that the officer was empathetic and knowing that gold could buy strange friendships—even for the wily Phillip de Cordoza.

''Give me some time to dig around in the land office for your initial petition. If I can find it and have a private talk with the governor, perhaps he'll approve it and not force the issue before the Superior Council.''

''Even if I have to buy it, I want title to that piece of land so I can begin my home,'' Jean Pierre assured him earnestly. ''I've furs to sell and other business to attend to, then I'll come back to see if the petition has been found. I'm not eager to remain very long in New Orleans.''

There seemed little else Jean Pierre could do but place his faith in the lieutenant and give him some time to search through the records, and he was soon on his way to the fur-trading center. The hot summer sun beat on his face with a fury when he headed back toward the Plaza de Armas, doing little to cool his temper over what appeared to be a final insult from Phillip de Cordoza. At least, he told himself as he paused at the sidewalk café beside the river to fortify himself with coffee, there was no record that someone else was applying to receive the desired land. And the price for his pelts had been generous. Even so, he felt depressed.

"Why so gloomy?" came a familiar accented voice. "I should think you'd be smiling at just being alive."

"Beau Bradford," Jean Pierre exclaimed, rising to shake the Englishman's hand, then motioning for him to join him as Beau asked all about what had happened in the North Wilderness and listened with surprise to a brief account. Jean Pierre added then, "Rose told me you called at Attakapas and gave her your report."

"That's right, though I've received more information since then to pass on to you." Not ready to let the subject of Jean Pierre's near-death go, the big man said, "I could hardly believe it when I was over at the Cabildo and Lieutenant Leyoso mentioned that you were in town to see about a land petition. You're one lucky Frenchman!"

At Beau's insistence, Jean Pierre told the details of Rufus's attack and the following miserable weeks of waiting in the Indian camp for his leg to heal.

"What caused the man to jump you?" Beau asked when the strange tale was over.

"I don't know. If I thought there'd been a way for a certain Spaniard to have met up with that mean rascal, I'd know why he tried to kill me," Jean Pierre remarked musingly.

"Would you be referring to Phillip de Cordoza?"

"Why do you ask? Do you know him?"

"Not exactly," Beau replied. "After I left you in Natchitoches, I returned to New Orleans. In a riverfront bar, I heard this drunken Spaniard bragging about who he was and how much he'd pay to make sure a certain Cajun trapper from Attakapas never made it back from the woods in the spring."

"And somebody took him up on it, yes?"

"No, he was too drunk for anyone to pay him any attention. If someone had, I guess I would've asked a few questions, but it was August—and hot as Hades. Nobody in town but a few men hoping to find berths on the next ship." Beau grinned before going on, "Within a week, my friend over at the Cabildo, Lieutenant Leyoso, told me how the governor packed his nephew back to Spain and told him not to come back. Seems he'd stirred up so much trouble in the few months he was here that Governor Unzaga was having a hard time trying to keep him from turning all the colonists against the Spanish officials. I doubt it was worth the telling. He seemed no better than a weasel."

Wondering if the governor's brusqueness at their meeting might have come from embarrassment over another likely instance of his nephew's vindictiveness, Jean Pierre leaned forward and changed the subject. "I appreciate your finding out about Rose's family."

"She had no doubts about deciding she wanted to stay in Louisiana, even that day I saw her when she thought . . ."

"Yes, she told me," Jean Pierre said, not liking to recall Rose's tearful account of how touched she had been at his thoughtfulness in hiring the barrister. "She said you advised her to go along when you return home, to meet everyone and look into her legacy. I figured you'd already gone."

"I sail on the *Talisman* in a week. The offer still stands; only this time, I guess I'd take you along, too." The blue eyes twinkled.

"Thanks," Jean Pierre answered dryly, smiling at the friendly Englishman. "I would insist on our going if I didn't expect to get title to my land in the next day or so. We're eager to get back and clear our land and start a home."

"Want to come to my room tonight and see the latest information my father sent, Jean Pierre?" Beau was rising. "I've an appointment now that'll last till after dinner."

"I believe I'll take you up on the offer. Rose and I might be gone before we could find a time to meet, and I want to talk with you, as well as pay your fee."

After Beau gave directions to his hotel room, the two parted.

Figuring that Rose might not like the idea of spending the evening alone, Jean Pierre didn't tell her of his plans until after they had eaten the food Maria served in the bricked courtyard. A slight evening breeze had reduced the mugginess, and the two had a pleasant meal.

"You'll be back soon, though, won't you?" Rose asked when he told her he was going to meet Beau to settle his account and read the reports from England. The heat had drained her all day, and she looked forward to relaxing upon the cool, linen sheets in the bedroom off the upstairs balcony. By the time Jean Pierre returned, the night would be pleasant and they could make love, she reassured herself. A coquettish smile lit up her face as she kissed him goodbye at the gate opening onto the street. That a passing sentry averted his head at their impassioned embrace brought a smile to her face. And across the way, she thought she saw a man standing on the shadowy corner turn away, as if not wishing to be caught staring. What was wrong with a man kissing his wife goodbye in public? she wondered with a feeling of brazenness, especially when there was no light except for the dim glow of the whale-oil lamp on the street corner and a smaller one inside the courtyard. She lifted her unbound hair off her shoulders to catch the little breeze and went back inside, scolding herself for feeling sad at Jean Pierre's absence.

Jean Pierre had an enjoyable hour with Beau and felt that the fee he charged was fair for such a wealth of information. After talking to the lawyer, then ruminating as he walked the deserted streets to the Brearde apartment, he was no longer sure that he should accept Rose's assurance that she would never want to know her family in England. Should he, perhaps, insist on taking her now, so that when they became busy rearing their children, she'd not entertain doubts?

Just as he let himself in the gate to the Brearde townhouse, he heard footsteps in the darkness behind him die away. A dog howled in the next block, the mournful sound reminding him of the lateness of the hour. He moved across the courtyard to climb the curving metal staircase to the bedroom, promising himself to curb his impatience at having to wait to learn about the land he wanted. The thought of Rose's waiting for him buried his musings and hurried his steps.

Chapter Twenty-Two

"Not a trace?" Jean Pierre asked Lieutenant Leyoso the next afternoon at the Cabildo. "De Cordoza must have destroyed all papers on me." A contemplative look claiming his face, he said, "There's nothing to do but fill out a new application." If he ever saw that scoundrel Phillip again—!

Lieutenant Leyoso laid out the proper forms on his desk, watching the Acadian wrap his control about himself as he wrote. When he could find no record on Jean Pierre yesterday, he had felt even more compassion for the young man than at first. That something far more serious than imagined must have taken place between the governor's nephew and the Acadian seemed more than a mere suspicion now, he mused. It seemed clear that Jean Pierre's original claim was gone. He knew Governor Unzaga was aware of the streaks of ugly arrogance in the son of his wife's brother and that the old man had sent Phillip back to Spain.

But the lieutenant also recognized that the governor felt a degree of loyalty to his kinsman and wouldn't be quick to admit that Phillip was capable of such pettiness that seemed evident in the case of Jean Pierre Guilbeau's petition. The lieutenant had little doubt that if the Acadian could substantiate Phillip's wrongdoing, the old man would bend. He could cite many cases in which the governor had shown that he was a genuine diplomat, even a bit of a peacemaker. Had his superior been well enough to keep regular office hours, Lieutenant Leyoso would have talked with him informally about the problem, but the governor was laid up with gout that day.

"There," Jean Pierre said, sliding the completed papers toward the officer. "That should suffice. Mayhap Governor Unzaga can approve this new petition without my having to wait until the October meeting of the Superior Council. I'm eager to return to the bayou."

"The governor won't be in today. He's not feeling well," Lieutenant Leyoso said, not surprised when the Acadian's face took on a new look of anger and disbelief. He had seen Jean Pierre walking that morning with the beautiful blonde and guessed from their affectionate looks and touches that they were newlyweds. Widowed but retaining vivid memories of those early sweet weeks with his own bride, Lieutenant Leyoso wondered at the Acadian's impatience to leave New Orleans. It seemed to him that to have such an exciting place to show one's lovely wife would be a perfect way to spend a honeymoon.

"Is there any way things can be speeded up?" Jean Pierre asked, exasperation marking his face.

The Spaniard met the young man's troubled eyes with a wary glance. A fleeting memory of the way he had seen the petite blonde lean her head against her husband's arm that morning, a gesture reminding him of his own bride's impulsiveness, chipped away at his objectivity. Young people sometimes needed help with obstacles. He cleared his throat and said softly, "I'll send this new application to the mansion and ask the governor if you might call tonight after dinner for his decision on the matter. I can't say that he'll take license to approve it, but who knows. . . ." His voice died away at the sound of footsteps in the outer office.

"Thank you, Lieutenant," Jean Pierre said, rising to shake the solid hand proffered. "I'll await your message."

Jean Pierre asked Mark to bring the carriage around that evening after Rose and he shared an early supper in the small dining room off the courtyard. In answer to her teasing questions, he explained, ''We'll ride out to Lake Pontchartrain before dark. It's a pretty drive, and I want you to see it.''

Rose enthused over the large homes and exotic flowers beside the wide carriage road. The lake impressed her with its small whitecaps and gray reaches rising to meet the horizon. Her low, melodious laughter and chatter delighted Jean Pierre, and he tightened the arm resting lightly around her shoulders. On their way back into town, they could see dark, low-lying clouds in the fading light. Even though a quickening of wind caused the moss in the giant oaks along the road to dance and sway, the heavy cloud mass seemed to be suspended over the curving Mississippi up ahead.

''We might be treated to a New Orleans rainstorm tonight,'' Jean Pierre commented as they watched the sky grow blacker.

''I'm not afraid of rainstorms,'' Rose assured him, loving him with her gaze. Sometimes she still had difficulty realizing he was truly alive and back with her. What was a bit of wind and rain after all she had endured when she believed him lost to her forever?

''Good,'' he replied. ''A messenger came this afternoon to tell me Governor Unzaga will see me tonight, and you'll be alone, except for Maria and Mark.'' In the near darkness he couldn't read her expression.

''Why do you have to meet him at night?'' Rose asked when they had returned to their bedroom at the apartment. ''It seems to me that business should be conducted in the daytime.'' Rose pouted, despite the realization that he was attending to a matter of great importance to both of them: land along the Bayou Teche for their future home. Even so, her eyes accused him of wanting to leave her alone.

''I'll not be gone long. The man has gout and didn't feel like going to the office today,'' Jean Pierre stated with finality. She might have a point, but he knew he must show up at the mansion as agreed, or there would be no chance that the land could become theirs before early fall. Surely she wasn't jealous, he thought, didn't suspect him of even glancing at another woman. It had to be something else. "If you're afraid of the rainstorm, I'll ask Maria to—"

"I'm not afraid," Rose declared, angling her chin even higher. Stubbornness ruled her, forbidding her to throw her arms around his neck and plead with him to stay. Not that she feared the storm building outside, she told herself. But something gnawed at her, begged her to keep him beside her. She turned a deaf ear, clinging to her earlier resolve to remain aloof. When his face wore that air of introspection as it had ever since he had told her of his plans, she felt cut off.

Her lack of response to his farewell kisses chilled Jean Pierre, and he left with a half-hearted pull at the bedroom door leading out to the balcony. When she made up her mind to believe something, he might as well bow out, he reflected as he slammed the outer gate and stalked off into the stormy night. For some reason he chose not to examine, he didn't ask Mark to drive him to the governor's residence, hadn't even informed the slave that he was going out. He pulled his cloak of treated broadcloth closer against the gusts of wind and hurried on his way.

Not needing Maria to help her get ready for bed and not wishing to have to put on a false smile for the kindly slave, Rose idled while preparing for the night. The whitewashed walls of the cheerful room mocked her dark mood. While working the brush through her windblown tangles, she took time to study the paintings lending an air of sophistication to the bedroom, smiling at the antics of a maid and her suitors, captured within a gilt-edged frame in splashes of soft blues and greens. Was the whole world enamored of the whimsical moods of lovers? She dropped her brush and gave up trying to trick her mind into a lighter disposition. Despising herself for fretting over Jean Pierre's absence, she climbed into bed and fell into a deep sleep in spite of the heavy thunder.

A sound close by jerked Rose out of a tenuous dream. Thinking at first that it might be Jean Pierre returning, she lay still. A sense of danger hung about, though, and she knew instinctively that he was nowhere around. Warily she opened her eyes and tried to focus them in the darkened room. She held her breath when streaks of lightning through the window revealed a shadowy form moving toward her. Her screams echoed through the room and down into the courtyard as a man pounced on her there in the bed, but rolls of thunder drowned them. Noticing that he reeked of strong spirits, she rolled out from under him and started for the door. Two brutal hands grabbed her at the waist and threw her back upon the bed. One hand pinned her hair against the mattress, and she flinched from the pain. She screamed again and again as she fought, bit, and scratched at his face and pinioning arms, her struggles no less violent than the storm raging outside. Her assailant's wet mouth silenced her, bruising her lips while he ripped away her gown. A great roll of thunder echoed her rage and frustration, drowning out her moans.

"Shut up!" hissed the man, moving his repulsive mouth barely enough to speak. "You won't escape this time, Rose Guilbeau. Phillip de Cordoza isn't the only one who desires you as much as he wants to kill your husband."

The insidious words terrified Rose even more. Who? —but an immediate jag of lightning showed her the contorted face of Thom Keller, the drummer she had bested in Natchitoches last year, the man who had run off with young Mimi Dibert after making the hateful insinuations about incest to Jean Pierre and her. With renewed force Rose struggled to free herself, but her strength couldn't compare to his.

Brutally he held his ravaging mouth over hers in such a way as to prevent her from biting him. One of his hands held both of hers over her head against the mass of hair, his weight forcing her down as he fumbled with his breeches with his free hand. Paying no attention to her tears of pain from the attack on her hair, he tried to force her tightly clamped legs apart with an impatient, punishing knee. She writhed anew, desperate to escape in spite of the tearing at her scalp. Some part of her noted that a loose shutter banged in rhythm with the screeching wind.

All at once the attacking body and hands went slack, and the man collapsed, rolling partly off Rose's nude body.

"Jean Pierre!" Rose yelled once, twice. Thom Keller had mentioned Phillip, had said something about wanting Jean Pierre dead. New fear overtook her. Had Thom attacked him beforehand? No voice answered, but she knew that someone else was in the room. Shocked but grateful to have the assault cease, she tried, without success, to pull herself from under the sweaty weight holding her down, fully expecting Jean Pierre to come into view. She let out another scream as, in the eerie flashes of lightning, she watched a woman plunging a knife into Thom Keller's back again and again, each stroke slamming his inert body against Rose and pushing her down against the mattress. As though from a far distance, she heard the door crash open, and she saw a pale light from the lamp in the courtyard below seep into the room.

In stark terror she stared at a wild-eyed Mimi Dibert holding a huge, bloody knife. Her racing pulse took over her ears, threatening to stamp out all other sounds.

"Maybe now the world won't be so evil," Mimi said, her eyes fixing on Thom's inert form. "Ever since he met up with that Phillip de Cordoza and saw the bag of gold he was offering for somebody to kill Jean Pierre, the devil has owned him."

Before either woman was aware of another presence, a big hand grabbed Mimi and led her aside. "Rose," Jean Pierre said, grappling at Thom's body and sliding it to the floor, "are you all right?"

"Yes, I think so," she managed to answer, so relieved to see him alive and to have the gruesome body off her that she sobbed convulsively. "What was Mimi saying about . . . about his meaning to kill you? And even *he* mentioned Phillip. . . ." She couldn't go on.

Across the room, Mimi leaned against the wall, letting out shuddering gasps, as if trying to catch her breath, before slipping silently down into a crumpled heap. A nightmare, Rose told herself, not missing one of Mimi's movements. None of this could be happening. In a new streak of light from the noisy storm, she glimpsed the painting above the woman's head, something perverse in her bringing peals of hysterical laughter. A smiling young woman fondled the sharp horn of a mythical unicorn, blissfully unaware that behind a nearby tree, a leering man spied upon the idyllic scene.

"Rose, darling, it's all right now," came Jean Pierre's voice for the second time from right beside her, only then penetrating the din in her ears. When he lit the candle on the nearby table, the artist's depiction of innocence and evil lost its hold on her. The bedroom jumped back into focus. She clamped back the mad laughter and fell weeping into his arms. Rain assaulted the window and the courtyard below in deafening sheets. While she sobbed against his beloved neck, his crushing arms and comforting words soothed her tortured mind and trembling body.

Once her tears slackened, Jean Pierre dabbed at her eyes with his handkerchief and said, "My darling Rose, it's all over. Don't be afraid. I'm here with you now." Still holding her within the circle of one arm, he stooped to pick up her robe and drape it around her nakedness. Pain and guilt rode his heart now that his fear had faded. "I never should have left you alone tonight."

Still staring at Thom's body on the floor, Mimi said, "He's been out of his mind ever since we got to New Orleans at Christmas and he found Phillip de Cordoza had gone back to Spain. I doubted his wild tales that Phillip had offered him money to kill somebody, till today when I found an old letter from him in Thom's things."

"What did it say?" Jean Pierre asked, still sitting on the bed with his arms around the trembling Rose.

"That he'd not send any money till he heard if the man Thom hired had really done away with you."

"What man? Did he name him?" Jean Pierre watched Mimi bury her head in her hands. "Was it Rufus Bedlow?"

"Yes. It was Rufus." Mimi wept loudly then.

"Did Thom hear from Phillip again after everyone believed I had died in an accident?" he asked when she quieted.

"'No, I don't think so. I couldn't find but the one letter," Mimi replied, lifting the sad doe-eyes. "I never dreamed that he was counting on collecting money for having someone killed, least of all somebody I knew.'' Tears ran down her face but she seemed unaware of them. ''After he knocked me down and made me lose my baby, I came to hate him. But I couldn't earn enough money as a cook's helper to go home. He just hung around drinking and waiting to hear from that Spaniard.''

Rose hiccuped and grabbed the handkerchief from Jean Pierre's hands, wiping the last of her tears just as Maria and Mark burst through the doorway, both jabbering at the same time, their eyes wide and staring.

''What's all the noise about?'' Maria asked, her eyes round from fright. ''I fetched Mark from the carriage house 'cause I was afraid something awful had happened.''

Jean Pierre related what had taken place, to the best of his knowledge, and sent Mark to fetch a street sentry.

Within a brief time, two soldiers came into the room, close upon the slave's heels. From a stone-faced Mimi they unraveled the sordid story.

Still in shock, Rose sat on the settee beside Jean Pierre and watched the pathetic Mimi Dibert in the circle of candlelight. She was no longer pretty, no longer even looked young. Her thin body suggested she'd not eaten well in a long while, and Rose's heart went out to her. The big, dark eyes stared from within deep sockets accentuated by half-circles underneath. In the same unemotional voice she had used to relate Thom's evil doings and connection with Phillip, Mimi answered the soldiers' questions.

Mimi told how she had worked as a cook's helper at the hotel after they had settled in New Orleans at Christmas. When she had become pregnant, she had begged Thom to leave his wife in Natchez and marry her, but he had laughed at her and beaten her. His blows had caused her to miscarry only weeks ago.

For the first time, Mimi's features showed grief, and she hid her face in her hands. Sobbing then, she went on, ''He began cursing me and beating me worse than ever. I was glad when he began sneaking out of our room at night after he thought I was asleep. This afternoon I came across the letter from Phillip de Cordoza, and when he threatened to kill me if I tried to warn Jean Pierre, I took a knife from the hotel kitchen and followed him when he left tonight." Then the vacant look returned to her eyes; the tears stopped. "I had asked around and found that this was where the Guilbeaus were staying. I watched him jimmy the gate to the courtyard and sneak inside after Jean Pierre left." She paused to swallow with noticeable pain. "I didn't know he meant to attack Rose."

One of the soldiers sent her a look of concern, and took the glass of water Maria had brought and handed it to the young woman. "And then?" he asked once Mimi had drunk and given him back the glass.

"I reached the courtyard before I heard Rose scream. I rushed upstairs, following the sounds, and stabbed Thom as he struggled over her." She looked at her bloodstained hands as if she had never seen them before. "I was glad to see him collapse, glad he was dead."

"Sergeant, Mimi saved my wife from a man who had threatened her own life as well as mine," Jean Pierre said. "She deserves praise, and I intend to reward her."

"I don't deserve a reward," Mimi declared. At Jean Pierre's puzzled frown, she asked, "Don't you know what the two of you had to do with all of this? Thom had it all planned that I was to try to get you to marry me last summer, Jean Pierre, even though you'd never shown me much attention. Then, while you'd be off trapping most of the year, he and I could be together. That way, he said, if I became pregnant, I would have a husband to name as father." The unbelieving gasps from Rose and Jean Pierre made no impression on the big-eyed young woman. Her eyes burned with torment, though she focused them on some distant, unseen object.

Rose asked the soldiers, "Can Mimi stay here tonight?"

"We would be responsible for her," Jean Pierre added.

"No," Mimi said, her voice as expressionless as her eyes. "I want to be alone. I want to go back to my room, unless these soldiers mean to take me to jail."

Jean Pierre and the soldiers conferred, then the one who seemed in charge said to Mimi, "We'll escort you back to your room for the night and post a guard outside until we can take you to tell your story to a magistrate tomorrow.''

Rose rushed to put her arms around Mimi. ''Thank you for saving Jean Pierre and me. You're the bravest person I've ever known. Both of us will go to the magistrate's office in the morning, and we're going to take care of you.''

Rose and Jean Pierre stared with compassion at the obviously tortured Mimi. Numbed, they moved to the far end of the balcony while Mark and the other soldier removed Thom Keller's body, unmindful of the little showers of rain the lingering storm blew on them. Shortly a third soldier came and asked them to sign brief statements relating the happenings of the evening. Left alone at last, they embraced without words.

Maria returned after she and Mark let out the soldiers, assuring the couple that the gate was once more secured. To be certain that all was safe for the rest of the night, Mark announced that he would keep watch from the front room downstairs. Directing Rose and Jean Pierre to another bedroom which she had hastily prepared, the black woman washed the blood from Rose's body and helped her slip into a fresh gown. It was there in the bedroom down the hall from their original one that the exhausted Rose finally fell asleep in her husband's arms.

Jean Pierre watched with raised eyebrows the next afternoon when Louis appeared in the arched doorway leading from the back section of the building into the enclosed courtyard, his saddlebags still over his shoulder. Not that Louis's appearance was such a surprise; after all, he had told them the day of their departure from Grenfall that he would be traveling into New Orleans soon. But the fact that his wife rose from the table where they sat idling over tea and rushed to throw herself into Louis's arms and burst into tears did grab Jean Pierre's attention.

''Rose is doubly upset at all this messy business,'' he confided to his friend when Rose allowed Maria to escort her upstairs to lie down and rest before dinner. Since he was no longer jealous of Louis—well, he allowed privately, maybe a little—he believed he understood her need for added reassurance that all would be well.

"No wonder Rose looked unusually pale," Louis remarked, his mind boggled from the stories that both Jean Pierre and she had told him upon his arrival. He couldn't forget the way Rose had hugged him and whispered over and over in a broken voice that only Jean Pierre's fortunate absence had kept her husband from being the victim of Thom Keller's madness, that she had no idea that anyone could be as evil as Phillip obviously was. "I well remember Rufus from our run-in with him over his trap last year, and I met Keller at Ma Dibert's when you did, but I never would have guessed they were that rotten. Frankly, I hadn't expected Phillip to be so set on revenge as to hire someone to do away with you. Damn! I'm glad he was sent back to Spain. No telling what he'd try next if he were given the chance."

Jean Pierre nodded thoughtfully. "Rose seemed to be taking everything in stride until a soldier came early this morning to tell us that Mimi must have had poison stashed in her room. When they knocked about dawn to rouse her but got no answer, they went inside and found her dead on the floor. She left a note telling about Thom's dastardly deeds and of her wish to leave the world." His brow furrowed and he went on in a troubled voice. "I feel guilty for not insisting that the soldiers let her stay here last night."

Louis jumped in then with questions, motioning for Maria to bring a bottle of brandy as he listened to all that Jean Pierre had been doing in New Orleans. As Jean Pierre gave a report of his second meeting the previous night with Governor Unzaga and his failure to get a quick decision on the land request, Louis drained his glass of brandy.

"Damn!" Louis said, rising and pacing across the brick floor of the courtyard. "I know how much you two wanted to return to the bayou and begin your home."

"Not badly enough to have last night's actions take place," Jean Pierre replied.

"You can't blame yourself for that."

"If I hadn't given in to my infernal impatience at the

ponderous workings of the government, Rose wouldn't have been alone and vulnerable last night. How can I ever make it up to her, Louis?'' His eyes begged for answers.

"How would I know?'' his friend rejoined. "I never thought I had much talent when it came to understanding the fairer sex.'' Wanting to erase the solemnity from the face across from him, he added with a little chuckle, "My talent with the ladies lies in a far different field.''

Jean Pierre responded with a weak smile before returning to his brandy.

"Chomping at the bit isn't going to make the Superior Council meet any earlier,'' Louis pointed out. "From what you say, the governor won't show you special favor and sign the title, but neither is he going to try to influence the council members to vote against approval. You know there's nothing on your record, or Pierre's, to keep that grant from being made. Try to set your mind on something else over the next few months—like bringing back the smile to your wife's pretty face.''

Jean Pierre relaxed a little about the problem of receiving title to the land. What Louis said about both the land grant and Rose made sense. She did need to have something nice happen to her. All afternoon, one corner of his mind kept straying upstairs to the beautiful blonde who seemed to be struggling hard to accept the ugliness she'd had to face during the past twenty-four hours. He had no idea that her thoughts about how near he had come to suffering death or serious injury at the hands of the obviously deranged Thom Keller formed a basic part of her inner turmoil.

Forcing his thoughts back to Louis, Jean Pierre asked, "What are your plans?''

Louis smiled and said, "I'm going to leave this fall and travel to see part of the Old world. Father says he's going to turn over the running of Grenfall to me next year and take Celeste with him to visit family in France. If I'm to get a chance to give the women in Paris a whirl before I settle down at Grenfall, then this is the time to do it.''

"Maybe a long trip is what you need,'' Jean Pierre said, his thoughts running back to Louis's bouts of depression all winter over his botched-up marriage, and then the blow of losing his wife and unborn child. "Guess Jarrette won't like seeing Celeste take off with her father for a long visit in France next year, though."

"Father and I both favor the way Jarrette seems to bring out the best in my flighty little sister. If they still have eyes for each other when she returns, I suspect Father will give them his blessing. We both want her to marry for love." He didn't need to say more; both men recalled too well the tragedy of Louis's forced marriage.

They sat in companionable silence awhile, sipping their brandy and watching the shadows lengthen on the bricks of the private courtyard.

"While my leg healed I spent some time thinking about the future of our fur business, Louis. Yesterday I went to the trading shed to sell the pelts I had stashed before Rufus jumped me, and I began liking that idea of renting a warehouse of our own better and better. What about you?"

"Sounds like a worthwhile idea," Louis responded. "The reserve in our account convinces me that we've done well."

"While I was with Beau Bradford last night, we got to talking about the fur business. If what he says is true—and as you likely already know, the man seems very knowledgable —the trading companies in England are suffering from a lack of good pelts now that the colonists across the Atlantic have taken up arms against the British. He said that they've been sending theirs secretly to France over the past couple of years. If we could find a direct buyer for our furs over there, allowing us to bypass the dealers here, we could make a far bigger profit. So long as the British ships have access to the Mississippi, we'd have no problem with shipping."

"And with Jarrette planning to trap a couple of years more with Arlee Simpson, we'd be guaranteed trustworthy representatives to trap and buy for us," Louis added, his mien showing his approval. "What does Rose think of your plan?"

Jean Pierre jerked his head toward his partner in surprise. "I haven't discussed it with her. This is men's business." He poured himself another brandy, becoming interested in studying the facets of the cut-crystal decanter in the fading light before returning it to its place on the table. Swishing the amber fluid in his glass with unnecessary force, he sent a questing look toward the Creole. "Why do you ask?"

Louis let out a quiet chuckle, not ducking his friend's piercing look. "From all that I've learned about your wife, she might not agree that everything you do is your business alone. I gather she's not your typical young woman from bayou country." He wondered how much he should tell Jean Pierre about Rose's keen interest in the partnership when it appeared that Jean Pierre was dead. Even he had been surprised at the sharpness of her mind and her grasp of what her husband was now referring to as "men's business." Deciding that to mention such details would indeed be none of his affair and that he might already have overstepped the bounds of friendship, Louis scuttled the idea of bringing up anything more to add to that hint of jealousy on his partner's face. He sipped his brandy. "You're a lucky man."

"I'm well aware of that, and I've an idea how I can put that smile back on Rose's face."

By the time twilight was creeping inside the courtyard and the two parted to go up to their bedrooms, Louis to dress for a call upon a young widow who had sent him an invitation to visit the next time he was in New Orleans, and Jean Pierre to see if Rose's nap had made her feel better, both wore smiles at the thought of the plans that Jean Pierre had revealed.

Mimi's funeral the next afternoon was a dismal affair. At the Cabildo, Beau Bradford had heard about the deaths of Mimi and Thom Keller and the incident involving the Guilbeaus and had hurried to call upon Rose and Jean Pierre. Shocked at what he learned, Beau volunteered to accompany Louis and them to the cemetery, where Jean Pierre had bought space for Mimi in one of the eerie-looking tombs above ground. Authorities in attendance at the brief ceremony reported that they had shipped Thom's body upriver to his wife at Natchez for burial.

Afterward, with tears sometimes threatening to blur the

ink, Rose had written a letter to Ma Dibert and tucked
Mimi's farewell note to her inside. She felt sure that
the sad-faced Ma would like knowing of Mimi's declaration of love for her mother and sorrow at the grief she had
brought her.

Not until the following evening did an air of normalcy
return to the Brearde townhouse on Bourbon Street.

"How much longer will we be in New Orleans?" Rose
asked that night when Jean Pierre and she returned from
dining at an elegant restaurant beside the Mississippi. They
had chosen to remain in the second-best bedroom, where
there were no reminders of Thom Keller and that stormy
night.

Jean Pierre cocked his head and leaned back against the
upholstered chair, missing not a movement of his wife as
she made ready for bed. Just that afternoon, the new
gowns had been delivered, and, to his supreme delight,
she had worn one to dinner. He watched her slide the blue
taffeta off her shoulders and let it whisper to the floor.
Stirrings inside him sent extra warmth to his eyes. "We're
leaving the day after tomorrow." From behind a curtain of
pinkish blond, her eyes peeked at him before she retrieved
the rustling gown and hung it up. "Would you go with me
anywhere, Rose? Or only back to bayou country?" he
teased.

"Anywhere, yes," she replied, sliding a coquettish look
at him from beneath half-lowered lashes while shedding
petticoats and chemise to stand unclothed a moment before
reaching for a nightdress. The way he seemed never to tire
of watching her prepare for bed pleased some wayward
part of her, called up the trace of a wanton he had stirred
within. A sudden awareness of him quickened her heartbeat and led her to listen to his breathing. His very
presence permeated the dimly lit room. Her breasts warmed
from the heat of his gaze, and her fingers fumbled as they
lifted the garment over her head.

"Don't," he begged in a voice thick with desire. He
had shucked his own clothing, except for underdrawers.
"Come to me just as you are." The lift of her breasts

when her arms carried the garment up seemed to be an act of pure feminine grace, and his breath caught in his throat. His hands already sensed the way the curves of her hips would feel beneath their touch. Deliberately he had made no attempt to make love to her since the night of violence, wanting to give her time to regain her former serenity. In the glow of the candlelight, his love for her stretched between them like a cord, beckoned her to him as surely as did his words.

Rose saw the fullness of his mouth and felt the force of him wash over her, draw her, set her pulses skipping. With hair flowing across her naked breasts and shoulders, she moved in a trancelike way to where he sat upon the oversized chair with open arms, lips smiling, eyes promising. When he cradled her against his virile body and buried his head in the blond cloud half-hiding her breasts, she closed her eyes and arched her neck across his hard-muscled arm. Her blood became coursing fire, even before his mouth closed over a nipple. The roughness of his tongue upon the tight bud called to secret senses, and when his dark head moved to reward the other nipple in like manner, an audible purr eased from her throat. That feeling of enveloping warmth which always came when he held her in his arms soothed away any leftover fears, and she hungrily pulled his mouth to hers, drinking in his obvious passion for her. Her kiss-dampened breasts swelled and throbbed against his furred chest, their firm softness acquiescing to the masculine planes in titillating invitation.

As a loving forefinger traced Rose's delicate profile, then returned to linger a moment at the fuller upper lip, Jean Pierre worshiped Rose with his eyes. He sighed when he realized he could never express the depth of his love for her and said, "I love you more than anyone has ever loved before."

"Not more than I love you," she countered, nibbling at the hand caressing her face, loving the smell of his skin.

"I'll bet I do." One hand fondled her breasts while he claimed her mouth again. Lifting his face, he whispered against her lips, "I'd prove it if I knew how."

Rose reeled from the play of his hands. Sitting across

his lap there in the chair, she could feel the warmth of his arousal and the bubbling of her own throbbing need. The paths of his hands upon her breasts and stomach sizzled, even after their creators moved on to more daring patches. A slow trek down the outer curves of her legs and an even slower one back up the inner lines to the pulsating apex dizzied her, brought a moan low in her throat, made her press closer with new breathlessness, made her own hands clutch convulsively at his hair, his neck, and then move down to ease in begging circles against his chest. The knobs of his nipples seemed as turgid as her own.

Their exchanges of uneven breaths, hot, wet kisses, and unabandoned caresses fueled inner fires into demanding flames. Standing with Rose in his arms, her mouth maintaining its hold on his, Jean Pierre took her to their bed. With one quick movement he shed his undergarment, standing before her in what she deemed magnificent splendor. His manhood taunted her as he lay beside her, and she reached to encircle him with her fingers, gripped with a roar of desire at the feel of the velvet-sheathed warmth, awed at his obvious surrender to some compelling, inward pleasure. And then she lost herself in his renewed, devastating interest in those secret places leading directly to her center. Imitating his own bravery in ferreting out new ways to create thrills for her partner, she explored the lean hips, the hard buttocks, the manly crevices, her hands at last returning to that fascinating proof of his manhood. All at once, Rose wanted him inside her, felt she would explode if he denied her.

When she pressed closer, a great shudder and worshipping moan from Jean Pierre signaled his readiness, and he accepted her invitation with an energy that quite took their breaths away and set already racing pulses to new paces. Exquisite agony led them in their rhythmic search to ride and conquer the waves threatening to drown them. A burst upon a final crest hurled them into that glorious abyss of pure sensation they sought, where they clung as one being before accepting their despised separateness. Still close, still joined in a withering tenderness, they nestled like just-hatched birds in an untried world.

Jean Pierre felt his heart had no edges, so filled was it with love for the young woman he held. The memory of Thom Keller's cruel attack a few nights ago tortured him, but not as much as the guilt of his having left her unprotected that night. How could he have faced another day if he had lost her or found her injured? With his head he nudged hers upward so that he could kiss her. "I love you." His voice came out in a whisper because it could manage no surer tone.

Responding to his kiss with passion-bruised lips, Rose replied in like breathlessness, "And I love you." Her eyes measured the dormant love in his, and she suddenly felt compelled to hug him closer. Without him she had no purpose in life; that she had already found out.

"I've thought of a way I can prove how much I love you," he said, his voice feathering warmly across her face and caressing her ears with its bass vibrato.

"How, darling?" Was he going to name a bauble or bit of frippery found in one of the many shops they had visited? But no, she realized, there was a grave look in those dark eyes.

"I want to take you to England to let you meet your relatives and see where your parents came from." Jean Pierre watched black pinpoints swim within her blue eyes and heard her catch her breath in surprise.

"I don't feel a need to go to England, but I appreciate your thoughtfulness." When his determined expression didn't alter, she asked, "Anyway, could we afford the time and—"

"Yes," he interrupted. "We'll have to hold up on starting a home till we get title to our land, and that's going to be in the fall after the Superior Council meets and rules."

"What about Maman and—"

Again he didn't let her finish her excuse. "We'll write a letter and tell them I'm taking you on a honeymoon. And you did say earlier that you'd go anywhere with me, didn't you?"

She propped herself up on an arm and rested her head on her hand, never taking her gaze from his face. Now that he had mentioned a honeymoon, she liked the idea better. "You're the most surprising man I've ever been in bed with," she teased, liking the way he leered at her silly remark. "When would we go?"

He filched a hidden curl from beneath her neck and pulled it forward to wrap lightly around her breast. Dipping his head then to kiss the silken-framed spot, he said, "In two days. We'll sail on the *Talisman* with Beau. He went with me this morning to book passage." The ruby pendant caught his eye in the flickering light, and he lifted it from its nestling spot at the top of her breasts, sliding it back and forth across the chain as he had seen her do so often.

A smile and a little squeal of delight at the thought of having him all to herself told him of her acceptance. An impulsive hug and kiss added a kind of thanks. Then a soft "Thank you" filled his ears as well as his heart. Playfully she rumpled his hair, laughing to see the curls fall in greater number across his forehead. If to give her the trip pleased him so, why not enjoy it? After all, she felt guilty that he had suffered Rufus's attack; for if she had not allowed herself to get into the awkward situation with Phillip de Cordoza that night in the pergola, none of the ugliness would have taken place.

"If I'd known the idea would please you so," he intoned after capturing her in a bear hug and rolling her to rest atop him, "we would've already been on our way." Like a slight wound freshly cut, the knowledge that it was his fault that she had been assaulted smarted. If he hadn't flattened Keller after his vicious insinuations . . . if he hadn't gone to meet that night with the governor . . . And then his thoughts ran to the way her softness curved against him, the way her tongue dueled with his and stirred the embers into new life. She charmed him, thrilled him, gave back to him measure for measure. Love lived in the room again, its magic a balm to their spent bodies after they again became lost in ecstasy.

The next evening while Maria and Rose flitted about packing garments into the trunks Jean Pierre had purchased, he sat on the patio and smoked a cigar. The realization of a period of enforced inactivity on the ship, and possibly another one once they arrived in England, weighed upon him. Accustomed to the simple, uncluttered life of a trapper in the wilderness and to that of a Cajun on the bayou, he found it hard to imagine how one with his curse of impatience might spend his time in England at those times when Rose might be involved with kin.

His looking into the prospect of finding an English market for pelts from Louis's and his warehouse seemed the perfect solution. Not that he would ignore his wife, he reassured himself when Rose's voice or laughter floated down from the bedroom above where Maria and she were packing, for there would be time to care for her needs as well as those of his business interests. Waiting on the Spaniards to grant him title to the land next to Papa's would not be so bad now that the trip to England was a reality.

Rose stood between Jean Pierre and Beau at the rail of the *Talisman* the next afternoon, waving at those who had come to see them off—Louis, Maria, and Mark. Feeling the motion of the ship taking them farther away from her beloved Louisiana filled her heart with all kinds of misgivings, and she gripped Jean Pierre's arm tighter. What lay ahead in England? she wondered silently. Should she have given in to her handsome husband's invitation—or had "demand" been more like it, she thought, remembering that he had already booked passage before telling her of his plans. But since the trip was obviously for no reason except to please her, she couldn't say she found his high-handedness in this matter totally displeasing. Only that morning she had assured him again that she would be content to live on the bayou with him without knowing anything about her heritage; his quiet insistence had moved her, made her see again what a wonderful man she had married.

The loving Marie and Pierre had taught all their children that God was in his Heaven, with sure and complete control over their destiny. Her job, Rose reflected as the ship rounded the last curve in the Mississippi that shut off the view of New Orleans, was to accept and make the best of what came her way—even if she had to make a few alterations here and there.

Chapter Twenty-three

Made up mainly of older businessmen, the passenger list for the *Talisman* was small. Rose, Jean Pierre, and Beau found that they preferred their own company to that of their more sedate fellow travelers. Both Rose and Jean Pierre turned out to be good sailors, once they left the unstable waters off the shore, and the voyage from New Orleans to Portsmouth proved uneventful. Only one minor storm hindered the sturdy vessel.

Since the young people shared a table in the small dining room, they came to look forward to mealtimes. Jean Pierre and Beau liked comparing notes on what they had learned about the various Indian tribes, though the Acadian found it hard to believe that a grown man would desert his law office in New Orleans at sundry times just to explore Louisiana. Often the three exchanged stories about their growing-up years, sometimes ending up in bursts of laughter at the differences in the customs of the British and the Acadians. At times Beau related unusual cases from the law books he read, and Rose especially drank in every word. When he offered to share some of his books, she accepted eagerly and could be seen sitting on the top deck poring over the thick volumes while the restless Jean Pierre wandered about the ship, as often as not lending a hand to the sailors. Beau began joining Rose in the afternoons, and their earnest discussions would continue even after Jean Pierre came to lie on the deck near them and listen.

Rose made certain that Jean Pierre and she were on deck when the ship glided into Portsmouth. She tucked a gloved hand into his hooked arm and stared at the land of her parents, feeling a little rush of emotion at the strange thought that she might have just "come home."

And then it was time to set foot upon land. Pulling her fur-lined cape of blue velvet about her to ward off the damp, cutting wind, Rose followed Jean Pierre and the porters carrying their trunks down the gangplank. In the gray fog, she could barely see Beau's head above those around him as he waited for them up ahead on the crowded dock.

By the time they reached the Hart Inn on the far side of Portsmouth, its white-plastered walls striped by dark brown boards in precise curves and angles no longer seemed unusual to the newcomers. Rose's first view of the alien architecture, which Beau had designated as Tudor, had filled her with awe, but after passing blocks of the same basic style, she had accepted it as the natural way for English buildings to look. She realized that if she had not visited New Orleans, she would have been surprised at the narrowness of the streets, the proximity of the houses to one another, and the cobblestoned walkways and thoroughfares.

Jean Pierre made Rose feel special by ordering a hot bath set up for her in front of the coal fire glowing in the grate of the fireplace in their room. She dawdled in the scented water while he went downstairs to acquaint himself with their new surroundings. Carefully she unpacked the gowns from Madame de Pointerre's shop, choosing a pale pink silk. With her shining hair coiled low in a loose chignon and her elegant new gown rustling about the pink satin slippers from Natchitoches, Rose gave in to the excitement of being in England.

"Are you feeling better?" Jean Pierre asked when he came to escort her down to the inn's dining room. The pinched, white look on her face when they docked had bothered him, and he was glad to see that her bath had restored most of the pretty pinkness to her skin. All the while he had been exploring the inn and the section of the

city it occupied, he had fought down the image of her
loveliness as it would appear as she bathed. Even as he led
her into the dining room, his eyes sparkled with his plans
for after dinner. And small wonder, he mused, when her
own eyes sent such blatant invitations.

"I'm glad your husband and you are comfortable, Lady
Rosalind," Beau said, purposefully using the proper form
of address to gauge her reaction. Her eyebrows arched in
question, and he added, "You'll have to become accustomed to being addressed in that manner now that you are
to be at Heatherlee."

Rose glanced from Beau to Jean Pierre and back to the
blond barrister. "I can't be 'Rose' anymore?"

"Only to your husband, close family members, and
friends." Her look of wide-eyed disbelief brought a smile.

"Then you, Beau, will continue to call me Rose," she
announced, her voice serious and light at the same time.
With a secretive smile at her husband, she said, "And you
can call me Cajun Rose." A deep pink tinted her face
when he shot her a knowing look and a slow smile.

Jean Pierre had never used the endearment except at
times of intense emotion during or after lovemaking, and
his shock that she would mention it aloud, much less in
front of Beau, showed in his rugged face, brought the soft
look to the area around his mouth. Was he destined to love
her more with each passing day? He wrenched his thoughts
back to the food being served.

It was still early the next morning when the threesome
met in the common room of the inn and set out on the
journey northwestward. The hired carriage, piled high in
back with their trunks, soon left the port city behind and
began its uphill climb toward the hamlet of Wanington, its
driver a kind-faced man with a patch over one eye.

"How far from Wanington is your home?" Jean Pierre
asked Beau.

"Two or three hours by carriage, less by horseback. My
family lives near Salisbury. My father keeps offices both in
Portsmouth and Salisbury, but our main residence is on the

family's land. My grandfather was a squire, seeing to the planting and harvesting himself.''

"You did tell us that your business in Louisiana is concluded, yes?'' Rose asked.

"Then we'll expect you to visit us at Heatherlee while we're here,'' Jean Pierre said when Beau nodded. The thought of not knowing anyone with knowledge of Louisiana shook him. Rose would be engrossed in getting to know about her family, but what would he—With a smile, he recalled his plans to search for an outlet for Louis's and his pelts.

"You can depend on it,'' Beau assured him. "Also I'm going to insist that Father allow me to handle Rose's affairs so that I'll not run out of reasons to call.''

At her first distant view of Heatherlee through the trees, Rose couldn't decide if Beau's decision to keep mum about her father's ancestral home rated as a blessing or a pox. A hint would have helped her to accept that what he was now pointing out to Jean Pierre and her was truly where her father and his people had lived for centuries— since the rule of Edward I in the thirteenth century, according to Beau and the books Father Sebastian had loaned her.

They had been traveling for some time in gently rolling hills. Dense forests lay between farmland and occasional villages. From a closer rise, Beau indicated the huge building of pink stone towering above the trees as Heatherlee. As they drew nearer, Rose could see that the house was larger than any she had ever seen or even imagined, having three stories and innumerable chimneys topped with clusters of what Beau had identified in Portsmouth as "chimney pots.''

Beau was explaining further, "Each pot connects to a separate fireplace.'' He was having misgivings about not preparing Rose for the shock such grandeur was bound to cause in a person from a newly settled land. She seemed pale and agitated.

"Who builds that many fires?'' asked the practical-minded Jean Pierre, as astonished as Rose at the sight before them.

"And for whom?" Rose asked. Even Grenfall, the biggest place she had ever seen up close, had only eight chimneys, while she guessed Heatherlee had twenty.

"There are great numbers of guests at various times. Friends and relatives often come and stay for days at a time. They live such distances apart that it makes sense to visit awhile before making the return trip. The men often hunt, while the women play games or do needlework," Beau explained. "And there would have to be many servants in such a stately home."

"Servants?" Rose asked. "Do you mean slaves?"

"Not slaves, only servants." The Englishman smiled at her naïveté. "Many live inside the manor in their own quarters, while others live in small houses out back and nearby in the forests. Some may even come, when needed, from the tenant houses in Wanington, the village we just passed through."

Rose burst out, "I don't belong here. Everything overwhelms me." She reached for Jean Pierre's hand on the carriage seat and shook her head. Even the contact with him failed to allay her doubts as to the wisdom of having come to England. Her only consolation lay in the reminder that this trip was a gift from him and that he wouldn't be out of her sight.

They entered the grounds then and Rose could see the corner turrets in detail above the surrounding brick wall. Just past the columned entry through the wall, she saw identical circular fountains on manicured green lawns, one on either side of the cobblestoned drive. The stone mansion had no welcoming porch, only wide, curved, marble steps leading up to massive twin black doors, where gleaming brass lions held giant loops in their mouths for handles.

Rose could never remember for certain how she managed to live through her introduction to Heatherlee. Beau had sent a messenger from the village to alert the household, and by the time they entered, the entire staff stood lined up in the receiving hall to welcome them, their uniforms giving the Louisianans little hint as to their duties.

Gentlemanly, charming, and apparently bowled over by
the beauty of his grand-niece and the commanding appearance of her husband, Sir Thomas Atwood eased her
through the necessary introductions in record time. He was
the only permanent resident at the moment, he told her.
Rose clung to the names of the first in the long line of
servants: David Dunston, chief steward; Agnes Hanley,
chief housekeeper; Anna Carruthers, chief cook. But after
those few, the faces and names of the twenty-odd persons
serving the house became muddled.

When a pert, red-haired girl remained, bobbing and
curtsying again after Sir Thomas had dismissed the others,
he informed Rose that she, Kitty Banyan, would serve as
Rose's personal maid; but at the old gentleman's presenta-
tion of a young man to attend Jean Pierre in the couple's
assigned apartment, the square-shouldered Acadian refused
in a positive manner, cutting a look toward Beau for
assistance. Sir Thomas made no comment and dismissed
the servant.

After Beau left to travel the additional three hours to his
home, Rose and Jean Pierre accompanied Sir Thomas on a
quick tour of the main receiving rooms on the ground
floor. By the time they arrived at their own quarters on the
first floor, Kitty had unpacked their trunks and prepared a
bath for Rose in a small room opening off the bedroom. In
addition to separate bathrooms, dressing rooms, and the
large bedroom, complete with window balcony and carved
marble fireplace, their apartment included a sitting room
appointed as elegantly as any of the larger ones on the
ground floor. Everything about Heatherlee seemed to Rose
to be grandiose, ornate, elaborate—too much, she thought,
her mind in a whirl.

"Your father grew up in an imposing place, didn't he?"
Jean Pierre asked Rose that night when they returned to
their rooms after having dinner with Sir Thomas. Jean
Pierre had done a better job of concealing his shock over
finding themselves in such grandeur than she, but inside,
his surprise equaled hers. He sank wearily upon the settee
before the fireplace in the living room, having shed his
cravat and coat. "Why is your great-uncle the only one

living here? I thought the uncle owning it had been dead for some months.''

''I gather my cousin Ashley, who inherited, is only sixteen and hasn't moved here yet with his mother from his former home,'' Rose replied, backing up to stand before him for help in unfastening her gown. The maid Kitty had seemed hurt that Rose had sent her away upon their return and not allowed her to assist in the preparation for bed.

When Jean Pierre had freed the fastenings on the gown, he pulled her onto his lap, where she nestled against him, murmuring contented little sounds. ''Tomorrow I need to check out the horses Sir Thomas told me I might enjoy riding,'' he said against her hair. ''I've had about all the inactivity I can stand.'' He slipped the pins from her hair, letting the cascade of pinkish blond bury his hands. Cupping the bones of her skull in both hands, he tipped her face to bestow a kiss on the tempting mouth. The sibilance of her silk-clad breasts as they met his leanness called up a warm fullness down low. A sudden need to hold her naked against him and reclaim that tantalizing body washed over him, a need interweaving with a shadowed doubt nagging at him ever since he had first seen Heatherlee. Was she still happy that she had married him now that she saw what kind of life she had been born to live? Would their visit in England harm their marriage? The thought of losing even a fraction of her love roared through his brain with a drive akin to the storm building in his loins.

Rose sensed a new urgency in Jean Pierre's kisses but had no inkling as to what created it. True, they had made love infrequently on the voyage, due to the roughness of the sea, but both seemed to have accepted the circumstances. When he ripped off her gown and chemise and carried her to the bed in the darkened bedroom off the sitting room, she stared at him in wonder, caught up in his apparent inner turmoil as though it seeped through her pores and became hers as well. He had seemed oblivious to the sounds of tearing fabric, seemed obsessed with devouring her breasts with tongue and mouth as he walked with her held high against him. When they lay with bodies entwined, she realized she had never seen him so impassioned, so forceful. Again and again he caressed her yielding body with something like frenzy, tasted its satiny curves and recesses with devastating thoroughness, bringing jolts of searing ecstasy she had never before experienced. Weak with love, with delicious wanting, drinking in the hoarse words of worship, Rose trembled for him, sought to return a measure of the intense roiling that seemed to be overwhelming him, driving him to possess more of her than ever before.

Like a tempest, Jean Pierre swept her into his private turbulence when he rose above her and made his riotous claim on her womanhood. Rose surrendered, offered all, unable and unwilling to deny the cataclysm raging within them, driving them in some new, tumultuous rhythm. A tremendous force she could sense in every cell, but couldn't identify, spewed them into a timeless moment of delicate savagery, leaving them speechless, breathless, all run down, clasping each other as though to let go would create disaster. With tremulous exchange of endearments, they sank into dreamless sleep.

Gowned and coiffed daily by the insistent Kitty, while Jean Pierre tried out several horses from the stables and explored the countryside, Rose spent her waking hours the next few days with Sir Thomas. He seemed to enjoy acquainting her with her new world. Gradually she relaxed and began to feel that something unknown had drawn her to Heatherlee.

Without the slim, white-haired and -mustached Sir Thomas, she doubted she would have made the transition so readily or so painlessly. Only as she allowed him to see that she was receptive did he fill her in on family history and affairs. Each day brought new revelations from each, and Rose sometimes had difficulty in sorting and cataloging all the information. From time to time, she could tell that her great-uncle found it equally as tedious to follow the accounts of her own life both before and after her marriage to Jean Pierre.

"You say my grandparents, Lord and Lady Winstead, have another daughter still living?" Rose inquired after breakfast the third morning after their arrival. Jean Pierre seemed taken with the fine horses and the open fields of the estate, and she was glad he had found an activity to enjoy while she tried to learn about her family. At night he still made love to her, but he had become more restrained after that first night at Heatherlee. "Where is she and why did she not inherit?"

"She lives on her own estate in Scotland with a large family nearby. In England, the legacies always pass through the oldest male line," Sir Thomas replied.

Rose nodded, recalling her readings aboard the *Talisman* in Beau's law books about entail and primogeniture. "I understand that my father's oldest brother, Uncle Percy, inherited everything after my grandfather died. And when he left no children at his death earlier this year, the land and title went to the next son or his heirs."

"Quite right, my dear," the old gentleman said. "And since the next son was your father and you turned out to be a young lady, the legacy now moves to his younger brother, George. George's death came prematurely, I'm afraid, but he did leave a son to take on the title and lands."

"When will I get to meet this cousin? Why doesn't he live here?"

"You'll meet Ashley soon. He's only sixteen and still a ward of the courts and his mother. Neither she nor the lad seems to be in a hurry to leave the manor house George built for them on a far corner of the estate. I doubt they will be moving here until nearer Ashley's eighteenth birthday."

"My father's older sister, the one I was named after, died last year, did she not?" Rose felt she was about to get the facts of her father's family straight. "Is she the one who left funds to find me and bequeathed me some jewelry?"

"Quite right, my child. I believe you have it all sorted out now," Sir Thomas replied, nodding happily as he sipped his third cup of tea and smiled across the table at her. "Rosalinde doted on your father and always dreamed of meeting you someday. When the letter came from a

Pierre Guilbeau, telling of your birth and the deaths of Charles and his family, she was eager to sail across to find you and bring you back here to rear. But her father and her husband forbade it, saying that she had no assurance you could be located. And of course she had her own children to consider.''

''Do they live near here?'' she asked, not sure she liked hearing that she might have been snatched away from Marie and Pierre and brought up in England. How then would she ever have found Jean Pierre?

''Her oldest son and his own son live within a half-day of here. Rosalinde's husband was a viscount, and her son is now holder of that title and the lands accompanying it.'' He added, ''Had you been a man and had a son, first you and then your child would have become the next earls of Wanington.''

Rose laughed, the first good laugh she had had since her arrival in England. She could tell that her companion was a bit nonplussed by her outburst, and she quickly controlled herself. She could not have told if she was amused at the idea that she could have been a male or at the idea that a person reared as a Cajun could hold a British title.

''My dear, I cannot tell you how delightful it is to have you here. When my wife died some years ago and your grandfather, my brother-in-law, invited me here to live, I never dreamed that one day Charles's daughter would be sharing meals with me. I met your mother once just before the marriage, and you are even more lovely than she was.''

''Are any of my mother's people in the area?'' She still felt awkward asking about her parents; Marie and Pierre had filled the roles so well and so naturally.

''I fear not. Your mother was an only child. Your grandfather was a silversmith in Salisbury, and your grandmother was frail, not living long after your mother married Charles and left for Maryland, if I remember correctly. We might take a day trip over to look about the place and check the headstones in the cemetery. To see the old cathedral is a treat in itself, and there may be records of interest there.''

Rose nodded her agreement with his suggestion, watching

the old gentleman dab lightly at his mustache with his
linen napkin before rolling it into a tube and inserting it in
the monogrammed silver ring alongside his plate. She
followed his example, and they moved to the library where
a roaring fire invited them to sit and continue their visit.
Jean Pierre rarely returned from his jaunts until noon.

"Lady Rosalinde's son and family should be arriving
today," Sir Thomas said. "I took the liberty of sending
them word of your arrival."

"They'll be the ones wishing to verify my ruby pendant
as part of the Winstead jewelry controlled by Lady Rosalinde,
yes?" Rose asked.

"Please do not think anyone doubts your identity; however, since Lady Rosalinde removed the piece—a favorite
of hers, I understand—from her own neck to give your
father as a gift for him to give his bride, the viscount, her
son, would readily recognize it," he said a bit defensively.
"Sketches from the goldsmith who created it are in the
hands of Beau's father, Lady Rosalinde's retainer, so there
is really no problem." As he spoke, his eyes lingered on
the ruby showing plainly just at the top of Rose's décolleté
gown of dark blue wool. "The pieces left to you have been
reposing in the viscount's safe ever since his mother's
death. I'm sure he will be bringing them to store in the
Heatherlee vault until they are officially presented to you."

"I've told Beau, as barrister and as friend, and I'll tell
you, Uncle," Rose said, her eyes narrowing with her
earnestness. "I have no need or desire for valuable jewelry. My coming to visit has nothing to do with any legacy
my aunt left me."

Late that afternoon from the bedroom window Rose
watched several fine horses and carriages enter the grounds.
After urging the already-dressed and fidgety Jean Pierre to
go on down early to share a glass of sherry with Sir
Thomas, she asked Kitty to help her prepare an especially
unique toilette for the occasion. Chatting easily, both
decided that Rose should wear the champagne-colored
watered-silk purchased in New Orleans, a gown that blended
prettily with her blond hair and pale skin.

After one more critical look at her elaborately styled

coiffeur and the becoming pale gown with its matching lace flowers re-embroidered on the bodice and petticoat, Rose allowed the maid to drape the matching shawl across her bare shoulders. Never had the ruby glowed with more fire. She was ready to go down to meet her kinsmen. With a trace of a grin on her face as she descended the curving staircase, she practiced opening and closing the fan Kitty had fetched.

When all the talk ceased at her entrance into the room called the Great Hall, Rose almost lost the newfound courage that Sir Thomas had helped her build. But Jean Pierre's reassuring wink and the old gentleman's warm, appreciative eyes as they rested upon her saved her.

Lady Rosalinde's son, the Viscount of Lombard, must be older than Papa, Rose guessed. Solemnly he examined the young woman when Sir Thomas presented her.

"I remember that your mother had hair of that remarkable shade of blond," the viscount said. He continued to appraise her. "My mother's young brother Charles showed excellent taste in choosing a beautiful wife. You resemble her a great deal, my dear, and I am proud to claim you as a first cousin."

"You're very kind," Rose said, flushing a little from his close scrutiny.

"Even from where I stand," the viscount intoned with certainty, "I recognize the ruby you wear as the one my mother often wore when I was a lad." With no warmth in his pale blue eyes, he added, "May you enjoy your visit here in England."

Following her husband's lead, the viscountess civilly but coolly welcomed her husband's kinswoman to England. A stout woman with broad shoulders, she in no fashion looked the way Rose had thought a viscountess would look, despite the lavish display of sparkling emeralds and diamonds above a large expanse of bosom.

Right away Rose liked Ashley, the teenaged son of her father's younger brother George and heir to Heatherlee. Gangling and awkward, he blushed furiously when she paid him special attention. His widowed mother, Catherine, a seemingly sensible, down-to-earth type among the other

aloof, reserved callers, won Rose's instant admiration by
doing no more than smiling warmly upon being introduced
and asking in a sincere way if her husband and she had
become rested from their long sea voyage.

"How far away is Ashley's and your home?" asked
Rose, hoping to get to know the young widow better.
"I've been looking forward to meeting both of you."

"An hour's ride," Catherine replied. "Mayhap your
husband and you will come and visit soon? Although
Ashley is heir to all of Heatherlee, he is still in need of my
guidance. If it were not for his having inherited his father's
business acumen, I would fear for him more than I do. It is
my fervent prayer that he gains in both stature and wisdom
over this next year of schooling so that we might go ahead
and take up residence here in the main house."

Harold, son of the viscount and viscountess, made no
inroads into Rose's affection, despite the fact that they
were second cousins. Thirtyish and unmarried, he hovered,
it seemed to her, like some vulture waiting for a meal.
When even Jean Pierre seemed to be having trouble
conversing with Harold, Rose knew that the slight blond
man was truly unapproachable. Brazenly he eyed her
cleavage, and at every halfway decent opportunity he
touched her—her arm, or hand, or bare shoulder—even
while Jean Pierre stood near. Never during the long dinner
did she look up and not find his strange, amber-colored
eyes studying her. She wondered, with an inward shiver, if
his eyes might not glow green in the night like those of an
animal. Was he perhaps angered that his grandmother
hadn't left him the Winstead jewels? A glance at his
bejeweled mother told her that he had no reason to be
coveting valuables. Obviously Harold, as the eldest son,
would someday come into his father's title and estates and
be an entity in his own right. Then why the scrutinizing
looks at her?

Merilyn Fenton, a cousin so far removed that Rose
could not make the connection even when it was explained,
seemed as fascinated with Harold as Rose was repelled.
Rather plain and a bit taller than the slight, pale man, she
hovered at his side and hung on his every word, having to

stoop to look into his pasty face. She appeared not much younger than Harold.

The twenty-odd remaining guests were, like Merilyn, distant cousins. While pleasant enough, they made no lasting impressions on their newly discovered relative from Louisiana. Rose gathered from Sir Thomas that the group would remain for a few days at Heatherlee before returning the great distances to their homes. Fervently she hoped that in time she might find some of them more congenial. Thankful that the ladies wished to retire early after their long carriage rides, Rose returned to her rooms, leaving Jean Pierre to join the men in the library for cards and whiskey. It was long past midnight before she tired of waiting for Jean Pierre and stilled her whirling thoughts enough to be able to slip between the fragrant linen sheets and sleep.

While the men hunted deer in a nearby forest the next day, the ladies gathered on the second floor in the room called the salon, its great length covering over half the width of the house. Rose recalled Sir Thomas telling her it had been designed to offer indoor entertainment during the cold, wet English winters. She had found the room so beautiful and intriguing that he had taken extra time to explain all he knew about its contents. Numerous groupings of chairs were placed randomly and there were writing tables and armless gilt chairs on both sides of one of the several window alcoves, both tables inlaid with tortoiseshell on brass.

If she had been asked to select a major point of interest in the salon, Rose thought that morning, she would probably choose the massive, white marble fireplace. The mantel was supported by sculpted muscular figures and topped by additional sculpture arranged in a sylvan scene. As this was only her second visit to the salon, she found herself still captivated by the decorative ceiling with its heavy squares of gilt molding serving as frames for the miniature oil paintings covering the vast area overhead, each of a different yet similar floral design. That she seemed the only one awed by the splendor of Heatherlee puzzled Rose.

She found before the day was over that she was enjoying the company of one of the distant cousins, pretty, auburn-haired Roxley Lindley. Chatting easily, the two young women rested on neighboring chairs at one end of the salon after having tired themselves at learning to play whist.

Merilyn Fenton, the woman who had seemed so attached to the unappealing Harold, had covertly watched Rose all day and done little to make the newcomer feel welcome. At tea that afternoon, Rose, as hostess appointed by Sir Thomas, tried to remain as calm and efficient as Celeste had when she presided at Grenfall. Merilyn questioned her about life in Louisiana.

"I understand that handsome husband of yours was presumed dead earlier this year while you were at some uncivilized fort in Indian territory, Lady Rosalind," Merilyn said after asking a few ordinary questions and appearing bored with Rose's replies. "You must have been unprotected a long while before you returned to your home. Were you not at the mercy of all kinds of savages and uncouth people?" she asked with a feigned air of simple curiosity, smugly aware that conversation lagged and Rose's answer could be heard.

"Hardly," replied her hostess. "I do prefer to be called 'Rose,' ladies." She lifted her chin and smiled at the women sitting around her before turning back to Merilyn. "In the bayou areas of Louisiana where I grew up, Miss Fenton, young women are usually chaperoned. Although I may not have so many years as some," Rose said, looking the obviously older, plainer woman in the eyes, "I was judged a widow at that period, not an unmarried woman with scarcely enough sense to recognize the uncouth and stay out of their way."

Merilyn's face flushed with anger at the polite but marked put-down. She stirred her tea noisily, remaining silent but ever watchful of the beautiful blonde. Her suspicions that the cousin from Louisiana posed a threat to Harold's well-being showed on her plain face. Almost everyone there knew that Harold had always had an eye for beautiful faces, but over the years he had returned to

Merilyn for company when his affairs soured, as they always did.

Merilyn welcomed Harold's pouring out of his secrets and troubles to her, believing that he would someday realize how invaluable she was. Her dowry was generous, and she was equipped to handle the duties of being Harold's wife and hostess until that time when he would become the viscount. There was no doubt in her mind that she would make an impressive viscountess. The major problem seemed to be Harold and his procrastination in asking for her hand, she mused that afternoon in the salon. And now there was another obstacle to delay her goals further. The unsuspecting Rose would soon have the power to bring about Harold's—and thus her own—downfall.

Rose joined Sir Thomas at the entry hall on the morning of their guests' departure. Roxley Lindley, the cousin she had taken such a liking to, promised to return soon to visit and play whist. Young Ashley grasped Rose's hand briefly, then lunged with a blush to peck her cheek before echoing his mother's invitation to visit them.

But Harold held back, making certain that he was the last of the departing group. He held Rose's hand overly long and fixed her with a piercing look from amber eyes. With his other hand he slapped at his boots with his riding crop, an evil-looking wand of thin black leather with a long, flayed tip.

"Mayhap I could return soon and show you more of Heatherlee's acres?" he asked, his eyes plundering her face. "The stables here have many choice mounts—or don't you ride?"

The last question seemed to suggest to Rose that one not born and reared in England couldn't possibly know about horses. She bristled. "I ride, yes," she answered in a manner more clipped than normal. "My husband goes out each day, as he has already done this morning. He'll show me the estate."

"There are many areas one can view only from horse-back," Harold said, a flicker of his eyes the only sign that he knew of her agitation. Though he still wondered how the narrow-eyed man knew so much about the cousin he'd figured would never come to Heatherlee, Harold confessed to himself that the Spaniard he had been gambling with over the past month in Portsmouth had been right: Rose was a rare, perfect beauty. "If your husband wishes to go along, he is invited as well. But I, as one who visited here often with my grandmother and roamed about the place, might be better suited to showing you the family holdings."

Harold's words made sense. Rose decided she might be overly suspicious of his actions and gave a more courteous smile and response. Why not let him show Jean Pierre and her the estate and tell them what he knew of the area? The thought of riding over the land her father must have known well as a young man perked up her spirits and brought a decided sparkle to her eyes, an addition that the conceited Harold mistakenly believed had been caused by his promise to return.

Like a distant bell, a faint feeling of impending danger invited Rose's attention as she watched her cousin mount his horse and bring the riding crop down upon the rich chestnut coat. But she refused to acknowledge it; in the distance she could see Jean Pierre on a handsome bay coming toward her over a hill, and she ran out into the sunshine to meet him.

Chapter Twenty-four

"Why would you need to stay in Portsmouth for the next few days?" Rose asked Jean Pierre one night soon after the visitors had left. They had returned to their rooms after dinner, and his casual announcement stunned her. She had sensed that he was becoming restless, but she had not realized that he might choose to go elsewhere . . . without her. "I thought this was a kind of honeymoon." She paused in brushing her hair to follow his mirrored reflection as he undressed. In the candlelight he seemed more handsome than ever, and she smiled.

"I asked Beau to arrange meetings with several trading companies to see if any might be interested in buying furs from our company," Jean Pierre replied, climbing into bed and propping himself up against a pillow to watch her. About the only times he could have her to himself and receive her full attention came late at night in their rooms, he mused, enjoying the sight of her sitting before the vanity brushing her hair, her body barely covered by one of the sheer peignoirs he had chosen for her back in New Orleans. The sight of her beauty changed the rhythm of his heart. During the two weeks they had been here, Rose seemed so engrossed in poring over family histories and portraits or conversing with her great-uncle or other relatives who seemed to drop by almost daily, that even if he remained in her presence she barely had time to give him a glance—or so it seemed to him. Across the dimly lighted room he could see her blue eyes darken in the mirror.

"When did this idea come up?" Rose watched in the mirror while he stretched and yawned, admiring the ripples of muscles on his bare chest and arms, feeling that little tug at her heart that often came when she thought of being in his arms. Maybe he had been more bored than she had thought and had let his mind search for ways to stay busy. Her conscience tweaked at the thought. Perhaps she really had been spending too much time with family.

"I talked it over with Louis before we left New Orleans." Their eyes met and held in the mirror in front of her.

"Why with Louis and not with me, pray tell?" Rose turned to face him then, her face tight, her chin lifted.

"It's men's business . . . and it doesn't concern you." Her haughty stare infuriated him. Did she think she could dress him down as she could some of the scads of servants around this elegant . . . dead-house? All at once he'd had enough of her excited squeals over some praiseworthy tidbit a family visitor might offer about an exalted ancestor of two centuries back. That he might be jealous never occurred to him. "It shouldn't concern you at all, Lady Rosalind," he added with cold deliberation.

"What do you mean by those hateful words? You know I despise being called by that title," Rose hissed, snatching up the hairbrush and once more working at her tangled curls. "I'm your wife, and if something concerns you or a business *we* own, then it concerns me." She brushed harder. "Damn you for shutting me out of your life, Jean Pierre!"

"What common speech for one of your breeding," he retorted with a cynical cluck of his tongue. "And look who's talking of shutting the other out!" he yelled, stung at what seemed the unkindest, most inaccurate accusation ever. When she pretended to ignore him, he went on, "How can you accuse *me* of shutting *you* out when it's bound to be obvious to all those hordes of people—God only knows where they come from—traipsing in and out of this . . . monstrosity of a house that *you* have shut *me* out?" The deep voice resonated around the huge room. Facts were facts, he assured himself, and it was time she faced some of them. The as yet unrecognized hurt of his finding during the past two weeks that his wife had interests in addition to him had crystallized into raw anger. That little seed of uncertainty planted at his first sight of her ancestral home had mushroomed into a tremendous doubt. Could she ever be happy again with him back in Louisiana? His insides churned, and not only from the recognizable anger.

Rose gasped and stalked toward where he lay lounging against two plump down pillows, his arms crossed in front of his chest like some—her mind raced to come up with a comparison—like some lord looking down his nose at the lower classes. Her long strides belled the full skirt of the peignoir before her. Blue fire flashed from her eyes. "Monstrosity? You call this—" As if out of breath, she broke off to look around the luxuriously appointed room, her hair whipping about her face and shoulders as she examined each corner. She repeated in an unbelieving voice, "You dare call this a 'monstrosity'? I might have known that the first minute the world stopped revolving around you, you'd kick up a fuss. You're as self-centered as you ever were. You haven't ever really changed from that bully of a cousin who used to order me about just to see me jump, have you?'' Rose stood right beside him before she was halfway through, her words aimed to wound. ''You don't bother me anymore,'' she lied, glaring to hide the truth even from herself.

Jean Pierre lay still, recoiling inside from her anger, but letting his own build. ''You're the one who has changed, Lady Rosalind,'' he drawled with an exaggerated Cajun accent. ''Had I known what royal blood flowed in that beautiful body, I might never have stepped in to stop Phillip de Cordoza.'' Her contorted face and staring eyes warned him, but he was too wound up to backtrack then. ''Maybe you would have been better off to have married him and returned to Spain where someone might be impressed with your ancestors.'' He left the bed in a nonchalant way, hitching up his drawers over his flat belly and carefully walking around where she stood as if frozen. Stooping to pick up his discarded clothing, he padded across the thick rug. At the door, he turned to say over his shoulder, ''Because, dear wife, I don't give a damn where you came from.'' With a slam of the enormous door, which reverberated from the tall ceilings and assaulted Rose's ears, he disappeared into the sitting room.

Rose unclenched her hands and wheeled around to follow him, but a glimpse of her wild face and eyes in the mirror stalled her. Why give him the satisfaction of seeing her in such a state? She tiptoed to the door, hearing noises through the keyhole that sounded as if he were thumping the pillows on the settee. *Good*, she thought with a grim smile. *Let him squirm on the settee for a while*. With his long frame, he would find little comfort or sleep there. Her hurt and anger did not ebb quickly, and she tossed upon the lonely bed long after the candles had burned down.

Jean Pierre was unable to sleep, blaming his restlessness on the too-short settee. Before daylight, he came to his senses enough to leave Rose a note on the tea table in the sitting room. But the message was terse, telling her only that he could be reached at the Hart Inn in Portsmouth during his absence. He made no apology—indeed, he

assured himself, he owed none; it was she who needed to
apologize—and signed his name with no tender message.

When she awoke late the next morning, Rose found the
note. That its brevity indicated he was still angry bothered
her, but not so much as the thought of being unable to see
him for several days. The remembered anguish of those
months when she had believed him lost forever tore at her,
banishing to a hidden corner the hurt his words of last
night had produced. With great care, she hid her inner
problems and went down to face the days looming ahead.

Both Kitty and Sir Thomas, each at different times over
the next couple of days, pleaded with Rose to give in to
European custom and learn to ride sidesaddle. While in
New Orleans on carriage rides with Jean Pierre, she had
watched ladies ride in the wooded area near Lake
Pontchartrain. To her way of thinking, the sitting of a
horse in such a manner looked unnatural. She had no
desire to master it. Not easily daunted, Kitty brought one
of the customary black habits kept on hand for guests and
altered it to fit Rose's petite figure. She found boots and a
hat small enough and cajoled her young mistress into
trying them on. Grudgingly Rose gave in to the only two at
Heatherlee who seemed interested in her personal happiness and went with her great-uncle to the stables.

She wondered what Jean Pierre would say when he saw
her in the outlandish costume with its graceful sweep of
skirt. An image of Jarrette's old breeches and shirt that had
served as her riding habit those many days on the trail
flashed into her mind, and she grinned. Already too able at
sitting a horse in an ordinary saddle to be hampered long
by the new experience of sitting sideways with one leg
hooked over the side horn, Rose was cantering on Tandee,
the chestnut beauty chosen for her, before the day was
over.

On the fifth day of Jean Pierre's absence, Sir Thomas
rode with Rose in an open-topped carriage to Salisbury. In
the huge, old cathedral there she found the record of the
marriage of her mother's parents. Visiting the silversmith
shop her grandfather had once owned lent reality to his

existence. But because Jean Pierre wasn't there to share these experiences, part of the joy seemed diluted.

As Sir Thomas helped her down from the landeau at Heatherlee's front door that afternoon, she heard a horse approaching. Someone called, "Rose?"

She whirled about. "Beau! I'm so glad to see you that I could cry." She beamed her pleasure at the tall blond man handing his horse's reins to a groom.

"I much prefer a smile," Beau said, after greeting her and Sir Thomas. "I was in Wanington and rode by to see if my friends from Louisiana are well." He frowned to see faint smudges underneath her eyes and a wan look upon her face.

"Of course, silly. Do I look sick?" Could he tell she had slept little the past few nights?

"You look as though something is troubling you. Where is Jean Pierre?" He looked around as if expecting to see him.

"He went to Portsmouth a few days ago on business. Mayhap I don't sleep as well when he's gone." She pretended not to see the men's exchanged glances and began chattering about the members of the family she had met since he had left Jean Pierre and her at Heatherlee a little over two weeks ago.

"A penny for your real thoughts," Beau told Rose after Sir Thomas excused himself and went inside. Her face was too pale. Her normally twinkling eyes were sad, as they'd been that day he called upon her in Attakapas, he realized.

"I'm just missing Jean Pierre," she replied with total candor. Speaking his name cheered her not at all. She pulled her shawl closer. Suddenly the warmth of the day had disappeared. "Won't you come in for tea or coffee?"

Beau declined, saying, "He'll likely be back soon."

"Would you think I'm imposing on a friendship to ask you to go to Portsmouth and see if he's all right . . . mayhap pretend you had to work at your office there and just happened to run into him?" Rose liked the idea even more once she spoke.

"Well, I guess I could find something to do down there," Beau remarked after a moment's thought. He recalled her telling him aboard ship about her strange dreams during the time when everyone believed Jean Pierre dead. Was she having some kind of premonition that all wasn't well now? "I'll leave for Portsmouth the first thing in the morning—but only if you promise to stop worrying."

Rose's smile and thanks led Beau to hope his agreeing to her request was the right thing to do. But the prickly question of what his friend might think of his spying, no matter how well intentioned, ran through Beau's mind as he mounted his horse and rode off.

In Portsmouth just at nightfall, Jean Pierre completed his first worthwhile business meeting since leaving Heatherlee in a huff. The man he had just left seemed trustworthy; he was glad Beau had appeared in the city that very day and found him at the Hart Inn, as he was eager to ask about the importer's local reputation when the two met as agreed at a popular bar and gaming house near the wharves.

Taking a shortcut through narrow, dark alleys, Jean Pierre mused over the way several of the importers he had called on in the waterfront area since arriving six days ago had been leery of him and his strange accent. Some had shown no interest in handling furs. And some he hadn't wanted to deal with after visiting with them and explaining his need to have a guaranteed market for Louis's and his furs. From the dim light of a street lamp down the way, he made out the sign THE LOST ANCHOR and pushed open the door there on the cobblestoned alley.

"Didn't I tell you this place was unique?" Beau asked after Jean Pierre and he took their mugs of beer over to a small table to get away from the large, noisy crowd around the bar. "There's about as much dealing going on between importers and sellers here as in those offices you've been calling on. We might get lucky and run into the very man you need to talk to." His eyes scanned the dimly lighted room.

Jean Pierre also studied those in the bar. Most seemed to be dock workers. "If you hadn't told me so many dealers end their days here, I would almost have feared for my life to be caught in such a place.'' His fascinated gaze wandered on past the front room into the brighter gaming room . . . and stopped, ''My God, Beau,'' he exclaimed. ''Isn't that Phillip de Cordoza over at the corner table?''

''By damn, it is! What could that weasel be doing here?'' It was not unusual to find all nationalities in the gaming places in the port city, but still it seemed more than coincidence to see that particular Spaniard there, he reflected.

''Looks like he's gambling.'' Jean Pierre felt the rage against Phillip's attempts to bring harm to Rose and him boil up inside. ''I think I'll go over and surprise him.''

Beau grabbed his beer and followed, not at all sure that approaching the Spaniard would benefit anyone. He stepped beside his friend and took in the scene: Phillip was as drunk as when Beau had seen him in New Orleans last summer, and the arrogant sneer still claimed his long, thin face.

''Well, Phillip, we meet again, and this time your being Unzaga's nephew doesn't carry one stone of weight, does it?'' Jean Pierre asked the tight-lipped young man staring up at him. ''How did England get so lucky as to rate a visit from you?''

''Jean Pierre Guilbeau,'' Phillip replied with a disdainful air, ''how nice to see you at last. I thought I might have to send you an engraved invitation to join me at the gambling table. That is why you're here, isn't it? Or has your lovely wife forced you from her family's estate near Wanington?'' Obviously pleased to note shock upon Jean Pierre's face, he added, ''I still have good sources in New Orleans who keep me posted about matters that concern me.''

Jean Pierre was already angry, but to hear that Phillip knew far more about Rose and him than he knew about Phillip threw him off balance. A sixth sense whispered that it was more than chance that brought the devious Spaniard to the city near Heatherlee. The man was more than drunk; he was obsessed. Something tried to tell Jean Pierre to walk away, but he chose to stand his ground. ''And what would you know about my wife that you'd say in my presence? I've heard some of the sly remarks you made to

Thom Keller. Care to repeat them?'' He noted that the three men with whom Phillip had been playing cards raked coins into their hands and left, barely making noise when they slid back their chairs on the wooden floor.

Phillip darted looks of aggravation at the departing gamblers, saying, ''I don't know what you're talking about. I never met a Thom Keller.'' From his sliding glance at Beau standing a distance behind Jean Pierre, it was obvious that he had no recollection of ever having seen the Englishman.

''You're lying! You met him at Acadian Point last summer, probably the day after I beat you up at Grenfall.'' Jean Pierre leaned menacingly, one hand on the table. ''Did you think he'd not turn yellow and talk, especially after you wouldn't send him the money for hiring Rufus Bedlow to kill me?''

Phillip's olive complexion was rapidly turning sallow, and he retorted, ''You've no proof of anything you say.''

''I've got all the proof I need, right up here in my head.'' Quite a few gamblers had stopped pretending interest in their games and were openly watching and listening as the two young men talked angrily at the corner table. ''If you weren't drunk, I'd beat the hell out of you right now. As it is, I suggest we meet tomorrow morning at the Hart Inn, where I'm staying, and hash out our differences—unless you plan to sail at dawn for Spain.''

Phillip's eyes slid to the walls of the gaming room. Huge pegs served as storage places for the dock workers' tools while they drank and gambled: baling hooks and tongs of varied sizes and shapes. ''I'm not drunk, you Cajun, and I've no need to wait till tomorrow to talk with you. Talk away.''

''Tomorrow morning, Phillip. You owe me a hell of a lot of explanations.'' Jean Pierre turned away then, his face contorted with the effort of refraining from jerking Phillip up and smashing his fist in his face.

But Phillip jumped up from his chair and clutched Jean Pierre's arm, yanking him around and yelling, ''Now! You talk when *I* say. Your wife's cousin Harold thought he could put me off, too, and he learned you don't cross

Phillip de Cordoza and get away with it." An evil smile rode his angry face.

Surprised at the mention of Harold, but far more angered at the grasp on his arm, Jean Pierre shoved the drunken man, freeing himself. "Shut up and sit down. We'll discuss our differences tomorrow." He again turned away.

This time Phillip grabbed Jean Pierre's arm and swung his fist at the same instant, clipping him behind his ear and cursing at the near miss. Jean Pierre delivered a far more telling blow to Phillip's cheek, then a second from the other fist to his chin. Reeling with a snarl back against the wall, his head banging against metal, the Spaniard reached behind him and yanked down a baling hook as long as his arm and curved into a sharp point at the end. At exclamations from Beau and the nearby gamblers, Jean Pierre grabbed at the tool, blood shooting up from a wound in his palm. He moved quickly to wrest the hook from the wild-eyed man, trying to lift the aiming arm above Phillip's head and push it against the wall.

Phillip reached behind him blindly, muttering curses and searching for another weapon with his free hand. He couldn't remove it from the peg, managing only to turn the pointed curve of the grappling tool toward his back. At that moment, Jean Pierre pinned Phillip's hand grasping the baling hook to the wall and socked him squarely on the jaw, the crack of the blow resounding in the gaming room, silent now, as was the bar.

A piercing scream came from the Spaniard's twisting mouth; his eyes rolled with agony. Only then did Jean Pierre and Beau realize what the gamblers watching from nearby tables had seen: midway down the left side of his back, in the area of his heart, Phillip had become impaled on the sharp, curved point of the grappling hook he had tried to remove from the wall. Blood was already spurting from his mouth before the hideous screams drowned, before two men at the next table could get there to free the dying man.

Chapter Twenty-five

The day after Beau's departure for Portsmouth, Harold returned to Heatherlee, leading a gleaming chestnut horse. Speechless at his gift, Rose examined her cousin's face for an ulterior motive but found only bland impassivity. She took the proffered reins, feeling as if she were entering a dark, unexplored pool of water, but not finding any logical reason for refusing the gift.

"What is her name, Harold?" Her fingers moved across the velvety nose.

"Star Princess." He watched her intently, tapping at his boots with his quirt.

"She's a real beauty," Rose said, taking in the proud lift of its head and perfect stance, totally unaware of Harold's measuring of her own body in similar manner. "I wish Jean Pierre hadn't had to go into Portsmouth on business. He loves horses as much as I." It was the sixth day of his absence, and she dreaded the loneliness of their rooms at night.

"Would you like to ride now?" Harold asked.

"Yes." Why not? At least a couple of hours would do more than drag by.

Rose gloried in tasting and feeling the chilly wind. Star Princess seemed unusually perceptive to its new mistress's moods and responded to the slightest leg pressure or hand movement. Each rise upon the route Harold chose offered Rose new scenes of the land her father had known. As soon as Jean Pierre returned, she promised herself, she would ride with him over the arpents—no, she corrected herself: the English measured land in acres, not arpents.

Her conscience bothered her at the memory of the times he had urged her to accompany him. She would not put him off again. They had been in England three weeks, and she was finding that little spurts of homesickness nagged her at odd times.

Watching from her side but remaining silent, Harold noted his cousin's rising color and curving lips with increased yearning. She might be married . . . and a threat to him . . . but she was breathtaking. How could he best get her to overlook the missing items in his grandmother's jewelry collection when it was officially opened and presented to her? It seemed a certainty now that she would be present the following week when that last bequest was read and carried out. Would she keep quiet if he could coax her into his arms?

"Shall we rest here?" he called to Rose from a hilltop, gesturing with his quirt to the edge of the trees.

Rose turned from where she had reined in to look down on the vast acres below. She had kept to herself and her own thoughts all during the ride, barely answering when Harold offered explanations about the estate or country-side. Still wary, but realizing she had no basis for being suspicious of her cousin, she consented. Harold helped her to dismount, but she refused to allow him to guide her to the edge of the trees for another view of Heatherlee's back fields. She noted with repulsion a flayed spot on the rump of his horse and glanced at the hardened leather strips on the tip of the riding crop dangling from his saddle horn.

"What do you think of the ancestral acreage now that you've ridden over some of it?" Harold asked, moving closer.

"Heatherlee is beautiful," Rose replied. "Beau didn't prepare me for such sights."

"Oh, that fellow. I hardly know the Bradfords. Not titled, of course. Not my cup of tea. Do you see him often?" Had she retained the man to represent her at the reading of his grandmother's will next week? Why would she need counsel, unless his secret had leaked out? he pondered.

"Beau will be back when we all meet next week." She

despised his slurring of Beau and his family. She sneaked a look at him from beneath her lashes. Maybe he did resent his grandmother's bequeathing anything valuable to an unknown niece, and maybe if she told him—"Harold," she began, her voice softened with compassion for his imagined plight, "I want you to know—"

Instantly Harold was at her side, pulling her into his arms, mesmerized by what he deemed a coquettish look from beneath her lashes. Caught off guard, Rose was seething.

"Please, Harold. I believe you forget yourself." She looked up into the amber eyes as she attempted to disengage herself from his hold, not liking what she saw there. Her heart tried to jump into her throat,

"Rosalind, my dear Rosalind," Harold grated, ignoring her words and her attempts to draw away. He tightened his hold.

Rose ducked, knocking off her riding hat and causing his attempted kiss to land in the air. Harold was breathing heavily like an animal gone mad. His mouth aimed for her ears, her forehead, even as her hands beat against his face and chest and she called him vile names.

"You intoxicate me," he muttered hoarsely between his attempts to kiss her and escape her blows. "You're the most beautiful, desirable woman I've ever seen."

Rose trembled with renewed indignation and anger. How dare he think she might be receptive to him? No longer the gullible innocent that Phillip de Cordoza had tried to molest, she drew up her knee and aimed for his groin, kicking his shin too, for good measure, before he flinched away. When he released her with a black look and a snarl, she followed with a kick to the other shin, delighting to see him double over from his dose of agony and to hear him let out a moaning curse before she ran to her horse. Without a backward glance, she mounted and galloped toward the stables. She knew she had done nothing to encourage Harold, unless it had been to accept the horse she now rode at breakneck speed, one she would return when she reached safety.

Nearing the stables, Rose could hear the crack of Harold's

quirt as he whipped his mount in frenzied chase. She never pulled in her heaving horse until she was in the stable yard.

As luck would have it, Sir Thomas was in the sitting room on the back side of the house. If he was shocked to see Rose enter the room in such a state, he didn't show it. Instead, he treated her unladylike entrance and appearance as casually as he did the noisy one Harold made a few seconds later.

"Did you two have a nice ride?" he asked in his calm manner. His glance jumped from one to the other. "You're just in time for tea." With a doting smile, he accepted Rose's offer to tug the bell pull near the door for a servant.

"Uncle," Rose said, once she was near the door to the main hall, "please excuse me. I prefer to have coffee in my room." Without waiting for his reply or even glancing in Harold's direction, she darted into the hallway and fled.

Storming up and down in her rooms, Rose flung off her clothing one item at a time, tossing each at the bed as if it were the object of her fury. Relieved that Kitty was not around to wonder at her mood, and not daring to let herself wish for Jean Pierre, she flung open the armoire. With disinterest she reached for a gown to wear.

The brightness of the blue brocade gown did little to dispel her dark mood. With a critical eye she viewed the smooth sweep of the fitted bodice across her breasts and small waist, eyeing with little interest the silver threads weaving patterns on the stomacher. In the privacy of their bedroom back in New Orleans, she had loved putting on the handsome creation, she reflected. Her inner voice taunted her: *Because Jean Pierre was there then.*

To her great relief, Harold had departed by the time Rose went to dinner. In guarded language, she let Sir Thomas know what had transpired between Harold and her.

"Harold has always been self-centered. And in his earlier days he had no trouble charming the young women— what with his promising future as a viscount," Sir Thomas said after digesting her story. "But during the past few years he has taken to spending more time and money than he can spare in gambling down at Portsmouth with all kinds of unsavory men. He is greedy and has reportedly made several snide remarks about his grandmother's decision to leave her jewels to you. I would not put it past him to want to gain mastery of you as a part of some devious plan.''

''He can have the jewels. I've said before that I don't want them.'' Her doubts as to the wisdom of having come to England had grown ever since the quarrel with Jean Pierre, and now they seemed to have become even larger. Where was he? Had something happened to him? Surely Beau would have sent a message if all was not well.

Rose might as well not have spoken, for Sir Thomas moved on with his thoughts. ''Lady Rosalinde despaired over Harold's wasteful ways and told me some time before her death that she found his behavior despicable.''

''I never want to see him again!'' Rose shook her head with vehemence, not really surprised at what she had heard.

''You will have to, though, because he is family,'' the old gentleman remarked. ''Just as we all do. As you know, you cannot escape family here. Haven't I told you that everyone will begin gathering early next week to go grouse hunting?'' When she made no comment, he added, ''I'm hoping that nice young man you married will be back long before then.''

Rose had no word from Jean Pierre until Beau returned at the first of the following week to find her in the music room. She was so eager for news from Portsmouth that she hurried to pull him to sit beside her on the settee, questions popping forth.

''Yes, he told me to tell you he's fine and that he'll be back within the next few days,'' Beau told her, not quite able to meet the trusting blue eyes. Determined to follow Jean Pierre's demand that he not upset her with news of the messy business of Phillip's death and the two days they had spent in court to clear up the matter, he said with a purposefully light tone, ''Sit back down at the harpsichord and close your eyes. Jean Pierre sent you a surprise.''

Rose did as he requested. All that afternoon she had idly hunted notes on the harpsichord in an attempt to play a recognizable melody, not admitting that what she sought was the one Jean Pierre had composed for her. Even to herself she couldn't confess how utterly miserable she was over his prolonged absence. She had steeled herself to have him gone no more than a week, and now the second was almost past. She felt a warm bit of fluff in her lap and jerked open her eyes. A tiny blond dog with a darker face lay gazing serenely up at her.

"Jean Pierre sent him for me?" She looked up into Beau's smiling face. "I've never seen a puppy with such a wrinkled little face." She hugged the warm puppy to her, her fingers fondling the smooth, short-haired coat. She felt better already. "How is my husband? When will he be here?"

Glad that Jean Pierre's thoughtfulness had pleased her, Beau said, "In a day or so. He's not quite through in Portsmouth."

"I'll name him 'Monte,' " she said, not liking that Jean Pierre hadn't returned, but delighted to learn he was all right and apparently no longer angry with her.

After that, no one saw Rose without Monte either trailing after her on short legs or contentedly resting in her arms. Rapidly the puppy became so possessive of his new mistress that he allowed few to come close to her without a show of tiny teeth and a menacing growl.

Another surprise came the next day. Roxley Lindley, the cousin Rose had taken such a liking to, stopped by Heatherlee on her way home from Portsmouth.

"I promised I would return soon," Roxley said with a smile at Rose's obvious pleasure at seeing her. She gestured toward the tall woman behind her, saying, "My maid Winnie and I went to shop for winter clothes and decided to stop by."

"Winter is indeed getting close," Rose mused, distracted for a moment from her joy at seeing Roxley. What if bad weather delayed Jean Pierre even longer? "Tell me what you found in the shops," she said, forcing herself back to the moment.

When Beau and Sir Thomas returned from their walk through the back gardens, they found the two young women laughing and chattering like old friends, with Monte perched on Rose's lap as if listening to every word. Roxley's curly auburn hair gleamed with dancing red lights from the steady glow of the fireplace as she leaned toward Rose with an animated account of a visit to a milliner's shop. Excitement brought unusually high color to her pretty, round face.

Stimulated by Roxley's visit and gossipy accounts of her trip to Portsmouth, Rose had relaxed a bit. After introducing Roxley to Beau, she reflected on her good fortune to have visitors to help her endure Jean Pierre's absence.

"Why is it I haven't met Beau Bradford before?" asked Roxley that night before dinner. She had completed her toilette early and had stopped by to accompany Rose downstairs. "Is he someone special?"

"He says he's been in Louisiana and the Atlantic colonies for the past few years," Rose answered. She sat at her dressing table while Kitty piled blond curls in pretty profusion on top of her head. "And yes, he's very special. He's my barrister as well as Jean Pierre's and my friend."

Roxley primped in front of the gilt-framed mirror standing on carved feet in the corner, eyeing her green velvet gown critically as she rearranged the folds of the draped panniers. The heavy skirt flared out from a tiny waist. She turned this way and that, as though disapproving the slender image facing her. The dark color contrasted with the fair skin of her stylishly exposed upper bosom and neck and made the hidden lights in her auburn hair sparkle into a deep red. Some inner excitement added a new liveliness to her widely spaced gray eyes. "Does Beau have a special . . . lady friend?"

"Why do you ask?" Rose turned to look at her cousin, ignoring Kitty's indrawn breath at the sudden movement during a crucial moment of forming a curl at the base of her neck. "Are you taken with him?"

"Not if someone else has already taken him," Roxley replied, turning to laugh along with Rose at her ridiculous play on words, but evading the questioning eyes.

"We may be good friends, but I've never heard him talk of affairs of the heart," Rose told her. She turned back for Kitty to finish her coiffeur, not that she much cared how she looked without Jean Pierre there to see her. He *had* to return on the morrow, she agonized, or she would die.

"I think he might be the nicest and most charming man I have yet to meet," Roxley said, coming to stand behind Rose. Their eyes met in the mirror. "Do you think he noticed me?"

"But of course he did," Rose replied enthusiastically. She moved to make a final inspection in the standing mirror Roxley had used. Perhaps spurred on by the presence of her pretty cousin, or perhaps by the need to lift her spirits, Rose had chosen to wear a taffeta gown of tiny navy and pale blue stripes that she had been saving for a special occasion. Bias ruffles topped the low-cut bodice and extended over her arms to form the tops of tiered, three-quarter-length sleeves, leaving her pale shoulders exposed. With a slight grimace that her beloved would not see her looking so fashionable, she fluffed the crisp overskirt to stand out even farther from her small waist and asked Roxley if she was ready to join Sir Thomas and Beau on the ground floor.

By the time they left to go down, both were excitedly planning how they would arrange for Roxley and Beau to have some time together. Their high spirits and chatter as they drifted down the wide stairway kept them from noticing Dunston's opening the front door to a heavily cloaked figure until they were already in the large entry hall.

Rose paused in speech and step as she saw, in the poorly lighted area by the door, a hat being handed to Dunston and a familiar dark head leaning conversationally toward the chief steward. And then, as though answering some unvoiced call, the tall figure strode into the lighted area.

"Rose," came the beloved voice. Jean Pierre held out his arms, still burdened with the cloak.

"Jean Pierre!" Rose could find no other words to add to her greeting, but he seemed not to mind. He enveloped her within his cloak and held her close. When she would have pulled away to look up at him, he enfolded her once again with her blond head cradled against his heart, the fragrance of roses enhancing her natural, sweet smell.

Upon hearing the commotion, Sir Thomas and Beau came from the drawing room, glasses of sherry still in their hands. They added their own greetings to Roxley's, once the obviously delighted couple separated and admitted others might truly exist. Their eyes caressed each other all during dinner.

"Tell me what kept you away so long," Rose said when they finally were alone in their rooms. "Beau was so secretive, saying you were terribly busy." Dinner and conversation had become a blur after his return. Every inch of her seemed keyed up at the sight of him, at the sound of his deep voice with the rich bass vibrato, at the warmth of his gaze on her face and neck. Neither had wasted any time in undressing and sliding into bed.

"Do you think I'm going to waste time talking when I can make love to my adorable wife?" Jean Pierre asked, his lips feathering over hers. From the moment he had seen her in the hall so exquisitely coiffed and gowned, a lightheadedness had claimed him. The ugliness of their quarrel had long receded; even the doubts lay hidden. The fingertips itching all evening to trail across her face and lose themselves in the pinkish gold curls went berserk with pleasure, now that they had lovingly removed all the pins and rosebuds. They traced the shape of a perfect ear, found a resting place on a satiny lobe.

Rose felt her body was no more than a musical instrument being stroked by a master's touch. That old melody of passion that he knew so well how to create in her swelled and sang through her blood, stealing her breath, playing havoc with the beat of her heart. The delicious feel of his nakedness against hers set up a throbbing inside her womanhood that threatened to rob her of sanity. Impatient to have their share of caresses, her breasts ached and swelled against his furred chest. And when his hands seemed content to cup her face and ears, she pulled one to fondle her breast, delighting at his indrawn breath almost as much as at the sudden singing deep inside some secret place. Her mouth begged for more; her tongue demanded. Her overpowering love for him gave her a new boldness. She sent soft hands to find the hard shape of him before his mouth had completed its sampling of her budded nipples. The instrument seemed to be leading the willing musician.

Lost in the agony of the senses Rose titillated with her unabandoned caresses, Jean Pierre let his mind sink out of sight and surrendered to that part of him crying out for the completion only her body could offer. Warm curves melting against his hardness created a drumming of wild anticipation in every cell. To find her eager to lead him in the love game excited him to a new height. Her hands worked wondrous magic, and a fleeting thought that his must be doing the same for her surfaced as she moaned and writhed against him. Something new, more wanton than before, seemed to be directing her movements. As if attuned to his every need, she received his fervent kisses but gave them back with more telling intensity. If he touched her hips and rounded buttocks with reverent awe, she placed a fiery pattern on his flat stomach and hips. If he stroked a velvety patch at the gateway to her core, she fondled the pulsating length waiting to enter.

And when hearts reached a fever pitch, and her frenzied invitation could no longer be postponed, Jean Pierre accepted what she offered and made them one in age-old harmony. Her little cries of ecstasy sounded like a snatch of a love song there in the enveloping darkness. The exalted rhythm of their joining carried them to that apex they sought, and they soared into that private heaven reserved for lovers. Caught there in perfect unity, their spirits communed before the flesh once more made itself known. An embracing silence and a stillness born of consummate fulfillment reigned and soothed.

"Never go away from me again," Rose whispered in a ragged voice. She tightened her arms around his neck as he held her against him.

"Never, my Cajun Rose." His heartbeat still not settled, Jean Pierre tucked her head beneath his chin. There were many things he needed to tell her, but he was too satiated to want to talk. With arms and legs entwined, they slept.

To Rose's disappointment, the morning brought heavy, overcast skies, and her plan to ride with Jean Pierre had to be postponed. That she had hoped to talk with him at length about all she had seen and done in Salisbury, and what he had accomplished in Portsmouth, dimmed her happiness a little at having him back. There would be time for private talk later, she assured herself. For now, she floated on a cloud of bliss to have him near. She drank in the sight of him in a full-sleeved white shirt gathered into a simple band at the wrists and topped by a black vest with gold threads forming tiny fleurs-de-lis. "Black on white," the prophecy had said, and for the moment she gloried in recalling that night at Fort Arkansas when she had seen her pale hair against the midnight black of his and realized their love had been foretold. Her heart full, she forced herself to join in the spirited conversation at the breakfast table.

With Beau and Roxley, they lingered in the library after a leisurely meal, talking about the upcoming grouse hunt. Jean Pierre remarked that he was looking forward to trying his hand at the sport.

Parties of kinfolk and their friends arrived all that day, their laughter and gay talk enlivening the spacious receiving rooms. Arriving along with his parents, Harold greeted Rose and Sir Thomas with distinct coolness. When he fixed his frosty amber eyes on Rose, she shrank inwardly from the appraisal she saw therein. He made no mention of the return by Heatherlee's groom of Star Princess to the viscount's stables the day after his departure. Except for the intense stares directed at Rose, he seemed to have erased from his mind that previous visit.

Merilyn Fenton came in with a later group and Rose barely noticed when Harold and she wandered toward a back sitting room. Merilyn had hoped that Harold might be upset that she had not arrived earlier, but he had greeted her with his usual peevishness over some imagined personal insult. As always, the problem centered around another woman.

Stalking up and down in front of where Merilyn sat on a settee in the private room, Harold rubbed his forehead with agitated fingers. "She is not fit to wear the Winstead jewelry," Harold fumed, ending a monologue about Rose's shortcomings. He had suffered ever since his failure to charm Rose by giving her the horse and coaxing her into his arms. Time was running out.

Remembering how taken with his cousin he had seemed at their previous visit, Merilyn was confused. However, her years of conniving to get him to marry her had sharpened her wits. Like the sudden slam of a door, the knowledge that he must have visited Heatherlee alone and been repulsed by Rose jarred her. Each passing year made her more desperate for Harold to propose, and she had a birthday coming up soon—too soon. She made all the expected soothing sounds and persuaded him to sit beside her so that she could massage his aching temples. When the dinner gong sounded, they left the room arm in arm.

The guests' activities kept Rose and Jean Pierre from retiring to their rooms early enough to allow her to talk with him about anything of a serious nature. And early the next morning the boisterous group of hunters, Jean Pierre among them, left soon after breakfast. All were commenting on their good fortune at having a sunny day so that the ladies might join them at noon for a picnic lunch in the fields after their shooting.

With well-filled hampers of food and jugs of drink, several servants had already gone ahead in wagons to the picnic shed set deep in the woods by the time the ladies rode out from Heatherlee. Before they had traveled far, Jean Pierre and Beau appeared over a hill.

"Your returning to ride with us was thoughtful," Rose told her smiling husband after he assured her that nothing was wrong, that Beau and he had tired of shooting and decided to seek out the ladies. To see Roxley's face light up at the sight of Beau had brought an extra sparkle to Rose's eyes. *They make a handsome couple*, she thought.

"Not really," Jean Pierre said, glancing ahead to make sure the large group had gone. He already knew that Beau and Roxley lagged even farther behind: "I wanted to see how you looked riding sidesaddle in that outlandish costume." Dark eyes raced over her with devilment and a flirty look of knowing what lay beneath the somber black. "Frankly, I don't find it an improvement over Jarrette's old breeches and shirt."

Rose smiled at his obvious ogling and lifted her head with pretended disdain. Apparently having become warm, he had unbuttoned his coat and the top of his shirt and she could see the curls on his chest. The sun overhead brought gleaming lights to the black hair falling across his forehead. She could feel the force he exerted over her reaching from his horse to hers and exulted that they shared a love like no one else's. Would she ever tire of seeing the flash of his teeth in his tanned face when he talked or smiled? "If I didn't know better, sir, I would think you were making advances," she taunted, sending him a coquettish look.

"How bold of you, my lady," he shot back. When her eyes teased him like that, he always felt his heart jump. The saucy black hat against her upswept hair made it look blonder than ever. In fact, he couldn't remember when she had looked more appealing. He loved her more each time he saw her.

"Probably not so bold as some of the ladies in Portsmouth over the past week." Rose had carefully refrained from asking how he had spent his evenings. Somehow neither had wanted to force talk about his absence, and yet she was dying to know what he had done every minute he had been in Portsmouth.

"Or so bold as some of the gentlemen who must have been hanging around my wife while I was away." Jean Pierre watched a rise of color add new pinkness to her cheeks. Exactly what had taken place to cause her to blush? She had been reluctant to explain her activities while he was gone, saying only that the days and nights were about the same as before he left. From such an answer, he had assumed that Sir Thomas had taken up most of her time with even more stories. But now his curiosity was aroused and he asked, "Who besides Beau called during my absence?"

Trying to be casual, Rose filled him in on the several callers. In detail she told of the trip to Salisbury and her failure to learn much about her mother's people. She saw no reason to mention that Harold had brought Star Princess to her since the horse had been returned so soon afterward. And because she assumed from Harold's air upon his arrival yesterday that their clash was to be forgotten, she did not tell her husband of that incident on the hilltop.

"So the only unusual happening was the appearance of Monte, the fierce protecting puppy?" he asked when her recital ended. He must have imagined the blush, he decided. "I'm glad you liked my surprise. I suppose I should count myself lucky that I'm one of the few he'll allow around his mistress." Beau had teased him about buying the puppy for Rose, but now that the fair Roxley seemed to have Beau enthralled, Jean Pierre was finding that his English friend could be as lovesick as any man when the right young woman came along.

"Tell me of your unusual happenings in Portsmouth," Rose invited. The ardor of his lovemaking since his return left her little room for suspicions that he had sought out another's arms.

Jean Pierre stared at the countryside for a moment. "I met with more than a dozen owners of trading companies, but I found only two who struck me as honest men I might like to do business with." Wanting to avoid tipping her full measure of temper again, he added, "That *our* company—Louis's, yours, and mine—might like to do business with." He had given her complaint careful thought after recollecting Louis's account of her interest in and bright comments about the future of the company when she thought he was dead. Admitting to himself that he might have placed her in a category she would never fit into, that he truly had no desire to force her into, he asked, "What would you think if we signed a contract to double the pelts we supplied this year?"

"I don't care to help you make business decisions, Jean Pierre," Rose said. "That was never my complaint. I just don't like it when you treat me as though I don't have sense enough for you to talk over your ideas and plans with me.''

He digested her words, then said, ''I hate serious topics when we're on our way to a picnic, but I've put off telling you something too long already.'' At her little frown, he went on, ''I ran into Phillip de Cordoza in a gaming house and—''

''Oh no!''

''Don't be upset, my love. We had a fight . . . and Phillip was killed.''

Rose's eyes and mouth widened as Jean Pierre fleshed out what happened in The Lost Anchor, ending the sordid tale with, ''Thank God Beau had come to Portsmouth and saw the whole thing. He went with me to the police station that night and again when I had to appear before a magistrate to clear things up. I asked him to let me tell you about it.''

''Jean Pierre, you could've been the one who was killed!'' After he had soothed her, he suggested they slow down and wait for Beau and Roxley to catch up with them.

Roxley shot Rose a look that reiterated Rose's suspicions that Beau had indeed ''noticed'' her pretty cousin and was letting her know of his interest.

Rose and Jean Pierre talked at length about Phillip's villainy in their sitting room that evening before dinner, longing to put the matter behind them. Then he played with Monte, laughing at the little dog's efforts to catch Jean Pierre as he took long strides around the settee, trailing a piece of rope.

''Wouldn't you love for Robert to see my puppy?'' The thought of the little boy back home brought a lump to Rose's throat.

''Are you missing Louisiana?'' he asked. He'd not heard her mention anyone from home since the letter had come from Marie on the day of his return. He felt relief that Rose seemed all talked out about the nasty business of Phillip de Cordoza.

''Every day. Aren't you?''

''Yes, but I had no idea you were. How much longer

will we need to stay here, Rose? Has the business of your inheritance been cleared up?'' Letting Monte catch up then and tug at the rope with his teeth, he wondered if now was a good time to tell her of his plans.

Rose thought of the contents of Marie's letter, smiling at the news that word had come from a ''very nice Lieutenant Leyoso'' that the land title was now in Jean Pierre's name awaiting his signature.

''Tomorrow is the date for the reading of the part of the will that applies to me,'' she said, reaching to put her arms around him. ''Now that Maman has told us that the land next to theirs is now yours—no, ours—would it matter if the whole dreary bit were over or not?'' Her lips moved against his.

''It might,'' he said, dropping the rope, forgetting all but her. ''I don't want you to leave here until you are completely satisfied that you've done all you want to do.'' Her nearness intoxicated him, and he buried his face in her hair.

With a contented Monte in the curve of one arm, Rose went down the staircase with the other arm hooked lovingly into one of Jean Pierre's. The silver buckles on his shoes caught her eye, and she admired his manly calves encased in white stockings. Delighted to feel him tighten his arm about her, she whispered to him that he had never looked more handsome than in his brown velvet jacket and fawn-colored breeches. What he whispered back brought a blush to her face.

Harold and Merilyn watched as the handsome couple mingled with the other guests for drinks and conversation before going in to dinner. They stood apart from the others beneath some family portraits in a secluded corner.

''She'll be there for the reading tomorrow, the little upstart,'' Harold complained, tearing his eyes from the alluring Rose to meet those mute cow-eyes tilted down to his level.

''You should have tried to charm her.''

''What do you mean by that?''

''Ha!'' Merilyn knew him too well. ''If I'd snitched

jewelry to pay gambling debts to that Spaniard who threatened you if you kept putting him off, I would have tried somehow to win over the one who owns the jewelry. When the barristers open that box, you're in trouble—not only with them, but with your father, the viscount. Do you think he's going to favor what you've done?''

In a tone revealing his lack of confidence in what he was saying, Harold remarked, ''There's nothing Father can do but leave everything to his only son.'' With a touch of arrogance, he straightened his apple-green waistcoat and tried to stand taller.

''But he seems in excellent health,'' Merilyn pointed out. ''And how will you live if he cuts you off at the discovery of your thievery? He will be furious that while his mother's jewelry was in his safekeeping, a choice piece or two disappeared into the hands of his son. What if I were to tell him what I know? De Cordoza may have been the only one forcing you to pay up, but what about the Englishmen who are holding notes until you become viscount?'' She saw then that she had gotten his attention. His face had paled another degree. It was at that moment that she noted the awful clash of the green of his coat and the blue-green of her gown. She made a mental note to speak to his tailor.

''You wouldn't dare!'' Harold's amber eyes fixed her with the penetrating gaze of an eagle, a ruse that had always caused her to retreat. Until now.

Without batting an eyelash, she said slowly, as if for emphasis, ''If I were your wife, you would have my dowry to live on even if your father cuts off your allowance, which I have no doubt he will tomorrow. And also, I wouldn't be tempted to tell more than is necessary to keep you out of jail.''

''Jail?'' he asked, not believing his ears. ''Rose won't file charges. Father will pay up before he . . .''

''Humph!'' she replied when he couldn't finish his statement. When she continued to stare at him boldly, almost mockingly, Harold knew he had stumbled into her lair and, for the first time in the years they had known each other, he lowered his eyes in partial defeat.

When Monte kept squirming in her arms, Rose set him down at the end of the big room. The little dog wandered among the guests, sniffing and examining those gathered in little groups, and, for the most part, being ignored. When he reached the end of the Great Hall where Merilyn and Harold had just finished their heated conversation, he stopped and bristled.

Growling and baring his teeth, Monte made a lunge at Harold's silk-clad ankles and received a kick. The puppy didn't retreat far; instead he set up a louder fuss and tried to attack a bony calf. Almost everyone in the hall turned to see what was going on, and then laughed to see Rose hurrying to retrieve her pet before he caused serious damage.

"Get away from me," Harold hissed, kicking out again. "I despise dogs. Make him stop, Merilyn."

"I'll make him stop," Rose assured him, stooping to pick up Monte. As if he sensed he had only one more chance, the dog sidestepped Rose's hands and leaped onto the top of Harold's slipper, sinking his teeth into the soft leather, snarling and shaking his head. Only when Rose grabbed Monte and held him next to her did he calm down, though he still protested and bared his teeth at Harold. "I am terribly sorry," she said to her red-faced cousin. "He's only a puppy."

"The funny thing is, though," said Beau, who stood nearby in a group including the auburn-haired Roxley, "he attacks only those people he thinks are a threat to Rose." He wore an amused smile as he spoke, one echoed on the faces of those around him.

"Where did you find such an unusual dog?" Merilyn asked, wondering if Beau had overheard Harold's and her conversation.

"Jean Pierre gave him to me." When Merilyn's eyebrows angled upward in haughty query, she added, "Beau brought him back from Portsmouth."

"Naturally such an 'old friend' could call whenever he chose, could even bring a gift of his own," Harold said, his sarcastic tone letting Rose know of his humiliation at having had Star Princess returned.

"Of course," she replied, wishing Monte's aggression had not forced her into conversation with the couple. She hugged the puppy closer and sought a safer topic. "You two have been friends for a long time, yes?"

"We're going to be more than old friends soon, aren't we, darling?" replied Merilyn, simpering and peering into Harold's shocked face.

"You mean you're engaged?" Rose asked. She tried to hide her surprise and force an interested smile. "I wish you much happiness." She noted that Merilyn smirked but that Harold merely stared. Monte's irritation increased and, using the excuse that she must take him back to her room, Rose escaped.

Hatred for the dog, which was still sending little growls his way even as Rose walked away, shot from Harold's eyes, though he had to pretend he saw the comedy in the situation and fake a smile for all those watching the little drama.

Rose awakened early the next morning. She barely remembered when Jean Pierre had kissed her cheek and left for his usual morning ride. Pulling on a wrapper, she opened the door into the sitting room to let Monte in. When he wasn't in sight, she called softly. The dog was gone.

Kitty came right away in answer to Rose's agitated jerk on the bell pull. She assured Rose that when she had checked the previous evening after Jean Pierre and she had retired, Monte was asleep on his cushion and that she had, as usual, closed the entrance door to the sitting room. At Rose's insistence, the maid went searching.

By the time Rose had dressed in a pink day gown with tucked bodice and belled sleeves and secured her hair away from her face with a matching velvet ribbon, a solemn-faced Kitty returned with news. Monte had been found dead in the front entry hall downstairs. A distraught Rose insisted on seeing for herself, and when she hurried down and saw the tiny body beaten horribly with some weapon that had left stripes of blood and mutilated flesh, she wept.

Rose's heart pained her when she had to face up to the

obvious conclusion that someone at Heatherlee was responsible for Monte's death. No one who was questioned admitted to seeing the puppy during the night. Although many had seemed annoyed at the little dog's antagonism toward people around his mistress, no one had seemed excessively so. As far as she knew, Monte had never bitten anyone, but . . . She thought back to last night's unpleasant encounter with Harold.

In the privacy of her sitting room, Rose recalled everything that had taken place and, reluctantly, remembered something else: Harold's wicked-looking riding crop with the flayed end. The damage he had inflicted on his horse the day she had ridden with him had been in stripes. She buried her head in her hands and shuddered at the cruelty of the man, shed tears at the thought of what a painful death he had forced on her beloved pet. At first she wanted to run and confront him in the presence of everyone with what she felt was an obvious truth. After her tears dried, though, she could think more clearly and decided that nothing could be gained by accusing the wily Harold without proof. If he was that devious, he would have covered his tracks thoroughly. Thoughts of the peaceful bayou country in Louisiana shimmered on the horizon of her mind.

Chapter Twenty-six

Thinking that he would escape notice by going for a ride before anyone but the servants stirred, Harold sipped his tea in Heatherlee's smaller, informal dining room, where Merilyn found him. When he ignored her honeyed greeting, she dismissed a hovering servant and poured tea from the silver pot on the sideboard before taking the chair beside him.

"I believe you agreed late last night that we could announce our engagement today," Merilyn said, her eyes doting on him. Adding milk and sugar to her tea, but returning her gaze to him every few seconds, she watched him as a child eyes an unopened gift. For him to stalk from her last evening and leave her to find her own amusement after dinner had rankled her. She had spied on him after all the others had gone to bed, and had let him know what she had witnessed before allowing him to sneak to his bedroom. "Silence is consent, I assume," she went on when he continued to stare into his cup. "You can tell your parents alone first, and then the viscount can make the announcement to everyone else before the business of the will this afternoon."

"Very well," Harold answered after further silent sipping of his tea. With a clatter he returned the fragile cup to its saucer and rose, finally looking at her. There seemed to be a new sharpness in Merilyn's features and speech. Was its source the victory over him? What a revolting development to have fallen prey to the least attractive of the single young women he had known, albeit the wealthiest. But at the moment, not even the thought of her reputedly large dowry cheered him. He had no doubt that she would indeed tell what she knew if he dared attempt to wriggle from her grasp. His lips thinned in distaste.

"Harold," Merilyn said, rising and putting her hand on his arm, "I'll be a good wife to you. You have always found me a tower of strength when you needed a sympathetic ear. I will not fail you." She stooped to place her moist mouth on his and pressed against him, not having to fake the passion emanating from her. "Or allow you to fail *me*," she added with threatening emphasis. "I am the only one who understands you."

A cruel laugh that matched the miasmatic gleam in Harold's amber eyes rolled from his unresponsive lips when she stepped back. "We will be a very unusual couple, my dear," he said in a loud, cutting tone. "We will probably be the only married people in the world who completely understand each other.''

Just then Rose came from the hallway, and Harold rushed toward a side exit, picking up his riding crop from a chair near the door. In the ensuing silence, she could hear the sound of it rapping smartly against his boots, becoming fainter as he hurried away. Her resolve not to approach him with her suspicions about Monte's death wavered, and she almost called out to him. Instead, she centered her interest on the tall woman before her.

''Good morning,'' Rose said in the strongest voice she could muster. ''Did I interrupt a private breakfast?''

''Harold was just leaving for a ride,'' Merilyn responded, nervously pushing at a stray piece of hair.

''I don't recall having seen the two of you together after dinner last night,'' Rose said, watching a closed look take over the long face. ''I suppose you had much to talk about, with your upcoming engagement and marriage.'' Why was Merilyn fixing her with such a baleful stare?

''You're right, of course. We found a private sitting room and made plans.'' Was the upstart blonde making sly digs about the way Harold had deserted her, causing her to seek her own room for fear that others might notice that she had been left alone? ''We talked far into the night.'' Rose's intense study of her face made her add a second lie. ''We hadn't realized we were the last ones still awake until we went up to our rooms.''

''A lovers' tryst. I should have known.'' So Merilyn was willing to give Harold an alibi. That was that. Rose should have known that he was too devious to leave himself open for suspicion. ''Do you recall seeing my little Monte before you went up?'' Rose asked. When Merilyn shook her head, she went on, ''He must have come down sometime in the night to be let out for a nature call. This morning he was found dead near the front entry. It seems that someone had taken a whip to him.''

''How unfortunate,'' Merilyn managed. How would Rose know about Harold's whip? Fearful that she might reveal more to Rose than she already had, she made no further comment.

When she had entered the dining room, Rose had overheard Merilyn's last words to Harold, as well as his ugly retort. Right off, she had discarded any previous notion that a warped but mutual love might have brought about their engagement. And now as the obviously distraught Merilyn fixed her with a bright stare and swept from the room, Rose wondered at the strange ways in which justice can prevail. There was no need for anyone to seek vengeance against the hapless Harold; marriage to Merilyn would be his punishment.

Jean Pierre returned from his ride to find Rose brooding in their sitting room. When she told him that Monte had met with an accident and died, he pulled her into his arms and promised to buy her another puppy as soon as they returned home. As she decided not to tell of the strange marks on the animal or her suspicions that Harold's riding crop had inflicted them, he had no idea that more than grief at her loss gnawed at her.

Before they went down to eat their noon meal, Rose told Jean Pierre what she had overheard between Merilyn and Harold in the dining room. His wry comments on the faulty attributes of both of them made her smile, exactly as he had hoped.

Nearly all the guests had departed at various times that morning, and the dining room was considerably quieter. Sitting at one end of the long table with Roxley and Beau, Jean Pierre and Rose had a good time visiting and joking. Although Ashley, the young heir to Heatherlee and the title of Lord Winstead, and his mother, Catherine, had been unable to come for the grouse hunting of the past few days, they had ridden over in time for the meal. From where he sat across the table, Ashley seemed as smitten with his cousin from Louisiana as upon their first meeting, and his youthful contributions to their banter brought new laughter.

After they had eaten and Beau informed the group that his father would arrive soon to meet in the library with the family, Rose could find no reason to muster even a smile. Just the thought of assembling with her kin and going through the dreary business of hearing read and executed the section of her aunt's will pertaining to herself brought a feeling of uneasiness. An air of tension seemed to pervade the large room as all pushed back their chairs, the majority moving toward the library down the hallway.

Rose and Jean Pierre bade Roxley farewell near the front entry. Then Rose, glancing up at Beau, teased her, "For myself, I'm sorry you're leaving for your home now, Roxley. But I'm not sure you're doing the right thing to get to know this man better. The minute you're nice to him, he takes control. He's forcing me to hear the will read."

Roxley returned Rose's smile and sent a flirtatious look at Beau, saying, "I'll remember that when I return next weekend for the Festival Gaiety. And when he comes to spend the Christmas holidays at my home, I shall warn my father not to show him one whit of kindness." Her pretty face lighted up as she spoke of the big blond man gazing down at her with open admiration.

Jean Pierre watched the surprised look on Rose's face as she listened. Earlier he had heard Roxley and her discussing the upcoming, traditional Festival Gaiety held in Wanington. There was no way she could be astonished that the friendship between her cousin and her barrister was developing into something more romantic, so what had jolted her? Beau escorted her outside to her waiting carriage, leaving husband and wife alone for a few minutes.

Jean Pierre asked, "Didn't you write Maman that we would be home for Christmas?"

"Yes," she confessed, "and I hadn't realized until Roxley spoke of their plans for the holidays just now that it's scarcely two months away. We need to think of returning before long, yes?" She still warmed inside when his gaze caressed her in the way it was doing now. For a moment, she thought she saw a contemplative look surface in his dark eyes and that he had something important to say, but a noise at the front door prevented further private exchange.

Anthony Bradford, Beau's father, was coming in with his son, having arrived while Roxley was leaving. He was an older, more gentle version of his son, and both Jean

Pierre and Rose delighted in chatting with him as the four walked to the library. As the legal representative of Lady Rosalinde's estate, Mr. Bradford greeted those already gathered there and set his leather bag on a nearby desk.

Feeling out-of-place, despite the quiet assurances of Beau and Mr. Bradford, Rose glanced at her family. The viscount sat upon a heavy chair of carved rosewood and gleaming red damask near the black-veined marble fireplace. A walking cane with gold tip and knob lay propped against the side table separating his chair and the matching chair where the viscountess sat.

Rose and Jean Pierre sat upon the chairs Beau indicated and completed the near circle. Not being a blood relative, Sir Thomas had excused himself and gone for his afternoon rest. Ashley and his mother sat on a settee on the opposite side of the fireplace from the viscount and viscountess.

Harold and Merilyn perched upon a small settee next to his parents. As though dressed for a special occasion, Merilyn wore a purple-and-black-striped taffeta with black lace trimming the pagoda sleeves and edging the heart-shaped neckline and overskirt. She fidgeted with an ornate fan of purple and gold while Harold talked with his father.

Content to rest against the back of the settee, Harold was saying to the viscount, "I hardly see why Mother and you act surprised, Father, that Merilyn and I are engaged. You well know that we have known each other since our cradle days."

Mr. Bradford turned then from where he had laid out his papers on the desk. At the viscount's sudden announcement to the group about the engagement of Merilyn and Harold, he made all the appropriate comments and added, "Now I see why this lovely young lady has joined us on this occasion."

Merilyn preened. She opened her fan and examined the garish purple flowers. Closing the fan, she met his gaze then and recognized a shrewdness there. Anthony Bradford would not be hoodwinked easily. "My family's retainer will be contacting you soon," she told him, hoping to postpone a great deal of questioning. "Since my father's death a few years back, he serves as executor on my behalf until my marriage. He has been most kind to allow me a small voice in the handling of my affairs.''

Harold brushed at an imaginary piece of lint on his lemon-colored vest, then checked the pocket watch dangling from a silver chain. Only once had he glanced at Rose, and the venom in those animallike eyes had revealed his hatred.

After Mr. Bradford went to the door and motioned for his assistant to bring in a leather box tooled ornately with gold, one large enough to hold a lady's hat, he read the final portion of Lady Rosalinde's will. ''Attached herein,'' he announced afterward to those gathered before him, ''is the list of the jewelry left to Rose Guilbeau, the daughter of her brother Charles.'' Dismissing the assistant, he placed his hand on the handsome box and asked Beau to join him at the desk.

The crackle of the logs in the fireplace made the only other sound apart from the barristers at the desk. All eyes watched the simple process of unlocking the box. Beau lifted a tray and set it aside, reading aloud from the list his father held. The only items named that brought a sparkle to Rose's eyes were the ruby ring, earrings, and bracelet that matched her pendant. Without thinking, she fondled the gem on its familiar chain around her neck. But when the two men shifted their attention to the contents left in the bottom of the box, they paused and exchanged puzzled looks.

''There seem to be some discrepancies here,'' Mr. Bradford announced after a whispered consultation with his son. ''The Winstead tiara of diamonds and the necklace of emeralds are missing.'' His eyes went to the troubled, narrowed ones of the viscount. ''As Lady Rosalinde's son,'' Mr. Bradford said to him, ''you have held this box in your care until this day. Can you offer some explanation?''

''I have not opened it,'' the viscount replied in an ominous tone. His glance slid to his son. ''I brought it here to Heatherlee and placed it in the vault as soon as Rose arrived, according to your instructions.'' He coughed behind a shaking hand, still sending frowning looks toward Harold.

"Mayhap I can clear up this small matter," Harold managed to say after a noisy clearing of his throat. As soon as the jewelry box was set upon the desk, his face had become flushed. "I had no idea that Rose could be found and be persuaded to be here for this reading today." No one spoke. Harold went on, more agitated now than ever, "I took the liberty of borrowing the tiara and necklace."

"Borrowed the—" the viscount sputtered, his voice failing him for the moment. "What is this bit about 'borrowing'? You had no right to take anything from my vault," he said indignantly. He searched the faces of those assembled, his countenance reddening with each word he uttered. "I gave my word to safeguard the jewelry." Leaning toward his son and ignoring the warning looks from his wife, he said, "You may be my son, but you've become a scoundrel, just as Mother told me over the past few years. I suppose your gambling brought this on."

"It was just a matter of a small debt, Father," Harold replied, his voice squeaky despite his attempts at bravado. He hated knowing that all but one person stared at him with disdain. That Merilyn was on his side was his only consolation, as small as it was. He crossed and recrossed his legs, shaking one foot in a circular pattern. "I plan to make full restitution."

"Not with my money you won't," declared the visibly shaken viscount. Stooping down from his chair, he picked up his walking cane and stood it between his spread knees, his hands resting over the gold knob as if they needed something to hold on to. "You've drawn the last pound from me." The lift of his head and chin proclaimed his disapproval even further.

"May I speak?" Merilyn asked, turning first to the stiff-necked viscount and then to Mr. Bradford. Harold was cowering back against the settee, his face pale and sickly. When both of the older men nodded in puzzlement, she went on. "Harold and I have discussed this problem of the missing tiara and necklace. I will send my barrister to repay the cost of the items. It all came about from a misunderstanding about the existence and whereabouts of his cousin Rose. Harold had every reason to believe that on this date she would still be missing and that all of the jewelry would become his. Besides, a horrible Spanish person named de Cordoza showed up a couple of months ago at Harold's favorite gaming house, where he has always been able to cover his losses with notes, and threatened Harold's very life if he didn't come up with the money. He pawned the jewelry to pay off the debt. Surely you can understand his plight.''

A flurry of heated exchanges filled the room then as the viscount and viscountess talked in desperate whispers and Merilyn spoke to Harold. Beau and his father held a private consultation at the desk. Ashley tried to ask Catherine something, but she shushed him and kept her gaze on the lawyers. Her eyes wide with astonishment at all that she had learned, Rose eased her hand into Jean Pierre's. The thought that Phillip de Cordoza's evilness had touched so many people sliced through both their minds.

''Verbal commitment might not be acceptable to my client,'' Beau announced after the consultation with his father ended. ''Rose, what we have here, though it is inside the family, is a confession of theft of your property. What do you—''

''I've no wish to bring charges,'' Rose interrupted, not daring to look toward the settee where the engaged couple sat. She had already noticed that Merilyn had moved closer to Harold. That he was the one who had killed her dog was no longer a question in her mind. A shudder attacked her, sending goosebumps to trail up her spine.

Mr. Bradford spoke then. ''If the pieces can be retrieved and returned, perhaps this matter can be kept within the family.''

''Yes,'' Harold answered, cutting pleading looks toward his intended. ''Instead of accepting Merilyn's offer to pay the price of the jewelry, I shall ask her to give me the money to get them back from the jeweler in Portsmouth where I pawned them.'' A cold, forbidding look on Merilyn's face made him add, ''We may not have mentioned it, but we have already made plans to be married within the month. The business of dispensing funds then will be between husband and wife. Isn't that right, my dear?''

Merilyn beamed then, her large teeth exposed to the fullest. With an unbecoming blush and something akin to a girlish giggle behind her words, she said, ''Of course, darling. We will have the pieces back here within two weeks.'' She leaned to put a hand on his arm, exulting that he could not back away from her now.

An awkward silence took over then, broken when Rose ventured to say, ''Beau, I have no wish to claim the missing pieces. I'd like them to stay here at Heatherlee for Ashley.'' She sent a quick look at her visibly shocked young cousin and his mother before adding, ''Someday he'll marry, and I think his wife should be the one to wear the Winstead tiara and emeralds. As my attorney, can you handle the necessary arrangements?''

Beau nodded and once more spoke with his father while the others talked among themselves.

Rose whispered to Jean Pierre, ''I had no idea why Harold and Merilyn seemed to detest me. Now that I see they were hoping to keep me from being here today, I no longer want to refuse Lady Rosalinde's bequest. I doubt I'll ever have any occasion to wear any but the ruby pieces made to go with my pendant, and I'm tempted to take only those.'' She paused to look across at Harold. ''But I see everything in a new light now,'' Rose went on. ''From what I've learned about my father's oldest sister, she had definite ideas about family ties and morals. She could have left everything outright to her grandson Harold had she wanted him to have it. My receiving these special pieces must have meant a great deal to her. What should I do?''

''Whatever pleases you,'' Jean Pierre assured her, patting the cold hand he held. Even the pink of her gown didn't lend enough color to hide her paleness. The full upper lip had that trembling, vulnerable look that always touched a tender spot deep inside him. Swirling dark pinpoints in her blue eyes signaled her inner turmoil. *Damn the whole lot of them*, he thought. This entire business was upsetting her far too much. He should never have brought her to England. But then the guilt he had suffered from having left her vulnerable to Thom Keller's attack pestered him and made him hold his tongue. What was done was done.

Beau approached them and said in a professional tone, "Someday, Rose, Jean Pierre's and your children might enjoy owning this legacy from your father's people."

Rose searched Jean Pierre's eyes for answers, but all she saw was love for her and faith in her ability to make the right decision. "Very well," she told Beau and the others who seemed to be awaiting her words. "Except for the pieces I've asked be returned to Ashley, I will accept what my aunt wished me to have."

The barristers breathed audible sighs of approval. They drew up the proper papers for both Harold and Merilyn to sign to make binding their verbal agreement about returning the tiara and emeralds. A back log fell in the fireplace, causing showers of sparks to land on the marble hearth. Rays from the afternoon sun danced through tall windows and brightened the muted patterns of the Persian rugs into glowing, gemlike colors. In a mercifully short time, the unpleasant episode ended, and the library emptied.

Much later, after all the guests had gone to their respective homes, and after they had dined with Sir Thomas and returned to their rooms, Rose and Jean Pierre relaxed on the settee before the fireplace in their sitting room. She had already brushed her hair into a cloud of pinkish gold and slipped into one of the diaphanous peignoirs Jean Pierre had bought her in New Orleans. Its pale blue reminded her of the first gift he had ever given her, the lengths of satin ribbon the week before their wedding. She nestled against his chest, liking the feel of his hardness beneath his barely closed silk robe, sniffing contentedly at the familiar, beloved scent of him. The events of the day had left her edgy, uncertain of her feelings for her father's family. Her emotions seemed to be running amok.

"This has been quite a day, hasn't it?" Jean Pierre asked. He eased her head to lie across his arm so that he could look into her face and be charmed anew by the fuller upper lip dipping over the lower one. The fragrance of the

hair spilling across his arm captivated him. Not even
trying to resist, he kissed the inviting mouth, savoring its
full sweetness.

"Ummm," she murmured when his lips released hers.
They had discussed at length the nasty business of Harold,
and of Phillip, and even of Thom Keller. When she had
pointed out her belief that Harold would live a lifetime of
punishment being married to Merilyn, he had joined in her
bemused laughter.

"Would you like to go home now?" he asked, almost
sure of her answer. From beneath their bewitching, silky
lashes, her eyes beckoned. He could no longer put off
telling her of the plans he had made in Portsmouth.

"I'm not sure," she replied, her gaze suddenly getting
lost in an explosive flare of flame in the fireplace. She
didn't want to think about anything but snuggling in his
arms. Only there did she feel safe and secure, at home.

"After today, how can you not be sure?" Dark eyes
assessed her faraway look. Her answer was not what he
had expected.

"In a week they'll be holding the Festival Gaiety." Her
voice was dreamy, but inside she was still tense.

"I know, but I can't see why that would interest you. I
thought that you would've had enough of these simpering
relatives by now." Not trying to withhold the contempt he
felt for Harold, he was unaware that the emotion flavored
his stated opinion of the other kinfolk.

"Harold is the only one who is lacking," Rose said,
sitting up and fixing him with a haughty stare. Silk
meeting silk had created a sensuous sound when she
moved against him. The low neck of the peignoir dipped
from her movement, revealing the top of one breast,
except for its rosy nipple. Candlelight bathed her face and
lingered on the ruby pendant resting off-center above the
shadowed valley separating her creamy breasts. "Nobody
said you had to like my father's people. It was your idea to
come here. I resent your being petty."

"I'm not being petty," he denied, freeing her to flounce
away from him to sit at the far end of the settee. A show of
her shapely legs in the process did little to deflect his

attention. Those hurts and doubts festering since their arrival ascended to the surface. Was she feeling a stronger pull toward this ancestral home now that she had spent so much time here? "It's time for us to get away from here and go home. Maman's letter made it plain that the land we want is ours, and we need to get started on our house. We have wasted a month—"

"*Wasted* a month?" she asked, her eyes shooting sparks. With both hands she pushed her hair from her face, then angled her chin. "Oh yes, I remember now that before you left on your wild trip to Portsmouth, you called Heatherlee a monstrous dead-house. I thought you told me we could stay as long as I wanted to."

"We can, so long as that ends two days from now." Brown eyes aimed daggers of their own then, not a bit daunted by her mouth opened in astonishment. "I booked passage for New Orleans while I was in Portsmouth, and the ship sails in two days." As though to signal the end of the discussion, he crossed his arms across his chest and sat up straighter.

"Without consulting me, of course," Rose said, her voice rising. "Why do you insist on assuming you can make all the decisions about our lives by pretending I don't deserve any consideration? I've told you a million times how much I resent your high-handed manner, but you never seem to listen."

"That's not true."

"Isn't this the same quarrel we had when you announced you were going to Portsmouth on a business trip, one never discussed with me . . . because it didn't 'concern' me?" Her temper was storming her brain, digging up old pains to toss out. His set, angry face led her on to more insults, which her rational self knew were untruths. "And it was then that you let me know how sorry you were that you 'rescued' me from that awful Phillip. Who asked you to interfere in my affairs and make the grand gesture to make me your wife? Damn you! You've always loved to make my life a hell." How could he sit there and look so self-righteous?

"God! I must have been out of my mind to think I was

making the right move," Jean Pierre muttered, rising to pace back and forth in front of the fireplace. He fought at the black curls covering his forehead. "You've always been impossible to reason with. I should have known you would never be more than a spoiled, bad-tempered, foulmouthed little girl." Gritting his teeth, he pulled at the belt on his robe to tighten it, gaining pleasure from the pain it caused when he jerked it too tightly. What he had suspected was true, and his heart ached. She had no wish to return to the simple life he could give her in Louisiana. Her false accusations angered him, but he recognized that the anger he felt toward himself for having brought her to England was of greater intensity. He was going to lose her!

"If I'm spoiled, it's certainly not by you," she shot back with renewed venom. The memory of his threat to spank her in Natchitoches took its place at the front of her mind, and she left the settee to stand before him with her hands on her hips. "Why don't you threaten to spank me? Would that make you feel less put out for having had to marry me?" When he glared back but made no comment, she went on, "Get your belongings packed and take off for Portsmouth this minute, for all I care. I'll return when and if I get ready and not one minute earlier. You knew well that I wanted to be here for the Festival Gaiety, and I don't intend for you to deprive me of being with the people who've been nice to me here in England. You told me that you didn't care where I came from. Maybe you'd like to know that I don't care where you go!" Unreasoning rage controlled her now.

Jean Pierre took in the sight of this lovely young woman with the tumbling blond curls and sought for a way to rectify the misunderstanding. As strong-willed as he was, he could not manage the feat, could not even hang on to the earlier, half-formed thought that it was only a "misunderstanding." Doubts that she had ever truly loved him controlled every cell of his brain that anger had not already taken over. The blond hair and pale eyes were merely outward signs that she did not belong in the Cajun settlement back in Louisiana. Was her natural habitat here, amidst the formal splendor of Heatherlee?

No wonder he had suffered those doubts when he first brought her here, he agonized, as his eyebrows furrowed into a scowl. Even with the weighty sum he had accumulated from his sales of pelts, he could never provide her with the kind of life showered upon her at the ancestral mansion. There would be no elegant picnics in Louisiana prepared and served by countless servants, no grooms to care for the horses, no maids to help her with her hair and clothing, no Festival Gaiety—whatever the hell that would turn out to be, the angry part of him threw in. Not more than a few times in New Orleans when they might be there on business would there be any occasion when she could wear the ancestral jewelry. Sobered a little from his thoughts, humbled at the realization of how much he loved her, yet still testy from his tempestuous rage, he made a mocking bow and turned his back on her to stare into the fire.

"I'll leave early in the morning," he said over his shoulder. "You can, as you so plainly said, come when and if you choose. I'll leave money for one of the servants here to accompany you. We never should have come."

"And we wouldn't have if you hadn't insisted that the trip would be like a honeymoon," Rose yelled, no longer caring what she said as long as she could wound him as much as his threats to leave without her cut into her heart. "And all the time, you came to find a dealer to buy pelts. You could've at least been honest with me about why we came." She saw him stand straighter, stiffer.

"That's ridiculous!" Jean Pierre wheeled to face her. His tone was ominous. A part of him reeled from the half-truth she had hurled.

"I'm sorry I asked Beau to go to Portsmouth to see about you. I should've realized you never need advice or help from anyone."

Jean Pierre's temper goaded him to say, "That's right. I'll send for my trunk and pack tonight."

Before midnight, he had flung his clothing into the trunk and set it near the door. With a cold silence permeating the rooms, each went about separate tasks. When Rose climbed into bed and pretended to be asleep before he had collected all his belongings, Jean Pierre continued to act as though she were not in the room. Snatching his pillow and a quilt, he strode to the settee and stretched out as best he could to pass the hours until dawn. By that time he had come to the conclusion that not only did Rose deserve the motley collection of English relatives, but also her kinsmen deserved her. They were all a bunch of pompous hotheads.

"Goodbye, my boy," Sir Thomas told Jean Pierre early the next morning at the front door. "I shall see that your message of farewell to Beau is delivered. Rest assured that I will take care of Rose as long as she wishes to stay at Heatherlee." He studied the solemn faces of the couple and added, "I'll leave you now to say your private farewells."

Rose heard her great-uncle's steps fade away. Through the open door she could hear the sounds of the horses stamping their feet on the cobblestones while awaiting the signal to pull the handsome carriage to Portsmouth. Anger and hurt still reigned and smothered what her heart was trying to tell her. "Have a safe journey," she said.

"Thank you," Jean Pierre replied. He saw the shadows beneath her eyes and wondered if she had slept any more than he had. "If you decide to come, you can go to the Breardes' townhouse and send a message to me at Attakapas."

Rose nodded, afraid her voice would fail her. He took her arm as they walked down the steps, but she flinched and moved away. The grim set of his mouth and brows reminded her of that time he had come home from trapping when she was still an ignorant girl. If she had grown up, she agonized, why was she allowing him to leave? Not even when he leaned to peck her lips with a polite kiss did that soft look she had come to associate with some deep feeling for her rearrange the area around his mouth. It was over. If he had ever loved her, the feeling was dead. She no longer knew the man stepping into one of the smaller carriages from the Heatherlee mews. The family crest emblazoned in miniature on the door held open by the liveried footman seemed no stranger to her than did the handsome man with the faraway look in his dark eyes.

Rose offered him a final wave as the carriage left, the footman joining the driver upon the open front seat. In a state of shock, Rose stood on the steps and watched the silver trim on the black leather coach pick up the sun's rays until the vehicle disappeared over a distant hill.

Chapter Twenty-seven

Jean Pierre remained in a kind of emotional shock until the carriage had long passed the village of Wanington. Ever since the heated exchange of the preceding night, a haze of red seemed to fill his brain. Nothing made sense, and he found it difficult to recall all that had been said and done. The memory of Rose's waving goodbye there at the giant doors of Heatherlee haunted him. He had seen no sign of that vulnerable look about her lips that usually revealed inner doubts. With a sigh, he accepted its absence to mean that she had no qualms about staying behind, that his leaving had no major significance in her life, that she no longer needed him. But had she ever needed him or truly loved him? he asked himself with tormenting honesty. Hadn't he more or less forced himself on her?

His last view of her kept coming back. She had been wearing a deep pink gown that had picked up similar shades in her hair in the morning sunlight, and he knew that picture was etched permanently in his mind along with a thousand more. And there on the lonely road to Portsmouth, he stretched his legs across to rest on the empty, opposite seat and let other images and memories float to the surface of that mental screen to haunt him.

Rose dawdled in her bath when she returned to her rooms after watching the carriage pull out of sight. Then she took forever to decide upon wearing the favored blue silk trimmed in darker blue embroidery. She fidgeted while

Kitty arranged her hair into a stylish coiffeur. Earlier Rose had merely brushed it back and tied it with a ribbon to get through the business of trying to eat breakfast and seeing Jean Pierre off. Even the coffee, which had become a standard offering ever since her statement to Sir Thomas that day that she didn't care for tea, had tasted alien to her that morning. Without interest, she watched in the mirror as the talkative maid twirled a final curl.

And when Kitty inserted the ruby earrings into her ears, she managed a half-smile at the maid's excited announcement that they made the ever-present pendant glow more brilliantly. The matching bracelet felt heavy and cold on her wrist, but she allowed it to stay there, for her gaze seemed riveted on the ring below it. The band of gold Jean Pierre had placed there on their wedding day gleamed with new beauty and seemed to be sending some preternatural message. A childhood memory chased away her anger.

"Kitty," Rose exclaimed, rising and kicking her full petticoats and skirt out of the way to rush across the room and fling open the doors of the wardrobe. "Start packing my things. I'm going to Portsmouth to sail home with my husband."

At the desk in the living room, Rose hurriedly wrote notes to be delivered to all she wanted to bid a special farewell, then rushed downstairs. Patting the startled Sir Thomas's arm and assuring him that she did indeed know what she was doing, she asked him to order a carriage. Sir Thomas gave in and insisted that the largest, most luxurious one would speed her toward the port city. She took a few minutes to bid goodbyes to the household staff and gave both her great-uncle and the tearful Kitty giant hugs before she stepped up into the gold-trimmed coach. When the carriage topped the last hill, she was already envisioning what a marvelous reunion she would have with her husband and forgot to turn for even one final look at Heatherlee.

The quaint village of Wanington flew by, a blur of high-pitched gables thatched with straw, squawking geese and chickens trying to escape barking dogs, and the clatter of the rattling wheels of the big carriage hurrying through the main street. Sitting stiffly against the soft leather seat,

Rose barely noticed the sway of the coach suspended from its frame by thick leather loops. Her mind backtracked to the quarrel of the preceding night while she clutched the velvet-lined handhold and stared out the window at the still-green hills and partially defoliated forests. England was indeed beautiful, and there had been times when traces of a feeling that she had come home had filled her being with humbleness. But not any longer. Not when Jean Pierre wasn't here.

How could she have forgotten so quickly how miserable she had been when she had believed him dead, and again at Heatherlee while he was away in Portsmouth? She must have been out of her mind. That no place without him could ever be home was the powerful message her wedding ring had given while she sat having her hair coiffed, one she had no intentions of forgetting again.

Rose scolded herself for accusing Jean Pierre of making decisions without consulting her. What difference did it make if the decision was one she would have voted for anyway? And she was ready to leave England, had known it deep down even as she quarreled with him over his having reserved passage for the following day. Why had she refused to admit it when he had told her of his plans? With her free hand she toyed with her pendant.

Would Jean Pierre forgive her for letting her nasty show of temper mask her desire to be uppermost in his thoughts? All she wanted was to be the center of his world, just as he was the center of hers. Would he believe her when she told him that she would never act so childishly again? Or would he turn that handsome dark head away from her and leave her to sink back into the abysmal pit of despair she had sunk into after he left this morning—the one she had endured those months when she had thought him dead? Cheering her not at all was the realization that yesterday when she had asked for his advice about accepting the jewelry, he had given none. In fact, he had sent her a look of confidence in her ability to think for herself. Tears pressed behind her eyes, and a heaviness sat upon her heart.

"Why have we stopped?" Rose asked, jolted into the

present when she realized that the carriage had pulled off beneath some trees and that the footman was opening her door. Before the man could answer, she leaned out to see another carriage racing toward them from the crest of the hill ahead. Familiar silver bands shone from its tip in the afternoon sunshine.

Not waiting for the footman to alight and open his door, Jean Pierre stepped from the second carriage when it pulled alongside the larger one. He flung back his cloak and looked up at his driver, saying, "Frames, you and the others take the teams down to that stream beyond the trees and water them. My wife and I have some talking to do."

"Jean Pierre, you weren't traveling toward Portsmouth," said Rose, once the servants had led the horses out of sight. They stood alone, eyeing each other like wary adversaries. She had thought upon first seeing the coach rushing toward her that she would fling herself into his arms and beg his forgiveness. But that was before she had seen him up close and saw the steely look upon his features. She stood facing him beneath a bare-limbed plane tree, her fur-lined cape of blue velvet about her shoulders, its hood falling to form a partial frame for her face. Something new in his eyes probed at her, slashed at her ebbing confidence. "Is something wrong?"

"Nothing that hasn't been wrong for a long time," he snapped at her. The shock of seeing the big carriage—easily recognizable as the fine one he had seen in the mews at Heatherlee—coming down the road still unsettled him. He had feared all kinds of bad news might be chasing him. Once they reached the waiting vehicle and he saw her beautiful face, he almost forgot the reason he had told the driver to turn back toward Heatherlee. "And I'm going to straighten it out right now." He moved toward her.

"What do you have in mind?" she asked, taking a step backward. Those arms she had been dreaming of no longer represented a haven. Her heart pounded. He didn't look at all the way she had expected he would upon seeing her. There was no sign of levity on his countenance. If he was still angry, why had he been riding back toward Heatherlee?

"I'm going to give you that spanking you deserve for

your ridiculous behavior last night and take you home with me.'' He took another step closer. The swimming black specks in her eyes mesmerized him, as did the parted, full lips.

''Doesn't that seem rather stupid when you consider that I've already decided to join you?'' Rose swallowed hard. Her attempt to put him on the defensive had failed. When he kept staring at her with unfathomable looks, she said, ''Jean Pierre, I talked out of my head last night, and I'm sorry. I packed and came after you because I . . .'' Her voice faltered and floated away on a sudden gust of breeze. Somewhere nearby a bird trilled a husky note. She cleared her throat and began again. ''I realized I had acted as you said—childishly.'' Praying that his face might truly be thawing a bit, she moved toward him, a hand lifted imploringly.

''*Childish* is not the word I have in mind now, though,'' he said, his deep voice heavy with feeling. ''I've had time to think today, and I believe a better word might be *devious*.''

''How so?'' Instantly on the defensive at his tone and sure now that he was not ready to call a truce, she brought her hands to her hips and glared up at him. The hood fell farther back across her shoulders. What a fool she had been to think he would be delighted to find her coming to join him! All he wanted to do was argue. He no longer loved her—if he ever had.

''I let some of your telling remarks slide by me last night. But now I recall them well.'' He stomped his foot and walked up and down in front of her in that cocky, square-shouldered way she had come to love. She watched the way his tight pants revealed the play of muscles in his thighs and she caught a glimpse of his taut buttocks when his cloak flared from a sudden turn. All handsome virility and power, that was her husband, she exulted. ''*Devious* suits you perfectly. You work your devious charms on me and everyone else to get your way, then go berserk when I dare have an idea of my own. You took it upon yourself to make a decision about my life without consulting me at all—the same accusation you're always making against me, if I remember correctly." When she stood with lips parted and eyes staring, he ceased his nervous pacing and grabbed her arms. "I didn't need you to send Beau to Portsmouth to keep me out of trouble. I was never in trouble—and if I had been, I could have gotten myself out of it without help sent by you." By then he had pulled her so close against him that her little breaths fanned across his chin. He could see the hammering of the pulse in the hollow of her throat, could feel the trembling of her body, and could smell the delicious fragrance of her.

"You're hurting me," Rose protested, trying to wrench free of his grasp. The hardness of his body reminded her of the density of a brick wall.

"I'm glad," he muttered, fascinated all over again at her show of spirit. Did nothing ever daunt her? "You've hurt me by your unfair attacks on my failures to give you consideration when I make decisions that I feel are mine to make."

"And that's what you think I did when I asked Beau to . . . to check on you in Portsmouth?" Genuine puzzlement creased her forehead and clouded her eyes. She had never examined her actions in that light. She had based her choice on her love for him and her determination to protect him from what she feared might be danger. Were such thoughts the kind that had led him to buy passage home? Had he perhaps sensed that some harm might befall her or their marriage if they remained at Heatherlee?

"Was it much different than my making plans for us to return home? Isn't that what you did, Rose?" He could tell from the set of her fuller upper lip and the corner crinkles of her eyes that she was weighing his words.

"I didn't look at it that way," she confessed after a quick appraisal of her uneasiness at the time. Suddenly she wanted nothing more than to have him forgive her. She longed to have those compelling dark eyes drink her in rather than freeze her out. She wanted to melt that imprisoning brick wall into a loving, warm hunk of muscle. For an instant she glimpsed that softening about his mouth and let her hopes fly high. "Can you ever forgive me?"

"Maybe . . . in a million years, if you'll forgive me

also," Jean Pierre whispered just before he kissed her trembling lips. His heart skipped about in his chest, and he pulled her softness closer. As if they moved to some inner music, he walked her over to the broad tree trunk and leaned back against it, still keeping her within the circle of his arms. After some more fervent kisses and impassioned moans from both, he lifted his mouth to ask, "Are you sure you're making the right decision to come with me, Lady Rosalind?"

Rose didn't even flinch from the title, so lovingly was it whispered. She nestled her already-throbbing breasts closer against him and lifted a pale hand to fondle his ear, then tumble the black curls down upon his forehead. With that look from beneath her lashes, the one he had once confessed that he couldn't resist, she asked, "Don't you know who and what I really am?"

"You're Rose Guilbeau, my wife," his velvety voice told her. His teeth flashed whitely as his worshiping smile and dark eyes gave her more titles, titles she knew she would hear that night in his arms at the inn in Portsmouth.

"And you're just a plain ol' Cajun, yes?" When he continued to smile in that heart-stopping way and drown in her loving gaze without giving an answer, she went on, "Then how could I ever be anything but your Cajun Rose?"

The black head bent over the blond one again, and Jean Pierre said, "You're right, darling. And I'm taking you home to the bayou." Just before his eyes closed in ecstasy at the double delight of holding her close with his mouth upon hers, the blue ones starred for him in a way he had never seen, and his heart soared.

Even as she gave herself fully to Jean Pierre's fiery kisses there beneath the plane tree, Rose heard again the old woman's predictions that had snatched her attention back in the bedroom as she stared at her wedding band. The only two parts of the prophecy not yet fulfilled were unfolding: They would cross that "world of water" and share that promised "lifetime of love."